CW00515096

GRAVE
MOUNTAIN

BOOKS BY WENDY DRANFIELD

GRAVE
MOUNTAIN

WENDY DRANFIELD

Bookouture

Published by Bookouture in 2024

An imprint of Storyfire Ltd.
Carmelite House
50 Victoria Embankment
London EC4Y 0DZ

www.bookouture.com

Copyright © Wendy Dranfield, 2024

Wendy Dranfield has asserted her right to be identified as the author of this work.

All rights reserved. No part of this publication may be reproduced, stored in any retrieval system, or transmitted, in any form or by any means, electronic, mechanical, photocopying, recording or otherwise, without the prior written permission of the publishers.

ISBN: 978-1-83525-384-7
eBook ISBN: 978-1-83525-383-0

This book is a work of fiction. Names, characters, businesses, organizations, places and events other than those clearly in the public domain, are either the product of the author's imagination or are used fictitiously. Any resemblance to actual persons, living or dead, events or locales is entirely coincidental.

Dedicated to the readers who have stuck with Madison and Nate from Book 1.

PROLOGUE

Paris, France

The woman looks at her companion, an attractive thirty-two-year-old international pilot. The uniform used to turn her on, but years spent working as a flight attendant and countless layovers with handsome men have numbed the thrill she once felt. She still intends to fool around with pilots, not because of the fantasy, but because she can't enjoy sleeping alone. Not after what happened.

Now, she needs someone by her side as darkness falls. Otherwise, the bleakness of nighttime and the haunting silence trick her with random knocks, shadows in the corner of the room and, if she listens hard enough, the sound of someone else's breathing.

No. She'll never be able to sleep alone again, no matter how tired she is after working a long flight. That's where the pilots come in handy. And if they're busy with other girls, she always has her pick of bartenders from whichever hotel she's staying at.

With a deep breath, she unzips her overnight case on the bed of this fancy Parisian hotel as her companion gets dressed.

She needs a hot shower before meeting the other cabin crew downstairs for drinks. It's only the second time she's been to Paris, so they're planning to hit the town during their brief layover. There's safety in numbers. Safety can be found in foreign countries too, as long as you're careful and far enough away from home.

She feels strong hands around her naked waist. Warm lips on the back of her neck.

"Why won't you marry me?" he asks. This isn't their first shared layover, but it will be their last. He's getting too close.

Because if we marry, you'll die.

She doesn't say it aloud. Instead, she turns and smiles. His dark blue eyes sparkle with lust as she says, "Pilots shouldn't marry. You have too much temptation around you, and you *all* kiss and tell."

He grins. "I only have eyes for you, baby." He kisses her on the lips and forces her back against the wall. His warm torso under his open shirt presses against her naked breasts.

He *is* the kind of person she'd like to marry, but it's impossible. Marriage is off the table for her, and so are kids. It's too risky.

She gently extracts herself to save his life. "You should know by now that I'll never settle down, and I'll always see other people."

Other pilots. Because they're safe. They don't stay in one place long enough to be hunted like prey.

She smiles and tenderly runs a hand down his tanned face. "So, please, stop asking me."

He stares at her, frustrated. She waits for a parting shot, but instead, he picks up his tie and jacket and gives her a sad smile before exiting the hotel room.

There goes my future.

Tears come to her eyes. Life shouldn't be this way, but she can't dwell on it. She's already put a lot of time and energy into making peace with it. Besides, the crew flies out at 7 a.m. tomorrow, heading to New York City, and in the meantime, she needs to dress for a night on the town.

As she pulls a crumpled black dress from her overnight case, her cell phone pings with its distinct notification tone.

She stops dead.

She has two cell phones. One for work and everyday life, and a cheaper one for private matters. That phone only receives one text message a month, and she's already received this month's, so it should be silent for another two weeks.

Her heart pounds a little harder as she crosses the room to retrieve it from the drawer in the nightstand. The screen shows a number that's permanently etched into her memory. It belongs to the only person who has this number. She enters the four-digit passcode to read the message.

You need to run.

Her blood runs cold. She always knew this day would come, but it doesn't make it any easier. It makes things worse than they've ever been. She drops the black dress and spins around. Her instinct tells her to lock the door. To lock *all* the doors that lead to her.

And to never open them again.

CHAPTER ONE

Lost Creek, Colorado

Detective Madison Harper looks around the dimly lit diner at the distraught but determined faces of the people who invited her here tonight. She's at a support group meeting for those with missing family members. They want her to listen to their stories. Remember their loved ones. Search for the missing.

But there's only so much she can do. It's not up to Madison whether the Lost Creek Police Department reopens cold cases. If it were—and if new homicides could magically cease for the foreseeable future—she would work through each of these people's cases one by one until they were all reunited with their missing loved ones, and until support groups like this weren't needed in her hometown.

The icy December wind howls outside the windows. A shiver runs through her as sixty-one-year-old Vince Rader, owner of Ruby's Diner, walks by. He's preparing hot drinks for every-one. Vince closes the diner a little early one Wednesday a month, allowing this small group of distraught people the chance to support each other. He has a whole bulletin board dedicated to missing people. It's covered in the posters of those missing not just from Lost Creek but from nearby towns and cities. It's a subject close to his heart, because for six long and torturous years he was in these people's unthinkable position, until Madison helped find his wife and grandson last year. Eleven-year-old Oliver Rader is here tonight, helping his grandfather prepare the refreshments. Unfortunately, Vince's wife Ruby didn't make it home.

Local resident Robert Dorsey clears his throat. "My thirteen-year-old son disappeared five years ago," he says. Although only in his late forties, Robert's face is heavily lined, and his long black hair, which he keeps tied back, is sprinkled with silver strands. Several have escaped, giving him a disheveled appearance.

"Brandon was walking home from school one afternoon," he continues, his intense gaze fixed on Madison. "He saw his friend to her door and then continued on alone. Once he left her property, no one ever saw him again. I hate this saying because it's become meaningless in this country, but Brandon literally vanished into thin air, which is impossible." He swallows. "Someone knows something. Someone saw something. Someone *did* something. So why can't you investigate, Detective Harper? You could re-question everyone the department spoke to back then. Rewatch the surveillance footage. We all know you could have it solved in a week if you really wanted to."

Madison hesitates before responding. She can't tell him that the real reason she can't investigate his son's disappearance is due to a lack of resources. Lost Creek is a small mountain town in southwestern Colorado. The police department is also small, with only two detectives. Most days, the team struggles to cope with new and current investigations, so finding the time and resources to put into cold cases isn't always possible. Not unless something prompts it: a new witness coming forward, or a body being found.

Madison knows these people don't care about any of that. And neither should they. Their loved ones should've been found soon after they vanished and before they became cold cases. But investigations don't always work that way. And it's rarely down to the fact that the local police department or sheriff's office doesn't care about the missing. It's simply down to a lack of money. Which sucks, to put it mildly.

She looks around at the other people present. The enormity of their grief and frustration weighs heavy on her. "I know it sounds like that should be an easy task," she says. "So I understand your frustration, I really do, and I'm sorry you're still waiting for answers after all these years." She fixes her eyes on Robert as she adds, "I want to assure you that the Lost Creek Police Department remains committed to finding your son, Mr. Dorsey, and if you can bring me anything new to investigate, I will. I wasn't in the department when he vanished—"

Robert scoffs, cutting her off. "Right. We all know where you were. In prison. How are we supposed to trust an ex-con?"

One of the women gasps at his offensive comment.

Unrepentant, Robert continues. "The fact that Chief Mendes sent *you* here tonight instead of your male partner tells me everything I need to know about her so-called commitment to finding my son. We need someone on the case who doesn't have a screwed-up personal life, so they can focus on *us*, not themselves."

"Now come on, Robert," says Vince sternly. He hands Madison a decaffeinated coffee, due to the late hour. "That's unfair and you know it. You're not exactly giving her a reason to help you right now."

Madison leans back in her seat, trying not to let the comment affect her. It's true that she served time in prison for killing a fellow police officer, but that doesn't mean she was guilty, and everyone in this town knows her conviction was eventually overturned. But not before she served six long years of her ten-year sentence. It was a low blow from Robert Dorsey, and she knows she'll never convince some locals of her innocence, but she will only take so much before she walks out of here. She doesn't deserve to be treated like a criminal, no matter what this man is going through.

"I'm not going to dignify that with a response." She places her cup on the table. "If you'd like me to leave, I'll—"

"No, don't go," says Nancy Draper, an older woman who came with her husband, Doug. She's clutching what looks like a photograph in her hands. She shoots Robert an irritated look before turning back to Madison. "We're glad you're here, Detective. None of your predecessors would've agreed to come."

Vince disappears behind the counter to help his grandson with the drinks.

Robert sighs heavily. "Listen, I'm sorry, but being cordial has gotten me nowhere. I can't sit back and hold my tongue any longer. I'm at my wits' end! Aren't all of you?" He looks around at the others, but no one speaks. "I just need to know where my son is, even if he's dead! Even if I can't bury him! I just need to visit his remains and tell him how sorry I am." His voice breaks as he fails to hold back a sob. "I need to tell him how I should've been there to protect him from whichever sick bastard took him!"

Madison swallows the lump in her throat. She has a son who left for college a few months ago. He was only ten when she was arrested. He was taken from her by child services, and she wasn't able to be there to protect him from what followed. After having him back in her life for just a year and a half, she's lost him all over again, to college and adulthood. Things will never be the same now that he doesn't live at home, but at least she knows where he is, and she can call him whenever she wants to.

Robert Dorsey can't even do that.

She switches seats to be closer to him and rests a hand on his shoulder. "I'm so sorry," she says. Other than that, she doesn't have the words, because there are none. The likelihood of his boy being found alive now is slim. If she tells him that, he might give up all hope. She knows she would.

Robert gets up and walks to the counter for some space while he composes himself.

Madison looks at Nancy Draper. "Why don't you tell me what happened to your daughter?"

A fiercely private woman under normal circumstances, Nancy glances at her husband, whose arms are crossed tightly, a stern expression on his face. He doesn't want to be here. Whether that's due to Robert's display of raw grief or the fact that Doug Draper just doesn't like her, Madison is unsure. She and Doug got off on the wrong foot when they first met this past summer. He bought the salvage yard formerly owned by her sister, and she wasn't sure whether he was just as corrupt as Angie. She suspected him of murder. It turned out he wasn't involved, but there's still something about him that Madison doesn't trust.

Nancy squeezes the tissue in her hand as she glances nervously around. "Becky was nineteen when she went for a hike on Grave Mountain a little over five years ago." Her voice falters. "This is a photo of her that morning." She hands it to Madison.

A young woman is frozen in time in the hallway of a home as she glances at the camera with one hand raised in either a goodbye gesture or a self-conscious one. She looks like she's about to leave the house. Her straight brown hair is covered with a red woolen hat. She's dressed warmly in a thick burgundy jacket and black hiking pants over black boots. One strap of a backpack is visible on her left shoulder.

"That was taken right before her best friend drove them to

the mountain. They went there to meet this man." Nancy nods to a young blond guy sitting in a corner booth by himself. He's turned away from them, staring at his pale reflection in the window. "His name's Stuart Carpenter," she goes on. "He took Becky and Tasha hiking. He returned hours later, but my daughter and her friend didn't. They were never seen or heard from again." She meets Madison's gaze. "We believe he killed them."

Vince drops something behind the counter. It shatters loudly into pieces.

Madison is just as surprised as he is. She glances at Stuart, who remains silent. He's not even protesting his innocence. Her heart beats a little harder as it dawns on her why she was invited here tonight.

They don't just want her to listen to their stories. They want her to arrest this man.

CHAPTER TWO

A silence settles over the room. The only sound is the clock ticking and the rain lashing against the large window that, in daylight, looks out over the parking lot. Vince breaks the silence by sending his grandson upstairs to prepare for bed. When Oliver has gone, Vince sets to work cleaning up the mess behind the counter, but Madison knows he'll be eager to hear what happens next.

She looks at Nancy and Doug. "Mr. and Mrs. Draper, I... I don't know what you want me to do with that information."

"Sure you do," says Nancy evenly. "Take him in for questioning. Get him to fess up."

With a shake of the head, Madison says, "That wouldn't be appropriate. I know nothing about what happened back then, and presumably the investigating detective already questioned Stuart when your daughter and her friend failed to return home."

Their suspect speaks up for the first time. "You can ask me anything, but it won't do any good." Stuart's voice is soft. His expression conveys sadness. "I spoke to the cops at the time." His hands tremble slightly. He doesn't make eye contact.

Madison feels uncomfortable. If she feels ambushed, so must he. This isn't why she agreed to come here tonight. But if she's honest, she's intrigued about why *he* came here and what he knows. "So you *were* questioned?" she asks.

He sits forward and leans his elbows on the table in front of him. "By the black guy. He's dead now, right?"

She winces. Detective Don Douglas *is* dead. He's the person who arrested her for murder all those years ago, but he was a good cop, and she knows that if there was any evidence in this case, he would've solved it. He would've brought Nancy's daughter home, whether dead or alive.

She pulls out her pocket notebook and pen. "Tell me what happened on the day of your hike, Stuart."

The Drapers share a hungry look and shift in their seats. Madison hopes they don't think this means she's agreed to reopen the case. She just needs more details.

The only other person present, a woman Madison doesn't know and who hasn't said a word so far, goes to the counter, presumably to get another drink. Maybe she's heard all this before.

Stuart Carpenter runs a hand over his clean-shaven face. His red-rimmed eyes make him look close to tears, and Madison can tell that whatever happened on that hike has haunted him every day since.

"The day started out sunny," he says quietly. "It was bitterly cold, but the sky was clear. We thought we could beat the blizzard, since it wasn't forecast to come in until the evening. We set off at seven in the morning." He seems to find something amusing as he adds, "Becky wasn't too pleased about the early start, but it was the only way to fit the hike in before the weather changed."

Nancy smiles faintly. "I always had trouble getting her up in time for school when she was a teenager. She wasn't an early riser."

Madison feels for her. She doesn't know how the woman maintains her composure when sitting just inches away from her daughter's suspected killer. "How old did you say Becky and her friend were when they disappeared?"

"Becky and Tasha were both nineteen," says Nancy. "They worked together at the mall. I assume that's where they met *him*."

Her contempt for Stuart is evident, but Madison thinks they should give him some credit for turning up here tonight. He didn't have to.

"I was twenty-two," says Stuart. "It wasn't my idea to go on the hike, it was Becky's. I wish I'd never gone." His face clouds over.

The silent woman returns to her seat with a cup of coffee and sighs heavily, as if annoyed.

Madison raises her eyebrows. "Is there a problem?"

"I want to get home," says the woman. "But I guess I have to wait my turn, or you'll leave here without hearing about my baby."

Madison's stomach flips. *She has a missing baby.* She glances at the clock above the counter. It's already ten o'clock. "I'm sorry," she says. "I realize it's getting late. If I don't hear everyone's stories today, I can come back next time."

"They're not *stories*," says the woman with contempt. "They're *lives*." Her eyes well up. "I don't think you understand what it's like. We're living between hell and hope, all of us, and the only people with the power to get us out of our black hole are you cops, but you refuse to help us!"

Madison can only imagine what she's going through. Before she can say anything, Nancy Draper interjects as if the woman never spoke. She's determined to make Madison focus on her daughter.

"Tell the detective," she says to Stuart. "Tell her about the last time you saw our daughter. Tell her what happened to Becky."

The atmosphere in the room has shifted. Doug Draper might be silent next to his wife, but he looks like a coiled spring, ready to jump up and lash out at Stuart Carpenter at any moment. He must be in his early fifties, and he's tall and robust. He could do some damage to someone like Stuart. With emotions charged, Madison wishes her partner was here with her so they could split their attention between the grieving parents.

Stuart won't meet her eyes. He looks resigned to his fate as the prime suspect in the women's disappearance. He shakes his head. "I can never tell anyone what happened."

Doug suddenly leaps out of his chair, fists balled. "Then why did you even come here?" he yells. "You should leave before I do something I'll regret, boy."

Madison jumps up and stands between them. "You're not helping, Mr. Draper. Sit down."

"It's a support group, isn't it?" says Stuart behind them. "I need support." He swallows before looking up at them. "I wish I'd never come back from Grave Mountain. I wish I'd died up there too."

The room falls silent as he breaks down.

His words send chills down Madison's spine. Has he just let slip that the women *are* dead? She motions for Doug to return to his seat. He does, which surprises her, but his demeanor is so tense she thinks it's just a matter of time before he reacts violently again.

She looks at each person here—the Drapers, Robert Dorsey, Stuart Carpenter and the woman with a missing baby—and feels their conflicting emotions about the situation they find themselves in. They're bewildered that this has happened to them, angry that the police didn't find their loved ones and distraught at the thought that they'll never be found. They're afraid they'll never get the answers they need in order to try to rebuild their lives. It's unbearable to witness, so she can't even imagine how it feels for them.

She needs to ask Chief Mendes if they can find the money to hire another detective. One whose primary focus is investigating cold cases. Because someone needs to find these people's loved ones. And someone needs to bring Stuart Carpenter in for questioning, because he clearly knows something about what happened that day. She can't understand why he thinks he can't tell them about it. Unless he was involved.

The door to the diner suddenly bursts open behind her, making them all jump. Madison's partner, Detective Marcus Adams, appears. His face and black hair are dripping wet from the evening's heavy downpour. His eyes search the diner until he spots her.

"Sorry to interrupt," he says. "But we have a situation."

She can't leave now. These people will never forgive her. "I'm busy. It'll either have to wait or you can deal with it yourself." She tries to convey the seriousness of her current situation in her look, but Adams has never been one for picking up on signals.

"It can't wait, and I need you there, Harper," he says. "Human remains have been discovered."

Her heart beats a little harder, like it does every time a body is found. She hears murmurs around her, and Vince stops what he's doing behind the counter. He has a front-row seat to the drama tonight, but Madison knows he'd never repeat anything he hears.

Detective Adams doesn't know why she or these people are here, but he should've pulled her aside before blurting that out. Before she can stop him from saying anything else, he adds, "I hope you're up for a hike, because the body's on Grave Mountain."

Madison closes her eyes. *Shit.*

Nancy Draper yelps like a dog being pulled too hard on its leash.

Doug Draper jumps up and heads for Adams. "Are you serious?" His face flushes red. There's panic in his eyes. Panic that he could be about to get the worst answer imaginable to the question that's been eating away at him every day for the last five years.

Nancy clutches her gold cross necklace. "Please let it be Becky. Or both of them."

Madison realizes the woman is long past expecting her daughter to return home alive. She just wants to lay her daughter to rest. A grave to visit. She heads for the exit and tries to lower the Drapers' expectations before she leaves. "Please don't get your hopes up," she says gently. "This could be anyone. We all know it's called Grave Mountain for a reason."

Doug grabs her wrist as she passes. "I'm going with you," he says.

"Hey, buddy!" says Detective Adams, stepping forward. "Hands off."

Madison stops him. "Leave it, Adams. His daughter went missing on the mountain."

"I don't care," says Adams. "That doesn't give him the right to grab anyone, never mind a cop."

Doug drops her wrist and squares up to Adams. "I'll do more than that if you don't get out of my way."

Madison knows she's losing control of the situation. "Everyone, calm down!" she says, raising her voice. "You need to let us do our jobs and identify whoever this is. Unfortunately, that means waiting. It could be days, maybe weeks. The sooner you let us go about it, the sooner you'll know who it is. Okay?" She eyeballs Doug.

He reluctantly turns away.

Stuart Carpenter is standing now, with his back to them and

his shoulders hunched. Madison's gut tells her he might already know who they've found.

CHAPTER THREE

"You shouldn't have said that in front of them," says Madison as she heads to her vehicle, reluctantly leaving Stuart Carpenter behind in the diner. She can't take him in for questioning as she doesn't know enough about the case. She needs to see what's waiting for her on the mountain in order to understand what they're dealing with and whether it's related to the Drapers' missing daughter.

The rain soaks her in seconds. She stupidly left her jacket in her car as it wasn't raining when she arrived at the diner.

Adams follows her with his hood up. "How was I supposed to know they have a vested interest in bodies on Grave Mountain?"

She spins around and stops him as he wipes the rain from his face. Adams is a few years older than her at forty-one, and he takes care of his appearance. Some might consider him attractive. He's not Madison's type. Instead, he drives her insane.

"Look," she says, "I just had to listen to those poor people tell me about their missing loved ones and how I supposedly don't give a crap about what happened to them because I'm not out there searching every day. Now I have to go look at a dead body and figure out which one of those people gets the devastating news that it's *their* loved one we've found deceased. I don't need to babysit you on top of all that, Adams! *Think* before you speak. Can you do that for me?" She doesn't wait for a response. She turns and continues to her car.

This isn't their first argument. Adams joined the department a year ago after leaving a larger PD in Denver, where he worked as a sergeant. It's fair to say that, so far, he's not as dedicated to his job as Madison would like him to be, which is why she tends to lead their investigations. He can be insensitive and half-assed, but she thought he was making progress. Nights like this frustrate her because she can't be good at her job if he's not a team player.

"I'm sorry, okay?" he yells over the rain. "I had no idea why you were in there and who those people were. I'm not a mind reader!" He sighs heavily. "Look, it won't happen again. I'll pull you aside next time."

She turns and looks at him. His tie hangs loosely at the open collar of his shirt. His eyes are weary. They've both had a long day already. She takes a deep breath. "Fine. Take me to the body." She grabs her jacket from her car before they get into his Ford.

Once inside the car, Adams hands her some takeout napkins from the glovebox. "Here. Dry off while I drive."

She tries, but her hair is dripping wet, and he doesn't have enough napkins. As he pulls out of the diner's parking lot, she asks, "What do we know?"

He hits the gas. "The remains are skeletal. They're located east of the Juniper Trail, and a woman found them just before noon. Actually, her dog discovered them. He wouldn't come back when called, and when she tracked him down, she realized why. The recent storms must've unearthed things up there."

Madison thinks about Nancy and Doug Draper. Situations like this are conflicting. Is it better that it *is* their daughter, to end their suffering, or are they secretly harboring hope that Becky's still alive? Madison would want answers, no matter what those answers were, but everyone's different.

"If she discovered the remains at noon, why did she wait until now to call it in?" she asks.

Adams races through a red light. The windshield wipers struggle to keep up with the downpour. "She said she's never called 911 before and was scared she'd be blamed for her dog disturbing the remains."

Madison rolls her eyes. It was sunny and dry earlier today. "So she thought she'd wait for the storm to pick up and night to roll in before sending us up there. Great. Can we drive close to the scene?"

"Nope," says Adams. "The trail's only accessible by foot, unless you want to ride a horse or a mountain bike up there."

Madison sighs.

Adams glances at her. "Why's it called Grave Mountain anyway?"

"Because it's not unusual for hikers to get lost up there and go missing, more so in the old days. When I was younger, there was an urban legend about how if you saw the spirit of a missing hiker, you'd be the next person to die."

Adams raises his eyebrows as he focuses on the road. "Man, this town is something else."

She snorts. "There are all kinds of myths about the various trails because they adapt with each new retelling. All I know is, I wouldn't go up there alone."

The rain comes down even harder as they arrive on the dirt road with designated parking for walkers intending to hike the Juniper Trail. The only thing they can make out through the windshield is the blur of red and blue flashing lights ahead of them.

"Officers Vickers and Sanchez are already here," says Adams. "Along with the rookies."

Two new young officers have recently joined the department, fresh out of the academy. One male, one female, and both wildly different from each other.

Adams looks at her before opening the door. "I have an umbrella in my trunk if you want it?"

Madison scoffs. "I'm not an umbrella kind of girl."

She gets out of the vehicle and her breath catches when ice-cold drops from the heavy downpour make their way down the back of her jacket before she can even pull her hood up. She runs to the cruiser with the flashing lights and peers in at Shelley Vickers. Shelley's in her early thirties, with long brown hair that she keeps tied back when on duty. "Hey," says Madison. "Is Sanchez already up there?"

Shelley nods. "He's showing the rookies how to secure the scene. Alex just went up too." Alex Parker is their forensic technician. "I'm just waiting to take you up," she adds.

Madison nods. "Let's go."

Shelley exits the vehicle and takes the lead. The pathway is rocky, with dips and inclines, making it difficult to find a steady rhythm as Madison walks. It's only wide enough for two people to walk side by side for the most part, with some parts so narrow they have to walk in single file. The trail is lined with thick vegetation. Madison's boots weren't made for hiking, so she feels every stone and rock underfoot, making her grimace as she walks. She hears Adams slipping around behind her. His shoes are even less suited to muddy conditions.

It takes twenty-five long, tiring minutes for Madison, Shelley and Adams to stumble up the narrow trail with nothing but flashlights in the pitch black to locate the area where the remains were found. When they finally get close, they're off the main trail and in an area thick with underbrush. The densely packed trees offer enough protection from the rain for Madison to pull her hood off her wet hair. The wind can't reach them under here. It's a relief, as her face stings from the journey, but it means a cool, damp mist hangs in the air due to a lack of breeze.

In the distance, Officer Luis Sanchez waves to them with his flashlight. The two new officers are some way off, searching the ground.

As they approach, ducking under low-hanging branches, they find Alex Parker crouched over the remains. He's brought scene lighting with him, so they can see what he's looking at. Trying to catch her breath, Madison touches his back to let him know she's arrived. "Hey."

Alex stands and smiles. Originally from England, he's in his mid-thirties with black hair and a slim build. "Evening, Detectives." He pushes his glasses closer to his eyes and looks at the ground. "We have adult remains."

Madison crouches in the damp soil to get a better look. The strong earthy aroma mixed with the scent of pine needles is a relief, as she was expecting the smell of decomposition. The skeletal remains sit at the bottom of a tree trunk. They've been claimed by nature, leaving them partially hidden by a creeping vine weed that has grown over and around the tree, suggesting this person has been here for some time. It looks like the skeleton might be missing some bones—maybe a couple of ribs and a foot, no doubt scavenged by wild animals over the years. The skull is weathered and thin around the mouth area, with the scalp sitting at the base of the tree trunk. It has a noticeable bullet wound between the eyes. The exit wound must've shattered the back of the skull, as a plant is growing out of it and through the left eye.

Madison shudders as she stands. "They were shot."

"Yes," says Alex. "Or they shot themselves. Although to aim between the eyes would be unusual for a self-inflicted wound. I'll look for the shell casing, but given how long the body has been here, I'd be surprised if we find it. Besides, if this person was killed, it's likely the killer took the casing with them."

She nods. A noise behind distracts her, so she aims her flashlight in that direction. Detective Adams is munching on a granola bar.

"I hope that doesn't tempt the bears," says Alex.

Adams scoffs. "There aren't any bears out here."

"Actually, there could be," Alex replies. "Black bears. One would hope they'll be hibernating by now, but I brought this just in case." He shows them a can of bear spray attached to his belt. "It's best to be prepared. I wouldn't recommend eating anything pungent up here, especially if you ever find yourself alone. Hungry bears can be desperate."

Adams stops chewing and goes a little pale. Eventually, he slips the half-eaten bar into his pocket and nods at the remains. "Do we know whether they're male or female?"

Alex looks at the skull and shakes his head. "That's for Dr. Scott to determine." Dr. Lena Scott is the town's medical examiner.

"I'll give her office a call." Adams pulls out his cell phone and turns, quickly disappearing into the darkness.

Alex wanders away to fetch his camera equipment.

Alone with the remains, Madison looks around, trying to picture what happened out here, but it's too dark to see anything. The noticeable lack of background noise is unsettling, with no birdsong or squirrels rustling through the vegetation due to the time of day. It's easy to imagine how scary it would be if you were isolated out here with a killer. If that was what happened, the victim had nowhere to turn for help. Their screams would've gone unanswered. Were they lured here to be murdered? Or did they take their own life?

It's a good place to remain undiscovered if suicide was this person's intention. A lot of suicidal people choose somewhere they can't easily be found to avoid traumatizing anyone. Madison has attended homes with notes on the front door warning family and emergency services of what awaits them inside.

She thinks about Stuart Carpenter and how he said he could never tell anyone what happened up here on the day of the hike. She saw the conflict on his face. It could've been guilt. Did he make an unsuccessful pass at Becky or Tasha and, when rejected, see red? It's the oldest story in the book and therefore the most likely.

A chill runs through her as she realizes he's had a head start. He could escape. She needs to take him in for questioning immediately.

"Shelley?" she calls into the dark.

Branches snap nearby as Officer Vickers appears from the shadows. "Yes?"

"You need to keep searching." Madison lowers the flashlight's beam to the skull at her feet. "I think there's a good chance we'll find a second body nearby."

CHAPTER FOUR

Madison races down the Juniper Trail with Detective Adams close behind her. They try not to slip in the mud, but it's impossible as the ground is saturated, the rocks are slick with moss and they only have one flashlight between them. By the time they arrive back at his car, their hands, boots and clothes are covered in mud.

"Now I know why you wanted to take my car," says Adams, trying to wipe the mud from his boots.

Madison snorts. They've had some friendly vehicle rivalry going on ever since she wrecked his prized Chevy Camaro in pursuit of a serial killer. To add insult to injury, she was then gifted a black Dodge Challenger SRT Demon with a black and ruby-red interior. Adams can only afford a crappy Ford Taurus as a replacement for his Camaro, and he never lets her forget it.

She slips into the passenger side and buckles up, desperate to race back to the diner and take Stuart Carpenter in for questioning. When Adams appears more concerned with cleaning the mud off his clothes to avoid getting the car's interior dirty, she leans over, opens his door and yells, "Get in! Never mind the damn mud."

He's not happy. "Why can't you let me keep anything nice?" He slides in and starts the engine. "What's the hurry? Where are we even going?"

Madison explains how the remains on the mountain could belong to the Drapers' missing daughter or her friend, and how they might have been killed by someone present at the diner tonight.

"Why would he attend the meeting just to be openly accused of murder?" says Adams as he drives. Thankfully, the downpour has tapered off to a drizzle.

"I don't know," she says. "He implied he needed support too. I thought he wanted to clear his name, but he acted strange. Said he couldn't talk about what happened." She glances at the clock. It's almost midnight.

It takes another ten minutes to reach the diner, and the lights are already out. Everyone's gone home. "Dammit!"

Adams parks the car and turns the engine off. "What's his name? I'll call dispatch to see if they have an address for him."

"Stuart Carpenter." He told Madison he was twenty-two when he went on the fateful hike, and that was five years ago. "He's twenty-seven, but I don't have his DOB." She gets out and heads to her own car while he makes the call. She pulls a towel from her trunk to start drying herself off. She keeps it in there for when Brody, a former police dog, takes trips in her car. Somehow, he's always muddy or wet, even in the summer.

She looks up at the darkened apartment over the diner as she dries herself. Vince and Oliver have gone to bed, and Nancy and Doug Draper must've returned home. They won't sleep, though. They'll be awake all night.

"Madison!" yells Adams. "I have two possible addresses. Coming?"

"Keep your voice down!" She throws the dirty towel into her trunk and quietly closes it before going to his window. "Text me the addresses and I'll meet you there."

"Meet me there or beat me there?" He smiles as he revs his engine.

She rolls her eyes and gets into her own car. When his text comes through, she looks at the addresses to see which is closer. "We'll go to Mason Lane first," she says through her window.

"Got it." Adams pulls out of the parking lot before her.

She catches up with him before overtaking on a quiet road. She easily arrives at the address before him. She parks a short distance away and assesses the house from her vehicle. This is a rough, high-crime neighborhood where she spent much of her time as a rookie.

Adams pulls up behind her and they quietly get out of their cars.

"Ready?" she says.

He nods, leading the way.

The two-story house has no porch, just concrete paving slabs leading up to it. It looks run-down, with an overgrown yard. A light is on at the back of the house. They can see the orange glow through the frosted glass in the front door.

Adams knocks hard. A couple of dogs from neighboring properties wake from their slumber and bark nonstop.

No one comes to the door.

"What d'ya think?" asks Adams. "Should we go to the other address?"

Madison walks to the front window to peer in. The living room drapes are closed except for a narrow gap between them. She can't see anyone inside, just part of an empty couch. "Let's take a look out back before we go."

Adams goes ahead of her, and something makes Madison touch her weapon.

The backyard is in complete darkness, with no security lights. The neighboring houses aren't too far apart, and she sees someone glance out of their bedroom window to her left. They're looking to see what woke the dogs.

Madison holds up her badge so they know not to call 911 about a couple of potential robbers. The person disappears back behind their blinds and their bedroom light quickly goes out. Madison doesn't look away, though, and after a minute she sees a cell phone light pointing at her. They've returned to the window to record her and Adams, probably hoping to capture something good enough to go viral.

She rolls her eyes. "Bet they wouldn't bother if we *were* here to rob the place."

Adams stops and looks back at her. "What's that?"

"Nothing." She walks past him to the back door. She tries knocking, as she doesn't want to be shot by whoever is inside. "Open up! This is the police."

They wait in silence for a full minute and hear nothing. Madison doesn't like it. Her gut tells her something's off. Someone's deliberately keeping quiet. "Dispatch knows we're here, right?" she whispers.

"They don't know which address we came to first, but they know we're trying both of them," Adams says.

She thinks for a second. "Call for backup."

He frowns. "But the house is empty, isn't it?"

A thud from inside makes them jump. Madison glances at Adams. "We gave them a chance to answer the door."

He nods as he pulls out his service weapon.

Madison retrieves her own and tries the door handle with her spare hand. She's surprised when it opens. Without hesitation, she opens the door wide and enters. "This is the police! We're coming in, and we're armed. Make yourself known!"

The kitchen is clear. Adams flicks on the light. The small room is tidy, with just a single mug in the sink waiting to be washed. Sparse of belongings, it smells of mildew, with no signs of family life, suggesting this person lives alone. A doorway to their right leads to the room the light is coming from. As it's next to the kitchen, Madison assumes it's a dining room.

She heads toward it with her weapon held up in front of her. She feels beads of sweat under her arms from an adrenaline surge. "Who's in there?" she shouts. "Is that you, Stuart?"

The sound of heavy breathing starts. It's creepy. Madison walks toward the doorway and peers into the room. Her heart skips a beat. "Oh my God."

As she's blocking the doorway, Adams looks over her shoulder. "Put the weapon down, now!" he yells.

Stuart Carpenter is sitting alone at a large wooden dining table. The room is empty apart from him, the table and four chairs, and a floor lamp behind him. A single painting of a ship sailing stormy seas is mounted on the wall behind him. Stuart has several newspaper clippings spread out in front of him on the table. Madison can't read them from the doorway, but it doesn't take a genius to figure out they're probably about Becky and Tasha's disappearance.

Stuart's formerly pale face is bright red, and his eyes are bloodshot. His expression is one of overwhelming guilt. Madison realizes that the two missing women died on the mountain that day. All that's left of them now is skeletal remains. A ball of dread fills her chest as she pictures the Drapers' faces when she breaks the news to them later.

"You've finally found them, haven't you?" says Stuart without looking up.

Madison fixes her eyes on the sawed-off shotgun that rests on his seat between his legs. It's pointing upward. His chin hovers dangerously close over the barrels. "Listen, Stuart," she says. "Nothing is worth dying for. *Nothing.* You hear me?"

She feels Adams's hand on her back as he tries to squeeze by her, but she doesn't want him to spook Stuart, so she pushes her weight back to stop him. Like her, he keeps his gun trained on him. They remain in the doorway in case he decides he wants to take a couple of cops out before killing himself.

"Why don't you tell me what happened, and we'll see what needs to be done after that?" she says.

Stuart finally makes eye contact with her. "That's the problem," he says. "You wouldn't believe me if I told you. And I wouldn't blame you."

She swallows. Her mouth has gone dry. It's only been three months since another man took his own life right in front of her. That one decided to jump off the top of the downtown shopping mall. When she tries to fall asleep at night, she still hears the sickening thud of his body hitting the ground. She doesn't know what she could've done to stop him from jumping, and she could really do without someone else taking their own life in front of her.

"Stuart?" she says. "I'm no skeptic. You wouldn't believe half the things I've witnessed in my career. So why don't you try me?"

When he doesn't respond, she considers shooting him in the arm or shoulder to stop him from pulling the trigger and ending his life. She can't bear the thought of him dying without revealing the answers that Nancy and Doug so desperately need. From the way Adams subtly moves his weapon's aim, she figures he's considering the same thing.

"Please, Stuart," she says. "At least tell us why you killed your friends. That's the very least you can do if you're sorry about what happened."

He lowers his eyes and stares directly into the barrels.

Madison's trigger finger twitches, but she holds off as he opens his mouth to speak.

"I *am* sorry," he says. "But I can't undo any of it now." He takes a deep breath. "I can't un-kill them."

Madison pulls the trigger, but it's a second too late. Her shot scrapes Stuart's arm. *His* shot destroys his entire face.

She's deafened by the blast. It numbs her senses. She doesn't even have time to cry out to stop him.

Adams lurches forward to reach Stuart, but he's beyond help. The force of the gunshot blast has sent him and his chair backward. The contents of his skull now cover the wall and the painting behind him.

Adams is yelling something with his hands on the back of his head, but Madison can't hear him yet. Her ears ring loudly as her hands tremble uncontrollably.

CHAPTER FIVE

Nate Monroe wakes to the sound of a dog barking. It confuses
him. Dogs aren't allowed on death row. A black cat called Oreo
visits the inmates occasionally, when the warden allows it, but
never a dog. Bleary-eyed, he sits up and can instantly tell he's
not in his cell. He senses extra space around him. The walls
aren't close enough to touch. Confused, he checks the clock on
his nightstand. It's just after 2 a.m.

The barking continues, and he realizes his German shep-
herd–husky mix is trying to wake him, which quickly brings
Nate around. Brody runs downstairs, so Nate follows him, bare-
foot in just his pajama pants. He's not expecting visitors, but as
Brody's a former K9, Nate knows to trust his behavior.

A knock at the front door makes him jump. He switches a
light on and unlocks it. Madison's standing there. She's soaking
wet and her clothes are covered in mud.

He steps aside to let her in. "What's happened? Are you
okay?"

Brody goes to her with his tail wagging excitedly. Madison
strokes the dog's face before turning to Nate. She reaches for
him, and they hug with the door open. He doesn't care that she's

cold, wet and muddy. When she pulls away, she looks weary and troubled.

"I've had a rough night," she says.

He closes the door. "Come here." He kisses her before stroking her damp, tangled blonde hair away from her face. "Jump in the shower while I make you a hot drink."

She pulls her jacket off. It sticks to her arms and comes off inside out. "I need to make a call first. It won't take long."

Nate hangs her coat over the back of one of the breakfast bar stools and fetches a clean bath towel from the laundry pile. He wraps it around her shoulders before switching the coffee machine on and looking for clean cups.

Madison takes a seat at the breakfast bar and pulls out her phone. She readies herself before using it, taking a deep breath as if steeling herself for a battle. Nate realizes she's dreading the call. He wants to give her some privacy, so he heads to the living room, but as he passes her, she reaches for his hand, signaling she wants him to stay.

He stands by her side and gently rubs her back as she makes the call.

"Nancy?" she says when someone answers. "It's Detective Harper. I'm sorry to call so late. I figured you'd want an update."

Nate can make out the voice at the other end of the line. She says something about being relieved that Madison called. He thinks this is Nancy Draper. He knows she has a missing daughter.

Madison takes another deep breath. "I don't have anything concrete to tell you yet, it's just too soon, but I can tell you that only one body was found. They were some distance from the Juniper Trail. It seems they've been there some time, and due to the condition of the remains, we need the medical examiner to determine whether the person is male or female."

Nate's not surprised when he hears a sob. *Due to the condi-*

tion of the remains is a sentence no one wants to hear. It's the only polite way of explaining there's nothing left but bones, and maybe not even a complete skeleton. It means the medical examiner can only do so much in determining the cause of death and any injuries. There will likely be no remnants of the organs that once made the body thrive, along with little hair and certainly no skin. Maybe they can use dental records to identify the person, assuming Madison's team has found the skull.

He doesn't know how people live with picturing their loved ones that way.

Perhaps faith plays a part. Nate himself has been through some horrendous ordeals: his fiancée was murdered, and he served seventeen years on death row in Texas. He'd like to believe faith got him through it, as he was heavily religious as a young man, even hoping to become a priest. But the truth is, it was his faith that got him locked up, and now he's often left wondering whether he even believes in God anymore or whether he's just paying lip service when he says his silent prayers. Either way, he hopes the woman Madison's talking to has someone with her tonight. Whether that's a family member or a God she believes in, either is better than being alone.

"Dr. Scott will examine the remains first thing in the morning," says Madison. "She's extremely professional and will handle the situation sensitively. I'll be there, so I'll update you as soon as possible."

"That's the trail she was on," says Nancy. "The Juniper Trail."

Madison nods. "I need to tell you something else, but I don't want the press to learn about it yet. If I tell you, can you promise me you'll keep it to yourselves?"

Her back trembles under Nate's hand. It's concerning, as she doesn't usually get this upset over the discovery of remains.

"I went to Stuart Carpenter's house tonight," she says. "Once I was back from the mountain."

Nate can feel her holding back a sob as her shoulders tighten and her hand goes to her chest. He kisses the back of her head.

"I wanted to take him in for questioning. But..." She pauses. "He's dead, Nancy. Stuart decided to take his own life tonight."

Nancy relays the information to her husband. Nate hears Doug Draper exclaiming but can't make out the words. It sounds like Doug believes he's been robbed of justice.

Madison turns her head and shoots Nate a weary look. Her blue eyes are bloodshot, and her skin is pale, apart from her cheeks, which are pink and weather-beaten. He hates that she had to discover a dead body.

She shakes her head at something Nancy says. "I can't answer that yet. He was upset, and I'm reluctant to repeat his final words right now. I need more context before I can assign guilt to him. And we don't know for sure that Becky and Tasha are dead. The remains discovered could belong to someone else." She takes a deep breath. "Just, *please*, don't tell anyone about Stuart. I need to notify his family as soon as we can locate his next of kin. And once the media gets involved, you'll be harassed by reporters. So let's try to figure all this out privately while we still can."

The woman asks when she'll have answers. When she'll know whether the remains found belong to her daughter.

"I can't give an exact time frame, I'm sorry," says Madison. "As soon as I know who this person is, you'll know. Okay?"

Nancy gives her thanks and reluctantly ends the call.

Madison places her phone on the breakfast bar and lowers her head with a long exhale. "It never gets easier, Nate. *Never*."

He gently spins her stool and sits in front of her on the next one. "That was Nancy Draper, I take it?"

She nods before telling him about the support group meeting she attended at the diner, and how the guy who killed himself was there.

He's stunned that Stuart Carpenter would attend if he's a suspect. "So while you were on the mountain, he killed himself?"

"No," she says. "He shot himself at his home as Adams and I tried to talk him out of it."

Shocked, Nate pulls her to him. At times like this, he wishes she weren't a cop and he weren't a PI. With the compensation payout from his wrongful conviction, neither of them needs to work another day in their lives. Their relationship is still new—they've only known each other for almost a year and a half—but after everything they've been through, Nate knows he wants to protect this woman for the rest of his life. But he also knows policing is in her blood, and she probably wouldn't give it up for anything.

As she pulls away, he glances at the clock on the wall. It's 2:30 a.m., and Madison has an early start ahead of her.

He stands. "Come to bed."

CHAPTER SIX

Madison hovers outside the entrance to the medical examiner's building. Miraculously, last night's downpour cleared over the early hours and has left a beautiful morning in its wake. It's the kind of sunny, bitterly cold day you dream about in the depths of a midsummer heatwave. The ground glistens with a fresh layer of frost, and she can see her breath.

She pulls her gloves off to check her phone for the time. 8:14 a.m. She asked Detective Adams to meet her here at eight. Maybe he's busy tracing Stuart Carpenter's next of kin, or perhaps it was his turn to take the kids to school. With a sigh, she decides to go inside without him. The guy behind the front desk calls Dr. Lena Scott to let her know that Madison has arrived.

Lena makes her wait. It's 8:28 before she appears, and she offers no apology or smile, which is unlike her. Things have been a little awkward between them ever since Lena expressed an interest in Nate right before Madison and Nate started seeing each other. But now Lena's dating Sergeant Steve Tanner, so Madison doesn't know what the woman's problem is, and she could really do without the high school drama today.

"Follow me," says Lena. She's already in her scrubs and white coat. Her formerly long brown hair has recently been cut into a shoulder-length style and is tied into a small ponytail at the back of her head.

Madison enters the cool morgue and helps herself to a surgical mask. The familiar, unsettling aroma of death greets her, which always takes a minute to get used to. Lena's assistants busy themselves as she pulls back a sheet from the skeletal remains laid out on the mortuary table in front of her.

Madison steps closer. The bones are clearly weathered from exposure, as they're stained brown, with noticeable degradation.

Lena pulls her surgical mask up over her nose and mouth. "I've recorded all the bones that were found, and it appears we're missing several, which isn't surprising considering how long this person went undiscovered."

"How long was that?" asks Madison. "Can you tell?"

"*I* won't be able to tell, but a forensic anthropologist might if it comes to that."

"Can you tell their sex?"

Lena takes a deep breath. "Well, skeletons don't fall neatly into two categories, but it's easier to determine the sex of adult skeletons than children. There are several morphological differences between males and females. The easiest place to start is the pelvis." She points to it. "A male's is narrower and more U-shaped than this one. A female's is shallower and broader to facilitate childbirth."

Madison checks her phone quickly.

"Am I boring you?" says Lena sharply.

"No, sorry." She pockets the phone. "It's just that Detective Adams should be here by now. I'm wondering if something else has happened. The officers are still searching the trail where this person was found, so he could've been called to another body."

"You're expecting more?"

"Maybe. You have someone named Stuart Carpenter here, right?" she says.

Lena looks over at one of her assistants, who nods.

"He's being processed in the next room," says Skylar. "We only got him an hour ago because Alex was doing his thing."

Alex would've wanted to document the scene at the house in case someone—perhaps a family member or their lawyer—insinuates that Stuart was murdered. It sounds ridiculous when the suicide was witnessed, but it happens. Some people can't accept their loved one chose to die, which is understandable.

"I'm considering the possibility that he's responsible for the murder of two women on Grave Mountain," says Madison. "One of whom might be this person. They disappeared five years ago. But it depends on what you tell me and whether we find a second body up there."

Lena focuses on the remains. "Well, to get to my point a little faster than I intended, this *is* a female. It's not just her pelvis that leads me to that conclusion, but her skull has female characteristics too. Females have smaller skulls with more rounded eye sockets than males, and she has a smooth brow ridge and several other feminine identifiers." She looks at Madison. "We basically use a sliding scale of differences to determine the sex of the remains, and I'm confident this is a female."

Madison learns a lot in her job, and she finds the majority of it fascinating but equally depressing. "I see some of her teeth are intact, so would dental records be the easiest method of identification?"

"It would certainly be the quickest and cheapest. DNA's a little harder to extract from older bones, due to degradation, so it would take longer to match a comparison sample, and to find someone to give that sample."

Madison pulls out her pocket notebook. "Now that I know this is a female, it could be either of the two women I have in mind. I'll track down their dentists and see what I can find."

Lena picks up a clipboard and pen. "What are their names? Because I can make a note of this person's presumed-to-be name."

"Becky Draper and Tasha Harris. Both were nineteen when they disappeared." Lena makes a note as Madison asks, "Is there any way of aging the remains?"

"There is, but as I said earlier, we'd need a forensic anthropologist for an accurate range, and that won't be necessary if we manage to identify her through her dental records."

If this isn't Becky or Tasha, Madison will need to look through all of the department's cold cases and see if she can match a missing person to the remains.

"Was the bullet wound between her eyes enough to kill her?" Madison's seen enough cases of people surviving gunshot wounds to the face to know it's not a stupid question.

Lena picks up the fragile skull, which has separated into fragments since being removed from the mountain. Lena has pieced the fragments together like a jigsaw puzzle, and the ones on the table show a large exit wound. She returns the front of the skull to the table in order to examine the rest of the bones.

"I haven't found any other injuries yet. That doesn't mean she wasn't also stabbed, or shot more than once. Without her tissue and organs, it would be impossible to tell unless a knife or bullet pierced or scraped the bones. The only obvious wound is the one on her head, and a gunshot at that angle could certainly result in death." She pauses. "I'm guessing you want to know whether it could've been self-inflicted?"

Madison nods. "Alex said suicidal people usually position the gun elsewhere. I'm guessing in the mouth, under the chin, or maybe to the temple, right?" She suddenly experiences a powerful flashback to Stuart's suicide. The blast of the shotgun roars in her ears. She closes her eyes for a second.

Lena doesn't notice. "It would be unusual to point the gun between the eyes, although that doesn't mean it wasn't suicide, as she may have been aiming for her forehead. Generally, people flinch when pulling the trigger on themselves, which means the shot should be off-center, but it isn't. It's difficult to know the range of fire, as she has no tissue left to reveal the necessary clues, but the entrance site suggests to me that this wasn't a contact-range gunshot, meaning it wasn't self-inflicted. Which also suggests that whoever shot her had a good aim. You'd need a ballistics expert to gauge how far away they were when they fired the shot."

Madison nods. She doesn't think that's necessary yet. "So her killer was experienced with guns and perhaps hunting."

"Right."

Stuart obviously had access to firearms, because he used one on himself, so it's not unreasonable to assume he owned one at the time of the hike. "Can you tell what type of firearm was used?"

Lena shakes her head. "I haven't had time to check yet. I'll need to get back to you on that."

"Sure." Madison looks around the room. "Do you know if any clothes or a cell phone were found with the remains?"

Lena removes her mask. "Alex told my team he'd unearthed some other items, so maybe, but he hasn't passed them to us. They'll probably go to the crime lab."

Madison needs to check in with the team as soon as possible to see what other developments have happened in the few hours she spent trying to sleep. She steps away from the remains and removes her own mask. "Thanks for this. It's useful to know the victim is female and we're dealing with a homicide."

When Lena doesn't reply, she asks, "Lena, have I done something to upset you? It's just that you seem a little off lately."

Lena takes a sip from her water bottle before responding. "No. I'm just stressed right now, that's all." She offers a weak smile.

"How are things with Steve?"

Sergeant Tanner keeps his private life to himself, but the truth is, until recently he didn't really have one. He spent all his time at work. He's in his mid-forties and has never married. If he's not working, he's working out, and he's a great team member; reliable, trustworthy and excellent at his job. Since dating the medical examiner, he's had a spring in his step, and Madison hopes the relationship works out.

"Good. It's still early days." Lena turns her back on Madison as she busies herself with some autopsy tools. It suggests she doesn't want to talk about it.

"Glad to hear it," says Madison, sensing it's time to leave. "I should get out of here. I'll keep you updated with the investigation."

She heads for the exit, relieved to get some fresh air. Once outside, she pulls a hat over her hair and scans the parking lot, but there's still no sign of Detective Adams. She has no missed calls either. Sensing that something's wrong, she gets into her car and heads to the station.

CHAPTER SEVEN

Madison is keen to notify Stuart Carpenter's family of his death as soon as possible, and she'd like Detective Adams to come with her. But as she heads to her desk at the station, she learns that Adams is sick and is staying home today.

"He feels terrible," says Sergeant Steve Tanner as he finishes his coffee and stands. "He thinks it could be viral and he doesn't want to spread it around the station. Apparently, he caught it from one of his girls."

Adams has twin nine-year-olds.

Madison is unimpressed. He's either bailing because what they witnessed last night is too much for him to deal with, or he really is sick, which means she's likely to come down with whatever he has. "Hopefully it's just a twenty-four-hour thing," she says diplomatically.

She looks around the open-plan office. Stella and Dina, the dispatchers, are busy on the phones. Chief Carmen Mendes is alone in her office, and several uniformed officers come and go on their way to fetch coffees and paperwork. She watches the two rookies for a second.

Officer Lisa Kent is a petite five foot four, with bright dyed red hair tied back in a bun. She's laughing at something the other rookie has said, but he looks puzzled by her reaction. They're both twenty-seven, but that's where the similarities end. Officer Corey Fuller is tall, muscular and serious for a young guy. He comes across as introverted, and Madison wonders whether he's right for the role. Kent is a little too playful with him, making him blush a lot. She's heard rumors that the young woman likes to flirt with anything in pants.

They exit the building behind the department's more experienced officer, Gloria Williams. Madison smiles to herself. Gloria must be on rookie duty today.

Chief Mendes gets Madison's attention through her glass-paneled wall. Madison nods and says to Steve, "We're being summoned."

He follows her into Mendes's office. They don't bother closing the door behind them. The office is big enough for a large desk, some filing cabinets and a few chairs, and it's kept impeccably tidy, like the woman herself.

Chief Mendes's long dark hair is slicked back into a ponytail. She removes her reading glasses and sits back in her chair to look at Madison. "How are you after everything that happened overnight?"

"Well, my ears took forever to stop ringing. He used a shotgun in a small room."

"That's not what I mean," says Mendes. "What you and Adams witnessed was traumatic. Do you need time off to process it, or do you want to speak to Julien? I'm sure he could squeeze you in."

Julien Adler is a therapist from a local clinic who's agreed to accept referrals from their department. Madison has been instrumental in highlighting the need for someone to provide mental health support to the team, but until recently, she was told they couldn't afford it.

"I don't think so," she says. "It was shocking, of course, and I didn't manage much sleep when I finally got to bed, but I'll see how I go. I'm just tired." That's not the whole truth. She dreamed about the moment Stuart's head exploded against the wall behind him. But she figures that's normal, given what she witnessed.

Nate said she had been talking in her sleep when she finally dropped off at around 4 a.m. But it's not just the flashbacks and the dreams. She's feeling more anxious than she would've expected. As if her life is at risk somehow. But it's not, and it never was. Stuart never threatened her or Adams at any point. The evidence suggests he might've been a killer, but she was never in any real danger, so she can't understand the tightness in her chest or the ball of dread in her stomach. It feels like something bad is imminent, and she needs to stay alert to ensure she isn't caught unawares.

She attempts a smile. "It's reassuring to know support is there if I need it."

Mendes's gaze remains on her a minute longer than necessary as she considers whether to order her to see the therapist. She must trust Madison's opinion, because eventually she says, "What did you learn at the morgue?"

Madison takes a deep breath. "Well, our victim is an adult female who was killed by a single gunshot wound to the head, *not* self-inflicted. Lena doesn't know how long she was on the mountain, but I believe I might know who she is." She explains everything that happened at the diner last night as Mendes and Steve listen in, surprised. They hadn't known she planned to attend the support group meeting.

"How long have they been meeting?" asks Steve.

She shrugs. "Probably years. When Nancy invited me, she implied the group has gotten smaller over time. Last night, it consisted of the Drapers, Robert Dorsey, Stuart Carpenter and a woman with a missing baby. I didn't get her name."

Steve frowns. "So the Drapers openly accused Stuart of

murder and he immediately went home to kill himself because he couldn't face being arrested?"

"It looks that way," she says. "Uniforms are checking his house for a suicide note and anything that might tell us whether he was involved in Becky and Tasha's disappearance. He had newspaper clippings on the table in front of him, all about their disappearance, so combined with everything else, it seems he's our guy. I'm not expecting a note to be found as I think his decision was impulsive."

Chief Mendes nods. "Unfortunate though his death is, at least it might mean we can close a cold case and provide answers for two families."

Madison isn't sure that will help any of the parents, given the likely outcome is that both their daughters are dead. "I've got officers scouring the trail for evidence and other possible remains, but we need to set up a formal search."

"I'm not sure that's worth starting until we confirm who the remains belong to," says Mendes. "Because if the body in the morgue isn't Becky Draper or Tasha Harris, then a full-scale search of the mountain would be a waste of resources. It's too big an area, and presumably it was already searched after they disappeared."

Madison knows she's right, but it's frustrating. "Fine." She takes a deep breath. "Well, I need to notify Stuart's family of his death, then update the Drapers and track down Tasha Harris's family. Tasha's parents don't know anything yet. I'd rather have an ID for the remains before I tell them, but I need her dental records for that."

It dawns on her that Tasha's parents weren't at last night's meeting. She wonders whether they used to attend and stopped for some reason. Maybe a support group wasn't for them. Not everyone wants to share their grief with strangers.

"Is Detective Adams at either scene?" asks Mendes.

"No," says Steve. "He's out sick. Virus, he thinks."

Chief Mendes taps her long fingernails on her desk for a few seconds. She looks like she's about to make a difficult decision. "Since I have you both alone, tell me honestly: how's Adams working out?"

Madison shares a look with Steve. She can tell he's thinking the same as her. They're not sure how honest they can be considering the chief chose Adams over Steve for the vacant detective role. Apparently, Mendes once worked with Adams's hotshot brother at the Colorado Bureau of Investigation and assumed Adams would be just as good. Unfortunately, she was wrong.

"Your expressions tell me everything I need to know," says Mendes with a sigh. "Is he incompetent or just lazy? Because I want to know what I'm dealing with before I consider his future here."

"He's not lazy," says Madison carefully. "And I don't actually think he's incompetent. He just doesn't want to be here. He never has. He hates living in Lost Creek and would much rather be back in Denver."

"So why'd he leave?" says Steve. "I don't get it. He acts like he was forced to come here."

Madison's cell phone rings. It's Alex. "I should take this," she says.

"Sure," says Mendes. "We can discuss Detective Adams another time."

"Just don't do anything drastic," says Madison. She feels sorry for the guy since he's not here to defend himself. "Let me talk to him and see what's going on in that head of his."

"You'll catch his virus," says Steve.

She scoffs. "I think we all know he's not really sick." She accepts Alex's call as she leaves the office. "Hey, Alex."

"Morning, Detective. I'm currently at the crime scene on the mountain and wanted to know whether you or Detective Adams will be joining me." His voice comes and goes. The cell service isn't great up there. Madison can hear the wind whistling down the line.

"Adams is out sick," she says. "And I'm busy. I've been to the morgue. Lena says the victim was an adult female. The gunshot wound wasn't self-inflicted, so we're treating it as a homicide."

"Understood," he says. "I found some clothing near the skeleton, so I'll send that..."

She loses him for a second. "Alex, you're breaking up."

"I said..." Before he can repeat himself, the line goes dead.

Frustrated, she shoots him a text for when he has service.

I'll be there as soon as I can. Text me what clothing you found.

She takes a deep breath. If either the Drapers or Tasha's parents recognize the clothing, they'll be devastated. Which means today's going to be even worse than yesterday.

Her phone buzzes, but it's not Alex, it's Nate.

Dinner at my place tonight?

She smiles, hoping she'll be able to take him up on his offer. It all depends on whether they find anything else on Grave Mountain. Her phone buzzes again.

PS Don't forget I love you.

She blushes. It's been years since she was in a relationship, and her troubled past made her believe she'd never meet anyone who'd be willing to take her on again. The fact that she's found love with someone she's not only attracted to and has a great time with but who she also respects seems too good to be true.

A heavy feeling of dread washes over her again. She should be happy, but instead, she feels like it will all be taken away from her. Maybe because now she has something to lose. She shakes her head. She's not going to think about anything negative when it comes to her relationship with Nate. She replies.

Can't wait. Love you (and Brody) too.

When she sits at her desk, the bright morning sunlight coming from the nearby window dazzles her. After getting up to close the blinds, she starts her computer and searches for Stuart's next of kin. His family will be devastated, and they'll have many questions, but she's hoping they'll be able to answer some of her own. Like: did they know their son was a killer?

She finds a cell number for the person who owns Stuart's house: Bryan Carpenter. It could be a brother or his father. Another search finds Bryan's current address. She learns that he also owns the Pine Shadows Lodge on the other side of town. Before she leaves to pay him a visit, she runs a quick background check on Stuart. He had no history of arrests, but she finds a record of Detective Douglas's interview with him about the women's disappearance. Attachments include photographs of the three people who went on the hike. She opens Stuart's first. He looks the same as when she met him last night, just a little younger. Becky's photo is the same one Nancy showed her, where she's dressed for the hike right before she left home.

Madison opens the image of Tasha Harris. It's the first time she's seen her. Tasha has long, wavy blonde hair. The photo was taken on a beach. She's wearing a pink bikini, visible from the waist up. Sunglasses obscure her eyes, but she's smiling widely at the camera. Her skin is tanned, and she looks youthful and at ease.

Madison needs to read Stuart's witness statement, but it's more important that she notifies his family of his death first. She'd hate for them to find out from a neighbor that something happened at his house in the early hours, although all the neighbors questioned by officers said they didn't know who Stuart's friends or relatives were. Apparently, he wasn't very open. That could just mean he was a private person. There's no law against that.

Dreading his family's reaction, Madison grabs her car keys and heads out of the station.

CHAPTER EIGHT

The Pine Shadows Lodge sits in front of a breathtaking panoramic backdrop of the mountains, making it one of Lost Creek's most popular wedding venues. It's surrounded by acres of woodland, with a crystal-clear creek running alongside it. The midmorning sun glistens off the water. It's so pretty that it makes Madison yearn for a vacation. She and Nate have promised themselves they'll take one as soon as things are quiet. Maybe once this current case is wrapped up, she can finally tell him to book something. With Christmas just over three weeks away, she considers whether to fly somewhere hot and sunny for a change.

She quickly dismisses the thought. She can't go away because Owen is coming home from college. She's only seen her son once since he left in August to study law at Arizona State University, and he didn't even return for Thanksgiving. He's not far away, but she's trying to give him space to settle in and become his own person. And she has regular video calls with him. It's not the same, though. She misses his mess around the house and his sarcastic sense of humor. Bandit misses him too. The cat still sleeps on Owen's bed most nights.

Not wanting to think about how much she misses her only child, Madison gets out of the car and zips her jacket up to stop the biting cold from making her want to run inside as fast as possible. Before she can go anywhere, her phone rings. She has a feeling it's going to be one of those days when it never stops, especially as she doesn't have Adams to share the load.

"Hello?" she says, turning to face the chilly breeze to keep her hair out of her face.

"It's Stella," says the dispatcher. "I know you're busy, but I've got a man named Robert Dorsey on the line. He's eager for an update on the body found on the mountain. Want me to tell him you'll be in touch later?"

Madison sighs. She could leave it until later, but it seems cruel as he's seeking reassurance about his missing son. "No, that's fine. Put him through."

"Okay."

When the line clicks, Madison slips back into her car, leaving the door open. "Mr. Dorsey? It's Detective Harper. I understand you're calling about last night."

His voice is thick with emotion as he says bluntly, "I need to know whether it's Brandon."

"Sure, I understand," she says. "The medical examiner believes the remains are female. It isn't Brandon."

The line goes silent, and Madison thinks he might hang up until he says, "Is it the Drapers' girl? I'd be happy for them if it is."

"We're trying to confirm who it is as fast as possible, but the truth is we don't know yet. I'd appreciate it if you wouldn't mention this to anyone, especially the press. We'd like more time before upsetting anyone unnecessarily."

It sounds like a sob breaks free from Robert. The disappointment of knowing he's no closer to answers about what happened to his son must be crushing.

Madison wants to help, but there's no way she has time to

reopen his son's case right now. She has another solution. "Mr. Dorsey, I have a friend who's a private investigator." She should probably refer to Nate as her partner or boyfriend, but it still feels weird. "I don't know whether you've already tried that or would even be open to it, but I could ask him to get in touch with you and see how he might be able to help."

Quietly, Robert says, "I can't afford a PI. My home is in foreclosure. I suspect I'm about to be laid off from my job too."

She takes a deep breath. "I'm sorry to hear that. I don't think it'll be a problem for Nate. I have a feeling he'd be happy to help regardless." It's not unusual for Nate to work cases for free.

"That would be Nate Monroe, I take it?" he asks.

"Right." Madison frowns. In the diner last night, Robert made it clear he knows about her past, so it's not a stretch to assume he also knows about Nate's time on death row. She wonders if he'll let that stop him from accepting help.

It takes a long time for him to reply. "I just want my son back," he says with a deep sigh. The pain in his voice is still raw, even after all these years.

"Text me your number," she says. "I'll explain the situation and ask him to call you."

She reels off her cell number, and he thanks her before hanging up. No matter how reluctant he may be to accept help from a former felon, he texts her his number immediately. She's glad. She'll speak to Nate later, but for now, she puts her phone on silent so she can deliver a death notification undisturbed.

The landscaped driveway leading to the lodge's entrance is almost as grand as the building itself. Madison's never been inside. This place is out of her price range, probably even for just a drink. She finds herself wondering how much it costs to get married here, but not because she expects to ever get married. She's intrigued by how the other half live and what they spend their money on. A large lobby with an open fireplace and comfortable-looking soft leather couches gives a good first impression. The front desk is made of solid pine and looks as though it was built from one of the trees dotted around the property.

It's busy. About fifteen animated guests are hovering around the lobby with hot drinks and plates of enticing pastries in their hands. Despite it only being 11 a.m., there's a party atmosphere with lots of laughter, suggesting the guests know each other. They're slowly making their way to what seems to be an impressively decorated restaurant.

"Can I help you?" asks the man behind the desk.

Madison approaches him. He looks like he comes from money, with his thick brown hair, tanned skin and perfect white teeth. Dressed in a crisp pale blue shirt open at the collar and smart beige pants, he has an air of authority about him.

"Hi. I'm Detective Madison Harper from the Lost Creek PD. I'm looking for Bryan Carpenter."

The man's smile falters. His eyes flicker to the gold badge on Madison's waistband. "I'm Bryan. What is it? What's happened? Is Mel okay?"

Unsure who he's referring to, Madison says, "I'm here about Stuart Carpenter."

"Stu? He's my son." His hand shoots to his mouth. "Oh God. What's happened?"

Madison hates this part. "Do you have somewhere private we could talk?"

Before they can go anywhere, an attractive young couple enter the lodge and approach the registration desk. The man is dressed in suit pants with a white shirt. He's holding an iPhone out in front of him as he says into the camera, "We're finally here!"

He walks around the desk to warmly embrace Bryan on camera. "Hey, Dad. Good to see you." He pulls away and says, "I've just noticed Aunt Edna's BMW outside. She must be doing well to afford that thing." He laughs before noticing the look on his father's face.

Madison swallows as she realizes this is Stuart's brother and that these guests are here for some kind of family gathering or reunion. That's why the younger man is filming their arrival. She couldn't have picked a worse time to show up and deliver bad news.

"What's wrong?" says Bryan's son. He's tall, with dark hair, probably in his mid-thirties. The woman he arrived with is beautifully dressed in stylish pants and a cream-colored silk blouse. She has a visible baby bump.

"This detective is here to tell me something about Stuart." Bryan looks at Madison. "This is my other son, Jay, and his fiancée, Mel."

Madison nods before saying, "It's not good news, I'm afraid."

"Oh no." Mel reaches out to grab the front desk.

Jay's face instantly drains of color. He lowers his phone and reaches for his fiancée's hand with his spare one.

Bryan quickly leads them to his office, just left of the lobby. Once he closes the door behind the four of them, Madison glances at Mel and considers telling her to sit down.

"Please," says Jay Carpenter. "What's happened?"

"I have some bad news about Stuart." Madison takes a deep breath. "I'm afraid he took his own life earlier this morning."

There's a sharp intake of breath all around before Jay reaches for his father's arm as if he needs help standing.

Bryan yells, "No! That's not possible. Stuart wouldn't do that!" His voice is deep and booming, and for a second, the audible merriment outside the office stops, before continuing a few seconds later.

Mel bursts into tears and takes a seat at Bryan's desk.

Jay collapses onto a small couch, dropping his phone face-down on the seat next to him. Instead of filming a joyous celebration, he's captured what will surely be the most devastating event this family will ever experience. He leans forward, his head in his hands. "This isn't happening." He looks like he might vomit. A hand shoots to his mouth as he involuntarily gags.

Madison takes a step back as his father passes him a bottle of water from his desk.

Jay glances at it and shakes his head, unable to stomach even a sip. After a few seconds, he looks up at her with red-rimmed eyes. "Are you sure it was Stu? Where was he when it happened?"

"He was at his residence on Mason Lane. It happened just after midnight."

Mel has tears rolling down her face. Bryan's expression is one of bewilderment, as if bad things shouldn't happen to people with money.

"When my partner and I entered his unlocked home," says Madison, "we found Stuart in his dining room. He was alive, but he was holding a sawed-off shotgun under his chin."

"No!" Jay gets up and turns away, his hands on the back of his head in disbelief. "This cannot be happening!" His legs visibly tremble with shock.

His fiancée goes to him and slips an arm around his waist.

Madison has to continue. "Shortly after our arrival, and despite our best efforts, he pulled the trigger. I'm so sorry." She hears the gunshot blast again. The ringing in her ears. She remembers how the sea in the painting behind Stuart's head turned from blue to red in a heartbeat.

The room falls silent as they take it all in, until Bryan turns and glares at her. "How could you let that happen?" He takes a step closer. "If you were there while he was still alive, you could've stopped him from pulling the trigger. Isn't that your job?"

It isn't surprising he'd want someone other than Stuart to

blame for this, but it doesn't feel good for Madison. "Mr. Carpenter, we tried to talk him out of it."

"Wait," he says, suddenly confused. "Why were you even there? Did he call 911 for help?"

"No," she says. This is where it gets tricky. "We were there to question him. I'm afraid your son implied he had some involvement in the disappearance of two young women five years ago."

"What?" says Jay. "That's ridiculous. He didn't have anything to do with their disappearance. He was already questioned over that!"

"Stuart wouldn't harm a woman," says Mel quietly. Her mascara is smudged now. "He wasn't like that, Detective. You must've misunderstood whatever he said to you. You've jumped to the wrong conclusion."

Madison doesn't know how much to tell them right now. She'd rather give them time to let the news sink in before going into detail, especially as she doesn't have all the facts herself yet.

Jay looks at his fiancée. "Thank God Mom isn't alive to hear this. It would kill her."

Bryan's face flushes red. "If you made my son believe he was going to be arrested for harming his friends, then this is on you," he says to Madison. "I demand an immediate investigation into his death."

Her heart sinks, and she immediately questions her actions. Did she push Stuart into pulling the trigger? Did he only do it because of something she said?

A knock at the office door makes her turn. Through the glass panel, an older couple hold up breakfast pastries with smiles on their faces to suggest Bryan, Mel and Jay are missing out. They haven't registered the haunted looks on their loved ones' faces, or the fact that a stranger is present.

Bryan waves to suggest he'll be out soon. Beads of sweat cover his brow. "Jay and Mel are supposed to be getting married here later this week," he explains. "The whole family has come to town in preparation. Today was supposed to be a joyous family reunion."

Madison lowers her eyes. She's ruined the lives of this entire family. They thought they were assembling for a wedding. They had no idea it would be for a funeral.

CHAPTER NINE

When Madison finally returns to her car, it's just after midday and she's already emotionally drained. Jay talked about canceling the wedding and she doesn't blame him. He and his fiancée can't go ahead knowing the happiest day of their lives will be forever linked with one of the worst. It's good that their extended family is here to support them.

Jay and Mel volunteered to notify the rest of the family about Stuart's death while Madison stayed behind in Bryan Carpenter's office to get some information about his younger son. After his initial shock wore off, Bryan's hostility faded somewhat, and he answered her questions.

She learned that Stuart worked as a dishwasher and sometimes bartender at Joe's Saloon downtown, and he wasn't in a relationship. According to his father, Becky and Tasha's disappearance—and the subsequent suspicion cast on Stuart—had a devastating impact on the young man's mental health, suggesting he turned into a different person almost overnight. As a result, Bryan was insulted at the thought of Stuart's name being dragged through the mud again.

Madison did what she could to reassure him, but she'd

noticed a text from Steve informing her that news vans had turned up at the mountain, so it's just a matter of time before word spreads about the body and Stuart's potential involvement. When she left, she promised to keep Bryan updated and to let him know when he could bury his son.

Now, ignoring the rumbling in her stomach, she's headed to see Tasha Harris's mother. Lunch will have to wait.

Downtown is busy as she passes the small law firm where Nate works part-time. She spots his Chevy Traverse outside and wishes she had time to drop by. Instead, she continues her journey. When she locates Tasha's mother's house on a quiet street lined with winter-bare trees, she pulls up outside. It's a nice neighborhood with well-kept yards and clean sidewalks. A blue Nissan sits in the driveway.

Madison gets out of her car and crosses the sidewalk as she approaches the yard. A black cat sits on the step outside the door. It doesn't move as she braces herself and knocks hard.

A slim blonde woman in her late twenties opens the door. She's dressed in yoga pants and a silk blouse that look mismatched. A headset sits on her hair with an unhooked wire dangling down her chest. "Help you?" she says with an impatient smile.

Madison clears her throat. "Hi, I'm Detective Harper from the Lost Creek PD. I'm looking for Sharon Harris."

The woman removes the headset, her eyes immediately concerned. "That's my mom, but she passed away recently. Can I help? I'm Susie Harris."

The resemblance to Tasha is evident. Both sisters are attractive, with that all-American, girl-next-door look that certain fashion designers love.

Madison steels herself as she says, "Can I come in for a minute? It's about Tasha."

Once she absorbs the shock of hearing her sister's name, Susie steps aside to let Madison in. The hallway is bright, and one wall is lined with photographs of family and friends. Madison spots numerous photos of Tasha as a teenager, and both sisters on various vacations as young girls.

A large desk takes up one whole corner of the stylish living room. A laptop sits open, and three faces watch Madison with interest from windows on the screen.

Susie goes to her desk and plugs her headset in before saying into the mic, "Sorry, guys. I've gotta go. We'll reconvene later." She doesn't wait for a response before taking her headset off and closing the laptop. She turns to Madison. "Sorry for the mess. I work from home and I was in the middle of a meeting." She crosses her arms as if hugging herself. "Are you here because you've found my sister?"

Before Madison can answer her, a hesitant knock at the door makes them turn.

Susie sighs impatiently and mutters, "Not now." She leaves the room to see who it is, and seconds later, she greets someone in surprise. The unexpected caller enters the house. When they come into view, Madison sees Nancy Draper.

"I'm sorry. I didn't know you were here," says Nancy. "I was coming to tell Susie about what happened last night. Doug told me I should leave it to you, but I was going out of my mind with worry, and I wanted to know if Susie had heard from you."

Madison nods. It's actually better that she can update both families together. She's a little surprised that Nancy has left her home, though. One of Doug's employees once told her that the woman was agoraphobic, except for attending the support group meetings at the diner, which are obviously incredibly important to her. "That's fine," she says. "I've only just arrived myself."

Susie's clearly confused. "What happened last night?"

Although it's not her house, Madison motions for them both to take a seat. They choose the couch while she takes the armchair. "Susie, I came to let you know that human remains were found on Grave Mountain yesterday."

The young woman gasps. She looks at Nancy, who nods sadly. Turning back to Madison, she asks, "How many people?"

"One adult female. And I'm sorry, but in order to identify whether it could be Becky or Tasha, I'm going to need to obtain their dental records."

Nancy lowers her eyes at the words no one ever wants to hear.

"Do either of you know which dentist they went to?" Madison presses.

Nancy nods silently. Susie has tears in her eyes as she says, "Tasha and I had the same dentist." She retrieves her cell phone from her desk and scrolls her contacts.

Madison writes down the name and number in her notebook before Nancy takes it from her and scribbles the details for Becky's dentist. As she does that, Madison gets a text. She quickly checks it. It's from Alex. Her throat tightens when she sees what it says. No cell phone has been found at the scene, but he does have an item of clothing.

"My forensic technician has just informed me an item of clothing has also been recovered." She can barely bring herself to say what it is because she recognizes it from a photo of one of the missing women.

"What is it?" asks Susie.

Madison looks at the older woman as she answers. "A red woolen hat."

Nancy squeezes her eyes shut against the instant tears that form. Her face wrinkles as grief takes hold. Her daughter was wearing a red woolen hat in the photo of her leaving the house on the morning of the hike.

Susie slips an arm around the older woman's shoulders. "It could be anyone's, Nancy. Think of how many hikers go up there every year. I lose hats and gloves all the time."

Madison is touched by her attempt to lessen Nancy's pain. "Do you know whether Tasha was wearing a hat that day?"

Susie looks at her. "She left hers at home. It was found next to the front door. She must've forgotten it."

It's looking even more likely that the body discovered belongs to Becky Draper. That means Madison can get a search team on the mountain to look for Tasha's remains. She doesn't think it has occurred to Susie that if one of them is dead, it's likely the other one is too.

Re-reading the message from Alex, she says, "There isn't a label in the hat, so we're not sure what brand it was."

Nancy says, "Becky always cut out her labels. She found them too itchy against her skin."

Madison nods. There's nothing she can say that will comfort this woman right now. Instead, she tells Susie about Stuart's suicide and how he's the department's prime suspect. She relays his last words before pulling the trigger. "He said, 'I *am* sorry. But I can't undo any of it now. I can't un-kill them.'"

The women lower their eyes.

"If Stuart was guilty of this," she says, "it's clear his family had no knowledge of it. They were devastated when I told them why my partner and I had gone to his house this morning." She leans in as she adds, "Did you ever suspect him of being responsible for Tasha's disappearance?"

Susie wipes her damp eyes. "My parents thought he killed them, but they were so devastated at losing Tasha that they tried to forget it ever happened. They stopped discussing her and put all her things into storage so they wouldn't be confronted with it daily. I'm sure the stress of it killed my dad. Then, once he was gone, Mom got sick. I felt like she gave up on life." She shakes her head sadly. "Some parents of missing children turn their pain into a search to find answers. To put someone behind bars. My parents weren't like that. It turned them inward. They became ghosts." She leans over to the coffee table and helps herself to a tissue. "As for Stuart being responsible... I guess it makes sense. He was the only one who came back. I bumped into him once, in the library downtown."

Nancy looks at her as she wipes her face. "Did he say anything?"

"He said I looked just like Tasha. That was it. He left immediately after, but I worried he could've followed me home, so I took a different route and visited a friend on my way. I guess I hoped he'd get bored of waiting for me to come out."

Madison makes a note of the encounter. It sounds like Stuart was odd. It makes her wonder why Becky and Tasha agreed to a hike with him. "Do either of you know how they met him? I'm wondering how they formed a friendship and whether he was dating one of them."

Susie shrugs. "He wasn't dating Tasha, but she told me he wanted to. He came on to her once, but she said he was awkward about it. I know she wasn't interested in him, but I got the impression she liked the attention. I don't know how they originally met."

"I suspected Becky was dating someone, but not him," says Nancy. "I think she met Stuart when she started getting interested in hiking. Other than that, I don't know. I wish I'd asked her, but she had so many people in her life that it was difficult to keep up."

"Of course," says Madison. "I'll pass the dentists' details on to the medical examiner immediately so she can obtain their records, and I'll be in touch as soon as I know anything." She stands and glances out of the window to see a vehicle pulling up in front of hers. She thought it might be a news truck, but it looks more like a neighbor arriving home.

Susie stands too. "How long will identification take once the medical examiner has the records?"

"It shouldn't take too long." Madison's phone rings. It's Adams. She looks at the women. "I need to take this. I'll see myself out." She leaves through the front door and answers her phone on the way to her car. "Hello?"

"Hey, it's me," says Detective Adams.

"Hey. How're you feeling? I heard you've got a virus."

He exhales. "I've got something, but it's not a virus. Can we meet? Not at the station."

He sounds so depressed that she immediately agrees. She was planning to visit Stuart Carpenter's boss, so she suggests it as a place to meet. "Joe's Saloon in ten minutes?"

"Sure," he says before ending the call.

Madison looks at her phone. She has a horrible feeling Adams is about to quit.

CHAPTER TEN

Nate's morning has dragged. His boss is in court, the office manager is taking a day off and their only intern, Madison's son, left for college months ago. As a result, the office is empty and time passes too slowly, so he decides to drop by Ruby's Diner for lunch and some conversation.

As he approaches the counter, he's greeted warmly by Carla Hitchins, the diner's longest-serving waitress. In her mid-fifties, with long chestnut hair that she keeps tied back in a bun, she's the friendliest woman in town.

"Hey, Nate. How are you?" she says. "And where's that beautiful hound of yours?"

He smiles. "Brody's taking a nap at the office. How're you?"

"Oh, I can't complain too much." She picks up a full coffee pot. "Will Madison be joining you?"

Amused, he says, "If that's your way of checking whether we're still together, the answer's yes, and everything's great."

She beams. "That's what I like to hear."

An older gentleman approaches from behind Carla. He's wearing glasses with the thickest lenses Nate's ever seen. He's the same height as the waitress, about five-seven, but heavier. His shirt buttons strain at his gut.

"You've met Hank before, right?" says Carla.

Nate has witnessed him flirting with her numerous times in here. "Not formally." He nods. "Hi. Nate Monroe."

"I hope you're not hitting on my fiancée," says Hank with only the hint of a smile. "Don't let my current physique fool you. I played football for years and could probably still beat your ass in a fight."

Nate ignores the odd comment and looks at Carla. "You're *engaged*? I didn't even know you guys were dating."

She laughs. "You and Madison are invited to the wedding, of course."

"Well, congratulations," says Nate. "I'm happy for you. It's about time we had some good news around here."

Vince Rader joins them, carrying a big stack of clean dinner plates from the kitchen. "You've told him the news, I see."

"I just heard," says Nate. "I guess I'd better buy a suit."

Vince frowns. "A suit? What are you talking about?"

"He means our other news," says Carla, flashing her engagement ring. She turns back to Nate. "Vince has decided to retire at last. Hank and I are buying the diner from him."

Nate's stunned. He never thought Vince would give up this place. He bought it with his late wife, so it holds a lot of memories for him. He lives in the apartment upstairs with his son and grandson.

"Where will you go? You're not leaving town, are you?" Nate leans in as he adds, "Come on, Vince, we're the only sane people in Lost Creek. Don't leave me alone here with the locals." With both of them being outsiders, they have a unique view of the goings-on in the town.

Amused, Vince bats the question away, suggesting he either hasn't thought about the logistics or doesn't want to. "There's plenty of time to figure all that out."

"What can I get for you, Monroe?" says Hank. "The old ball and chain is showing me how to work this place, so I might as well take your order."

Carla slaps his arm playfully.

Nate smiles, but he's not keen on the guy. Maybe Hank will grow on him like he did on Carla. Or perhaps she was just worn down by his relentlessness. "I'll have a chicken sandwich and coffee, thanks."

Carla pours his drink before leaving to serve a family. Hank heads to the kitchen.

When they're gone, Nate sits at the counter. "You kept that quiet," he says.

Vince nods. "I'm getting too old for running this place. It's physically demanding. I'm about ready to retire."

Nate studies his face. As a US Navy veteran, Vince is still in great shape, so he can't use that excuse. "Is that the real reason you're selling?"

Crossing his arms, Vince says, "No. It's not. It's all the true-crime stuff. It's mentally taxing. I've decided to end my podcast, take down the missing person posters and focus on my own life for a while. I only started it because I was looking for Ruby. Now that I know what happened to her, I need to move on."

Nate thinks that's a shame. The diner won't be the same without Vince and his weekly true-crime podcast, which has become more infrequent over the past year. "You're not seriously considering leaving town, though, right?"

"We'll see." Vince is noncommittal. "Carla's happy about buying this place, so it's not like I could back out of the deal even if I wanted to."

Nate glances over at the kitchen. "What do you know about Hank? Their relationship seems a little rushed, doesn't it?"

Vince scoffs. "Not everyone takes a whole year to ask a woman out, you know."

Nate smiles.

"To tell you the truth," Vince leans in, "I'm not a fan of the guy. He's a confirmed bachelor, so how come he suddenly wants to marry now?" He stands straight. "You know, when the Snow Storm Killer was terrorizing the town last year, I thought Hank Goodman made an excellent suspect."

"Seriously?" says Nate, amused.

"Sure! He lived alone, had never married and had a roaming eye with the women in here... But now I've gotten to know him a little, I know he couldn't kill anyone."

"Why's that?" Nate believes anyone's capable of murder given the right circumstances. He was tested himself when the opportunity presented itself to kill the person responsible for landing him on death row. Every bone in his body wanted to shoot Father Connor when the so-called priest was sprawled at his feet while Nate had Madison's gun in his hand. Connor had damaged him and the people he loved so much that Nate wanted revenge. He felt like he'd earned it.

He's glad Madison talked him out of it at the last minute. But that's why he refuses to carry a firearm, no matter how much Madison thinks he should. He won't risk being re-arrested for murder. If he shot someone defending Madison or her son, and the perp died from the wounds he'd inflicted, not only would he never get over taking someone's life, he could end up back in prison. And this time, he would have more to lose.

He may not be in Texas anymore, and Colorado recently abolished the death penalty, but he has nightmares about the power-hungry guards from the Polunsky Unit finding a way of getting him back there one day. It might not be a realistic fear, but if he can reduce the chances of it ever happening by not carrying a weapon, then that's what he'll do.

"I know Hank could never kill anyone," says Vince, "because Carla's been nagging him to get contact lenses, but he refuses because he's too squeamish to touch his own eyeballs." He scoffs. "If he can't even touch his own eyeballs, how on earth could he touch a dead body? Besides, he has a small dog he treats like a princess. Serial killers hate animals. It's been proven to be true in a high percentage of cases. Add to that the fact that the guy's lazy, and I just know he doesn't have it in him. Not many people realize it, but killing involves a lot of work."

Hank overhears Vince as he approaches with Nate's order. He slides it across the counter with a knife and fork and says, "You can say that again. I watched a documentary detailing how tough it is to clean up biowaste. You know, blood, saliva and other DNA." He looks back and forth between Nate and Vince. "Those guys who kill in their own homes are dumb. They're guaranteed to get caught. You gotta do it outside somewhere. Someplace no one will stumble across you. Like deep in the woods or on top of a mountain. And if you do it in winter, chances are the body won't be found until the snow thaws in the spring, giving you more time to get away *and* for the elements to destroy the evidence." He winks as if he's a mastermind.

Vince shares a look with Nate.

Nate stifles a laugh. He thinks his friend might've just changed his mind about Hank being harmless.

Hank suddenly looks apprehensive as someone approaches the counter.

Vince straightens in recognition. "Good to see you, Dennis," he says. "You don't know me, but I know your dad. He and your brother were frequent diners before..." He doesn't finish the thought.

Nate turns to look at Dennis McKinney, the guy who recently sought his help to get out of prison. Dennis was serving a life sentence for the murder of a local baby who vanished fifteen years ago. Madison reopened the case a few months back, when the baby's real killer showed up.

Dennis nods at Vince before looking at Nate. "I believe I owe you a drink, Mr. Monroe."

Nate's only ever spoken to the guy over the phone—while Dennis was locked up—but it's easy for Dennis to recognize him, given the extensive press coverage of Nate's own wrongful conviction. "I was just doing my job, Mr. McKinney. Detective Harper did more than me. I'm just sorry about what you came home to."

The guy's family will never be the same after what happened. They probably thought Dennis's wrongful conviction was the worst thing they could ever experience. Turns out life had a whole new hell in store for them.

Dennis shakes his hand, but words appear too difficult.

"Go take a seat," says Vince. "I'll bring coffee and a menu."

Dennis nods as he walks away. The entire room has fallen silent as the other diners stare at him. Showing up in the town's most popular place for gossip after being released from a long sentence is difficult, to say the least. Nate remembers the cold stares and hostile comments. He was all over the news for years, and the attention ramped up again recently with the death of Father Jack Connor, so he still gets recognized. But the locals are more accepting of him since he stuck around to help Madison with several cases.

"Looks like a killer to me," whispers Hank.

"Don't be stupid," says Vince. "The guy was framed. He had nothing to do with it. The case is closed, and he's suffered enough."

Hank crosses his arms with a self-righteous smirk. "Just because he didn't kill that baby doesn't mean he's not a killer."

Nate glares at him. It's people like Hank Goodman who make life unbearable for others because they'd rather believe salacious gossip over the truth. He picks up his plate and chooses a seat away from the counter. If Vince does sell the diner to this guy, Nate will need to find somewhere else to eat.

CHAPTER ELEVEN

Madison steps into Joe's Saloon on Main Street and spots Detective Adams sitting by himself at a small round table. It's one thirty in the afternoon and she's glad to see he's opted for soda rather than beer. He *is* meant to be on duty, after all.

She nods to him, then approaches the bar to get a drink and speak to the bar's owner. She knows Joseph Manvers a little, having questioned him about a friend of his in the past.

"It's a little early for cops, isn't it?" Joe smiles at her. He has jet-black hair and olive skin, and Madison thinks he's around her age: thirty-eight.

"Actually, I'm here to discuss one of your employees," she says. "Stuart Carpenter."

He frowns. "He's the last person I'd expect you to ask me about."

Madison checks over her shoulder before saying, "Unfortunately, Stuart died earlier today. He took his own life."

Joe stares at her open-mouthed for a few seconds. "*What?* Why would he do that?" After a couple more seconds of disbelief, he pours himself a whiskey and downs it.

She can tell he's genuinely upset. Suicide doesn't just

impact the person's family; it has a far-reaching ripple effect on everyone who ever met them. "I know it's a shock, but I wanted to ask your opinion. Did he seem unhappy to you? Did he have any burdens that you know of?" She doesn't mention how Stuart admitted to murdering two women.

Joe rubs his jaw. "I mean, he was quiet. Preferred washing pots to tending bar, but he'd help out wherever he was needed." He thinks for a second. "You know, I'm suddenly realizing how little I knew about him. Some people don't give much away, which is refreshing when you work in a bar."

"Was he working yesterday?" she asks.

"Yeah. He did a couple of hours in the afternoon but said he had somewhere to be in the evening."

Presumably, he meant the support group meeting. "Did he ever confide in you about anything?"

Joe shakes his head. "He'd stop for a beer most days after his shift, so he never seemed in a hurry to get home or anywhere else. But he kept conversation to things like politics, the news, movies... that kind of stuff, you know?"

She nods. "Did he ever talk about his family?"

"Now you mention it, yeah. His mom passed away years ago, and from what he told me, his dad sounds a little overbearing. I think his name's Bryan. I know he thought Stuart could do better than this job, and he was right. Stuart was intelligent." He shakes his head as he thinks about it. "I always wondered why he never went to college, especially as his dad could afford to help him out. Did you know Bryan owns the Pine Shadows Lodge?"

She nods. "I've notified his family. He has a brother too."

"Yeah, Jay's cool. He's been in a few times to shoot the shit with Stu while he worked. He tips well. I think he works in banking, in some city. The whole family is well-off, as far as I could tell, apart from Stu. Even though there was a nine-year age gap, the brothers were obviously close, unlike me and my brother. I only see mine at Christmas, and even then it's too much. Know what I mean?"

Madison thinks about her sister, Angie, who's currently incarcerated and awaiting trial. "I do."

"Shit. Jay must be devastated."

"He took it badly," she says, "but he has people around him."

Still clearly shocked, Joe sighs. "You just never know what someone's going through, do you?"

"You can say that again." She takes a deep breath. "Do you know if he liked to hunt?"

He frowns. "Not that he ever mentioned. I know he had firearms, but I don't know what kind and what he did with them." A look of realization washes over his face. "Has his death got anything to do with what's going on up at Grave Mountain?"

Madison straightens. "I can't answer that, sorry. Thanks for your help. If I need anything else, I'll let you know. Can I get a Diet Coke?"

"Sure." Joe selects a glass and fills it. As he hands it to her, he says, "I guess I need to hire a replacement."

Madison nods before taking her drink over to Adams, who's scrolling on his phone. He turns it face down when she sits opposite him. "Hey," she says. "We should have an ID for the person found on the mountain soon. Lena's going to contact Becky's and Tasha's dentists for their dental records."

He nods without responding.

Madison frowns. "What's going on with you?"

Adams rubs his face with both hands before letting them drop. "I think I'm gonna quit my job."

Her shoulders sink. Looking at him, she sees how miserable he is. Something is going on behind his weary eyes. Something he's never told her about. "Why? Am I that difficult to work with?"

He shakes his head. "No. I just want to leave Lost Creek and forget I ever heard about the place."

Considering how vocal he's been about hating it here, it doesn't come as a surprise, but it is disappointing. If he leaves, Madison will be on her third detective partner in just over a year. "How does Selena feel about that? Aren't the girls settled in school?"

He shoots her a hard stare. "You know what? I don't give a damn how my wife feels about it because she's not coming with me."

Madison's taken aback. She had no idea they had marital problems. Adams has always kept his private life private. She's only met Selena and his twin daughters once, and that was by accident. "You're *separating?*"

He sips his drink. "Ever wonder why I left Denver PD?"

"Of course," she says. "But I never thought you'd tell me." She doesn't mention how the entire department has various theories on what caused him to leave behind a job he supposedly loved for one he seemingly detests. Based on how he has performed since he took the role, she thinks he was squeezed out of his last job due to his incompetence.

"Selena cheated on me."

She takes a deep breath and leans back. "With another officer?"

"Nope," he says bitterly. "With my *brother*. You know, the one Chief Mendes has such a high opinion of."

Madison is stunned. "I'm sorry, that sucks." She thinks about it for a second. "So you thought moving away from Denver would, what, stop their affair?"

He shrugs. "I thought if I could get her away from him, we'd have a chance. She said it was over, but I didn't trust her, so I told her to prove it. We moved here for a fresh start, but no matter how hard I try, I just can't trust her anymore. And our marriage sucks now. We're different people to when we got married." He sighs heavily as he adds, "Everyone in my old department knew about it before I did. They all knew my brother because he consulted on some of our cases. The entire department was talking about my wife and my brother behind my back, and not one of the assholes had the decency to tell me what was going on. Once I found out, I was humiliated."

Madison doesn't know what to say. She sips her drink. "We have a department therapist now. Why don't you go for a session with him and see if that'll help?"

Adams looks at her. "Is he going to stop my wife from cheating again?"

"No, I guess not. Is Selena sorry about what happened?"

He shrugs. "Who knows? And how long until she strays again? You've met her; she's stunning, right?"

She nods. Selena has the most alluring green eyes she's ever seen on a woman. "Do you still love her?"

His shoulders slump forward as he touches his glass. "I can't imagine my life without her. My chest physically aches at the thought of it. But the fact she cheated on me tells me she doesn't feel the same way." His face darkens. "It doesn't help matters that I don't fit in down here. Those things combined make me want to leave as fast as possible."

"What do you mean, you don't fit in?" she says, concerned.

"You guys don't want me on the team. I know you think I'm useless."

Madison touches his hand. "No, Marcus. We don't. But you've never given this job a hundred percent, making *our* jobs harder. You never told me that's because you're distracted by your home life, so what was I supposed to think?"

He lowers his eyes and stares at his drink. "I feel like none of you gave me a chance. It was obvious when I started that you all wanted Steve in the role. No one ever invites me for drinks after work or tries to get to know me properly. Between not fitting in at work and the tension at home, these last twelve months have been hell." His eyes redden as he looks away.

Madison realizes just how much he's been suffering. His attempts at humor over the past year went down like a lead balloon because he always managed to put his foot in his mouth, but now she knows he was just trying to fit in.

She moves her seat around the table so she's next to him. "I'm so sorry. I've completely misjudged you. I wish you'd told me all this sooner. Trust me, you're not being left out of anything. None of us go for drinks because we're all too exhausted. We're not excluding you from anything. We're just sad bastards who'd rather sleep than drink when we get off work."

He takes a deep breath and glances over his shoulder. A couple of young guys are playing pool behind them. No one's paying them any attention.

"What would it take for you to stay?" she says. "I mean, I can't fix your marriage, but I can try to improve your work life."

He slowly tears up a coaster. "I need to move out of my place. I think we'll all be happier."

She nods. His twins are almost ten years old. "Kids notice everything. If you and Selena are having issues, your girls will know. It's better for them to see their parents getting along but separated than living together in a bitter, loveless marriage. I can help you find somewhere to live if you like."

He looks at her, surprised. "Seriously?"

"Sure. In fact, I have a spare room at my place if you need to get out fast. I spend half my time at Nate's place anyway, so it's not like we'd get in each other's way. You could feed Owen's cat for me when I'm not there." She smiles.

He looks away. "Thanks. I'll see what happens once I've spoken to Selena. I don't think I can put it off any longer." He slowly shakes his head. "I never thought she'd cheat on me. And with my own brother."

"Trust me," says Madison, "I know all too well how much siblings can suck. Have you cut him out of your life?"

Adams nods. "He calls every now and then, but I won't answer. I'm still too mad, even after all this time. I'm afraid of what I'll do to him."

Madison's phone buzzes with a text, but she doesn't even glance at it. Adams looks so miserable, she's worried about him. "I know everything sucks right now, but it won't be like this forever." She smiles as she adds, "Look at it this way: you're going back on the market. You could have a hot new girlfriend in a matter of months."

He snorts. "Yeah, right."

"Just don't make any drastic decisions about your job, okay?" she says. "Come back to work this afternoon and talk to Selena tonight."

He looks at her with suspicion in his eyes. "Why are you being so nice?"

She shrugs. "Because I don't want another new partner. It took me months to break you in."

He smiles. "You don't want a new partner?"

"Are you kidding?" she says with a grin. "You're so bad at your job that you make *me* look good! If you're replaced with some hotshot, Chief Mendes will realize I'm not half as good as she thinks I am."

"Oh, great," he says. "Thanks a lot."

She nudges his arm. "I'm just messing with you."

Her phone rings, and when she sees it's dispatch calling, she knows she has to take it. "Sorry," she says to Adams.

He nods.

She accepts the call. "Hello?"

"Detective, it's Stella. Officer Vickers has asked me to let you know they've found more remains."

Madison's heart skips a beat. "Another body? Where?" She looks at Adams, who perks up.

"On Grave Mountain," says Stella. "Apparently there's something unusual about the scene, but Officer Vickers didn't want to elaborate over the radio."

Madison swallows. She doesn't like surprises. "It must be Tasha Harris. Was it found near the other body?"

"I don't know details, sorry. The phones are pretty busy right now with reporters calling for information. Officer Vickers said she can meet you in the parking lot and take you to it. Should I let her know you're on your way?"

"Yes," says Madison, standing. "I'll be as fast as I can."

She slips her phone away and looks at Adams. "They need us on the mountain immediately. I can update you on the case when we get there."

He doesn't move.

"Listen," she says. "Just put your all into this case for me. Don't let your life go to shit just because your brother's an asshole. Show Chief Mendes you're good at your job. I guarantee you'll enjoy it more if you do, and besides, you need the income. My spare room doesn't come cheap." She crosses her arms over her chest and smiles. "Come on, Adams. Are you in, or are you out?"

Adams takes a deep breath and eventually stands. "Alright, alright. But I've gotta tell you, Harper, you really wouldn't make a good motivational speaker."

Madison snorts. "It's a good thing I'm an excellent detective then, isn't it?"

CHAPTER TWELVE

The midafternoon light is fading, and all traces of sunshine have vanished behind thick gray rainclouds by the time Madison, Detective Adams and Officer Vickers reach the location of the second body along the unforgiving Lovers' Peak Trail.

Madison knows nothing about hiking or the mountains, really, so she doesn't know the origins of the trail names. All she knows is that this route has a steep rocky incline, which makes her breathing heavily labored. She tries hard not to pant, but the fact that she's approaching forty, was incarcerated for six years and is a former smoker means her lungs aren't at their best. She's finally quit the cigarettes, but she always struggles with inclines.

She turns to look at Adams on the path behind her. He's stopped for a second, squeezing his waist with his hands, and the look on his face suggests he wishes he'd quit his job while he had the chance. The thought makes her smile.

He catches her staring. "At least we know we're looking for someone fitter than two middle-aged detectives."

"Hey!" she says. "Less of the *middle-aged*."

He laughs, which she takes as a good sign. Maybe he'll at

least see the day out before he quits. She needs to let the rest of the team know to cut him some slack, including Chief Mendes.

He does have a point, though. They know Stuart enjoyed hiking, which only adds to the list of reasons as to why he makes the perfect suspect for the two murders.

"It's over here," says Officer Vickers breezily. Shelley's still young and enjoys keeping fit, so she's not as affected by the hike. She continues onward.

After a couple of minutes, they pass two males descending the trail. Probably in their forties, they're both dressed in shorts, sandals and T-shirts. Madison would think they were crazy if she weren't from Colorado, where it can be snowing in the morning and like spring an hour later. Although not today. It's cold, but she's still sweating by the time they reach a large clearing at a cliff face overlooking the town. From up here, the huge Wonder Wheel at Fantasy World amusement park looks tiny. On a clear day, the view must stretch over the whole town.

She and Adams follow Shelley through a pine thicket. Several of the trees have rectangular white paint marks on them, and she wonders whether that indicates which trail they're following. They find Alex several feet from the well-trodden path, crouching in front of a cluster of large trees. Shelley leaves them and joins the other officers searching the area.

The forensic technician stands as he greets them. "Afternoon, Detectives. Glad to see you're feeling better, Detective Adams."

Adams nods.

Madison looks at the ground and can't see anything that resembles human remains, just overgrown vegetation. "I thought we'd found someone else."

"We have," says Alex. He kneels and points to a woman's sneaker that's half buried under a plant.

She crouches next to him, and so does Adams. They lean in

to take a look. The sneaker was probably once white, but is now covered in a thick layer of dirt. The faded pink laces stand out against the evergreen shrubs. A label stuck to the bottom probably once held a clue as to where the shoe was purchased, but not anymore. It's completely washed out from being exposed to the elements for so long.

"Is this all there is?" asks Adams.

"No," says Alex. With a gloved hand, he pulls the sneaker's tongue open, revealing a skeletal foot inside.

Madison leans back on her heels as she considers what another body means.

Alex points from the foot toward the bottom of the nearest tree trunk. "There's at least one tibia under there too."

Adams stands. Frowning, he says, "So we just have legs and feet?"

"No, Detective." Alex gestures to where three tree trunks have merged together over the years, with only a narrow gap between them. They must have been planted too close together, or maybe they sprung up from fallen seeds. He picks up a flashlight and switches it on, then kneels close to the trees. At waist height, he presses the flashlight to the space between the trunks. "Look inside."

Adams looks first, bending forward. After only a second, he turns away. "Oh God."

Intrigued, Madison rests her left hand against the rough bark and peers in. She's greeted by the hollow face of a skull. The skin has long since decomposed, but several strands of matted hair still cling to the scalp. A deserted bird's nest sits on top of it. The skull seems to be attached to the rest of the body, and it looks as though the person was sitting on the ground when they died.

Her mouth goes dry as she considers what happened to this poor individual. "How the hell did they get in there?"

Alex switches his flashlight off. "I think they've been there some time. Years, probably. It looks as though the clothes have deteriorated along with the body. Once I've taken photographs and checked for evidence, I'll need a tree surgeon to help me cut out an opening big enough to retrieve the remains." He looks up at the trees forlornly. "It's a shame to destroy them."

Madison takes a step back to assess the scene. "It's almost as though they sat down to take a breather and the tree claimed them as they rested." She shudders. "That's a creepy thought."

"Maybe they were messing around," says Adams. "Playing hide-and-go-seek, or just trying to see if they could fit inside the gap in the trunks. My girls do that kind of thing all the time. Drives me insane. It's all fun and games until someone gets stuck and the fire department is dispatched."

Madison thinks about it. "Or maybe they were hiding from a killer. They could've died from fear or stress while waiting it out. If this is Tasha Harris, she might have witnessed Becky's murder and then tried to find somewhere to hide."

Adams nods. "Either that or the killer stuffed her body in there so it would never be found." He sighs heavily. "I'll get the ME's team up here, then meet you back at the station." He pulls out his phone and walks away, dodging branches and rocks.

She looks at Alex. "I know you didn't find a cell phone with our first victim, but did you find anything else—a wallet, or any clothing other than the red woolen hat?"

"No wallet," he says. "Just some shreds of deteriorated clothes and two hiking boots. I've sent it all to the crime lab, but I wouldn't hold your breath. It's unlikely they'll yield anything useful in terms of evidence after being exposed out here for so long."

Madison wonders whether the young women even had their wallets and phones with them on the hike. Maybe they left them behind in Tasha's abandoned vehicle. She'll need to check the investigation notes to see what evidence the car offered, if any. She also needs to check in with Officer Sanchez, who is searching Stuart's house. She doubts Stuart would be stupid enough to keep hold of the women's belongings, but you never know with killers. Some are compelled to take trophies.

A thought occurs to her then. What if Becky and Tasha weren't his only victims? What if Stuart had struck before or since the hike? A shiver runs through her. Maybe he killed thirteen-year-old Brandon Dorsey too. It doesn't bear thinking about. She wonders whether Chief Mendes would let her look into other cold cases from around the same time, depending on what else they find up here.

Alex starts photographing the remains from the sneaker upward. He leans in close and is meticulous about capturing everything, from the skeletal foot to the trees that have claimed the rest of the body.

Madison rests her hands on her hips as she watches. This might just be the oddest crime scene she's ever attended.

CHAPTER THIRTEEN

It's dark when Madison arrives at the station. Before leaving the mountain, she managed to call Susie Harris to let her know another body had been found and that both discoveries would be announced at a press conference shortly by Chief Mendes. Now comes the long wait for identification. Lena has arranged for a forensic dentist to check both victims against the dental records as soon as possible, but when Madison left the mountain, they were already losing daylight, and it's going to take a long time to extract the latest body from the trees.

After pouring two cups of coffee in the station's kitchen, Madison carries them to her desk. She looks around for Detective Adams and spots him in Chief Mendes's office with the door closed. She can only hope he's explaining why he's been distracted from his job and isn't in there quitting.

Steve approaches her. He looks over at Mendes's office. "I thought Adams was sick?"

Madison takes a deep breath. "No, listen, I need to tell you something while he's not here." Steve perches on her desk as she says, "He's having a hard time, so we need to cut him some slack."

"Why, what's going on?"

She doesn't think Adams would mind Steve knowing about Selena's indiscretion. Steve's trustworthy. She lowers her voice as she says, "His wife cheated on him with his brother, and that's why he left Denver and moved his family down here. His entire department knew about it before him. Adams was humiliated."

"With his *brother*?" Steve grimaces as he rubs his jaw. "Wait. Aren't Adams and his wife still together?"

"Well, kind of," she says. "It's clearly not working, because he told me earlier that he wanted to quit this job and leave town. He wants out of his marriage."

"Jeez. Sounds messy."

"I know, right?" She sips her coffee. "Adams also thinks we all hate him, so we've got to be nicer to him. Laugh at his jokes, ask how he is, that kind of thing. He was on the verge of breaking down earlier, so we've got to be more supportive. Okay?"

Steve nods. "Of course. I don't hate the guy, but he makes us look bad. I can cut him some slack if he starts focusing on his job."

She leans back in her seat and changes the subject. "So, how are things going with Lena?"

He shrugs. "Fine, I guess." He doesn't exactly sound excited, which surprises her, as she thought they were good together.

"She seems distracted at the moment. Know what that's about?"

"To tell you the truth," he says, "she gives me mixed signals. One minute she's happy to see me, the next I feel like I've said the wrong thing. I end up walking on eggshells around her, which isn't fun." He takes a deep breath. "I don't know. It's been a while since I've dated anyone, but being single was a lot less complicated."

Not wanting to pry, she looks over at Chief Mendes's office and studies Adams's body language. "Can you tell whether he's quitting or begging not to be fired?"

They stare for a minute until Adams stands.

"Shit, he's coming. Go!" Madison sits up straight and turns to her computer as Steve hurries to his desk. She types Stuart Carpenter's name into their database.

Adams approaches his desk. "This for me?" he asks with raised eyebrows. He's looking at the coffee.

"It sure is, partner," she says with a wide smile. "Come on over here next to me." She pats the desk beside her. "We can read our suspect's witness statement, taken the day after the notorious hike."

He frowns. "You're being creepy. I think I preferred it when you hated me."

She laughs a little too hard. "You're pretty funny, you know? Come on. Bring your chair." She waits for him.

As he grabs a pen and notepad, Officer Lisa Kent passes by. She's taking off her coat, and her uniform shirt strains at her ample chest. She has a large bust for a petite woman.

"Sorry to hear you've been unwell, Detective Adams," says the rookie with a flirtatious smile.

Adams glances at her, and his eyes go to her chest for the briefest second. "Thanks."

"If you need some chicken soup, I can go fetch it for you."

Amused, Madison raises her eyebrows at Adams, who says, "I'm good. Thanks."

"Sure thing. Catch you later." The young officer heads in the direction of the kitchen.

"What the hell was that?" whispers Madison. She can't blame him for glancing at the woman's chest. It's hard not to.

He shrugs. "Maybe she thinks I'm in charge of payroll or something."

She laughs. When he's seated next to her, she says, "You didn't quit, then?"

He keeps his eyes on her computer screen. "No. I told Mendes about what an asshole Sean's been to me. She's no longer his number one fan." Sean must be his brother. "She wants me to see the new therapist for at least two sessions."

Madison nods. "Good. I think it'll help. It can't do any harm, right?"

He sips his coffee. "I guess not."

She can tell he's done talking about his problems, so she changes the subject. "Is Mendes holding the press conference soon?"

"Yeah. She doesn't want them to know much, just that two bodies have been discovered and Stuart Carpenter has killed himself. She's going to be vague about whether the incidents are related."

Madison looks at the long list of attachments to the original investigation into the disappearance of Becky and Tasha. She sighs. "I guess we better get started on these."

CHAPTER FOURTEEN

Stuart Carpenter's statement was taken the morning after the hike five years ago. Madison double-clicks to open it, and they both lean in to read the contents.

I arranged to meet Becky Draper and Tasha Harris yesterday morning at the Juniper Trail parking lot. It was Becky's idea to go on the hike. I immediately agreed because I was attracted to Tasha and liked spending time with her, but we aren't—and have never been—romantically involved.

I arrived first, and they arrived just after 7 a.m. in Tasha's red Honda. Within a few minutes, we started on the path that led to the trail. We only passed three other hikers on the way. After maybe thirty minutes, the weather came in on us earlier than expected. By that, I mean a thick fog, and the wind picked up. Tasha mentioned we should head back down the trail to leave. I didn't care either way, but Becky was eager to keep going. She'd never done this trail before, and since we'd already gotten so far, she wanted to go farther before turning around.

"Remind me what trails our two bodies were found on," says Adams.

"The first victim was discovered near the Juniper Trail," says Madison. "The second—the one in the trees —was found near the Lovers' Peak Trail."

"When we were up there, they seemed to run almost parallel to each other, right?" he says.

She nods. "You could easily start on one and cross to the other if you know the area well." Which means the second victim could've witnessed the first murder and tried to get off the Juniper Trail in a bid to escape.

They keep reading.

The dense fog advanced alarmingly fast, and as Becky was ahead of us, we soon lost sight of her. When she didn't respond to her name being called, Tasha ran ahead to try to tell her we were turning back, but then she disappeared too. I spent at least twenty minutes calling for them, but it reached the point where the weather made it impossible to stay. I didn't feel safe and I didn't want to risk getting lost by going after them. I didn't know how long the storm would last and I thought they might be playing some kind of prank on me, which pissed me off.

I eventually turned back and exited the trail. Ours were the only two vehicles in the parking lot. It was the kind of weather that drove hikers off the mountain, no matter how experienced. I saw that Becky and Tasha hadn't returned yet, so I waited in my car. After an hour, they still hadn't appeared, so I went home. Once home, I sent Tasha a couple of texts and assumed they would be back by lunchtime, but I never heard from them. I called Becky's house midafternoon to see if she'd arrived home and not bothered to tell me, but there was no answer. I fell asleep and woke up at around eight. Their moms, Mrs. Draper and Mrs. Harris, were banging at my door. They wanted to know where Becky and Tasha were, and that's when I realized they never made it home. It was at that point that their moms made me call the police.

Madison leans back in her seat. "He waited a long time before contacting the police."

"That's because he killed them," says Adams. "It's obvious. Sounds to me like he probably made a pass at Tasha, and she wasn't interested, so he lashed out. And if you kill one, you have to kill the witness, right?"

"Let's see what Detective Douglas thought." Madison reads his most recent notes on the case.

The suspect agreed to remove his shirt so we could check for scratches and bruising that could've been obtained during an attack, but no wounds were found. None of the three adults wore fitness trackers, and the women's social media accounts logged no activity from the day they vanished and haven't been used since.

Stuart Carpenter states that Becky offered to carry Tasha's cell phone in her backpack with hers. Apparently, both women switched their phones off on arrival, as they wanted to enjoy their hike undisturbed. Cell phone data corroborates that, and neither phone has been recovered. The phones haven't been used since their disappearance and there was nothing of interest in their call history in the build-up to that day. Stuart left his cell phone at home.

A search of the Juniper Trail was conducted, with nothing of significance found. Tasha's vehicle was processed, and a mixture of fingerprints were found, some unidentifiable. Stuart Carpenter's weren't on there.

"You know," says Adams. "If I hadn't been up there myself,

I would be asking why the search team never found the first body, since it wasn't buried. But now I can appreciate how vast an area it is to search."

Madison nods. "And the frustrating part is, you never know when to give up in an area that large. You can search for weeks and unknowingly stop just a foot or two away from finding the body. You never know how close you got until some dog walker stumbles across it just outside the search perimeter." It goes back to resources. If the department had more money, the bodies would've been found sooner.

They turn back to the screen.

A request for a search warrant for Stuart's house and cell phone was refused by the judge, mainly because the suspect has remained cooperative throughout and willingly spoke to us in his living room, where nothing appeared out of order. He declined to allow us to search his property, but we didn't find evidence of a clean-up operation and felt it was more likely that if the women were dead, they would've been killed on the mountain. Stuart appears visibly upset by what's happened. He didn't allow me to take his cell phone. He stated he felt his privacy would be violated, and as he hadn't taken it on the hike, there was no reason for us to search it. His father, Bryan Carpenter, later contacted us to state that an attorney would be present at any future questioning. Unless new evidence emerges, we've exhausted Stuart Carpenter as a suspect for now.

Adams scoffs. "Who leaves their cell phone at home when going on a hike?" He doesn't wait for a response before answering his own question. "A *killer*, that's who. He didn't want anyone to pinpoint where he hid the bodies."

Madison keeps reading.

The only eyewitness who could be located was a local resident, Mary Butler, who confirmed she was one of the people the group passed that morning. She stated that the three friends appeared happy and were joking as they passed her, with no obvious signs of animosity. They all greeted her, and they were the only people she saw during her hour-long hike.

"So let's see if I've got this right," says Adams. "Stuart Carpenter took two young women on a hike, emerged *alone* an hour or so later and never heard from the women again. He then waited *all day* before being convinced to call the cops. Then, five years later, he blows his brain out after one of the bodies is found with a gunshot wound to the head. Hmm..." He makes an exaggerated thinking face. "I just can't begin to guess who killed those poor women."

Madison takes a deep breath. "Fine. He did it. Assuming the remains belong to Becky and Tasha."

Steve approaches, cell phone in hand. "Lena just called. She says the victim she has in the morgue doesn't match Becky Draper's dental records. It isn't her."

"What?" says Madison, surprised. "But she was wearing Becky's hat."

"It must be Tasha, then," says Adams. He sounds less sure of his theory now. "Maybe Becky let her borrow her hat. Which means Becky could be the person we found between the trees this afternoon."

Steve shrugs. "I guess we'll know once they've extracted the body and taken it to the morgue. Lena said she's still waiting for Tasha's dental records to come through."

"Okay," Madison says. "Check Stuart Carpenter's phone records and bank statements from around the time the women vanished, would you? I want to see what he spent his money on and what kind of relationship he really had with them. His texts should give us an insight."

Steve nods. "Sure."

Madison wanted to remain open-minded until the bodies were identified, but it seems that Adams is right. Everything points to Stuart Carpenter being the killer. After all, why would he take his own life if he wasn't guilty of murder?

She stands. "Before we finish for the day, let's check out his house."

CHAPTER FIFTEEN

The scent of decay greets them at Stuart's house. His blood and tissue will still be clinging to the walls of the dining room. Every overhead light is switched on to counter the lack of daylight, and the heating has come on as normal, enhancing the smell.

Stuart's father already has a crime-scene clean team ready to come in once the search of the house is complete. He's also desperate to claim Stuart's personal belongings, which leaves Madison wondering whether that's because he's worried about what the officers might find. Perhaps he wants to try to protect his son's reputation.

Officer Luis Sanchez approaches. He's wearing blue latex gloves and a white protective suit over his uniform. Madison and Adams are similarly suited. The living room is messy from where every item has been pulled out and examined. Several couch cushions are upturned on the floor.

"Evening," he says. "We're just finishing up." Sanchez is a few months younger than the two new officers, but he's been with the team for almost two years now and is proving to be a committed cop.

"Find anything?" asks Adams.

"Not really," says Sanchez. "Nothing that looks like it doesn't belong to the resident anyway. He has photos of his mom in the drawer of his nightstand. None of his dad though."

"His mom's deceased," says Madison. "Maybe Stuart missed her."

"Or maybe he's got mommy issues," says Adams. "Let's face it, most male killers have."

"Any computers or phones?" asks Madison.

Sanchez shakes his head. "Nope. It makes me wonder whether he ditched them first, knowing we'd go through his online history after his death. Aside from the shotgun he used to kill himself, he also owned a licensed semi-automatic."

"That should go to Alex or Lena," says Madison, "so they can establish whether it was the weapon that shot our first victim."

Sanchez nods.

Detective Adams locates an air freshener above the fireplace and sprays it in front of him. He's weird about smells. He never seems to acclimate to the smell of blood or decomposition, no matter how long he's at a crime scene.

"The dining room smells even worse," says Sanchez. "But it's empty of belongings, so there's no point going in there if you can't handle the smell."

Adams raises his eyebrows, offended. "I *can* handle it. I just don't *want* to."

"So what's upstairs?" asks Madison. "Any sign that Stuart had a girlfriend or a roommate?"

"No," says the officer. "Just a bed in the master bedroom, male clothing in the closet and a few toiletries in the bathroom. He lived pretty cheaply from what I can see. Wasn't a big spender."

"That's probably because he washed dishes for a living," says Madison. "He wasn't bringing in a lot of money. Which is strange considering his dad's loaded." According to the records,

Bryan owns this house. "Maybe Stuart didn't feel he needed to earn much, knowing his father would always have his back."

Adams scoffs. "Not all parents share their wealth. My dad made me work the minute I turned fourteen, and he never once loaned me money, even though the son of a bitch had it."

Madison shares a look with Sanchez. Adams seems to have daddy issues on top of everything else.

She changes the subject. "Thanks for searching. Just straighten this place up before you leave, would you? His family will be by in the morning to collect his personal belongings. It'll be difficult enough to witness the dining room in that state; I don't want to make them feel even more violated when they see the rest of the house like this."

"Sure thing," says Sanchez.

They hear footsteps on the stairs. Officer Corey Fuller approaches.

"I just found this under a floorboard in the bedroom," says the rookie gravely. He's holding a driver's license.

Madison's heart sinks as she takes it from him. Tasha Harris smiles back at her from the photo.

"Well, that's that then," says Adams. "If he were still alive, we'd be arresting Stuart Carpenter for murder right now."

"Does this mean we need to tear up the floorboards and do a more thorough search?" asks Fuller.

Madison nods. "Good work finding this. I'd like to find Becky Draper's license too, and their cell phones. We need as much evidence as possible to prove to Stuart's family that he was responsible for the murders." Part of her worries that Bryan Carpenter is the kind of person who might sue the department for causing his son's suicide. People with money sometimes view lawsuits as the answer to everything.

Fuller nods and turns to Sanchez. "Let's go."

Sanchez glances at Madison and Adams with an amused expression. When Fuller is out of earshot, he says, "The rookie's giving *me* orders?" He laughs. Luckily, Sanchez is easygoing. He follows Officer Fuller upstairs.

Madison turns to Adams. "Well, I guess we should be grateful Stuart's not alive to kill anyone else."

Adams nods as he checks his phone for the time. "I need to go. Once the kids are asleep, I'm going to have *the talk* with Selena."

Madison feels for him. It won't be easy. "Let me know if you want to move into my spare room. I can stay with Nate more often to give you some space." The house is too empty now Owen's at college. Too silent. And the problem with silence is that it's filled with memories.

Adams leaves. Madison watches through the living room window as he drives away. Before she can follow him out, Bryan Carpenter skids to a halt outside in his expensive Audi and approaches the house at full speed. He looks pissed.

Madison tenses. "Guys?" she shouts up the stairs. "I think we may have a problem."

Sanchez and Fuller are down in seconds, just as Bryan lets himself in. He ignores the uniforms and heads straight for Madison.

"What the hell is going on?" he yells. "I have reporters at the lodge accusing me of harboring a killer! Why would you announce my son's suicide on TV?"

Chief Mendes must have held the press conference.

Sanchez steps forward. "Sir, I need you to calm down."

"Don't tell me to calm down!" says Bryan. He's got six inches over Sanchez. He turns to Madison. "You're ruining my family's reputation! I could lose my *business* over this. Isn't it enough that I've already lost a son?"

Refusing to be intimidated, Madison says evenly, "Mr. Carpenter, we're obligated to comment on serious incidents when questioned by the press, and the fact is, your son took his own life after remains were found near the spot where two of his friends vanished. We believe the incidents are related."

"No," he says. "Stuart took his own life because he was devastated that someone murdered his friends. It could've been *him* who was killed that day! He was lucky to get away."

Tasha's driver's license sits in Madison's palm. She doesn't want to devastate him, but she has to tell him what they know. She holds it up for him to see.

He squints at it. "Why are you showing me this?"

"You know who Tasha is, right?" she says.

He nods.

"We found her driver's license under a floorboard in your son's bedroom."

Bryan scoffs before glancing at Sanchez and Fuller. The color drains out of his face. "That doesn't prove anything."

Madison clears her throat. "Mr. Carpenter, your son was the last person to see the women alive, and now we've found this in his house. Stuart also admitted guilt right before he ended his life."

Bryan gulps back some air. He visibly shrinks as his shoulders sag. "You're lying."

"I'm afraid not. I'm sorry." She takes a step closer. "I know this is the worst thing you could hear right now, but Stuart's last words were an admission of guilt. He said he was sorry for what he did and that he couldn't undo it. All of this together means that if he were still with us, we'd be arresting him for the murders of Becky Draper and Tasha Harris."

The older man turns away and runs a hand over his hair. "This isn't happening."

Madison turns to look at the officers. She nods to the stairs to let them know they should return to their search.

Bryan remains silent until his phone rings. He automatically answers it. "What?" he barks. She can't hear what the caller says, but he spins around to look at her. "But the baby won't make it. It's too soon." He listens for a second. "I'm on my way." He ends the call and heads to the door.

Madison follows. "Has something happened?"

He spins around. "Jay's had to take Mel to the hospital. She's having contractions, but she's only five months into her pregnancy. It's the stress. She started spotting as soon as you told us Stuart was dead. She's been having cramps ever since, so the doctor put her on bed rest. Jay's beside himself with worry." He pauses. "You're trying to kill my entire family with this garbage, Detective."

Horrified, Madison steps forward. "No, that's not the case at all. We can support your family through this."

Bryan glares at her. "If my first grandchild dies, you'll be hearing from my lawyer." He leaves.

Madison watches him climb into his car before he speeds away from the house.

CHAPTER SIXTEEN

Nate pours Madison a glass of white wine and sits beside her on the couch in his living room while a salmon risotto simmers in the kitchen. He can tell she's had a stressful day because once she'd updated him on her current case, she went quiet, lost in her thoughts. He's learning more about her the longer they date, such as the fact that she needs time to decompress after work. She needs to process everything that's happened and mentally prepare herself for everything she needs to do the following day.

Nate wouldn't wish the life of a detective on anyone. At least being a PI means he gets to pick which cases he works on and who he works for. Madison has no choice, and each case seems more horrific than the last.

"Thanks." She smiles as she takes the glass from him.

"Want a foot rub?" he asks.

She looks at him like he's insane. "Ew, no. Why would you want to touch my feet? Have you got a weird fetish I need to know about?"

Amused, he says, "Are you telling me no one's ever given you a foot rub before?"

"No," she replies with raised eyebrows. "I've never asked for one! I don't expect anyone to touch my feet. I'm not a monster."

He picks up her feet and turns her body so that she's lying on the couch. She immediately giggles like a schoolgirl.

"Stop! That tickles!"

He gives her a stern look. "Madison, hold still. You'll love it, I promise."

She stills her tense foot in his hand as he removes her sock and starts kneading.

Her expression turns from a grimace to pleasure, and her foot relaxes in his grip. "Oh my God." She rests her head against the couch. "Seriously, oh my God. Where did you learn how to do that?" She pauses and looks at him funny. "Not in prison, I hope?"

Surprised by the comment, Nate laughs. She's probably the only person he'd allow to make jokes about his time inside. "I'm just rubbing your foot."

She starts making groaning noises. "Well, don't stop. That feels amazing. I can't believe you could've been doing this to me the whole time I've known you." She suddenly looks at him. "I hope you're not expecting me to reciprocate. Because I don't do feet, Monroe."

He laughs again. "No. I'm good."

They sit in silence for a while as Nate continues to massage her foot.

Eventually, Madison looks at him. "Do you ever get the feeling this is too good to be true? You know, us being together."

"Of course."

"So, do you ever wonder whether that feeling is normal? Whether we'd feel this way if we hadn't been so badly treated in the past?"

He switches feet. "I guess we'll never know. But it does make me even more grateful for what we have. Maybe we would've taken it for granted otherwise, or maybe it would never have happened. We would never have met if you hadn't wanted my help after you were released from prison."

She nods. "I almost didn't contact you. I didn't think you'd be interested in my case. That's why I offered to work for you as a PI, to hook you in."

"Once I learned you were an ex-cop, I wasn't interested," he says. "I tried to walk away, but you wouldn't let me."

She snorts. "Come on! You make it sound like I forced you to help me."

"You did force me!" He stops rubbing. "I could tell you were trouble, and I didn't want to get on your bad side."

She grins. "I *am* trouble. But only if I don't like you." She sips her wine. "Remind me of your first impression of me," she says. "Were you attracted to me back then? Because if you were, you didn't show it. You acted like I was annoying."

He looks at her. "You were extremely annoying. And controlling."

"*What?*" she says. "No I wasn't!"

"You wanted to work that case in Shadow Falls as though you were still a cop. You were bossing me around and acting like you were in charge. Trust me, it was annoying."

She narrows her eyes. "Yeah, well, maybe you needed to be controlled."

Nate laughs. "Maybe. Despite that, yes, I was attracted to you right away."

She blushes. "Well of course you were. I mean, look at me! I'm a catch." The way she gestures to her current appearance— sweatpants, flannel shirt and messy hair—suggests she's joking.

He leans forward and pulls her to him so he can kiss her. "You're the best thing I've ever caught."

She rolls her eyes at the cheesy line. "So, are you working on any cases at the moment?"

As well as working for a local lawyer, Nate has a website

offering investigative services. He focuses mainly on cases of wrongful conviction. With a shake of the head, he says, "Not right now. Why? Have you got something for me?"

She takes a deep breath. "There was a guy at the support group meeting I went to last night. Robert Dorsey. His thirteen-year-old son went missing a while ago, and as you know, Chief Mendes doesn't let me reopen cold cases unless I have new evidence. Robert's a little hostile toward me because he can't understand why I won't help him, so I said I'd mention it to you and see if you had time to look into it."

Nate could do with something to get his teeth into.

"He can't pay you, though," she adds. "Apparently, he's about to lose his home, so he's desperate right now." She shrugs. "I just thought he needed someone to take him seriously so he doesn't lose all hope and do something stupid."

He nods. "Sure. I'll meet with him and see if I can help." Working as a PI has never been about earning money for Nate. He's lucky not to need an income, if you can call what he went through to get his compensation payout lucky. For him, it's about keeping his demons at bay.

He stands and holds his hand out. "Let's eat."

They walk to the kitchen and Madison takes a seat at the dining table while Nate serves the risotto and brings it to the table. When Madison's phone buzzes, she lights up as Owen's face appears on the screen.

Nate moves around the table and sits next to her to be included in the call.

"Well, hello!" says Madison playfully. "Who is this stranger I see before me? You can't be my son because he's vanished off the face of the earth. In fact, I have a BOLO out in twelve states for him."

Owen flicks his blond hair out of his eyes. "God, Mom, you're so dramatic. It's only been six days since I last called."

"Yeah, well," she says, "time works differently for empty nesters. Cut me some slack."

"You're lucky she hasn't turned up at your dorm again," says Nate with a smile.

Owen looks happy, which is a relief. You never know whether a kid's going to settle into college life. Being away from home can be stressful for some.

Nate suddenly feels a wave of sadness hit him out of nowhere. He's envious of their bond. Because there was a time before his arrest when he assumed he'd be a father one day. He wanted children with Stacey Connor, but then she was murdered, and he spent decades in prison, which robbed him of his ability to start a family. Maybe that's why he enjoys spending time with Owen. It gives him a brief glimpse into what life with kids is like.

He watches Madison as she talks to her son, and surprises himself by wondering whether she'd be open to having another child. She's only thirty-eight, and he's forty-one. Is he too old to be a father now? And would the age gap between the baby and Owen be too big? He dismisses the idea. He doubts Madison wants more kids anyway. Her son leaving for college traumatized her enough.

Nate can see Owen's dorm room in the background, and it looks messy, with textbooks strewn all over the bed and clothes hanging off the back of his chair. He's lucky he doesn't have to share it with anyone. His roommate dropped out and went home to Wisconsin after just a few weeks.

"Where's Bandit?" asks Owen. "You haven't left him home alone, have you?"

Madison points the camera at the large rug on the floor where Owen's white cat is curled up on top of Brody's thick neck.

"Hey, Bandit!" Owen calls. The cat looks up with interest

and offers a weak meow before going back to sleep. Brody's tail wags, but he's too comfortable to get up.

"They don't care about me anymore," says Owen, disappointed. "I bet they won't even recognize me when I come home."

"Of course they care about you," says Madison. "They've been winding each other up for the past hour, so they're exhausted, that's all. Anyway, what have you been up to? How are your classes?" She eats a forkful of food.

"It's all good," he says. "Pretty boring at this stage, but we've been promised it gets more interesting. We have a field trip to a court downtown later this month, and I have tons of projects I should be working on." He yawns loudly.

"Are we boring you?" says Madison.

"No, I was out late last..." He stops. "I was studying late at the library and now I'm paying the price."

She rolls her eyes. "You must think I was born yesterday."

He laughs. "I should go. I just wanted to check in."

"That's it?" she says, disappointed. "Well, before you go, I need to tell you we might have a house guest soon, so if you ever think about turning up out of the blue to surprise your old mom, bear in mind there could be someone else at the house."

Owen frowns. "Who?"

Nate doesn't know about this either. He's intrigued.

"Detective Adams is going through a potential marriage breakup," she says. "I told him he could stay at our place until he figures things out."

Nate's surprised she'd let him stay with her. He didn't think they got on that well. "Is that why he's never fully invested at work?" he asks.

She nods. "Right. It's a long story. I'll tell you later."

"He's not staying in my room, though, right?" says Owen. "I don't want him going through my things."

Madison puts her fork down. "First of all, I'm glad you still consider it your room. You might want to check in on the place every now and then. And secondly, no, he can take the spare room. As for going through your things, I'm pretty sure he's outgrown video games and moldy pizza, so you don't have to worry about that."

Someone knocks on Owen's door, and they hear a girl ask him if he's coming to the party. Owen points the camera at the ground as he whispers something in response. Nate smiles. He suspects Owen won't get that early night he wanted.

When he points the camera back at his face, he's blushing. "Sorry, Mom. I gotta go. I'll call you in a few days."

"Yeah, yeah." Madison sighs. "Don't stay out too late."

With a grin, Owen shouts, "Bye, Bandit!" Then he's gone.

Nate returns to the seat opposite Madison and picks up his fork. "He's happy. That's all you need to focus on."

She nods as she places her phone on the table. "I'm just glad he's coming back for Christmas. I'm actually excited about doing his laundry."

He laughs. "That won't last long."

After a few more mouthfuls, she says, "By the way, that's why I brought more things with me than usual." She nods to the bags by the front door. "In case Adams needs my place tonight. He's having a heart-to-heart with Selena."

Nate thinks about Madison sharing a house with someone else, and how she has to carry fresh clothes back and forth when she stays here. He takes a sip of wine before reaching across the table for her spare hand. "Move in with me."

She stops eating. Her blue eyes meet his to see if he's serious. She's silent for a while. "We've only been dating a few months."

He shrugs. "Even before we dated, we shared the odd hotel room, then I lived in your spare room for a while, and now you're splitting your time between here and your place." He strokes her hand with his thumb. "I don't like it when you leave. The silence is unsettling." He smiles sadly. "I used to crave silence, back when, you know..." He doesn't need to finish his thought. She knows what he means. "I used to crave space too, but I don't need all this room just for me and Brody. It's too much. When you're here, this place feels like home."

Madison looks at her food. "What if it doesn't work out?"

One of the many consequences of being badly betrayed in the past is considering the worst-case scenario in any given situation. But, unusually, Nate hasn't even considered that their relationship might not work out. He knows this is the woman he'll be with for the rest of his life, given the chance. "It will. You're my reward for seventeen years on death row."

She snorts. "Some would say that sounds like more punishment."

"Not me." He waits for her answer, but she leaves him hanging while she eats. "You could let Adams move into your place properly," he adds. "Become a landlady. Let the house go to ruin around him while increasing the rent every six months." He smiles.

Madison still doesn't answer. A ball of dread builds in Nate's chest. Does she have doubts about him?

"If you don't like this house, I could move into your place," he suggests. "Or we could look for somewhere new."

Madison lowers her fork and leans back in her seat before fixing her eyes on him. "Let me think about it for a few days, okay?"

Slowly, he nods. "Sure." It's not the answer he was hoping for, but it's better than an outright no. Trying to hide his disappointment, he gets up and goes to the kitchen.

Madison cranes her neck to see what he's doing. "What've you got there? Is that apple pie?"

"Right. But it's only for residents. Sorry." He looks at the dog. "Brody? Pie?"

Brody immediately jumps up, leaving Bandit confused on the floor.

"Hey!" Madison throws a napkin in Nate's direction. "In that case, you don't get the dessert *I* brought."

He raises his eyebrows. "Oh yeah? What's that?"

She stands and starts unbuttoning her shirt. "Me."

Nate pushes the pie away and goes to her.

CHAPTER SEVENTEEN

The following morning starts bitterly cold and gray. Nate scraped all the ice off Madison's car while she showered, but it's accumulating again already. She pulls into the station's parking lot, and when she gets out of her car, she slips on some black ice and almost goes face-first into the ground. Chief Mendes catches her arm as she passes, even managing to keep hold of her coffee as she does so.

Embarrassed at having Mendes hold her upright, Madison lets her enter the building first. Inside, the station is toasty warm and smells of fresh coffee. They say good morning to the officer behind the front desk as they pass.

"So we like Stuart Carpenter for the two potential homicides?" says Mendes, removing her scarf as they walk.

"Right," says Madison. "All signs point to him. Hopefully, the second set of remains are with Lena by now, and she can confirm the victims are Becky Draper and Tasha Harris." They come to a stop outside Mendes's office. "I'll pay Nancy and Doug Draper a visit as soon as it's confirmed. And then Tasha's sister."

Mendes nods. "Keep me updated." She enters her office.

Madison heads to her desk and is surprised to find Detective Adams already here. He's never arrived at work before her, which means something's wrong. The day-old stubble on his jaw tells her he hasn't shaved, and his tie hangs loosely at the open collar of his shirt. It's clear he hasn't slept well. He's talking to Officer Kent, who suddenly straightens when Madison approaches. It makes her feel like she's interrupting something.

Adams looks at his screen as if he's suddenly found something interesting to read.

"Morning, Detective Harper," says the young officer before pulling on her black LCPD parka and heading to the exit.

Madison looks at Adams. "Hey," she says. "How did the talk go?"

Adams glances around to see if anyone's listening, but Steve hasn't arrived yet, and the other officers and dispatchers are busy going about their business. "Put it this way," he says gravely, "we're separating."

Madison removes her coat and then walks to his messy desk. She takes the empty seat next to him. "Shit. I'm sorry."

With a deep breath, he says, "Turns out she's wanted to separate for a long time, but she thought it wouldn't be good for the girls." He shakes his head. "I wish I'd known sooner. I wouldn't have uprooted my entire life and moved down here."

Worried for him, Madison says, "Bring some things to my place after work. I'll stay with Nate for a few days until we figure something out. You never know, it could be that you guys just need a short break from each other to put things into perspective. How long have you been together?"

"Fourteen years. But that's not it, she just doesn't love me anymore." He looks at her. "It's over, Harper. I could tell she's mentally checked out already. She looked relieved when I said I could move out quickly." He swallows hard. "Jeez, my chest hurts just thinking about it."

She thinks about her relationship with Nate and how she'd cope if they broke up. It's unsettling how fast you start depending on someone else for your emotional needs. Having been alone for so long, it scares her. What if they do break up? Adams obviously didn't see his relationship troubles coming. People change over time. Maybe it's better to stay single to avoid the kind of heartache he's experiencing.

"It's anxiety," she says. "You'll probably get chest pains and floods of panic over the next few weeks." She rests her hand on his. "You've got a big change coming your way, but you can get through it. Just think of your girls. You'll still get to see them every day." Her desk phone rings, but she ignores it for now.

"Selena said I can stop by whenever I want." He scoffs before adding, "Until she moves the next guy in."

Madison can tell he's devastated. He must be if he's opening up to her.

"Detectives?" Stella stands so she can see them over the top of the dispatcher's cubicle in the corner of the office. "I've got Officer Vickers on the line. Says she needs to speak to you urgently."

Madison goes to her desk and picks up the phone as soon as it rings. "Morning, Shelley."

There's a hesitation before someone says, "Madison?"

"Oh. Sorry, Lena." It's the medical examiner. She must've beat Stella to it. Madison looks at Stella, who's waiting patiently to put Shelley through. "I thought you were someone else. How can I help?"

"I'm calling because Tasha Harris's dental records came in yesterday evening, and my assistant emailed them straight to the forensic dentist. I arrived at work this morning to find his report waiting for me. It confirms they match the first victim found on the mountain."

Madison lowers her eyes. She'll have to break the news to Tasha's sister. "Understood. I think we can assume the second victim will be Becky Draper then."

"Probably," says Lena. "We should know for sure by lunchtime."

"Good," says Madison. "Keep me updated."

"Will do. Before you go, it appears the first victim was shot with a nine-millimeter bullet. Officer Sanchez brought me the semi-automatic pistol found in Stuart Carpenter's house. Alex and I both believe that type of weapon could've been used, but as five years have passed since Tasha was murdered, it would be difficult to say whether it was the same gun without getting a ballistics expert involved."

Madison makes a note. Given that everything else incriminates Stuart, and they can't arrest him now he's deceased, that shouldn't be necessary. "Got it. Thanks, Lena." She ends the call and signals to Stella that she's free to speak to Shelley.

Stella gives her a thumbs-up.

Madison's phone rings immediately. "Morning, Shelley."

"Brace yourself," says Officer Vickers.

"Why?"

"Because Officer Fuller and I have discovered another body."

Madison tenses. She looks at Adams, who's staring at her inquisitively. She puts her phone on speaker. "On the mountain?"

"Right. Skeletal remains. But, Madison?" Shelley pauses. "This one's missing its head."

Madison's lost for words. Could this be a *third* victim of Stuart's?

Adams stands as Chief Mendes joins them.

For the chief's benefit, Madison says, "So you've found a third body on Grave Mountain, but this one's missing its skull?"

"Correct," says Shelley.

Over in her cubicle, Stella stands again. "Detective Adams? Are you free to take a call from Officer Sanchez?"

Adams nods. Madison and Chief Mendes watch as he answers his phone.

"Hello?" he says, with a flicker of apprehension. There's a pause. "Yeah, Vickers just told Madison about that."

"Hang on the line a minute, Shelley," says Madison. "Sanchez has called Adams about something. Sounds like it might be what you've found."

"I don't know where Sanchez is," says Shelley, puzzled. "But he's not with us, so he can't know about the remains we found."

"*What?*" Adams looks incredulous. "You've found a dead *child* up there?"

Madison and Chief Mendes share a look. This is bad.

"Shelley?" says Madison into the phone. "Secure the scene. We'll be there asap." She ends the call.

Adams puts his phone down. He exhales heavily and runs a hand over his hair. "What the hell is going on?"

Madison's reminded of Robert Dorsey and his missing son. Her heart rate spikes. "That's *four* victims now." She glances at Chief Mendes. "It's starting to look like someone's been using Grave Mountain as a dumping ground."

Chief Mendes turns a little pale as she considers the implications. "You think Stuart Carpenter was a serial killer?"

With a deep breath, Madison says, "We can only hope Stuart was responsible. Because if it wasn't him..."

Adams's shoulders sag as he says, "Then we could have an unidentified serial killer on our hands."

Her mouth goes dry. She seriously hopes not. She thinks about her father, and how he was targeted by the Snow Storm Killer last year because of her involvement in that case. Relieved that Owen's safe in Arizona, she thinks about the only other significant person in her life who could become a target for a crazed psychopath.

Nate.

A shudder goes through her. She can't lose him.

CHAPTER EIGHTEEN

SEVEN YEARS AGO

Shannon Briggs laughs as she slips her sunglasses on to avoid eye contact with the two older hikers they pass. As the midday sun is intense, she can get away with it. Her married lover grabs her hand once they're in the clear and kisses her neck.

"Not here!" she says playfully. "We need to get off the trail."

They've been sleeping together for four months, having met through work friends. She's single and free to date whoever she wants, but he's married with two kids. She doesn't know who his wife is, and she's resisted the urge to search social media for answers. Having lived alone for so long, Shannon does her best to consider his wife's existence irrelevant. She's having the best sex of her life, and she intends to enjoy it while it lasts.

Her girlfriends know about her anonymous new man, and that he's married. They've predictably warned her that it'll end in tears by reminding her that married men never leave their wives for their mistresses. She can't blame them. It's what she'd say if one of them were stupid enough to find themselves in this situation. But Shannon's a big girl, and she thinks she can handle herself. She ignores the fact she's falling for the guy, even though she daydreams about him choosing her over his wife one day. After all, they get along so well, and the sex is fantastic.

Wouldn't he have left his wife by now if he felt the same way?

She shakes the thought away. She's a live-in-the-moment kind of girl, and in this moment, she's ready for some fun in the hot summer sunshine.

Occasionally, the meandering path reveals sun-blighted wooden signs disclosing where they are and what lies ahead. Her lover strides forward. She watches his tanned, athletic body climb over the rocks to the left of the Lovers' Peak Trail. He's finding somewhere secluded for them to go.

She follows him through dense thickets, swatting flies and bugs as her legs get nicked by thorns. She curses herself for buying the cheap bug spray, but as her work with vulnerable children doesn't pay well and she has no one to share her household bills with, she exists on a tight budget.

A line of blood runs down her shin from one of the minor cuts. "This isn't the kind of spot I had in mind," she says with an uncertain laugh.

He looks over his shoulder at her. "You'll take that back in a minute."

He's playing stern today. Taking the lead and treating her like she's been disobedient. She's noticed that the longer they're together, the rougher the sex gets. It was his idea to come here. They've exhausted all other locations where they won't get caught by anyone who knows his wife. He's never taken her to his marital home. That would be stupid, after all.

Shannon hears other hikers behind them, descending the trail in the opposite direction. She stops and turns to see if they've been spotted, but she can't see them through the pine trees, and she can't make out their words. Turning, she smiles and pulls off her shirt, tying it around her waist. The heat is scorching, and she worries that the more they walk, the sweatier she'll be when they eventually have sex.

Now half naked except for her sports bra and shorts, she continues after her lover. "Where did you go?" she yells.

"Over here!"

She hurries to catch up with him. It's dark under the trees where the sunshine can't break through. The occasional sounds of wild animals can be heard around them. Mostly birds and squirrels, but Shannon feels like she's being watched.

Finally, she sees him. As she reaches his location, it becomes clear why he brought her here. The view of Lost Creek is breathtaking. Lake Providence glistens in the distance, near the water tower. Fantasy World amusement park actually looks enticing compared to up close. And the mountains that border the town are majestic. "Wow," she says.

"I know, right?" He unties her shirt, grabs her waist and pulls her against his sweaty torso.

"How have I never been here before?" she says in awe.

"I come all the time."

She looks at him with raised eyebrows. "Oh yeah? Just how many women have you brought up here, lover boy?"

He smiles that devilish smile of his. The one she can't resist. "Only you. I swear."

She doesn't believe him, but in this moment, she doesn't care. He removes his baseball cap and throws it on the ground. His hands go to her neck, gently caressing, sending shivers down her spine. She closes her eyes as he pulls her damp hair back from her shoulders into a ponytail and tugs on it. Gently at first, but she knows it'll get harder.

She lowers her hand to his shorts and opens her eyes. "You really want me, don't you?"

"That's why I brought you up here," he says with a serious look. He spins her around so that she's facing away from him and pulls her arms behind her, clasping her wrists together with one of his hands and stroking her neck with the other.

She likes it when he takes control. "I'm missing work for this," she says softly, closing her eyes against the pleasure. "It better be worth it."

"Oh, it'll be worth it," he says menacingly into her ear.

She suddenly breaks out in goosebumps all over her body, as if an electrical storm is about to hit. But it's midsummer. No storms are forecast.

She questions whether she should've come here today. He's married. And he has no intention of ever putting her before his wife. She's just a cheap thrill for him. Disposable. His grip on her neck tightens, and a ball of dread builds in her chest. The feeling is so overwhelming she has to bite back a scream.

She tries pulling away from him, but his arm is locked around her waist, reminding her that he's physically stronger than her.

A quick flutter of movement through the bush to her left makes her listen closely. It's probably a squirrel. When it's followed by the sound of a branch breaking directly ahead of her, she looks up. There's no one there.

"Hey, relax," he says behind her as he removes her bra and cups her breasts, pulling her tighter into his grip. "It's just you and me out here."

But he's wrong.

Someone emerges from behind the tree directly in front of them, slowly at first. Her fear leaves her confused. All she registers is that they're wearing a ski mask on a hot day.

Then, when the stranger advances toward her, Shannon screams.

CHAPTER NINETEEN

PRESENT DAY

Nate turns up the collar of his jacket against the bitterly cold morning breeze. His hands feel like ice as he knocks on the door of a small one-story brick house in a cramped neighborhood.

He's come to meet with Robert Dorsey to discuss the guy's missing son. He's never seen Robert in person, just spoken to him on the phone, and when the door opens, he's greeted by a tall middle-aged man. His long black hair is tied back. It looks like it hasn't been cut for years, as the ends are thin and straggly.

"Hi." Nate holds out his hand. "Nate Monroe."

The other man shakes it, but his weary expression suggests he has the weight of the world on his shoulders. He steps aside. "Come in."

Nate has Brody with him and he's aware not everyone likes dogs. With Brody's size, he can look a little menacing to some people. "Would you prefer I leave my dog outside?"

Robert didn't even notice him. He sighs as he glances down at the inquisitive shepsky. "I don't trust dogs."

No one's ever said that to Nate before. In his opinion, animals are far more trustworthy than humans. He looks at Brody. "Sorry, buddy. Stay where we can see you."

Brody goes to the flower bed and cocks his leg.

Nate steps inside the house. The living room is sparse. All personal belongings appear to be packed into boxes and garbage bags.

Robert leads him to the breakfast bar in the kitchen. It's missing stools. "We'll have to stand." He assesses Nate as if cautious about allowing an ex-felon into his home, then pulls something from the back pocket of his jeans and hands it to him. "It's my son's missing poster. It contains all his details: height, eye color, the date he went missing. The photo was taken a month before he vanished. I intend to make a new poster and start getting them up around town, as it's been a while. People have forgotten him."

Nate unfolds the dog-eared piece of paper and looks at the thirteen-year-old boy staring back at him. Brandon is posing for a school photograph and smiling widely at the camera, which shows his braces. His blond hair looks freshly cut, and his blue eyes shine brightly. It looks like any other photo from a school yearbook and betrays no clues as to Brandon's mental state at the time of his disappearance.

"If you email me a few more photos of him, I can update this and get a whole bunch printed for you."

Robert nods. "That'd be helpful. Thanks."

Nate has a legal pad with him. He retrieves a pen from his coat pocket and rests the pad on the countertop. "As I said on the phone, I like to hear the full details of a case before I agree to investigate. It means I don't get anyone's hopes up if I think I can't help."

"And if you do help, you won't charge me, right?" says Robert from the opposite side of the breakfast bar. "Because look around, Mr. Monroe. I don't have anything left to sell."

"I understand. Are you working right now?"

"Yeah, as a carpenter. I build furniture." He glances over at the sparse living room. "Ironic, right?"

Nate offers a sympathetic smile.

"But I've been warned by my boss that he's letting people go over the coming weeks, and I have the kind of luck that makes me carry a target on my back."

"Well, I hope you're wrong about that," says Nate.

The man sighs. "The hardest part of packing everything away is packing Brandon's things. I'll need to pay to store them."

"Where are you moving to?"

"I'm sleeping on a friend's couch in their garage. There's barely enough room for a few clothes, never mind all this." He gestures to the boxes.

When Nate meets people like this, he feels guilty for his compensation payout. Sure, he did hard time for it, and his life was ruined for two decades, but he has trouble justifying being a millionaire when other people can barely afford to exist. He donates to various charities and offers to investigate for free in some cases, but it still doesn't feel enough. Because without that payout, he would be in this man's shoes. "Why don't you start at the beginning and tell me what happened the day your son disappeared?"

Robert looks out of the kitchen window, steeling himself to relive the day that's forever etched into his memory. "Brandon was in eighth grade. He used to get home from school between three forty-five and four thirty, depending on who he was walking with and whether he stayed back to talk to one of his teachers."

"Did he get in trouble a lot?" asks Nate.

Offended by the suggestion, Robert says, "No, not at all. He liked learning. He wasn't kept behind. He *wanted* to talk to them. He was an inquisitive kid." He takes a deep breath as he recalls his son. "He was like his mother that way. She died a year before Brandon vanished, when he was just twelve. She had heart failure." He lowers his eyes. "It just about destroyed our boy."

Nate makes a note. The loss of his mother could've given Brandon a reason to harm himself or run away.

"But we got through it," continues Robert. "I thought we were doing okay. His grades were great, and he had a close friend he spent all his spare time with."

"What was his friend's name?"

"Erin Martin. She lives a block away. Or she did. She's away at college now." His eyes glaze over. "At the University of Utah. Brandon wanted to go there too."

The despair coming from this man is overwhelming. Nate's been around many people with missing loved ones. They all exude a sadness that feels contagious. It changes the atmosphere in a room. It's so powerful it can make you feel guilty when you leave them because you're overcome with relief at being able to get away from it. Relief that it's not you in their position. He feels bad just for thinking it, but it's hard to appreciate the feeling until you've been in that position where someone is placing all their hope in you with something that literally means life or death to them and their missing loved one.

"Think she'd talk to me if I can get her number?" he asks.

Robert considers it. "I hope so. She was questioned by the detectives at the time because Brandon walked her home before he vanished. She was the last person to see him."

"And what did she tell them?"

He leans forward and rests his elbows on the counter. "Apparently, Brandon was joking around on the walk home. She said he'd had an *okay* day at school, whatever that means. They took their normal route home, and she didn't notice any suspicious vehicles following them. Once they arrived at her house, Brandon declined to go inside for a soda and waved goodbye. He turned left off her property, and that's where the trail goes cold. Erin's folks didn't have one of those doorbell cameras. In fact, no one in the neighborhood did. It was before they became popular. And none of the neighbors remember seeing him walk by. Given the time of day, most of them were at work."

"Were *you* at work at the time?" asks Nate. He doesn't know what this guy's alibi was, and just because he claims to want help finding his son doesn't mean he wasn't involved in his disappearance. He could be acting the grieving father role to cover his tracks.

"I was alone at my employer's workshop." Robert's eyes narrow. "Detective Douglas thought that meant I had time to kill my son, but he couldn't find anything to link me to his disappearance because there *was* nothing. So don't go down that route, Monroe. You'll be wasting your time."

Nate scribbles some notes. It would be good if he could read Detective Douglas's case notes, but he knows Chief Mendes won't allow him access. "There must've been some older people living on the street who would've been home. I wonder how many doors the police knocked on."

Robert shakes his head as if it's a pointless exercise. "In the following weeks, I spoke to practically every neighbor on Erin's street, whether they were at work that afternoon or not. No one saw a thing. Or if they did, they wouldn't tell me or the cops about it. And there haven't been any credible sightings of my boy since." He meets Nate's eyes. "No one pays attention to a damn thing anymore unless it's happening on their cell phone."

He's not wrong there. Eyewitness testimony is harder to come by these days. Sure, people will point a camera at something if they think it'll go viral, but no one catches the build-up to crimes. They're too busy watching crime documentaries indoors to spot it happening in their own neighborhoods. Nate tries not to be bitter about the popularity of true crime, but when he's had to deal with the bloodthirsty reporters, TV producers and armchair sleuths all spreading lies about him, it's difficult.

"Did Brandon have a cell phone on him that day?" he asks.

"Yeah, but the battery died while he was in school. He left it on charge in his locker, using a portable charger I bought him. It was still there the next day. Detective Douglas had it examined, but they didn't find any clues about what happened to him." Robert rubs his face as if tired. "My son wasn't being groomed online or anything like that."

It's starting to sound like Brandon could've impulsively left of his own volition. If he did, it's more likely his friend Erin would know about it. Nate needs to speak to her. Putting his pen away, he says, "I'll try to contact Erin and see what she can tell me."

Robert nods. "I've followed every lead that's ever come in, and every sighting, no matter how far-fetched."

"Do you get these tips through social media?" asks Nate.

"Right. I have a Facebook page dedicated to Brandon's disappearance, and I'm on all the other sites too." Robert sighs. "You name it, I've tried it. They've all gone quiet over the last three years, with barely any interaction. I was thinking of going on one of those TV shows about missing people to encourage new interest. What do you think?"

Alarmed at the thought, Nate chooses his words carefully. "I can understand why families go on them, and they probably do spark new tips and leads. But in the age of social media, I'd bet that the overwhelming majority of attention you'd get from appearing on one of those shows would be negative."

Robert straightens as he crosses his arms. "How so?"

"Well, if I learned anything from my experience in the spotlight, it's that people love to troll and people love to scam. You'd become a target for hate campaigns and malicious rumors. People will troll your social media sites, find your email address, and perhaps even stalk you at home, claiming that *you* killed

Brandon. They'll make it their mission to turn you into your son's abductor, all for the attention that a podcast episode or a retweet will get them."

Robert turns pale at the thought. "If that happened, I'd get the police involved."

"With all due respect to the Lost Creek PD," says Nate, "there isn't much they can do about that. The internet is mostly a cesspit of degenerates who are so unhappy with their own lives that they take it out on others. And then of course, you'll be targeted by scammers. Psychics and fraudsters claiming to know where Brandon is for a fee, which you can guarantee will run into the thousands. And you'll pay it because you're a loving father, desperate for answers. You'll take out loans, sell your vehicle and drive yourself crazy following fake leads." He stops, as he can see the man is sick just thinking about it. It's tough to be in the public eye when you're at the center of a mystery, because the public is mainly made up of assholes.

"I guess I won't be going down that route then." Robert rubs his jaw before looking Nate in the eye. "Given your experience, what does your gut tell you? What do you think happened to my son?"

Nate hates this question, but he can't avoid it. And he knows from the look in the man's eyes that he needs to be honest. "At this early stage of my investigation, I'll consider the two most likely options. First, that something was happening in Brandon's life that made him want to run away."

A flash of hope lights up Robert's face and he becomes animated for the first time. "That would mean he could be alive, right? If you find him, you have to tell him I need to see him. Even if he wants to remain hidden, he has to give me one conversation." His voice becomes gruff. "He owes me that much. I'm his *father*."

Nate nods, but he doesn't believe that's the most likely scenario, given the boy's young age and limited resources. "Of course. But I also have to be blunt with you, Mr. Dorsey. Given that no one spotted him walking away, boarding a bus or hitchhiking, I think it's more likely that Brandon was abducted."

In a split second, the look of hope is replaced with crushing disappointment. Robert looks away. "I don't see how. Someone would've seen something or heard him hollering for help. He wouldn't have gone easily."

"Unfortunately," says Nate, "it takes just seconds for a child to be dragged into a vehicle. And it happens all too frequently. Besides, it could've been someone he knew: a relative, a friend's parent from school or someone from around the neighborhood." Not wanting to leave the guy feeling completely hopeless, he adds, "But as you say, there's no evidence of that right now, so I'm going to work on the assumption that he's still alive. Because even if he was abducted, that doesn't mean the worst has happened. Kids get found years later, living under new identities. I had a case recently where a young boy had been missing for six years." He thinks about Vince Rader's grandson, Oliver, and the devastating impact of his disappearance, followed by the joy his homecoming brought Vince and his son.

"Detective Harper and I managed to bring him home alive." He takes a deep breath. "If this job's taught me anything, it's that each case is different, and anything is possible."

The look on Robert's face suggests he's trying to figure out whether Nate's offering false hope. "I'll text you some names," he says. "People who were in our lives at the time. I mean, I can't believe they would be involved, but after what you just said, who knows, right?"

Nate nods. "Stranger abductions are far less common than people think. It's often someone the missing person knows."

After digesting that, Robert Dorsey leads Nate to the front door. "Just keep me updated. If you learn anything at all, I want to know about it." He rubs the back of his neck. "I know I'm not in a position to be demanding anything from you, given I'm not paying for your services, but the not knowing has driven me crazy throughout all this. Even if I can't have my son back, I need answers."

Nate nods. "Of course. I understand. I'll be in touch."

He turns away from the house, and Brody joins him with an excited bark. As he leads the dog to his Chevy, that feeling of relief sweeps over him. Like he's removed himself from a pressurized chamber. But it's quickly replaced with dread in case he can't find the answers this man seeks. Or in case the answers aren't what Robert is hoping for.

He gets into his car and pulls his phone out of his pocket. He has a text from Madison.

We need Brody on Grave Mountain asap.

Knowing how much the dog loves to help in searches due to his cadaver detection training, Nate turns to look at him. He's in the backseat, alert and panting. "Looks like your mom needs us, Brody."

CHAPTER TWENTY

Madison hands Susie Harris a tissue from the box on the coffee table. She's just informed the young woman that her sister's body has been formally identified through dental records, and that they suspect they've also found Becky's remains.

"I'm so sorry," she says. "I wish I had better news."

She and Adams are seated on the couch in Susie's living room. A black cat made a beeline for Adams when they arrived, and it's now curled up on his lap. He keeps looking down at it to make sure it doesn't scratch him.

Susie drops the tissue in her lap, unused. "At least they were together when it happened. It means Tasha wasn't alone with the sick bastard. I hope they put up a good fight."

Madison's surprised by her calmness. She would've expected tears at least.

Susie sighs. "It's so predictable, it's practically a cliché."

"What do you mean?" asks Adams.

She looks at him. "Well, it's what happens in this world, isn't it? Women get killed every single day. By men, usually. I think I'm going to pretend my sister never existed. Make myself believe she was just a dream I had."

Madison resists looking at Adams for his reaction.

Susie takes a deep breath. "So we have Tasha back. How long will it take to ID Becky?"

"Not long, hopefully," says Madison.

Adams clears his throat. "We believe Stuart Carpenter killed them on the morning of their hike. Tasha's driver's license was found in his home."

Susie nods, expressionless. "I can't believe my parents wasted years thinking Tasha would find her way back to us. Hoping she was still alive. Thank God they aren't here to deal with this." She stands. "I'm glad it's finally over."

She's coming across as cold and uncaring. Madison thinks she could be in shock or trying to stop herself from breaking down in front of them. She stands too. "Do you have anyone we can call to be with you?"

Susie shakes her head. "That's okay. I guess I need to get busy arranging the funeral." She frowns as something occurs to her. "Is there anything left of her to bury after all this time?"

"Yes," says Madison, without going into any detail. "Once the medical examiner has completed her investigation, a funeral home of your choice can collect Tasha and help you with the planning." She pulls out a card from her jacket pocket. "If you have any questions once we've left, or need anything, just call me."

Adams moves the cat onto his vacant seat and walks ahead of them to the hallway.

Madison turns back to Susie before leaving. "Are you sure I can't call a friend for you?"

The young woman shakes her head. "No. I'll be fine. You have to remember, it's been five years. I've grown used to life without her. I've had to."

Madison nods. "We'll let ourselves out."

At their vehicles, Adams checks his phone and reads something before sighing. "Selena wants me to move out tonight."

Madison pulls her keys out of her pocket and removes the front door key. Nate has a spare. "Get a copy made. You can bring your things over later. I'll stay at Nate's so you can settle in."

He takes it from her. "You don't have to do this, you know. I could find a hotel."

She dismisses the idea with a wave of her hand. "It's fine. Nate's asked me to move in with him, so it's perfect timing."

"Oh yeah?" he says, surprised. "I'd say congratulations, but it'll probably end in tears if my experience is anything to go by."

Madison snorts. "Give it a few months, and I'm sure you'll be shacked up with someone new. Men always seem to rebound fast."

"Not me," he says. "I'm not that kind of guy." He takes a deep breath. "Want me to go to the mountain to check out the new sets of remains?"

She nods. "Get as many volunteers as possible to join you up there. Nate's bringing his dog to help with the search for evidence." She opens her car door. "I'll meet you there. I need to visit the Drapers before they hear anything on the news."

"Sure." He heads to his car as Madison slips into hers.

As it's almost lunchtime, she stops by Ruby's Diner on her way past to grab something to go, because it might be the last opportunity she gets to eat in a while.

When Carla flashes her engagement ring, Madison's shocked. "Wait. Who are you marrying?" she asks.

"Me," says Hank Goodman, approaching them with a bowlful of dirty dishes.

Madison knew they'd been dating, but she didn't realize it was this serious already. When Carla tells her they're also buying the diner together, she's stunned. "I didn't even know Vince was thinking of selling the place."

"He couldn't refuse our offer," says Hank. "That's what happens when you flash enough dough in front of someone."

"Don't be mean," says Carla. "Vince isn't like that." She turns to Madison. "I inherited some money when my mom passed, and Hank thought it would be a good idea to put it into a business. It means we can sell our places and live together upstairs." She beams as she says, "I mean, I'm here so often anyway, I may as well move in, right?"

Madison tries hard not to frown. A quick engagement and suggestions of how his fiancée should spend her inheritance ring alarm bells. But Carla's not stupid, and she looks ecstatic. She must know what she's doing. "I hope I'm invited to the wedding?"

The sound of persistent yapping suddenly starts. Madison has to lean over the counter to see what's making all the noise. It's a tiny tan-colored chihuahua.

Hank's face lights up as he gently picks up the little creature and cradles it in his arm like a baby. "Hello, Mrs. Pebbles. What're you doing in here?"

Madison tries not to grimace at the baby voice he puts on. The dog licks its owner's face, including his mouth. Madison looks at Carla, who doesn't appear to realize how disgusting that is, even though she's the one in line for sloppy seconds from her husband-to-be.

Hank turns the dog to face Madison. "Tell the detective what you think about law enforcement, Mrs. Pebbles."

The formerly happy dog bares her teeth at Madison and growls.

Carla and Hank laugh, but Madison sees meanness behind Hank's eyes.

A customer waiting next to her says, "That's gross, man. Don't let dogs near the food."

Hank shoots him a look of contempt. "You can leave. We don't serve morons in Carla's Diner."

Madison raises her eyebrows at the name change. They don't even own the place yet.

"Listen, jackass," says the guy. "If you want me to leave, you can remove me yourself."

"Maybe I will," says Hank defiantly. Mrs. Pebbles emits a low, guttural growl.

"What the hell?" says the young man. "I'm gonna call the health inspector on you."

Vince enters the diner just as things are heating up. He spots the dog immediately. "Get that thing out of here, Hank. It's not your place yet."

"He's refusing to serve me," says the young guy.

Flustered, Carla tells the customer, "Go take a seat, sweetie. I'll be right over with the menu."

Hank disappears with his dog, and Carla gets to work, clearly embarrassed by his behavior.

"You're selling this place to *him*?" says Madison when they're both out of earshot.

Vince sighs. "I didn't know he was an asshole when I agreed to it. Not that it matters. I guess his money's as good as anyone else's." Changing the subject, he says, "What's going on up at the mountain? I've never seen so many news trucks."

Madison leans in and speaks quietly. "Put it this way: I think some people from the support group you host will get answers about their loved ones over the coming days. But that's just between me and you."

He nods gravely, and Madison can tell he's thinking about his wife. He might've gotten his grandson back, but now he has to visit Ruby in the cemetery.

She rests her hand on his. "It could've been worse, Vince."

He smiles sadly. "I know. But it could've been better too. I would never consider selling the diner if Ruby were still alive."

She squeezes his hand. "I know."

CHAPTER TWENTY-ONE

Nancy and Doug Draper own a ranch in Gold Rock, a small town north of Lost Creek. The town is little more than a straight road with small stores dotted on either side, a saloon that looks like it's straight out of a Wild West movie set and some residential homes. Formerly a gold-mining town, it's now just a ghost town, with mostly only old-timers left. The Drapers' ranch was previously owned by Angie and Wyatt McCoy, Madison's sister and brother-in-law. When Wyatt met a gruesome death and Angie got locked up for their crimes, it was sold at auction.

Doug Draper now owns the two businesses that came with the land: a salvage yard and an auto repair shop. Madison doesn't bump into any of his employees as she makes her way to the front door of the house, but she hears them singing along to the radio over the sound of the car crusher smashing something to pieces in the salvage yard.

She climbs the porch steps and knocks on the large oak door, ignoring a flood of memories of her sister. She can't help wondering what happened to Angie's belongings after her arrest, as well as Owen's from his time spent living with his aunt while Madison was locked up.

"Nancy?" she says to the door. "It's Madison." Experience has taught her that Nancy Draper won't open up to just anyone.

After a long minute, she hears movement from inside the house and the door opens a crack. Nancy peers out, and when she's satisfied it really is Madison, she opens the door a little wider, but not much.

"Have you got news?" she asks. Even though she's only in her early fifties, grief has aged her. Her skin is pale from a lack of daylight, and her wrinkles are deeper than you would expect for someone of her age. She's wearing pale blue pajamas under a purple bathrobe. Madison knows she rarely gets dressed.

"Can I come in?"

Nancy turns and disappears inside, so Madison steps into the musty-smelling house. The door will only open so far because the downstairs is filled almost top to bottom with clothes, toys, purses and both opened and unopened packages from online stores. Nancy's a hoarder. She's almost managed to fill the property in the short time she's lived here, and Madison assumes it's due to the trauma of her daughter's disappearance.

It's only the second time she's been allowed inside the home, and she knows from last time that there could be rats under all these belongings, so she treads carefully as she follows Nancy to the living room. A narrow clearing leads to a couch with just one seat clear of items. Nancy sits there, leaving Madison no choice but to stand.

"Buying things helps," says the older woman. "While I'm doing that, I don't forget about Becky, but she's not my most prominent thought. I sit among my things and feel less lonely. You see, I buy things I know she would like."

Swallowing a lump in her throat, Madison says, "I understand that you have to do whatever helps you cope, but when it affects the way you live, it's time to get help."

Nancy ignores the comment. "We tried having a memorial for her two years ago. I purchased a casket and a plot, but when it came to it, I couldn't pretend she was in the box." She looks up. "I need her body back, Detective. I need to tuck her in and read her one last bedtime story."

Madison doesn't have any words to comfort her. And when she hears a sudden movement behind her, she turns to find Doug has joined them.

"Aren't you supposed to call first?" he says, squeezing by her to get to his wife. Although the same age, Doug appears younger and much fitter than Nancy, with a muscular frame and tanned skin from working outside year-round.

"Sorry. It's been a busy morning." With a heavy heart, she looks Nancy in the eye. "I came to tell you that the first set of remains found on Grave Mountain have been identified using the dental records we obtained."

Nancy squeezes the tissue in her hands.

"It's not Becky," says Madison gently. "It's Tasha Harris."

Uncertainty washes over Nancy's face. "What about the red hat you found?"

Madison's phone buzzes in her pocket. "We think Tasha must've borrowed it to keep warm. She forgot to take hers on the hike."

"So where's my daughter?" asks Nancy. "Have you found her yet?"

Madison thinks of the skeleton embedded in the tree trunks. "We've located another body. I'm just waiting for it to be identified." She doesn't mention the two latest discoveries found by Officers Sanchez and Vickers. Her phone buzzes again. "Let me just see if this is the medical examiner."

She reads the texts. One is from Nate saying he's with the search party. The other is from Lena.

The second victim isn't Becky Draper.

Madison frowns. She considers whether Becky could be one of the other two bodies found, but Sanchez believes one of them to be a child, and the other is headless, which means Becky's dental records won't help them identify it.

She looks at the Drapers. "I've just learned that the second person we found isn't Becky either."

Nancy's hand flies to her chest. "Oh God. I can't live like this. It's unbearable. It never ends. Make it stop, Doug. Please, make it stop." Her breathing becomes erratic as she tries to get air into her lungs. Doug soothingly rubs her back.

"I'm so sorry," says Madison, and she is. It's gut-wrenching to watch Nancy's pain. Knowing this couple are on a roller coaster of highs and lows, she hates that she can't end this horrendous ride for them. She considers telling them about the latest discoveries, but Doug steps forward, glaring at her.

"You're killing her by drip-feeding us information," he says. "I don't think you should tell us anything else unless it's about our daughter. My wife can't cope with all this upset."

Madison nods. He's right. Nancy's not strong enough. "As soon as I have any information about Becky, I'll let you know." She turns to make the laborious journey to the front door.

Doug follows her out of the house. He rubs his face with both hands and exhales loudly. "She's not eating enough. She's wasting away. Can't you just tell her you found Becky up there?"

Alarmed, Madison says, "We intend to identify every victim and notify their families. I can't say someone is Becky when they're not."

His expression shows he's conflicted. He's trying to protect his wife. It's clear he's at his wits' end. "But if there's anyone you can't identify for whatever reason, perhaps a homeless person..."

She crosses her arms. "I won't lie to her, Doug. You can't just bury someone else and pretend it's your daughter."

He nods, seeming to realize how ridiculous the suggestion is. After taking a deep breath, he says, "She watches the home shopping channels all day for the company. That's why she has all that stuff in there. I'm tempted to sue them. There should be a limit on how much you can spend."

Madison feels for him. Nancy's not the only person in America who needs the TV on all day for company or to drown out their thoughts. It's probably better than drinking herself to death.

"I'm not going to let her watch the news anymore," he says. "She sometimes gets fixated on that instead."

Madison zips up her coat against the cold. "I know you weren't living here when Becky vanished, but did Stuart Carpenter ever visit your previous home? Did you ever see him with your daughter?"

He shakes his head. "Not once. Nancy thought Becky was seeing someone, but she never brought a boyfriend home for us to meet. I don't believe she would've been seeing Stuart Carpenter. He was a loser, in my opinion. She could do better."

In his statement, Stuart implied he was attracted to Tasha, not Becky, so Madison agrees they probably weren't an item. "How did she seem leading up to the day of the hike?"

With a guarded look, he says, "What do you mean?"

"Was she experiencing any mental health issues? Trouble at work?"

"No, not that it's relevant. We already know who killed her, don't we?"

She takes a deep breath. "I'm just trying to build a picture of the twenty-four hours before the hike. I can't ask the two investigating detectives, as they're no longer with us." Images of Detectives Don Douglas and Mike Bowers come to her. The last time she saw Don, he was dead at his home, brutally murdered. The last time she saw Mike, he was holding a gun to his own head. She sometimes wonders whether she's destined to suffer a similar fate. Whether that's what this job leads to.

She tries to focus. "Was Becky home the night before the hike?"

"She was." Doug crosses his arms. "But you're asking all the wrong questions to the wrong person. She disappeared while she was on that mountain, not while she was at home."

Sensing he's done with her questions, Madison asks him one more. "Where were you and your wife on the morning of the hike? After Nancy took the photograph of Becky leaving the house?"

She's read both Nancy's and Doug's statements. They were taken the day after the disappearance. Doug was working as a truck driver at the time. His alibi must've checked out or he would've been a suspect, which he never was. The reason she asks him now is to make sure his story holds up.

He spits on the ground, clearly offended he's being asked for his alibi. "Don't pull that bullshit on me, Detective. I've got work to do." Before walking away, he adds, "Don't come here uninvited again. If you have any news, call *me*, not my wife."

Madison watches him disappear into the salvage yard.

CHAPTER TWENTY-TWO

With four bodies now unearthed, hiking alone on Grave Mountain is creepy, even in the afternoon and with the occasional walker passing Madison on their way up or down the Lovers' Peak Trail.

The silence, together with drizzly rain and low cloud, makes it unnerving. With the dense thickets of trees and foliage and the occasional rustle coming from all around her, it feels like someone's watching her from a distance. It doesn't help that she could be walking past discarded human remains. She grips her cell phone and keeps her holster unclipped in case someone should try something.

The snap of a branch close by makes her look up. Brody appears through the trees. He barks in recognition before rushing over. Nate probably sent him to escort her to the search team.

Madison stops to pet him as she catches her breath. His thick brown and cream coat is wet from the rain, and his panting mists the air before them. Her thigh stings where his tail excitedly whips her leg. Brody loves helping with investigations. Police work is in his blood. She smiles. "Hey, Officer Brody."

He barks again.

The physical exertion of reaching this point has warmed her, so Madison stands to unzip her jacket and pull it off. She ties it around her waist. The drizzle soon sticks to her skin, making her feel damp.

After accepting some attention, Brody runs ahead, eventually leading Madison to the others. Several volunteers in high-visibility jackets are spread out, searching the area around the latest crime scene. Madison heads to Nate and taps him on the shoulder.

"Hey, you made it." He turns with a smile before kissing her. "Water?" He hands her a bottle.

Relieved, she sips from it.

Alex and Chief Mendes join them. Most of the department is up here, and everyone except Mendes is wearing hiking boots or robust sneakers. The chief is wearing pumps, which may not be ideal for her surroundings but are more suitable than her usual high heels.

Two people Madison doesn't recognize approach behind Alex.

"This is Nora from the crime lab," says Alex, nodding to a short, heavy-set young woman with dyed orange hair, a nose ring and impossibly pale, unblemished skin.

Nora waves shyly, and Madison remembers that Alex seemed taken with the young woman when he worked with her up at the lab on a previous case.

Alex turns to the other person as he says, "And this is Dr. Conrad Stevens, her father."

Dr. Stevens is tall and looks to be in his fifties. He's wearing a beige suit, with a matching waistcoat and a patterned tie, and clutching a beige fedora. He looks like he's about to attend an archeological expedition on board a steamship on the River

Nile. In fact, he wouldn't look out of place in an Agatha Christie movie adaptation. And somehow, he's managed to keep his clothes clean of mud.

"Dr. Stevens is a prominent forensic anthropologist who will be helping Dr. Scott to recover and examine the remains," explains Alex.

Madison's impressed. "Thanks for coming, Doctor. It sounds like we'll need all the help we can get."

He shakes her hand. "Please, call me Conrad. I'm supposed to leave for vacation soon, but this case seemed more interesting than a seven-day cruise around Europe."

Madison wonders what kind of life he leads that makes a European cruise seem dull. "Okay, so what do we have?" she asks.

Alex takes the lead. "The third victim is an adult." He leads them to the site of the remains, which lie in a shallow grave about three feet deep. This skeleton ends at the neck.

Madison considers how the killer didn't bury the first two victims, although the second victim was found hidden between some tree trunks, possibly indicating an attempt to conceal the body.

"Obviously, we'll search for the skull," says Alex. "It could've been dragged away by an animal wanting to share the succulent skin with its babies."

Madison catches a glance from Nate. His eyebrows are raised at Alex's colorful description. Madison shrugs. She's used to it.

"Several items of clothing have also been found with the remains," Alex continues. "Nora will take them to the lab when she leaves."

Nora smiles at him before saying, "None of the clothing we've found with any of the remains appears to have been cut or torn off the bodies, which suggests the victims were clothed when they died and not sexually assaulted."

Madison nods. "Good to know." That isn't definitive proof, though. The victims could've gotten dressed after being assaulted and before being killed. Their attacker could've played with them. Let them dress and perhaps attempt to run for safety before he hunted them like prey.

"We've yet to find wallets or cell phones for any of the victims," adds Alex.

The scene in front of her is grim. Madison dreads notifying this person's family that their loved one has been found head-less. It doesn't mean they were decapitated, though. The head separates from the spine during decomposition if left undiscovered for long enough.

"Officer Sanchez said he found the remains of a child up here too. Is that right?" she asks.

"Well..." says Conrad. "Come take a look." He strides ahead to an area farther away from the trail and crouches in the soil. Brody rushes up to him, tail wagging, and sniffs the remains as Nate tries to pull him back by his collar.

Conrad appears amused. "Your dog can probably tell."

"Tell what?" asks Nate.

"These are the bones your officer thought could belong to a child, but actually, they're canine." Conrad stands. "In my experience, it's not unusual for hikers to bury their dogs on their favorite trail when the time comes for them to cross the Rainbow Bridge, as my daughter calls it. It gives the owners somewhere to visit them."

Everyone looks at Nate. He glances down at Brody, who's sitting by his side, panting and looking completely content among law enforcement. It's all in a day's work for the eager shepsky.

Nate strokes the dog's head. "That's not someplace you're visiting anytime soon, buddy."

Brody happily barks at him before running off to continue his search.

Nora has a tear in her eye. "Two of my rabbits crossed the Rainbow Bridge earlier this year."

Alex rests a hand on her back.

Conrad laughs. "Why so glum, everyone? We should be happy this isn't a child!"

"Pets *are* children for some of us, Dad," says Nora, affronted.

With an affectionate roll of the eyes, her father pats her hand. "I know, sweetie. I know." He looks at Chief Mendes. "Once the third set of remains are with Dr. Scott, I can begin my examination and try to age them and establish a biological profile. It'll be harder to identify the body without the skull, so perhaps your detectives should try to match it with known missing people from the area. The clothing found with it will provide a clue." He smiles widely at Mendes. "Not that I would dream of telling you how to run your investigation, Chief."

Mendes smiles back at him. "I'll ask Sergeant Tanner to do that."

Madison senses a spark between the pair. She catches Nate's eye and knows he's thinking the same.

Conrad folds his arms over his chest. "I get the impression your suspect for these unexplained deaths is someone who is no longer with us. Is that correct?"

"Right," says Madison. "He took his own life after the first victim was found."

"If you don't mind me asking, how old was he?"

"Twenty-seven."

"Hmm." Conrad considers it. "I'd hate to scare anyone, and I won't know for sure until I examine the bones properly, but my initial impression is that the third set of remains has been out here for some time."

"How long is some time?" asks Chief Mendes.

"I'd guess approximately a decade."

Madison frowns. "That would mean Stuart started killing at sixteen or seventeen."

Nate speaks up. "That's not unusual, is it? I mean, I'm no expert on serial killers, but don't they start torturing pets in their teenage years before moving on to humans? He could've killed this dog for all we know."

She nods. "The FBI believes that, so maybe... But Stuart didn't seem the type. He comes from a wealthy, loving family and was never in trouble with law enforcement." She shakes her head in frustration. "My gut tells me he wasn't the kind of teenager who was charismatic or devious enough to lure adults to their death."

A bright flash suddenly lights up the gloomy scene. The group turns in unison to see what caused it.

Someone ducks behind a tree.

"Reporter," says Madison. "There are a ton of them down by the entrance to the trail." She sighs. "We need to update them about the third victim, but we also need an officer stationed down there to stop them from getting this close."

"Officer Kent should be doing that," says Chief Mendes.

Madison frowns as Officer Fuller appears and briskly leads the reporter away from the area. "Where's Adams?" she asks.

Alex clears his throat. "Last time I saw him, he was chatting to Officer Kent."

As though he hears his name, Detective Adams suddenly appears from their left. He seems surprised to find everyone together, and Madison suspects the thought crosses his mind that they're talking about him.

"The fourth set of remains are canine," she says.

He nods. "Makes sense. I had a friend who buried his dog on a trail. I bet there are hundreds of them out here."

Far from being a depressing thought, Madison thinks it's sweet to know those dogs are resting in their favorite places.

"My friend joined him a few months later," says Adams.

"Shot himself in the chest. Couldn't bear to be without his canine buddy."

A silence falls over them as they exchange unsettled looks.

Conrad is the first to speak. "It wouldn't surprise me if the search party locates remains of people who've taken their own lives over the last few decades. This kind of place attracts the desperate. They know they won't be disturbed, and it's better than hanging from the rafters in their attics."

Another sobering image.

The sound of snapping branches makes Madison turn. Mark Fuller, the volunteer search-and-rescue leader—and Officer Corey Fuller's father—approaches. In his early sixties and with a wealth of outdoor experience, he's helped them with previous searches.

With a somber look, he says, "Sorry to be the one to tell you guys this, but we've found two more sets of remains over near the Juniper Trail."

Madison's mouth drops open.

"*Two?*" says Chief Mendes. "Are you sure?"

He nods. "Looks like an adult and a younger person to me. Maybe a teenager."

Shocked, Madison considers whether the teenager could be Brandon Dorsey. She looks at Detective Adams and Chief Mendes. "You know what this means, right?"

Adams turns away, rubbing his neck. "Not again."

Chief Mendes straightens. "Okay, people. There's now a good chance we're unearthing the victims of a serial killer. With that said, we can't assume that Stuart Carpenter was responsible and that there's no current threat to residents. Each scene should be thoroughly documented, examined and treated as an individual case." She turns to Dr. Stevens. "I'd hate to ruin your vacation plans, but would you be open to staying in town longer to help with more remains?"

He nods. "I'd be happy to."

The team disperses. Madison feels the rush of adrenaline coursing through her veins. She can't get the words *serial killer* out of her head.

When they're alone, she turns to Nate. "You're arming yourself immediately." She pulls out her phone. "I'll send you a link to an appropriate firearm and holster to purchase. You won't even know you're wearing it after a day or two."

Nate puts a hand on her cell phone to stop her. "Madison," he says, "I'm not used to guns. Besides, I have Brody. I'll take him with me where—"

"*Listen,*" she says, cutting him off and moving closer. "Serial killers are a different breed. If it turns out Stuart Carpenter didn't do this, then the killer's possibly still alive and at large. That means you and I both have targets on our backs. Owen's safe at college, out of harm's way, so the only other person the killer can hurt to get to me is *you.*" She stares him directly in the eye. "Which means you're getting a gun whether you like it or not."

It's no good. He's shaking his head. "No, Madison. I won't risk going back there."

She knows what he's referring to. "Colorado doesn't even have the death penalty anymore. Besides, you'd never be arrested for defending yourself. Chief Mendes wouldn't let that happen, and neither would I." Sensing she's not getting through to him, she adds, "And what if I need you to protect me?"

He smiles sadly. "Nice try, but you can protect yourself better than I ever could."

She sees the pain in his eyes. Mentally, he's back on death row.

"I'm sorry," he says. "But I'd rather die than risk going back there. I've been clear about that from the minute we met, so it shouldn't come as a surprise." He takes a breath. "Madison, you don't know what it was like."

He hasn't opened up to her much about the experience. She

hasn't asked. She knows what talking about it does to him. But she's so frustrated she could scream right now. His thought process is irrational to her. Carrying a weapon doesn't mean he'll need to use it, and it doesn't mean it will eventually result in his arrest for murder.

Her heart aches as she realizes what this means. "Look, Nate, if you don't arm yourself, then I can't be with you, because I know what'll happen." She blinks back tears. "Tomorrow, the next day or maybe next week, I'll get a call from dispatch or one of my team. And I know *exactly* how that call will go. Adams's voice will shake as he's forced to tell me how the killer got to you and how it was too late to save you because you were unarmed."

She knows it's a sign of how damaged they are that they've reacted this way. Why their feelings about this issue are on opposite ends of the spectrum. But it's infuriating because they both want the same thing. They want to grow old together. And for that to happen, Nate's chances of staying safe while she's investigating a serial killer are much better if he's armed. But he won't trust her, which proves he still has a wall up, even after all this time.

He breaks eye contact. "I'll be careful. You don't need to worry about me."

Her heart sinks. "I can't be with someone who wants to cause me unnecessary pain, Nate. I've been through enough already. So's my son." Before he can respond, she walks away. It hurts to look at him right now. Because by failing to arm himself, he might've just signed his own death warrant.

CHAPTER TWENTY-THREE

NINE YEARS AGO

"Look who just walked in. It's lover boy."

Maria Whitman glances up too fast. The man she's been flirting with for two weeks straight is approaching the bar and he sees her looking.

"Shit!" She quickly lowers her eyes.

Janie, her fellow bartender, laughs. "You need to learn how to use your peripheral vision, girl! Want me to serve him?"

"You do and I'll never speak to you again," Maria hisses. "Get your cute ass out of his sight."

Janie walks away with an exaggerated wiggle of her butt. She approaches an old-timer near the end of the bar, from where she will probably watch Maria's lame attempts at flirting. She and Maria have worked in this dive bar nestled in the shadow of Grave Mountain for years while raising their children. Both single moms, they differ only in their taste in men. Janie likes tough guys who don't return her calls. Maria likes monosyllabic cowboys.

She drops the dishcloth she's holding and steps closer to the bar. "Hey. What can I get for you?"

The cowboy removes his Stetson and smiles at her, showing

his straight white teeth behind kissable full lips. He leans forward on his elbows and looks bashful. "Ma'am, if you don't know by now, I must be doing something wrong."

She immediately blushes, unsure whether he's talking about her or the Budweiser he likes to drink. She turns to retrieve a bottle from the fridge. As she removes the twist-off cap, she keeps her back to him and watches his reflection in the mirror behind the bar. His eyes are on her body.

His thick hair is light brown, with sun-kissed highlights. His eyes are a rich chestnut color, and when they meet hers, a shiver runs through her entire body. They're knowing eyes. He knows she wants him. It's like an unspoken secret between them.

She's only seen him in blue jeans with a denim or plaid shirt open at the collar, exposing his dark chest hair. He always has at least a day's stubble on his square jaw. She doesn't know anything about him other than he's new in town and he drives a truck. He's been snowed in since the weather unexpectedly turned almost two weeks ago. She doubts he'll be around much longer, as the forecast is for higher temperatures from tomorrow, which means the snow will finally thaw.

She turns and hands him his Bud. "This one's on me."

He takes it from her while meeting her eyes. "Now there's an image to keep a man warm at night." He brings the bottle to his mouth and takes a slug, the liquid covering his tongue as she watches. Time stands still, and the loud country music playing from the stereo goes quiet. To her, at least.

Maria feels her heartbeat in her chest. It's been three years since she's been touched by a man. She imagines walking out of this dump and her life and traveling the country with this enigmatic stranger. They would sleep in his cab, making love at every stop. They'd be free to explore the country and each other. Thoughts of her two kids try to bring her back to reality, but she pushes them away.

She's allowed to fantasize, isn't she?

"Can I get some service around here or what?" shouts Bob Sanders from a few feet away.

Maria jolts back to the present, where the music suddenly sounds louder. "What'll it be, Bob? Whiskey sour?"

He nods as he pulls out a crumpled twenty-dollar bill and waits for his drink. Bob's local, and he's dull. He's here four nights a week to get away from his wife, and Maria has to listen to all his complaints about married life. He's everything she wants to avoid. While she fixes his drink, she watches the handsome stranger take his beer outside. He glances back at her before exiting the building.

Maria knows this is her only chance to feel his hands on her. She hands over Bob's drink before approaching Janie. "Cover for me."

Janie grins. "You lucky bitch."

The freezing night air takes her breath away when she opens the door to the outside. She didn't bring her coat, hoping the cowboy will keep her warm. The night is clear, making the glistening stars visible above the peaks of the mountains.

She doesn't see him until she feels his hand on hers. He's by her side, leading her over to his truck. His hand is warm, his grip tight. He wants her.

"I don't usually do this kind of thing," she says when they reach the passenger door and he presses himself against her.

He runs a finger over her lips. "Believe it or not, neither do I." He steps back and opens the door, helping her up into the cab. It smells of coffee and aftershave. As she scooches over, she notices the area behind the seats. A thick comforter covers his bed. The space is tidy, with no fast-food wrappers or dirty clothes.

She climbs into the back and sits on the mattress, her heart beating harder than ever. He comes to her. His large, warm hand is on the back of her neck as he gently pulls her lips to his. His kisses are slow at first, before becoming more passionate. He tastes of beer. His hands go to her shirt and undo her buttons as she lies back.

Maria closes her eyes as he moves on top of her and kisses her neck. The weight of a man is something she's missed the most. Something she thought she might never experience again. It brings a comfort like no other. She suddenly realizes it's time to find a partner. Not just so she can feel this whenever she wants to, but for companionship. She's put the kids first for long enough. It's time for her to live.

A clicking sound in the dark makes her frown. She quickly dismisses it. No one can see them back here. The lights are out, and a drape hides them from the front of the cab.

His hands go to unzip her jeans, and she opens her eyes and smiles. His eyes are filled with lust. When he moves his head to one side, her smile falters. A numbness spreads through her as her throat seizes.

"One word—one scream, even—and I'll kill him," says the masked person holding a gun to the back of her lover's head.

Maria couldn't scream if she wanted to. Her entire body has frozen in fear.

CHAPTER TWENTY-FOUR

PRESENT DAY

After spending hours on the freezing-cold mountain trail, and with the search set to continue overnight thanks to the volunteers, Madison and Adams have been told by Chief Mendes to get some sleep in preparation for getting up early to start a full day of investigation. By then, Lena and Conrad should have extracted all the remains from the mountain, and the department will be in a better position to figure out what happened to them. Chief Mendes intends to update the press about the latest gruesome discoveries.

Madison is tense on the drive home. The sound of the windshield wipers flashing back and forth in the heavy rain irritates her. A ball of dread builds in her stomach as she worries whether she and Nate can get over this latest setback. The earlier unease she felt after Stuart Carpenter's suicide has intensified. She still feels like something bad is looming, except now it's worse because Nate won't protect himself.

It's seven thirty by the time she arrives home, and Adams's car is already in the driveway. She gets out of hers and runs through the rain to her front door. Inside, she hears his footsteps upstairs. His twin girls are hovering in the hallway beside some boxes. They don't look much like Adams. He's dark-haired, and his daughters are blonde, with paler skin.

"Oh, hi," she says with a smile, closing the door behind her. She's met them once before, and only in passing. "Let me see if I can figure out who is who."

One of the girls grins at her. The other glares like a stroppy teenager. Madison knows Adams has trouble with this one. "You must be Summer."

Summer rolls her eyes. If ever a girl was misnamed, it's this one.

"I'm Lizzie," says the one dressed in cute dungarees with a yellow shirt over the top. Summer is wearing an oversized gray hoody over black jeans and Converse sneakers. They turn ten soon, on Christmas Eve.

"I'm Madison, remember? I work with your dad."

Summer walks away, uninterested. Lizzie and Madison follow her into the kitchen, where Bandit appears out of nowhere. Nate must've brought him home for her. When Summer sits at the dining table, the white cat jumps onto her lap, purring. Summer doesn't react at all.

"OMG. He's so cute!" says Lizzie. "What's his name?"

"Bandit, because the black strip of fur across his eyes makes him look like a robber. He's my son's cat, but Owen's away at college."

When Lizzie goes to stroke him, Summer turns away and cradles the cat herself. Bandit loves the attention. He sticks his ass in the air and wiggles it while having his neck rubbed.

"Help yourself to anything in the refrigerator," says Madison. "I better check on your dad."

Upstairs, Adams is sitting on the single bed in the spare room, emptying a backpack. He looks up when she walks in. "Hey."

"Hey," she says. "Do you need some hangers or more drawer space?"

He shakes his head. "This is going to be weird, Harper. Maybe I should've stayed in a hotel."

She can't deny it'll be odd having Adams on the other side of her bedroom wall, especially as she can't stay with Nate tonight thanks to their earlier disagreement, but she'll make it work. "Listen, I've shared a tiny prison cell with complete strangers, and I've showered naked in front of inmates and guards. If we can't spend the odd night together in the same house, that's on you, buddy."

He scoffs. "Jeez. I thought I had a hard life."

Madison smiles. "Your girls are cute. Is Summer still a handful?"

He nods. "Lizzie's trying to put on a brave face, probably so I don't get upset. Summer, on the other hand, thinks I've cheated on her mom, so she's not talking to me right now. I had to pay her to come here tonight. I thought it would be good for them to see where I'm staying and how it's not that far from our house."

"Good idea," she says. "She'll relax once she realizes you're both still in her life. Having separated parents isn't that unusual these days."

"Maybe not, but I didn't want this for them." He sounds despondent, like he can't believe his life has come to sleeping in a co-worker's spare room.

"Things will get better, Marcus." She sits next to him on the bed. "It won't always feel this crappy. Just take one day at a time."

He doesn't respond.

A knock at the front door makes her jump.

"I ordered pizza," he says. "There should be enough for you to join us."

She stands. "Thanks. Let's give them a pleasant evening before you need to take them home."

He takes a deep breath before following her downstairs.

Madison readies the dining table with plates and napkins while Adams pays for the pizzas. When her phone buzzes, she checks it quickly.

I wish you'd come over. Stay the night.

It's followed by a second text.

Stay forever.

They're from Nate. She glances at Adams as he plasters a fake smile on his face for his girls. She doesn't want to leave him alone on his first night as a single man. He's going to miss his daughters, and probably his wife too. He's vulnerable right now.

Maybe that's not the only reason she doesn't want to see Nate tonight. If she does, they'll have to talk about what happened earlier, but she can't do that without getting upset. She's still too mad at him for daring to risk his safety. If he's unwilling to take care of himself, how can he expect her to emotionally invest in his well-being? It's too hard.

She gets a flashback of her father slowly dying in her arms after an encounter with the Snow Storm Killer. She can't go through that with Nate.

I can't tonight. Adams is moving in.

She hits send.

"Can I feed Bandit?" asks Lizzie.

"Sure." She leaves her phone on the counter to open a can of Bandit's favorite food.

Lizzie joins her and scoops the strong-smelling concoction into his bowl. "It doesn't smell good."

Madison laughs. "I know, right? Apparently, the stronger the scent, the more cats love it."

Bandit jumps off Summer's lap and eats greedily from his bowl as if he hasn't been fed in days.

When everyone's seated at the table, Madison takes a bite from a slice of pepperoni pizza.

Summer eyeballs her. "Are you two going to have sex when we leave?" She looks at her dad for his reaction.

Madison almost chokes on her pizza. "Me and *your dad*?" She grimaces. "No way."

"Hey!" says Adams. "Try not to vomit at the thought, why don't you?"

She laughs. "Sorry." To Summer, she says, "He's not my type. And I'm seeing someone else." At least, she thinks she is.

"Listen," says Adams. "Your mom and I are figuring some stuff out, but neither of us will be seeing anyone else in the meantime, okay?"

Lizzie drops her pizza slice on her plate and slips her hand into his.

Summer narrows her eyes as if she doesn't believe him. "So why are you and Mom getting a divorce?"

Madison helps herself to more pizza, ensuring she stays out of this conversation.

"No one's mentioned divorce yet," says Adams. "We're just taking some time apart while we figure things out. It doesn't mean we don't love you guys, and not much will change other than you won't see me at home much anymore."

"But I'll miss you," says Lizzie with tears in her eyes.

Madison notices Adams is getting choked up, so she says, "You're both welcome here whenever you want to see your dad. You can even stay over occasionally if your mom allows it."

"Eat your pizza," says Adams. "I need to take you home soon."

Summer rolls her eyes in disgust.

Madison's suddenly glad she had a son and not daughters.

CHAPTER TWENTY-FIVE

Once Nate is showered and dressed, he makes toast for breakfast and tries not to dwell on how Madison refused to come over last night. He doesn't feel great about it, and he's realizing it was stupid to think their relationship would be plain sailing just because they want it to be. The house seems quieter this morning. Not just because she's not here but from the thought that she might never return.

While Nate eats, Brody licks his food bowl clean and then flops onto his favorite rug. They've already been out for a run this morning. Nate's trying to work out more. Now he's over forty, he has to work harder to stay in shape. Exercise also stops him from spiraling.

The morning sunshine streams through the kitchen window as he sits at the breakfast bar and opens his laptop. Last night, he tracked down Erin Martin, Brandon Dorsey's best friend, through her Facebook profile and sent her a message explaining how he's looking into Brandon's disappearance for his father. She responded thirty-six minutes ago, at 7 a.m. Considering she's at college, Nate's impressed she's awake this early. He clicks on her message.

This is amazing! I'll answer all your questions. I want to know what happened to Brandon.

She's provided her number so that Nate can video-call her. He replies to her message.

Great. Are you free now?

Her answer is immediate.

Yes.

He uses the camera on his laptop. While he sips his coffee, a smiling young woman appears. She's makeup-free and wearing a headscarf over her black hair. It looks like she hasn't been awake long. He can make out her tidy dorm room behind her. She appears to be seated at a desk using her laptop.

"Hi." She waves shyly at the camera.

Nate smiles. "Morning. How are you?"

"I'm good," she says. "Except I stayed out too late last night, and I have an early class this morning..."

She reminds him of Owen. "I'll try to make this quick." He takes a deep breath. "Why don't you start by telling me what *you* think happened to Brandon."

She turns serious. "It depends on what day you ask me, because some days I feel like he was abducted, and others I remember how unhappy he was, so I think he might've run away. But I don't want to believe he'd do that and never contact me again. You know what I mean?"

He nods. That's how everyone feels in a missing person case. But people do it. They walk out of their lives without confiding in anyone, no matter how close they are to their parents, siblings or friends. It's for the same reason that some people take their own lives. They're not thinking straight. Their thoughts are clouded by an overwhelming desire to escape whatever's causing them pain.

"I've spoken to his father, and he doesn't think Brandon was unhappy."

Erin scoffs. "With all due respect to Mr. Dorsey, he's either lying to you or to himself."

Nate makes a note. If Brandon did run away, he might be easier to find. "Tell me what was going on in Brandon's life at the time."

She exhales and pulls her knees up to her chest, hugging them to her. "Brandon was being low-key bullied at school. He didn't even realize it at first because the kids were pretending to like him. In reality, they were getting information to use against him online."

"How did he react when he found out?"

"Badly. He quit all social media to try to stop the worst of it. He seemed happier after that, but I found steroids in his locker. He was a skinny kid, and tall with it. He wanted to bulk up so he could take care of himself, but his dad wouldn't let him join a gym." She pauses to correct herself. "I mean, his dad couldn't afford a gym membership. Not once Brandon's mom died. He told him to join the soccer team instead, like it's *that* easy."

It sounds like Robert was out of touch with what his son was going through. "How did Brandon cope with his mother's death?"

Erin considers it. "I guess he was angry and in shock for a long time. But things slowly returned to a new normal. His dad returned to work, and Brandon returned to school. He stopped talking about her."

"Did he ever harm himself or talk about wanting to end things?"

"Oh, sure," she says. "He had suicidal thoughts all the time. What teenager doesn't, right? But that got a little better once he quit social media and..."

"And what?"

She hesitates for a second. "And started seeing me." She blushes. "We'd been friends since third grade and gotten closer over time. Eventually, he kissed me, and from then on we considered ourselves boyfriend and girlfriend." She straightens. "Don't go getting any ideas, though. We were both innocent thirteen-year-olds, Mr. Monroe. We only kissed and held hands. He was my first boyfriend. I was traumatized when he vanished." Her eyes brim with tears. "I honestly believe that if he hadn't disappeared, we'd still be together now."

"I'm sorry," says Nate. "I can tell how much you loved him."

She wipes her eyes. "His dad wasn't keen on his son hanging out with a black girl, though. At least that's how it felt. Brandon said his dad had no idea I was his girlfriend, but I think he did. Mr. Dorsey was never friendly toward me."

Nate writes: *Is Robert Dorsey racist?* It's a possible motive for Brandon's disappearance, because they could've argued about it. If Erin sensed Robert didn't like her, it's possible he was making his true feelings known to his son behind closed doors, and perhaps applying pressure on Brandon to break up with her. Robert could've given him an ultimatum and then lashed out when Brandon chose Erin. Or Brandon could've run away, knowing his father would never approve of his relationship. After all, young love is all-consuming.

He remembers Robert choking up when explaining how much he misses his son. If he feels that strongly about him, and if racism was his motive, then it's more likely he would've killed Erin. Unless it was unplanned.

"Tell me about the last time you saw Brandon. What happened?"

She lowers her eyes. "We walked home from school together, and he listened to me talk all the way home about homework and this girl in my class who was annoying me. After he vanished, I realized I didn't ask him a single question about his day." She wipes her eyes with the sleeve of her sweater. "Once we reached my house, he walked me to the front door and kissed me goodbye. He promised to call me later. If doorbell cameras were a thing back then, I'd have it on video to watch back." Her hand flies to her mouth, suppressing a sob.

Nate remains silent, giving her time to collect her thoughts.

With a deep breath, she says, "I went into my house as he walked away. I didn't wave or anything. I had no reason to believe I wouldn't talk to him later. I got a call from his house at five thirty, but it was his dad asking when Brandon would be home."

"How did he react when he learned Brandon wasn't with you?" asks Nate.

"He seemed confused, especially when he realized he should've been home by then."

Nate thinks about it. "And you didn't see anyone else in the neighborhood around that time? Robert told me you didn't notice any suspicious cars driving slowly."

"Nothing," she says. She picks up her cell phone and glances at the screen. "I'm sorry, but I'll be late for class if I don't leave soon."

"Sure. Just one more question, and try not to take offense at this." When she nods, Nate asks, "Do you really not know what happened to Brandon? You haven't had any contact with him since he left your house? I'm sorry. I have to ask."

She doesn't hesitate. "No. I wouldn't lie about something like this. Not even if I thought it was in Brandon's best interest. He was *thirteen* years old. That's far too young to try to be independent, even if his dad did piss him off occasionally."

"They argued a lot?"

She shrugs. "You remember being a teenager, right?"

Nate barely remembers that time in his life. He has a brother and a sister he hasn't seen since his arrest at twenty years old. His parents have long since passed, but he had a good relationship with both. He doesn't recall arguing with them, but he knows he was lucky on that score.

"So nothing out of the ordinary?" he says.

"Right. Everyone argues with their parents. The detective who investigated the case... I think his name was Detective Douglas. He said Brandon was high risk for being a runaway, but his dad didn't want to believe it." She stands. "I'm sorry. I should go. You can message me if you think of any more questions."

"Thanks, Erin. You've been a big help."

She smiles sadly. "I'd do anything for Brandon. Bye."

The screen goes blank, and Nate's left wondering whether Detective Douglas was onto something with his runaway theory.

CHAPTER TWENTY-SIX

Madison didn't sleep well last night, thinking about what to do next time she sees Nate. She heard Adams tossing and turning in the next room. She yawns as she enters the station. The temperature change from bitter cold outside to warm inside makes her shiver. She removes her coat but doesn't make it to her desk before she's stopped by Stella.

"Morning, Detective," says the older woman, turning in her chair and lowering her headset. "Thanks to the chief's press conference, Dina was inundated overnight with calls from people who have missing loved ones."

Madison's heart sinks. She hadn't thought about the broader repercussions of finding this many unidentified remains all in one go. Of course the families of the missing will want to know if this is the day they finally learn the truth about what happened. And each day they go without answers causes them more pain, which means Madison is under pressure to identify the bodies as fast as possible. "They want us to name the victims?"

Stella nods. "Right. I understand they're flocking to the Juniper Trail parking lot to talk with reporters and wait for answers. Oh, and the press has nicknamed the killer the Grave Mountain Stalker in today's coverage."

Madison's shoulders slump. "Great. That's all we need." Assigning a catchy but scary nickname just makes it more frightening for the community. "Thanks for letting me know." As she walks to her desk, she wonders how many concerned relatives they're dealing with.

Steve greets her. "Morning. Coffee?" He hands her a cup.

She smiles as she takes it from him. "You know me so well." She takes a sip and looks around the station. "There's so much going on that we need a team briefing."

"I'll gather the troops." Steve goes to fetch Alex from his office on the other side of the building.

Madison heads to the chilly briefing room with her coffee. It appears Alex has turned it into an incident room overnight. Photographs of each set of remains are stuck to a large whiteboard. Five of them. Only one has been identified. Tasha Harris. The body found between the tree trunks and the headless remains found in a shallow grave are numbered two and three. The final two victims discovered, an adult and a child, are four and five.

She turns as she hears voices. Detective Adams has made it on time after taking his girls to school. Steve and Chief Mendes are chatting as they enter, and they're followed by the rookies, Officers Kent and Fuller. Kent is chewing Fuller's ear off about something. He looks like he couldn't be less interested, but the young woman carries on regardless.

Alex and Officer Sanchez arrive last. Sanchez closes the door to drown out the sound of ringing phones.

"Okay," says Chief Mendes, folding her arms over her chest. "We have five victims and one deceased suspect. What's the latest from overnight?" She looks at Alex. "Are all victims now with the medical examiner?"

Alex nods. "I believe they were all extracted overnight.

Conrad will help Lena to examine them. The search-and-rescue team will return to the mountain this morning, but if any more remains are found, we'll need more volunteers, as the search area is fast expanding."

Chief Mendes looks at Madison and Adams. "So where are we at with the investigation?"

Adams speaks up while looking at his notes. "We know that the first victim—nineteen-year-old Tasha Harris—was shot with a nine-millimeter bullet between the eyes, likely on the day of the hike five years ago. Due to the precision of the shot, we're looking for someone who's experienced with firearms and fit enough to hike those trails at the time."

Steve clears his throat. "They only need to be fit enough to walk approximately thirty minutes up the trail, which, let's face it, most people can do at their own pace. And we don't know whether the killer lured his victims up there with him or whether he stalked hikers already on the mountain. So I wouldn't put much emphasis on physical fitness."

Adams disagrees. "He could've killed them elsewhere and carried them up there, in which case he'd need to be physically fit, so we're not looking for a senior citizen, right?"

"Actually," says Steve, "Lena told me last night that there's no way of knowing whether the victims were killed on the mountain or dumped there because of the time that's passed. So we can't assume he carried the bodies up there. I mean, it doesn't sound plausible to me."

With a roll of the eyes, Adams says, "Fine. Let me word it another way. We're not looking for a wheelchair user or someone with heart problems. Agreed?"

Madison raises her eyebrows at his attitude, but Steve brushes it off.

"Agreed," he says. "We can't narrow down an age for the killer until we know just how many bodies are on that mountain and how far back the kills went. Even though Tasha Harris only vanished five years ago, he could've started killing decades ago for all we know."

Mendes thinks about it. "If Dr. Stevens concludes that the remains of the other victims have been there for some time, then that probably rules out Stuart Carpenter as their killer. He was only twenty-seven when he died."

Alex scribbles *The Grave Mountain Stalker* on the whiteboard before turning back to the assembled officers. "Nora took several items of clothing from each crime scene to the lab," he says. "Maybe we'll get lucky with DNA."

"So we can't even tell yet whether the deaths are linked, right?" says Mendes.

"Correct," says Madison. "We could be dealing with individual murders rather than a serial killer. For all we know, Stuart might only be responsible for Becky and Tasha. I called Lena's office on my way here to ask that she prioritize the dental record comparisons."

Mendes frowns. "Why?"

"Well, we have Becky Draper's dental records already. If she can confirm that one of the unidentified adults is Becky, I can let the Drapers know. This whole investigation is causing them a lot of stress. I'm worried about Nancy." Madison sighs. "I think deep down they know she's dead, but they still need to know what happened."

Mendes straightens. "Of course."

Madison turns to Steve. "Any luck tracking Stuart's phone records and credit card statements from the time of the hike?"

He nods. "They were all in Detective Douglas's case files, and he found nothing of interest. I've double-checked them, and I can't find anything either." When his cell phone rings, he looks at the screen. "It's Lena. Give me a second." He leaves the room to answer it.

Madison considers how best to proceed. She looks at Adams. "What do you think we should do next?"

"Well," he says, "I don't think these five victims are the work of one killer. I just can't imagine Stuart Carpenter was smart enough to kill all those people. Not after how sloppy he was at hiding Tasha's driver's license in his own house and waiting so long to call the police about their disappearance." He looks at Alex. "Did you pull any fingerprints from the license?"

"Yes," says Alex. "Only Stuart's were on it."

Satisfied, Adams smiles. "I think he killed them because Tasha rejected him. But I don't think he was smart enough to kill five people, not if he started killing at age seventeen."

"So who killed the other three?" asks Chief Mendes.

"Someone who fits the profile of a serial killer," he says. "After the whole Snow Storm Killer fiasco last Christmas, I read the FBI's profiling research. It was fascinating. Now, if we begin with the obvious, I think we can all agree our killer is likely to be male, right?"

Everyone nods, including Madison. She read a study once that concluded less than ten percent of serial killers are female, and their motive is more likely to be financial than for sexual gratification or for the thrill of it.

"And from what I read," continues Adams, "I think we need to look for someone who"—he holds up fingers as he lists things —"lacks control in their personal life, hates animals, has a weird fixation with his mother, is socially inept and either leaves calling cards at the scene or takes creepy mementos from the bodies to relive his kills afterward."

Madison appreciates his research, but it all sounds too clichéd to her, like something from a bad made-for-TV movie. Murders aren't always the result of intelligent planning with reasoned motives born from a traumatic childhood. And crime scenes are rarely deliberately staged in a way to pique the media's interest. That takes too much time. Instead, the kills are more often brutal and rushed, the result of a frenzied rage that takes the killer by surprise. Sometimes, even they don't know why they kill, or why they're attracted to a particular victim.

Officer Sanchez speaks up. "We found several photos of Stuart with his mother in his nightstand drawer."

Adams crosses his arms, looking smug.

"Come on," says Madison. "What's wrong with keeping photos of your mom?" She sighs. "We didn't find any calling cards at the crime scenes, and I'm pretty sure nothing was taken as mementos. Was it, Alex?"

The forensic tech shrugs. "It would be difficult to know whether the killer took anything from the victims' bodies because we only have their bones."

"One of the heads was removed!" says Adams. "Maybe that's his thing?"

Chief Mendes dismisses it. "No. If only one head is missing from five bodies, that's not a pattern. What about the trails they were found on? Could the names be a clue from the killer?"

Madison's phone buzzes in her pocket. She ignores it. She thinks about the trail names. "The Juniper Trail and Lovers' Peak Trail..."

"Maybe our killer doesn't like couples?" suggests Adams. "Maybe he couldn't get a girlfriend, so he resents women, along with anyone who *could* get one, and killed them as some kind of misguided punishment."

"I don't know," says Madison. "Wouldn't we be finding dead couples if that were the case?" She takes a deep breath. "Given how vast the mountain is, I wonder if he limits himself to those two trails. Maybe he knows them better than the others."

Steve returns. He closes the door and takes a deep breath. "Okay, Lena says the forensic dentist has ruled out Becky Draper as one of the unidentified adults."

Madison's heart sinks.

He sees her disappointment. "But there's always the headless remains," he says. "She's going to arrange for DNA to be extracted from the bones to try to identify that victim. The good news is she's autopsied the body found between the trees and believes it belongs to a female, who was likely strangled. She mentioned something about the hyoid in the neck being fractured, which apparently suggests the cause of death was asphyxiation due to manual strangulation."

"Interesting," says Alex. "So now we have two different MOs: gunshot and strangulation. Plus, Tasha Harris's body wasn't hidden, whereas the woman in the trees was. At least, we think she was. The headless victim was buried in a shallow grave."

"Victims four and five were found exposed to the elements," says Chief Mendes. "Suggesting no attempt to conceal them."

Alex taps a whiteboard marker against his jaw as he thinks aloud. "It suggests either different killers or a serial killer who changes his MO to avoid capture."

Madison can imagine Stuart Carpenter shooting someone, but it's a little harder to imagine him strangling them. It takes a certain kind of person to grip a woman's neck tightly for several minutes until they stop struggling. That involves being hands-on and up close, and it's more violent than firing a weapon from a distance. But just because she can't imagine it doesn't mean he wasn't capable of it. "I think I agree with Adams," she says. "Stuart likely killed Becky and Tasha, but my gut tells me someone else is responsible for the other three bodies."

Adams nods in agreement.

"Well," says Steve, "I'm compiling a list of cold cases from the last decade. We should be able to cross-reference them and see if anyone fits the circumstances surrounding the people in the morgue." He looks at Alex. "I need a list of the items Nora took to the lab, in case what's left of their clothes matches what the cold case victims were wearing when they disappeared."

Alex pulls his phone out and types something, then looks up. "I've just emailed it to you."

"Fingers crossed we find some matches," says Madison. "Because then we can check the victims' inner circles and see whether they have someone or something in common."

Chief Mendes looks around the group. "Does anyone have anything else?"

Madison's phone buzzes again, so she retrieves it from her pocket. It's Vince. She frowns. It's early to be getting a call from Vince.

She looks at Mendes. "I don't have anything else. I better get this." She answers her phone as the rest of the team turns to leave the room. "Hey, Vince," she says.

"Madison. We have a situation at the diner." His voice is different. Thicker than usual.

Madison grips her phone a little tighter. "What is it? What's happened?"

Adams turns to look at her at the same time as Steve stops walking away.

"It's Carla." Vince gulps. "She's been stabbed. Repeatedly."

Madison gasps, covering her mouth with her spare hand. She looks at Adams and Steve. "She's still alive, though, right? You've called for an ambulance?"

Vince clears his throat. "No, Madison. You don't understand. I was too late. She's gone."

Her eyes go hot as she blinks back tears.

Steve steps forward. "Who?" he mouths.

She looks him in the eye. "Someone's killed Carla Hitchins."

CHAPTER TWENTY-SEVEN

Carla's deathly expression is locked in a grimace of pain. The morning sunlight illuminating her pale face somehow makes the grimace more horrific. More defined. Her white shirt is saturated in blood, which has soaked through the fabric and spilled onto the ground around her body. Her keys are still in her hand, and her purse rests on the ground less than two feet away, unzipped and discarded. A balled-up tissue is at risk of blowing away in the breeze, and her signature pink lipstick has spilled out.

Madison wants to tear her eyes away from her friend, but she can't until a warm hand on her back makes her turn. It's Nate. Vince called him straight after calling her.

Nate embraces her. His neck is warm against her cold face. She tries hard to swallow a sob as she hugs him.

When Detective Adams rounds the corner with Chief Mendes, Madison pulls away and clears her throat. Nate tries to take her hand, but she gently shakes him off. She needs to focus.

Carla's body is sprawled on the ground at the edge of Vince's property, directly behind the diner. A line of trees sits to her left, leading to the woods beyond. This spot is only just covered by Vince's surveillance cameras.

"Who would do this to a nice lady like her?" says Adams.

No one answers.

Several cruisers pull up behind them, and she hears Officer Sanchez ordering the rookies to tape off the parking lot. "Absolutely no press or customers are allowed on the property," he barks. "Got it?"

Officers Kent and Fuller nod dutifully, and Kent's eyes linger on Carla's body. Madison wonders whether she knew Carla. Most people in this town did.

Traffic builds up on the road out front. Several cars slow down as if intending to enter the lot to grab their breakfast or morning coffee, but they're forced to turn around and drive away. The customers who were already inside have been told to sit tight until they've been questioned by officers.

Alex Parker is the next to arrive. He approaches with a case in one hand and a camera around his neck. After crouching next to Carla's body, he looks up at them. "She's still fresh. This was recent."

"That should make it easier to locate her killer," says Chief Mendes.

Adams rests his hands on his hips. "Do we think this is related to the bodies on the mountain?"

Madison can't answer. She's too upset. Carla was one of the only people who welcomed her return to Lost Creek after her release from prison. Most of the other locals held a grudge and would often make it known while Madison tried to eat in peace. Carla wouldn't stand for it, often threatening to ban them from the place. She was excited for Madison's relationship with Nate to develop too.

The sound of a slamming door makes Madison look toward the diner. She shields her eyes from the morning sun as Vince appears from the rear exit. He marches toward her past the dumpsters, holding something in his left hand.

"No one inside saw a damn thing, which is why I put my trust in surveillance cameras instead of people," he says with barely concealed rage. "The camera out front caught a shadow of someone fleeing the scene." He hands her a flash drive. "Here."

Madison takes it from him. "Do you recognize who it was?"

He shakes his head. "Could be anyone. But you can pull footage from other businesses, right? Track the asshole all the way to his home?"

She takes a deep breath. "We can try. Thanks for this." She gives it to Adams. "Watch it all and see what other footage you can get from nearby."

Adams nods and leaves to head to his car.

Mendes calls Officer Sanchez over. He glances at Carla's body before he turns away. "Yes, Chief?"

"I need you and the new officers to secure the scene and interview the witnesses inside," says Mendes.

"Sure, Chief." He walks away.

Officer Fuller approaches with a blanket. He looks at Madison, who nods, so he carefully places it over Carla's body, hiding her from prying eyes. The diner's customers don't have a view of the rear of the property, but Madison thinks it won't be long before reporters get wind of what's happened and start finding ways to get back here, maybe even coming from the other direction, through the woods.

She looks at the ground and can't see a murder weapon. That doesn't mean it's not here somewhere.

Vince takes a deep breath. "The footage. It's..." His hand visibly shakes as he raises it to his mouth. "You can hear her scream."

Madison steps forward and rubs his back. "I'm so sorry, Vince."

He lowers his eyes to the heap under the blanket. "I thought she was just late to work, so I opened without her," he says. "I didn't look out back soon enough. If I did, I might've reached her in time. Stopped the blood flow."

"We don't know that," says Madison gently. "What time did you find her?"

He takes a deep breath. "About five minutes before I called you."

That would be around 8:30 a.m. Madison can double-check her incoming call log.

"One of the waitresses asked me where Carla was. She'd spotted her car out front," he says. "Once I realized her car was here and she wasn't, I approached the vehicle. It was empty and locked. Nothing looked out of place. I got a bad feeling then. So I walked around the back of the property." He swallows. "That's when I saw her." He's silent for a second while he rubs his neck, trying to compose himself. "I should've known she'd never be late. It wasn't like her. But since she's been dating Hank, she's changed."

"Where is Hank?" asks Nate.

"Oh God," says Vince. "I'll have to break it to him. And Carla's relatives. She has a sister in Idaho."

"Let us do that," says Madison. "Do you have the sister's contact details and Hank's address?"

He nods. "Come inside. You can watch the surveillance footage too. I kept a backup."

Alex stands. "I'll call Dr. Scott. We need to get Carla out of here before she ends up on the front page of tomorrow's newspaper."

Madison nods. Her heart aches as she considers how the waitress forced to listen to the news on repeat all day at work has now become a leading story herself.

CHAPTER TWENTY-EIGHT

Frightened faces greet them when Vince leads Madison into the warm diner. Plates of food sit untouched, and a couple of the younger waitresses are openly crying, probably thinking about how it could so easily have been one of *them* who was attacked.

That may or may not be true, depending on the killer's motive.

Madison notices the TV above the counter is switched off for a change. No one needs to watch the news when it's happening right in front of them, too close for comfort.

She tries to offer a reassuring smile to the group, even though she's also upset. "Officers will be in to take your statements shortly, then you'll be able to leave. I'm sorry for keeping you."

Several diners nod. Others lower their eyes. No one challenges her, which is something, at least.

She glances outside. Alex is focused on his forensic examination, and Chief Mendes is heading back to the station to notify Carla's sister of her death. Nate reluctantly left after asking Madison to come over tonight. She said she'd try, but she expects to have to work late.

Vince leads her behind the counter and up to his apartment above the diner. It's a cozy space filled with dark leather couches and walls lined with bookshelves. His son, Matt, and grandson, Oliver, are seated in front of the TV, but Matt stands when Vince goes to the kitchen to make drinks.

His eyes betray his fear. It must be unsettling to know someone was murdered so near to where his son was. "Do you know who did this?" he asks as he approaches. "Should we move out until they're caught?"

Madison unzips her jacket. It's warm up here. "We have officers stationed outside. If anyone tries to strike again on this property, they'll be stopped before they can cause any harm. But if you'd feel safer in a hotel or with friends, do what's best for you." She peers over his shoulder at the young boy watching TV. His backpack is on the floor at his feet, but Madison doesn't think he'll be attending school today. "How's Oliver? He hasn't looked out the rear windows, has he?"

Matt shakes his head. "Dad told me to keep him away from the windows and to distract him with the TV." He runs a hand through his hair. "Oliver loves Carla. What am I meant to tell him?"

"The truth," she says. "He'll find out eventually anyway, thanks to the news. Just ensure he knows he's not in any danger and that it was a one-off."

"*Was* it a one-off?" asks Matt.

She has no idea how to answer that. "Did you see or hear anything?" she asks.

He shakes his head. "Nothing. We were about to leave for school and work, going about our normal morning routine, when we heard Dad yelling outside. I looked out of my bedroom window and saw Carla. She was..." He swallows. "I thought it was a prank at first. Then I thought she'd passed out. My eyes didn't register the blood on her shirt. It looked like a pattern from up here."

"You didn't hear her scream, or any voices outside before she was found?"

He shakes his head. "Oliver was watching TikTok on his phone while eating breakfast, so I'm used to hearing screams and laughter coming from that. I couldn't tell you whether it was Carla or his videos."

She nods. "Sure. Try not to worry. We're checking surveillance footage and have officers searching for whoever did this. Someone's bound to report a guy fleeing the scene eventually, because he would've been covered in blood."

Matt's expression suggests he's skeptical, but he returns to the couch when Vince approaches. Vince holds out a cup of coffee for Madison. Even though it's only nine thirty, he's fixed himself a glass of Scotch to settle his nerves. She follows him into his small kitchen, where his laptop is open on the island in the middle of the room.

"Ready?" he asks.

She nods.

Vince downs the shot of whiskey and hits play. The footage is shrouded in darkness, and Madison can't tell what she's looking at. The video is time-stamped. This was recorded at 5:32 a.m. Four hours ago.

The outdoor security light senses movement and suddenly illuminates the area behind the diner. After a few seconds, Carla appears. She has a purse hanging from her shoulder and keys in her hand.

"Is five thirty her normal start time?" asks Madison.

Vince nods.

"And she always arrives alone, without Hank?"

"They don't live together yet," he says. "Hank's only been learning the ropes these last couple of weeks, and sometimes he arrives before her, but not very often. Some days, he doesn't show up at all."

Carla's back is to the camera that's mounted high on the

diner's rear wall, pointing at the dumpsters. Madison imagines Vince specifically aimed the camera to protect the waitresses as they took out the trash. Or at least to make them feel protected. Carla tentatively steps forward, as if someone's summoning her off-camera from the woods beyond. After a few seconds, she strides forward, confident and unafraid.

Madison shivers. "She knew whoever called her over."

Vince pours himself another Scotch. "Why were they hiding in the bushes?"

"Because they didn't want to be caught on camera," she says. "They planned this. Scoped the place out beforehand."

Carla keeps walking and eventually disappears from view. Almost a minute goes by before a single blood-curdling scream rings out. She doesn't reappear on screen. She'll be on the ground now.

Madison watches for the shadowy figure Vince spotted. "When does the suspect appear?"

"That was caught on the front camera." He leans in to close the clip and open a second one showing the view of the parking lot out front. "Watch here." He points to the tree line.

After a few seconds, a flash of black runs through the trees. It's so quick that Madison has to replay it several times to ensure it's human and not animal. She pauses at the best view of it, but it's just someone's shadow. Maybe Alex could tell how tall the perp is, but she doubts it.

She straightens. "Had Carla fallen out with anyone recently? Had she mentioned any customers who'd pissed her off?"

Vince doesn't even need to consider it. "No. She could take an insult like a champ, so she never got into a back-and-forth with troublemakers. Most people around here loved Carla. If she told them to shut up, they'd do it with a smile."

"What about Hank?" she asks. "He's not exactly charming.

Could *he* have pissed someone off? Someone who took their anger out on Carla to get back at him?"

Vince's face darkens. "If Hank's the reason behind her death, I'll kill him." He sighs heavily. "He's an asshole, so who knows."

"Think Hank could've killed her?" she asks.

He doesn't need to think about it for long. "He needed Carla in order to buy this place, and whatever I think of him, it's clear he's besotted with her." Straightening, he adds, "He accused Dennis McKinney of being a killer the first time Dennis came here after his release from prison. Maybe Dennis heard and took offense."

That's interesting. But she doesn't think Dennis McKinney would kill someone over a stupid comment, not after what it took to finally get his murder conviction overturned. Like Nate, he wouldn't risk going back inside, and besides, half the people in this town have been talking about him.

She watches the shadow on the screen again. Something springs to mind. She quickly pulls out her phone and calls Nate.

He answers almost immediately. "Hey. I'm still outside," he says. "I thought Brody could follow any potential blood trail from the weapon or the perp, so we're in the woods."

Madison smiles. "That's what I was going to ask you to do. I'll be there in a second." She pockets her phone. "Brody's looking for the murder weapon."

Vince nods. "Your department should hire him. Brody could be a real asset to investigations. So could Nate."

He's right, but Chief Mendes would never agree to it. She barely found the money to hire a department shrink, and Madison's still not sure how she made that happen. "I need to notify Hank before Carla's murder makes the news." She pauses. "Will you be okay?"

He looks at his empty glass. "I'll switch to coffee. I need to take charge downstairs and try to comfort the team." He takes a deep breath. "I'll close for the rest of the day, but I know people will want to come here to pay their respects to Carla, so is it okay if I open tomorrow? I feel like the locals should have somewhere to go."

She nods. "As long as Alex has finished his forensic exam, when you reopen is up to you. Just keep the TV off, would you? Carla would've hated the diners to watch her on the news."

He nods. "You can tell Hank that, once he's ready, we're here for him."

She tilts her head. "If he can scrape together the money, will you still sell him this place now Carla's gone?"

A look of distaste crosses his face. "Not if I can help it."

CHAPTER TWENTY-NINE

Brody doesn't look up when Madison approaches. He keeps his nose to the damp ground, focused on the job at hand.

"Hey," says Madison.

Nate takes her cold hands in his warm ones. The collar of his coat is turned up against the chill. He leans in to kiss her, then cups her face for a second. "You're freezing."

"I should've worn a thicker coat, but with all these hikes I'm doing up the mountain, I get too warm." She zips her jacket up and shoves her hands in her pockets.

Nate slips an arm around her waist as Brody leads them deeper into the White Woods. The morning sunlight illuminates the pale trunks of the aspen trees, but she spots approaching storm clouds off to the east. Her breath warms the air in front of her as branches snap underfoot.

"I can't go much farther," she says. "I need to break the news to Hank."

They stop.

"Sure," says Nate. "I think Brody was following the scent of Carla's blood, but he's becoming a little less certain of himself now."

They watch the dog, who, instead of progressing in a straight line, is now meandering back and forth in no discernible pattern.

Madison shivers. "The killer could've exited the woods at any point and made it onto the main road."

He nods. "Alex said he'll get the rookies to help him perform a more thorough search."

Brody is circling them, slower now. Less interested in scents.

Nate turns to her. "Madison? Are we okay?"

She looks at him. "We are until someone tries to kill you."

He reaches for her hands again. "Listen, you don't need to worry about me. Brody would alert me if I was being followed or if someone was hiding in my house."

"If I don't need to worry about you," she says, "then why am I even with you? If I didn't care what happened to you, I wouldn't be in this relationship." She shakes her head. "Look, I don't have time for this right now. I need to go." The disappointment in his eyes softens her. "We'll be fine," she says. "I just need to find whoever's killing all these people. Then I can relax."

He frowns. "You think Carla's murder is related to the Grave Mountain Stalker case?"

She nods. "I think he killed her to distract us. He wants the department thinly stretched so we're unable to solve those mountain murders." She shrugs. "It's just a hunch. I could be wrong. But I can't relax until I know for sure."

Her cell phone rings. It's Stella from dispatch. She looks at Nate. "I need to take this. I'll try to come over later, okay?"

"Sure," he says.

Madison ruffles Brody's fur before turning and retracing her steps through the woods. She accepts the call. "Hi, Stella."

"Hi, Detective. I have Mel Hewitt on the phone. Jay Carpenter's fiancée."

Madison stops. The last she heard, Mel was experiencing contractions far too early in her pregnancy. "Fine. Put her through." After a couple of seconds, she says, "Ms. Hewitt? Detective Harper here. How are you?"

"I'm out of the hospital, thank goodness. It was a false alarm. The baby's fine." Mel sounds anxious. "It took us so long to conceive that the thought of losing her now…" She trails off before adding, "We're going to name her Lucy, after Jay and Stuart's mom."

Madison smiles as she continues walking. "That's a lovely name. And I'm glad to hear you're both okay. So how can I help?"

Mel clears her throat nervously. "Detective, you need to tell the press that Stuart wasn't responsible for the deaths of those people you're recovering from the mountain."

Madison takes a deep breath, gearing up for a battle. "With all due respect, Ms. Hewitt—"

"Mel, please. I feel like I'm in trouble when you use my title." She laughs weakly.

"With all due respect, Mel, we don't know that yet. And I don't believe Chief Mendes has directly stated that Stuart was involved."

"It doesn't matter. Every news outlet around is implying it. They're saying he admitted it before he killed himself. Where did they get that from if not from you or someone in your department?"

Madison thinks the media are just trying to force the police department to disclose Stuart's last words. "Unfortunately," she says, "Stuart *did* admit guilt for the deaths of Becky Draper and Tasha Harris. And Tasha's driver's license was found in his house." She hesitates before gently adding, "I think you should prepare yourself for the worst."

"No," says the younger woman. "I'm sorry, but we can't do that. You're killing my father-in-law. His doctor has told him that if he doesn't lower his blood pressure, he's at risk of a heart attack or a stroke."

Madison feels for them, but she can't change the facts. "I'm sorry. I know how hard this is on you all."

"I don't think you do," says Mel, her voice thick with emotion. "Almost every guest who had a booking at the lodge over the next few months has canceled. It'll go bust at this rate. He just lost his son, Detective. He can't lose his business too." Her voice falters. "And then there's what all this is doing to Jay. He's distraught. I worry about his mental health. I've tried to make him see a therapist, but he's struggling just to get up in the morning." A sob escapes her as she breaks down.

It's clear she's under immense pressure as she tries to protect her loved ones.

Once she's composed herself, she goes on, "If it turns out that Stuart *was* involved, I don't think Bryan and Jay could take it. I don't think *I* could take it. He's the uncle to my unborn child. We were friends. I can't believe that about him. I just... can't." She falls silent.

Madison has no words of reassurance because she's still investigating Stuart's involvement, but her heart goes out to Mel, Jay and Bryan. Many people rightly focus on what a murder does to the victim's family, but there are devastating implications for the perpetrator's family too. They get zero sympathy from the public and little support from those around them as friends and acquaintances distance themselves.

Eventually, Mel says, "Our families have talked us into going ahead with the wedding."

Madison raises her eyebrows. "Are you comfortable with that?"

"Not really." She sounds uncertain, suggesting she's struggled with the decision. "But Jay's older relatives insist it's a good idea, and he's never been good at saying no to them. He would do anything to keep his family happy." Her voice turns quieter as she adds, "Besides, Bryan needs a distraction. He's always wanted to host our wedding. And my mom pointed out how everyone's already gone to the expense of traveling here from across the States, including Jay and I. Plus, the food has already been delivered at great cost to Bryan. I guess I won't fit into my dress for much longer either..." She runs out of steam as she tries to convince herself more than Madison.

Madison thinks they're trying to make everyone happy at the cost of their own mental health. "And Jay's okay with that?" she asks.

"He took some persuading, but he's hopeful that his brother will be cleared as a suspect by the time we go ahead."

Madison almost says, *What about Stuart's funeral?* But she doesn't. Everyone copes differently, and she can see how they need something to keep them going until the investigation is resolved. They can always renew their vows years down the line in happier circumstances. It occurs to her then that no one has asked when they can bury Stuart. Perhaps they're waiting to find out whether he's guilty first. It's not unusual for killers' remains to go unclaimed by their families. No one wants the trauma of being responsible for what happens to them.

"If I find anything that exonerates Stuart," she says, "you guys will be the first to know."

"Thank you," says Mel. "Once my father-in-law returns to the lodge, I'll tell him I've spoken to you."

Madison frowns as she ducks under a branch that's blocking her way. "Are you at the lodge now?"

"Yes. We're staying inside to avoid reporters and backlash from the locals, but it feels like we're in hiding. I think that's why Bryan went for a run earlier. He can't bear being cooped up."

Madison stops walking. "Is that his normal routine?"

"Right. He runs every morning."

"What time did he leave the lodge?"

Mel seems confused by the question. "I don't know. I only know that he'd already left before I came down for breakfast at seven."

Madison checks the time on her phone. It's ten fifteen. That's a long run. She can't manage twenty minutes without wanting to turn back. Maybe he decided to run some errands downtown afterward.

"Jay told him to take a break from exercise while he's stressed," adds Mel, "but he insists it'll help him relax."

Madison nods. "Well, I should get back to work."

They say their goodbyes. Madison tries to think. She doesn't want to jump to conclusions, but it's worth looking into Bryan Carpenter's route for his morning run to see if he was anywhere near the diner.

First, though, she needs to visit Hank Goodman.

Hank lives in a downtown apartment complex. It's not a wealthy area, and the walls of his building are covered in colorful graffiti, with a build-up of trash in the gated yard. Madison suddenly understands why he jumped at the chance of owning Ruby's Diner with Carla. According to Vince, he drives a black Toyota Corolla, but she doesn't see it in the parking lot.

His apartment is on the first floor. She approaches his door and knocks loudly. A dog barks ferociously in response, but the sound is high-pitched, nothing like Brody's deep, booming barks. Madison smiles. It must be Mrs. Pebbles. At least Hank has someone to comfort him.

When no one answers, she knocks again and looks around as she waits. Rain clouds are rolling in overhead. Perhaps a sign that the temperature will rise for a while. After a few minutes, she turns away. Hank obviously isn't home.

She calls dispatch to let patrol know that if anyone sees him, they should break the news about Carla or have him call her. Then she texts Vince to let him know Hank isn't home and to ask if he has any suggestions about where he could be. Vince is likely to know the guy's routine, and she'd rather tell him in person than over the phone.

She's heading back to her car when her phone buzzes. She has a text from Adams.

Lena and Dr. Conrad want us to swing by the morgue so they can update us.

She sends him a thumbs-up and gets into her car. Before pulling away, she calls Steve's desk phone. When he answers, she says, "Do me a favor, would you? Run a background check on Stuart's dad. Bryan Carpenter."

"Sure," he says. "Want to wait?"

"No, I need to get to the morgue."

"Leave it with me. You think his dad knew what he did?"

"I don't know. Probably not. But according to his soon-to-be daughter-in-law, Bryan went for a run earlier, and he's still not home."

"Interesting," says Steve. "I wonder if he's literally on the run."

Madison smiles. "You're as suspicious of everyone as I am."

"Well, duh," he says. "That's why we're cops, right?" He laughs. "I'll let you know what I find, but before you hang up, I took a call that came for you."

"Oh yeah?" she says.

"Yeah. But don't shoot the messenger, okay?"

She frowns as her stomach flutters with nerves. "Why would I?"

"Because it was about your sister. The prison warden called."

"Oh God. What's she done now?" Knowing Angie, it could be anything. Or it could be about her upcoming trial.

"She's getting out."

Madison's mouth drops open. For a few seconds, she's speechless. "Are you serious?"

"Afraid so. She's struck a deal with the DA. The warden didn't want to tell me too much, but it sounds like Angie's agreed to snitch on a couple of high-profile drug dealers. With time served, she could be out sometime in the new year."

She closes her eyes. The last thing she needs is her criminal sister back in town. *Thank God Owen's in Arizona.* "If Angie names the dealers, she'll have a target on her back."

"Right," he says. "She might need to leave Colorado and start fresh somewhere else."

Madison sighs. "I can only hope. Okay, thanks for letting me know."

"No problem."

She doesn't have time to worry about the implications of Angie's release right now. She starts the engine and hits the gas.

CHAPTER THIRTY

Madison spots Detective Adams waiting for her outside the medical examiner's building. He watches her car as she arrives, his thick winter coat zipped up to his chin.

She gets out of her vehicle and approaches him. "Hey. Find any more surveillance footage?"

He rubs his gloved hands together in a bid to keep warm. "I've been going door-to-door, checking whatever's available, but I haven't found anything useful yet. I do have a potential lead, though. An older resident who lives near the diner said her door cam woke her around the time Carla was killed. It alerted her to someone approaching the house, but she ignored it. Apparently, it's super-sensitive and picks up cats and wild animals."

"Did she let you watch it?"

He shakes his head. "She has no idea how to retrieve the footage, and she wouldn't let me in, but her son comes by every day at noon to check on her, so he's going to download it and email me a clip of whatever triggered it."

"Good."

"Also," he says, "Alex examined Vince's footage. He can't

identify anyone from the shadowy figure running away from the diner, but he said it might be useful once we have a suspect, as we can compare their heights and builds." He shrugs. "To tell you the truth, I think it's a long shot."

Madison agrees. She tells him what Mel said about Bryan Carpenter's morning run. "We should question Bryan as soon as we're done here."

He nods. "Sure, but why would *he* kill Carla? Did he know her?"

"I think everyone knew Carla. We can ask Vince if he frequents the diner." She looks at her watch. "It'll have to wait until we're finished here. Lena hates to be kept waiting."

Adams scoffs. "She's not exactly a ray of sunshine, is she?"

Madison stops and turns. "What do you mean?"

He shakes his head. "Steve was saying she's hard work. Sounds to me like she has a chip on her shoulder."

Madison rolls her eyes. "Or maybe she's just sick of men."

She enters the building. Conrad is waiting to greet them in the reception area.

"Good morning, Detectives." He shakes their hands. "I saw you'd arrived, so I thought I'd take you through."

They follow him into the morgue, where he slips a white coat over his scrubs. Lena's holding a bone. She puts it down with the rest of the skeletal remains in front of her and smiles at them. "Morning, guys." She checks her watch under the sleeve of her white coat. "Or is it afternoon?"

It's only 11 a.m., but she's probably been working since the crack of dawn.

Madison looks around. "How many of our victims have you managed to examine?"

"All of them," says Conrad. "But not in detail yet. I know you're incredibly busy, so I'll get straight to the point by giving you our preliminary findings." He walks to a whiteboard that has the victims listed one through five. Tasha Harris's name is next to victim one. "Victim two was the body found squeezed between the tree trunks. She didn't match Becky Draper's dental records, so she remains unidentified. I think Lena has already informed Sergeant Tanner that we believe she was strangled."

"Right," says Madison. She pulls out her notebook and pen to help keep everything straight. Five victims from the mountain—plus Carla Hitchins from the diner—is a lot to keep track of.

"Victim three is the headless body found in a shallow grave," says Conrad. "That's also a female. We need to extract DNA from the bones to know whether this is Becky Draper, and that could take some time." He pauses. "We believe she was also strangled. We may not have her skull, but we have another fractured hyoid with her remains."

Madison looks at Adams. "A pattern's emerging. Three females. One shot, two strangled."

He nods.

"Afraid not," says Conrad, dashing their hopes. "We then have the child's remains, which I'll return to, but first, I want to discuss the fifth set of remains we discovered." He leads them to another table containing bones. "This person is male, and his skull has a clear gunshot wound to the temple."

Adams leans in. Madison can see from her position where the bullet exited the skull.

"Now, a bullet to the temple usually, but not always, indicates suicide," says the doctor. "So I contacted Sergeant Tanner as I believe he's working his way through unsolved missing person cases, and we cross-referenced the clothing found with this man to that of the cold cases. His shoes were found with him. They were black leather, not the hiking boots or sneakers you'd expect from someone enjoying the mountain terrain."

Madison's intrigued. "Did Steve find a match?"

"He did," says Lena, taking over from Conrad. "Scott

Wilson. Thirty-eight years old. He was reported missing by his wife nine years ago. He set off for work one morning and never arrived. He was known to be suffering from severe depression caused by, according to her, financial concerns. She suspected from the minute she knew he was missing that he'd taken his own life, but his body was never found. Steve said that according to the investigation notes, the mountain was never considered a location of interest as Scott had never been up there before."

A wave of hopelessness washes over Madison. It's difficult to hear about suicides without thinking about the person's final moments. They're usually alone—through choice and necessity —and in the depths of despair. This man ended his life somewhere remote, leaving behind all his loved ones, probably assuming that his death was best for all concerned.

"We've since found his driver's license in a wallet discovered under his remains," says Lena. "His wallet was in his back pocket, which would've been protected from the elements by his body, and as it's plastic, it hadn't disintegrated."

Madison looks at Adams. "Would you mind breaking the news to his wife?"

He runs a hand over his hair, looking like he's drawn the short straw. "Fine. I mean, it shouldn't really come as a surprise, right? At least she'll finally have answers, and a body to bury."

Madison looks at the two doctors. "So we're down to four homicide victims found on the mountain, plus Carla Hitchins." She looks around the room and sees a gray foot poking out from under a white sheet on a table in the corner of the room. Lena's assistants are preparing it for autopsy. "Is that Carla?"

"Yes," says Lena. "She was brought in right before you arrived."

Madison's taken by surprise. Her eyes tear up, and she has to swallow back a sob. "Sorry," she says, turning away from them.

"No, I'm sorry," says Lena, stepping forward. "I should've moved her somewhere else."

Madison shakes her head. "It's fine. I just..." She doesn't know how to finish her thought.

"It sounds like Carla was well loved," says Conrad sympathetically as he hands her a tissue. "We'll take good care of her."

Somehow, that makes Madison want to cry harder.

Thankfully, Adams changes the subject. "So, the child. What are your thoughts on them?"

Conrad walks them to yet another table and uncovers the remains. They're much smaller than Scott Wilson's, but it's clear this child was no infant.

"Here we have a female teenager between the ages of thirteen and fifteen."

Madison's surprised. She thought this could be Brandon Dorsey.

"And if you look here," Conrad points to a rib, "you can see her rib has been skimmed by a bullet. She has no other marks on her. So it's our belief that she was shot."

"Like Tasha Harris," says Adams. "So, from the mountain we have four females. Two killed by gunshot and two by strangulation."

"And Carla was repeatedly stabbed," says Madison. "That doesn't mean we can rule out the Grave Mountain Stalker for her murder, though. He could be trying to throw us off the scent by using a different MO." She quickly texts Nate, letting him know the child found isn't Brandon Dorsey.

"We need to ID them asap," she says. "How long will that take?"

"Extracting DNA from bone material can be a laborious and time-consuming process," says Conrad. "But I'll start as soon as possible. In the meantime, you might find it quicker to link these people's clothing to the cold cases your sergeant is looking at. And once I've completed my thorough examination of their remains, I should be able to tell you how long they've been dead."

Madison turns to Adams. "I can help Steve with the cross-referencing while you notify Scott Wilson's wife of his death. I'll concentrate on the teenager."

Adams nods. "Sure. I'll chase that door cam footage too." He thanks Conrad and Lena before heading to the exit.

Madison follows him outside into a heavy downpour.

CHAPTER THIRTY-ONE

SIX YEARS AGO

Abby laughs as she watches her best friend dramatically stomp away from her after drawing the short straw to refill their water bottles from a stream they passed earlier. They've just spent an hour putting up and securing their cheap tent.

Being only fourteen, they shouldn't be camping alone on the mountain. No one knows they're here. Their parents think they're staying at another girl's house for a slumber party. That should've been the first clue for Abby's mom to realize they were lying because Abby doesn't have any other friends from school, just Lauren. They're not in with the popular crowd and don't want to be. Although, she secretly suspects Lauren would drop her in a heartbeat for a place on the cheer squad.

Now alone, she sighs. Part of her hoped their deception would be discovered and she wouldn't have to come camping. It was Lauren's idea. A fan of horror movies, Lauren's planning to document their overnight stay, like in the Blair Witch movie. She thinks that if they fake some creepy scenarios once the sun sets, she can make her footage go viral. Abby's only ever watched the Blair Witch trailer, which was terrifying enough. If she'd been forced to watch the movie, she suspects there's no way she would've agreed to this.

Right now, in the orange glow of the summer evening, the mountain isn't that scary. They've picked an opening with few trees around it to limit hiding places for any weirdos who might stumble across them, and their campsite overlooks the town below. Once the homes and roads are lit up beneath them at dusk, hopefully, it shouldn't feel like they're camped in the middle of nowhere.

She climbs into the small tent, which is already stuffy from the midsummer heat. Getting comfortable on her sleeping bag, she unzips her backpack and pulls out a wind-up flashlight she brought in case her phone battery dies. It shouldn't, because she charged it before leaving the house, but she's planning to take as many photos as possible tonight. Not for social media. Her dad won't allow her to have any accounts, which is probably a good thing judging by how much Lauren's upset her. She gets bullied in the DMs by some girls in her class.

Next, she takes out the sandwiches she prepared for dinner, along with a couple of candy bars and a huge bag of potato chips. Eating their snacks will probably be the best part of this adventure. She opens a sandwich and takes a bite. Ham and cheese. It tastes so good that she devours the whole thing and is hit with instant regret. The food needs to last all night.

Her arm hair suddenly stands on end, and she experiences a weird tingling sensation in her chest, like when she's dreading something: a test at school or reading aloud in front of the class. But this is different. She looks up.

Movement outside the tent makes her freeze.

She listens to see if it's Lauren, but there's no way her friend would've returned from the stream already.

The air falls silent.

Through the thin tent, she sees a large bird hopping away. Abby breathes a sigh of relief. Truth be told, she's a little afraid of the dark, and they've pitched their tent a long way from the main trail. She's hoping they don't come across any bears, or worse, any men. Her parents would freak out if they knew she was here with only Lauren for company. In hindsight, it probably is a stupid idea, but her mother's fond of reminding her that *you only live once*, so she thought she'd finally do something spontaneous.

Something tickles her leg. She looks down and finds the tent is filling with ants.

"Ew." She flicks one off her leg before removing a sneaker and squashing the rest. She won't be able to sleep if the tent fills with bugs. The hike up here was bad enough. She looks at her arm. It's blotchy from insect bites. Neither of them thought to bring bug spray. That's the kind of thing your mom remembers for you.

Her phone buzzes with a new text, making her jump.

It's creepy out here. You're getting the water next time.

Abby smiles. She responds with a face-palm emoji.

She peers up at the cloudless July sky through the unzipped flap in front of her. The sun is lowering, although not yet touching the mountainous skyline. They probably only have two hours of daylight left, if that. The sweet scent of an aromatic flower hits her, but she can't identify it.

She crawls out of the tent and selects the camera app on her cell phone. She snaps photos of the tent and their belongings before turning her back to the sunset and snapping selfies with the pretty view behind.

As she assesses them, she's reminded of how much she hates her looks. Her eyes are small and too close together and she doesn't know how to apply eye makeup properly. Her auburn hair isn't as thick as Lauren's, which means it's greasy and lifeless if she doesn't wash it every day. But her dad doesn't let her shower every day because it costs too much, so she has to use a ton of dry shampoo just to make it look clean. Someone at school told her dry shampoo causes cancer, so now she has that to add to the long list of things she worries about.

She takes a deep breath. Being alive is exhausting.

She takes one more selfie to see if she can find a better angle for her plump face. She snaps a final photo with the sunset and trees behind her, then quickly checks how it turned out. Unfortunately, she still looks like a dork.

Something in the photo makes her frown. "What the hell?" she mumbles.

She zooms in with her fingers. It looks like...

The snap of a branch behind her makes her freeze. She can't bring herself to spin around and face the person in the photograph.

"Abby?" she hears Lauren say. Her voice sounds as shaky as Abby's legs feel.

She looks at the photo again. Someone is standing behind Lauren, their hand on her shoulder. Lauren's light blue jeans are darker near her thighs. Something's terrified her so badly that she's wet herself. It hurts to see her friend like that.

"Abby, *please*," cries Lauren. "Please turn around."

Abby's heart pounds so hard in her chest she fears she might pass out. Against her better judgment, she slowly turns while holding her breath.

The stranger behind Lauren is wearing a ski mask and holding a gun.

Abby drops her phone as blood roars in her ears. Even though she's terrified, a thought occurs to her.

If I had social media, I could've uploaded that photo.

The police would know where to find my body.

A tear rolls down her face as she realizes she'll never see her parents again.

CHAPTER THIRTY-TWO

PRESENT DAY

Nate arrives at work at lunchtime. The office of Hope & Associates is almost empty. Richie Hope doesn't have any associates, unless you count the office manager and two investigators, but he likes to make it look like he's more successful than he is in the hope of attracting new clients.

Brody follows Nate inside and stops to shake off the rainwater that clings to his thick brown fur. The spray covers the oak reception desk and the antique rug on the floor, making the room smell of wet dog. Then he flops onto the rug for a nap. Nate smiles. He wishes his own life was half as chilled as Brody's.

Seated at the large reception desk, Richie greets them with a wide smile. White-haired and in his fifties, he tends to wear cheap gray suits with an off-white shirt and loud tie. "Good afternoon to my favorite shepsky."

Brody's tail comes to life, thudding the rug, but he doesn't get up.

"How come you're working out here?" asks Nate.

The lawyer motions his head backward to his office. "Justice stole my seat."

Nate looks over his shoulder. Through the glass-paneled wall that separates Richie's office from the reception area, he sees a black cat curled up on the seat behind the desk. Luckily, Justice and Brody get along.

Richie frowns. "What's wrong with Brody? He normally tries to steal my lunch right out from under me." A sandwich purchased from the deli down the street sits half-eaten before him. The lawyer's not one to make his own meals. He picks it up to take a bite.

Nate tells him what happened at the diner this morning and how Brody tried to help.

Richie's mouth drops open in shock. "That's terrible. Carla was such a lovely person. She always gave me extra onions on my burgers." Having lost his appetite, he drops his sandwich back onto its wrapper. "That must be why the deli was so busy today. Do we know who killed her?"

"Not yet." Nate sits on the leather couch opposite the reception desk and opens his laptop. "Anything you need me to do?"

Richie takes a deep breath. "Not unless you want to invest some of your hard-earned money in my law firm."

Nate's taken by surprise. "Things are that bad?"

The older man shrugs. "My clientele can't afford lawyers anymore. They'd rather serve time than get into debt defending themselves. At least they're fed and housed for free while inside."

The economy is bad right now; it has been for a long time, and small towns in the middle of nowhere seem to be the hardest hit, but Nate didn't realize just how bad things have gotten for Richie. "Could you try to find an equity partner?"

"I've been trying," says Richie as he pushes his glasses up his nose. "I've also considered working for someone else, but no one's hiring ancient relics like me. We haven't had anyone walk through those doors seeking representation in a long time, and truth be told, I'm bored. I need more excitement in my life." He smiles sadly. "You know, I always thought I'd die in court while in the middle of arguing a high-profile case. It seems I might be found dead at home instead, with half my face in my cat's belly."

"No," says Nate. "I'm sure Justice wouldn't do that. He loves you too much."

Richie scoffs. "I can tell you've never owned cats."

Wanting to make him feel better, Nate says, "You can help me with what I'm working on."

Richie gets up, intrigued. He pats Brody on his way to the couch and sits beside Nate. "What's the case?"

"A missing teenage boy. Brandon Dorsey was thirteen when he vanished five years ago." Nate explains the circumstances surrounding his disappearance.

Richie frowns. "Is he related to Robert Dorsey by any chance?"

Nate looks at him. "Robert's his father. Why?"

Wiping his fingers with a napkin, Richie says, "I represented Robert Dorsey's wife once. Must be a decade ago now." He makes a thinking face. "I can't remember without checking."

"Can you tell me why she needed representation?"

"Sure, seeing as she's no longer with us." The lawyer looks at Nate. "She claimed to be the victim of coercive control and emotional abuse. She wanted out of her marriage, but her husband wouldn't let her go without a fight. A *psychological* fight, that is."

Nate's stunned. Sure, Robert Dorsey is intense, but he spoke lovingly about his deceased wife. "Any claims of physical violence?"

Richie stands and walks to a large metal filing cabinet in his office. Nate watches through the glass. The lawyer finds the file he's looking for and returns. "Young Owen did a good job helping me go paperless, but we're only about eighty percent of the way there."

"You should hire another intern."

Richie sits. "If I thought I could pay them something, I would." He flips through the pages and reads the allegations made by Caroline Dorsey. "No claims of physical violence, but you and I both know that doesn't mean there was none."

Nate considers it. "What was your impression of her husband?"

"Put it this way," says Richie, "he looks like he wants to spit on me whenever we cross paths. I was based in Prospect Springs at the time Mrs. Dorsey approached me. She said she didn't want Robert to know she was seeking legal advice. Now that I'm here in Lost Creek, I tend to bump into him occasionally, and let me tell you, that man holds a grudge." He laughs as though it's funny. Richie has a strange sense of humor. He regularly receives death threats, and his last office was firebombed, which triggered the move south. None of it seems to bother him much. He thrives on the unexpected.

"Did Caroline go to the police with her allegations?" asks Nate.

"She decided not to in the end." Richie removes his glasses to rub them clean as he talks. "I seem to remember she was having health problems, and the stress was making it worse, so after three consultations, I never saw her again. I read about her death four or five years later. The article said she was survived by her husband and son." He takes a deep breath. "I didn't realize their son vanished. How long after her death was that?"

"A year. Brandon's girlfriend said he sometimes thought about harming himself, and there was some tension between father and son." Nate looks at Richie. "Do you think Robert's capable of harming his son?"

Richie slips his glasses back on and then stands. "I couldn't say either way." Given his job, he's careful about labeling someone a killer. "But if all other avenues have been explored, it's worth considering. I watched Chief Mendes on the news. She said a child's body had been found on the mountain. Could that be Brandon?"

Nate shakes his head. "Madison said the child is female."

"That's a shame. It's harder to convict without a body." Richie sits behind the reception desk again and takes a bite of his sandwich. Once he's swallowed it, he adds, "If I were you, I'd speak to the people around Robert Dorsey. Neighbors, co-workers and Brandon's teachers. Find out what they observed about his relationship with his son. And perhaps Madison could run a criminal background check for you."

Nate nods, but the detectives who investigated Brandon's disappearance would've already run a check. Robert must've been clean back then, but that doesn't mean he hasn't been charged with anything since his son's disappearance.

He stands. "Can Brody stay here for an hour or two?"

Richie smiles and pulls out the remaining slices of pastrami from his sandwich. Brody immediately sits up, ready to accept the food. "He sure can."

"Thanks." Nate heads back out into the rain.

CHAPTER THIRTY-THREE

After purchasing a poor-quality coffee at a busy McDonald's, Madison drives through the rain to get to Grave Mountain. She wants to speak with the bystanders to see if the parents of their unidentified teenager could be present. Hank's apartment complex is on the way, so she decides to stop by and see whether he's home yet. There's a good chance he's already heard about Carla's death by now, thanks to the news coverage, but she'd still like to check in on him as he isn't answering his phone, which bothers her.

After parking her vehicle, she rushes across the sidewalk to avoid the rain. She spots Hank's vehicle in the parking lot, thanks to Mrs. Pebbles, who's jumping up at the window and yapping loudly. The window is cracked open for air. Hank must be on his way out somewhere.

His front door is ajar this time. She knocks. "Hank? It's Detective Harper."

Something inside falls over with a bang. She leans in to listen and hears a male voice exclaim in annoyance.

Alarmed, she tries again. "Hank? Can I come in? It's about Carla."

After a short delay, the door opens wider and Hank appears. He's sweating and red in the face. His beige shirt isn't buttoned all the way up, suggesting he was interrupted while getting dressed. Perhaps by news of his fiancée's death. "What?" he says.

Madison frowns. "Everything okay?"

"No, everything is not okay," he says angrily. "My fiancée was killed."

"I know. I'm so sorry," she says. "I came by earlier, but you weren't home. Can I come in?"

He exhales heavily and looks behind him. "The place is a mess. I've been packing ready for the move into the diner. Turns out it was all for nothing."

"That's okay," she says. "I just want to talk." She's confused by his reaction. He doesn't seem upset about Carla's death, just angry. Maybe he's still in shock.

He steps aside. "Fine."

She walks past him into his living room. When she turns, she realizes he's trembling uncontrollably. Not wanting him to collapse, she says, "I think you should take a seat, Hank. You're clearly in shock."

Surprisingly, he does as he's told. He appears dazed, as though trying to come to terms with how drastically his life has changed in a heartbeat.

She considers fetching his dog to help calm him down, but her phone vibrates in her pocket. She pulls it out and sees Adams is trying to get a hold of her. She doesn't want to be rude to Hank, so she declines the call.

When Hank is seated, he says, "She must've been in so much pain." Finally, he breaks down. Tears spill down his face and he tries to wipe them away with his handkerchief. "This is the worst day of my life."

Madison's never seen this side of him. Gently, she says, "Can I get you some water?"

He stands. "I'll make coffee. I want to hear what you're going to do about catching the bastard who killed her." He gestures to the couch. "Take a seat. I'll just be a minute."

She watches him leave the room on shaky legs before sitting in the worn armchair, her back to the kitchen. She listens to the sound of running water. Hank might not be the friendliest person she's ever met, but it's clear he's suffering.

She looks round the room. Almost everything is packed away. The walls have light patches where paintings once hung. The wallpaper is tinged with yellow, making her wonder whether he's a smoker. It doesn't smell of nicotine in here. The carpet is threadbare in front of the couch where guests have rested their feet over the years. It looks as though Hank hasn't decorated in a long time. In comparison, the apartment above the diner is modern and well kept. Had it worked out, the move would've been a step up for him.

Her phone vibrates in her hand, making her jump. It's a text from Adams. She breaks out in a cold sweat when she reads what it says.

Hank Goodman killed Carla.

It's followed by a second.

The door cam footage shows him fleeing the diner covered in blood.

"No," she whispers, unable to believe it.

She hears a drawer opening in the kitchen. Hank wouldn't have invited her in if he thought she was coming to arrest him, surely? Maybe he stumbled across Carla's body and fled the scene in panic. That would make more sense. But if that's the case, why not call the police? Why not seek Vince out to ask for help? Could shock have stopped him from acting appropriately?

Maybe.

Not daring to move, her eyes scan the room for signs of blood from his clothes. She spots a small brownish stain on the beige rug by the coffee table. It could be blood, or it could be spilled coffee.

Her heart racing, she speedily replies to Adams.

I'm in his living room. He's here. Send backup.

She slips the phone away and stands. Before she can turn around, though, she senses him behind her. She reaches for her weapon.

A knife suddenly appears in front of her face, inching closer to her neck. Hank pulls her backward by her hair and brings the knife to her throat.

"No!" she yells. She grabs his arm and spins around to face him, twisting it as she does so. "Drop it, now!"

His eyes are filled with desperation. He intends to get away at whatever cost. As they continue to struggle, he takes her by surprise and headbutts her, his forehead making contact with her nose. The pain is excruciating. Everything goes white. While she's seeing stars, Hank twists out of her grip and flees the living room through the kitchen, dropping the knife as he runs.

Stunned, Madison raises her weapon. "Stop or I'll shoot!" She feels warm blood leaking from her nose. Her head has already started throbbing.

Hank disappears into the backyard. She follows him to the exit, and after a final warning, when she thinks she has a clear shot, she fires her weapon. He's fast for his age. He dodges the bullet by turning left and disappearing behind another apartment complex. Madison tries to chase him, but the effort makes her dizzy. Her head feels heavy as she leans forward.

Everything suddenly turns black as she hits the ground.

CHAPTER THIRTY-FOUR

Madison rests in the back of an ambulance while EMT Jake Rubio flashes a small light in each of her eyes. He's just pulled a bandage off her nose that was protecting her from getting covered in blood. Thankfully, the bleeding appears to have stopped.

Adams found her trying to sit up in Hank's backyard after having raced here when he saw her text. He's seated opposite her now, holding onto Mrs. Pebbles and making Madison feel claustrophobic in this small space. The dog has fallen asleep in his arms. She looks tiny and content. Animals seem to like him.

"Nothing's fractured," says Jake as he pockets the flashlight. "But you'll have bruising under your eyes for weeks, and your nose will remain swollen for a few days. If you experience any signs of a concussion, get someone to take you to the hospital. Do you need me to run through the symptoms again?"

Madison attempts to shake her head, but it's throbbing too bad. "Can I get some painkillers?"

"Sure." He rummages through a drawer and hands her two pink pills. "You can drive on these, but I wouldn't recommend it. They make some people drowsy."

She swallows them, knowing she'll be of no use to the team for the rest of the day. She can't work with this headache. "Thanks."

Jake's eyeing her suspiciously, clearly worried about a concussion. Eventually, he says, "Remain seated. I want to keep an eye on you for ten more minutes before I let you go. Just to be sure." He jumps out of the ambulance and hovers nearby while he completes the paperwork for her assessment.

Madison wonders how much this is going to cost her and whether she should've just asked Adams to buy her some painkillers from the nearby drugstore instead. "We need to run a background check on Hank."

"Already done," says Adams. "Aside from some traffic violations and parking tickets, he's clean."

Before she can reply, Vince Rader's pickup truck skids to a halt behind the ambulance. He hurries past Jake to the open doors. "Is it true? Hank killed Carla?"

Adams says, "Yeah. He tried to kill Harper too."

The blood drains from Vince's face. "How did I not see it? With everything I know about killers, how did I not see what he was capable of?"

Madison feels for him. "Nate told me you thought he made a good suspect for the Snow Storm Killer last year," she says.

Jake glances over at them at the mention of the SSK. His eyes lock onto Madison's, and she offers a sympathetic smile. He was more affected by that case than most residents. He looks away, not wanting to relive that terrible time.

"Which means you noticed there was something odd about him," she adds.

"Then I should have acted on it," says Vince. "Instead, I did what everyone else in this damn town does: I turned a blind eye and convinced myself he wasn't a violent asshole." He lowers his eyes.

"He fooled everyone, Mr. Rader," says Adams. "That's not

on you. Besides, we'll have him in custody within hours. He's an unfit man on the run with the entire police department searching for him."

"Chief Mendes has notified the media," says Madison. "He won't get far once his face is all over the news." There's no denying that Hank is dangerous, but Madison's confused by his motive. "Hank and Carla were buying the diner together and getting married. Why would he kill her?"

"Why would a confirmed bachelor suddenly want to marry?" says Vince.

Adams strokes the dog. "Assholes like him don't need a reason to hurt people."

Vince falls silent for a second as he considers everything that's happened. When he looks up, he asks, "Could he be responsible for the other murders? The ones on the mountain."

Madison looks at Adams. "We're not sure. I guess it's a possibility."

A tall blonde in heels and a blue pantsuit approaches them. Madison recognizes her as a reporter, but can't remember which news site or TV channel she works for. She's without her camera operator.

"Hi, Detectives," she says. "Could you give me a clue as to what happened here?"

"Sure." Detective Adams gently places the sleepy dog on the gurney before jumping out of the ambulance. "We have a killer at large. Fifty-seven-year-old Hank Goodman of this address." He nods over his shoulder. "Officers are currently searching his apartment. He should be considered armed and dangerous."

The reporter's eyes flicker to Madison's injuries before returning to Adams. "Is he the Grave Mountain Stalker?" she asks.

Adams rests his hands on his hips. "No. The so-called Grave Mountain Stalker is still at large, but he won't be for long.

We're confident we'll have him locked up, side by side with Hank Goodman, in a matter of days. Scumbags like him always get caught eventually because they're dumb. They make mistakes, or they have family members who secretly loathe them and eventually turn them in. Killers are hard to love." He smiles. "You can quote me on that."

Madison closes her eyes briefly. He shouldn't make promises they can't keep, and he shouldn't taunt the killer. It'll just end badly. "Don't quote him," she says. "We don't know whether we're dealing with a serial killer yet."

The reporter ignores her and offers Adams a wide smile. "Thanks, Detective. I appreciate your help." He watches as she walks away.

Madison's headache isn't going anywhere, and she's exhausted. "Vince? Would you give me a ride home? I need to lie down until the pain meds kick in."

"Sure," says Vince. He helps her out of the ambulance.

"You can leave everything to me," says Adams. "I'll update the chief and the rest of the team." He looks excited to finally take the lead in an investigation. "And I'll take the dog to the pound."

Madison glances at the tiny creature. "No, don't do that." Against her better judgment, she says, "Give her to me. I'll take care of her for now."

Adams ducks into the ambulance and emerges with the dog. Mrs. Pebbles wakes and bares her teeth.

Madison hesitates to take her off of Adams. "It's okay, sweetie. We're going to cuddle up in bed for a nap. Come on." She tentatively cradles the dog in her arms.

Unimpressed, Vince stares at the dog. "I think Hank trained her to hate everyone. I'd take Brody over a chihuahua any day."

Madison feels so ill she doesn't even care about the dog's behavior. She just wants to get home. "Adams, I'll call you later for an update. Oh, and both of you do me a favor. Don't tell Nate I'm injured. I don't want to worry him."

They nod.

"Come on," says Vince. He helps her into his car, where Mrs. Pebbles growls at her all the way home.

CHAPTER THIRTY-FIVE

Nate gets soaked as he goes door-to-door in the street Brandon Dorsey vanished from. He skips Erin Martin's house, since her parents still live there and they can't tell him any more about that day than Erin has already told him. They were at work when she waved goodbye to Brandon.

So far, every home he's approached has either been empty or the residents didn't live here five years ago. Next is a detached home five doors down and on the opposite side of the street to Erin's property. The yard is well maintained and tidier than others on the street.

He looks up when the door opens. An elderly man approaching eighty slips a pair of glasses on. "What are you selling?" he asks.

Nate smiles. "Nothing, sir. I'm a private investigator looking into the disappearance of a teenage boy. He was last seen leaving your neighbor's place five years ago." He points to Erin's house before looking back at the man. "Do you remember that?"

"Of course I do," he says. "The cops were all over the street for days. They wanted to search my house. I didn't want them in here, but Violet let them in."

"Do you mind talking to me about it?" asks Nate, hoping to be invited out of the cold.

The man slips a jacket on and joins him on the porch instead. They stand at the railing, looking out at the street. "What do you want to know?"

A white sedan honks as it passes, tires sloshing in the rain. The older man waves at the driver. "That's Susan heading off to work. She works at the grocery store and leaves her dog alone all afternoon, poor thing. But someone has to earn the money. Her husband has failing kidneys. He's in a hospice right now. Poor son of a bitch is only fifty-two." He takes a deep breath. "I always wonder why some go young and I'm left to suffer through to old age."

Nate has struck gold with this one. When someone knows all about their neighbors, it's a good bet they saw who was around during and after a crime. He holds out his hand. "Nate Monroe. I'm working for Brandon Dorsey's father, Robert."

"Gordon Humphrey." He shakes Nate's hand. "My wife, Violet, is no longer with us. Her Alzheimer's was progressing by the time the kid vanished. It's probably why the cops didn't pay her much attention."

Nate frowns. "Did she witness something?"

Gordon turns and points to a downstairs window. "Violet sat propped up in the armchair by that window every day during her final two years on this planet. She saw everyone and everything."

Nate's heart rate speeds up a little. "What did she see on the day Brandon disappeared?"

Gordon shrugs. "Well, now, that's the problem. She saw something alright. But it was all locked away inside of her on account of her condition."

Nate's shoulders slump. "She wasn't able to tell you anything?"

"Oh sure, she said stuff." The elderly man zips his jacket

against the chill. "But Detective Douglas and I didn't know what she meant. He even recorded her ramblings on the subject. There was one phrase she kept repeating in the days that followed."

Nate waits for Gordon to tell him what it was, but he's looking down the street, distracted by someone getting into their car. "There he goes, off to cheat on his husband. I knew they wouldn't last. The age gap is too big." He checks his watch and seems amused. "Everything plays out like clockwork in this street."

"What was the phrase?" asks Nate.

Gordon looks at him. "'He's in the car.'"

Nate shudders. It sounds like a possible abduction. Unless Brandon had arranged for someone to collect him from Erin's place after school. Maybe he'd organized a ride out of town to get away from his dad. "How confident are you that she was referring to Brandon Dorsey and not just a neighbor?"

"Pretty confident, because she had many lucid moments that month. But she couldn't answer follow-up questions like: What car? What color was it? Did he get in willingly? Did you recognize the driver?"

That's disappointing, but if Violet witnessed Brandon getting into a car, there's a good chance someone else on the street did too. Although, if his earlier attempts are anything to go by, it could be hard to track down the people who lived around here back then.

"Do you know which direction the car went in? I'm wondering if the cops pulled CCTV footage from nearby businesses and gas stations."

"She couldn't say," says Gordon. "But I remember that day because I was bringing her a cup of herbal tea and she was standing at the window looking right, as if following something with her eyes. It was unusual because she rarely stood up by herself at that stage of her illness. She'd made a clear attempt to watch whatever was happening." He chuckles to himself. "She always was a nosy so-and-so, my Violet."

Robert told Nate that Brandon had headed left from Erin's property, which, from Violet's position, would be right. It's good to confirm the direction he was going, at least. "Did you ask her what she was looking at?"

Gordon nods. "That's when she first said, 'He's in the car.'"

Nate considers why she found that interesting. She would've seen plenty of her neighbors and their friends coming and going over the years. The only reason he can think of is that it wasn't part of Brandon's regular routine. Maybe she was used to seeing him walking home, not being offered a ride. Perhaps she felt he was in danger. "I don't suppose the detective gave you a copy of the recording he made with your wife?"

Gordon looks at him. "I insisted on it. I've never trusted law enforcement, Mr. Monroe, so I didn't want them claiming Violet said something she didn't. That Detective Douglas guy seemed like a real hard-ass when I first met him. Although I have to admit, he grew on me the more I saw of him. I was sad to hear he was murdered. Seems to me it's dangerous to be a cop these days."

"Wasn't it always?" says Nate.

"Maybe. But I wouldn't let any of my family join law enforcement. Not in these times we're living in."

Nate's thoughts turn to Madison and how, if there really is a serial killer loose in town, she's at higher risk of danger than anyone else. "Think I could get a copy of the recording?"

Gordon considers it for a second before turning and entering the house. He's back in less than a minute. "Here." He hands Nate a flash drive.

"Thanks. I appreciate it." Nate slips it into his pocket and looks up and down the street, trying to figure out what happened to Brandon that day.

Gordon eyes him with an amused expression. "You've got

the same look on your face as the detective had at the time. You're one of us now, Monroe. This case will baffle you until the day you die unless you find answers. I'd love to know what happened to the kid. I feel like Violet and I have a vested interest. Know what I mean?"

Nate nods. Missing person cases have a way of getting under your skin, whether you're officially part of the investigation or not. He sighs. He should knock on more doors. There's got to be someone else who witnessed what Violet saw.

CHAPTER THIRTY-SIX

Madison wakes to the sound of banging. She has a crick in her neck from sleeping in the same position for too long. When she opens her eyes, the room is pitch black. Her head feels heavy and fuzzy for a few seconds until she sees the clock on her nightstand and realizes she's in her bedroom. It's midnight. She's shocked to find she slept through the entire afternoon and evening and didn't make it back to work. It must've been the painkillers.

She tentatively touches her nose and winces with pain. It doesn't feel like her nose. It's swollen and numb.

Something moves under her covers, making her jump in surprise. "What the hell?"

She lifts the blankets and sees Hank's chihuahua under there, yawning. Madison laughs with relief. "Hey, cutie. Did I wake you?"

Mrs. Pebbles growls softly before closing her eyes and ignoring her.

Unexpected footsteps outside Madison's room make her sit up so fast she goes dizzy. Startled, the dog dives deeper under the covers. When the room stops swaying, Madison reaches for the lock box under her bed. In the darkness, she unlocks it and pulls out her service weapon, listening for the intruder's location. She stops when she hears whispering voices.

Silently throwing back her covers, she climbs out of bed and pads to the closed door. The intruders are heading downstairs. Her heart is in her mouth as she tears the door open, weapon out straight.

No one's there.

She goes to the top of the stairs and peers down. Two shadowy figures hover near the front door. She flips the switch that lights up the downstairs. "Stop! Or I'll..." She frowns.

They turn to look up at her, shock on their faces. They're not as shocked as Madison is when she realizes it's Detective Adams and Officer Kent.

Kent is in the middle of slipping a T-shirt over her head. She pulls it down, looks away and quickly steps into her sneakers. "Sorry, Detective Harper," she says. "I didn't realize this was your house. I didn't know you two..."

Madison lowers her weapon. "Trust me, we're not." She sighs. "Adams. What the hell is this?" She tries not to be judgmental, but the guy's only just split with his wife. Besides, Officer Kent is fourteen years younger than him. He could lose his job if this ends badly, or if the rookie accuses him of abusing his position.

Adams opens the door for Kent to exit. They don't say goodbye to each other or kiss. It was a one-night stand. And not even a whole night.

Madison slowly walks downstairs. She smells alcohol on him as she passes. Maybe it was a drunken mistake. She heads to the kitchen and switches the light on. "You're not going to make sure she gets home safe?"

He follows her. "Madison, she's a cop. She can take care of herself."

Madison scoffs. "Such a gentleman." She switches the

coffee machine on and leans against the counter, watching Adams take a seat at the dining table. He's dressed in a blue T-shirt and dark jeans. "Wanna talk about it?" she asks.

"I didn't sleep with her. I came to my senses before it got that far." He runs a hand through his messy black hair. "I blame Steve."

She raises her eyebrows. "*Steve?* What did he do?"

"He suggested drinks after work. Said it was about time we got to know each other properly."

Madison smiles. She told Steve to cut him some slack, so it was nice of him to take Adams out. "Did he get as drunk as you?"

"I'm not drunk. I only had two beers and a shot of something. And Lena called Steve home for dinner, so he left after one beer. I stayed behind with Kent and her friends." He sounds regretful. Tomorrow morning will be awkward for him at work.

"Aren't you a little old to try to keep up with the rookies?" She selects some mugs and pours coffee.

He scoffs. "That girl sure can drink." He takes a mug from her. After a pause, he gives her a sheepish look. "You might as well know now that I've been screwed over by a reporter."

She's confused by the change of subject. "What do you mean?"

"The reporter who approached us at the ambulance earlier quoted me as saying serial killers are hard to love and even their families loathe them." He lowers his eyes. "It's getting picked up by other media channels and becoming a thing."

Madison snorts. "Wow. When you mess up, you like to go all in, don't you?" She joins him at the table. "It'll be forgotten in a few days. Hopefully. How did Chief Mendes take it?"

"She's pissed. Thinks I've put us all in danger."

She's probably right, but Madison doesn't want to make him

feel even worse, so she changes the subject. "Are you going to tell Selena about bringing Officer Kent back here?"

His face darkens. "Selena can kiss my ass."

Taken aback, Madison says, "Why? What's happened?"

He sighs. "I got into it with my daughter earlier over something stupid."

"Which one, Summer?"

"Right. And she took great pleasure in telling me that *Mommy's* been talking to Uncle Sean on the phone behind my back."

Madison leans back in her seat. "Jeez, Marcus. That sucks." She feels for him. It sounds like his wife is still seeing his brother. His bringing a woman home makes more sense now. It was still a stupid idea, but he was hurt. She realizes this separation could get messy.

"I guess we're heading for divorce."

She sips her coffee. "Just focus on your girls. Don't let things get hostile. If she finds out you brought a woman back here tonight, she might try to block shared custody."

Adams looks alarmed. His eyes go watery. "You think she'd stop me from seeing my kids?"

Madison's seen worse happen during divorces. "Listen, I don't know your wife, but I know that when people are jealous or hurt, they make horrible decisions to hurt the person they used to love, and the kids get used as pawns. Just try to keep things amicable. Don't tell her you know about her contact with your brother, and don't sleep with anyone until you're divorced. Keep things simple. Once the split is figured out, you can move on. In fact, I'd recommend you hire an attorney as soon as possible if you really think you're heading for divorce. I know a good one." She thinks about Richie Hope and wonders whether he's experienced in divorce law.

Adams runs a hand over his face. "I never thought I'd be in this position. And all because of my own damn brother."

Madison thinks there's probably more to it than that. His wife wouldn't have strayed if she was in a happy marriage. "Is Hank in custody yet?"

"No. He's still on the run."

Alarmed, she says, "There haven't been any more murders though, right?"

"Not yet."

She's hit with a wave of exhaustion. Her eyelids grow heavy. "Drink your coffee, then try to get some sleep. You can update me over breakfast on what I missed at work."

He nods. Madison stands before rinsing her cup clean and heading upstairs. As she slips into bed, her feet touch the dog, who starts growling again. She laughs. "Hey! It's *my* bed!" She lies down. "What kind of name is Mrs. Pebbles anyway?"

The growling stops, and within seconds, the dog repositions herself to lean against Madison's legs for warmth. It's strangely comforting, like when Bandit sometimes curls up next to her face on her pillow. She considers checking her phone to see if anyone tried contacting her while she was asleep, but she figures it's too late to respond now anyway.

She turns the light out and gets comfortable under her thick comforter, listening to Adams head into the spare room and close the door. Her eyes grow heavy as she hears his phone ring with a notification. She wonders if that's Officer Kent asking whether she's in trouble for coming here.

Adams exclaims. Something falls over in his room with a loud bang.

His door opens. "I'm heading out," he yells. "There's something I forgot to do." His voice is strained. "See you in the morning."

She sits up, confused. "Work-related?"

"No. Just personal. Don't worry about it." He runs downstairs.

Madison's intrigued. When he opens the front door and

slams it shut after himself, she mumbles, "Where on earth is he going at this time?" Despite being on the verge of sleep, she gets out of bed and approaches the window. She watches as he slips into his car and heads east.

She wants to know what's happened. It must be family-related or he'd want her to go with him. She considers leaving him to it and going back to bed, but something about the way he sped out of here fills her with dread. She quickly switches her pajamas for a pair of jeans and a sweater, slips her phone in her pocket and then takes a second to decide whether to take her service weapon. She pulls the holster on and inserts the gun. Better prepared than not.

Downstairs, she pulls on some boots and her coat. Outside, the night sky is clear, the earlier rain clouds having moved on. She backs out of her driveway. The roads are quiet, and she can't see Adams's vehicle, so she heads toward his home address.

As she drives, it occurs to Madison that he might be mad at her for following him, so she'll stay back and just make sure he's gone to his house before she heads home. After a few minutes, she catches up with him. A Chevy pulls out of a side road, getting between them as Adams slows at a red light.

If he's going home, he'll head straight at the intersection.

The lights turn green. Adams makes a right turn.

Madison frowns. "Where's he going?"

She loses sight of his vehicle more than once in a bid to remain unseen. She's considering calling dispatch to see if they've sent him out to a crime scene, but he would've told her if that were the case. She's sure of it.

When she spots him again, she realizes he's heading for the parking lot near the Juniper Trail.

A ball of dread swells in her chest. "Why the hell is he going there?"

CHAPTER THIRTY-SEVEN

Once Adams is out of his car and on the trail, Madison pulls over, keeping her vehicle hidden from view. She has a bad feeling about whatever's happening. If another victim has been discovered, he should've told her. Maybe he didn't want her to feel she had to attend the scene if she was feeling unwell, but officers would be present if that were the case. Instead, the entire area is shrouded in darkness, and no one is here but them.

Before getting out of the car, she checks her phone. She has messages from Nate asking if she's okay because he heard she'd had some kind of altercation with Hank. She figures she should call him so he knows where she is in case something goes wrong.

Even though it's 1 a.m., he answers quickly. "Hey, are you okay?" He sounds concerned and groggy at the same time. "I heard Hank was the one who killed Carla and that you tried to apprehend him. Vince told me you'd call me when you got a second."

"I'm fine, honestly," she says quietly. "I'll explain everything tomorrow."

"Why are you whispering?"

"Because Adams just got a text message, bolted out of my

house after being super shady about it, and now he's taking a hike all alone on Grave Mountain. I followed him. He's come to the Juniper Trail and I have no idea why. We're the only ones out here."

"You *followed* him?"

"Yeah. Something seemed off. I'm going to follow him up the trail to see what he's doing."

"No, Madison. Call for backup."

"If he wanted backup, he would've called dispatch himself," she says. "Maybe he's here to retrieve something he left at one of the crime scenes and it's all perfectly innocent. You know me; I have an overactive imagination. I'm only calling you to let someone know where I am, just in case."

"I'm coming to meet you," says Nate. "I'll bring Brody."

She knows there's no point arguing, and it would be the safest thing to do. He doesn't live far away. She just has to hope Adams isn't mad when he finds out they both followed him here. "Okay. But you need to be in stealth mode in case something's going down. I don't want Brody blowing my cover if Adams is on to something."

"Sure," he says. "I'd tell you to wait until I get there, but you wouldn't listen, right?"

"Depends," she says. "Do you have a weapon to protect me?" She can't resist the jibe.

"Madison—"

She cuts him off with a laugh. "Relax, I'm joking. Besides, all I'm doing is going for a midnight hike. What could possibly go wrong?" She doesn't wait for his response. "I'm setting off. See you soon."

"Be careful."

She smiles as she switches her phone to silent and dims the backlight. She doesn't want it ringing in her pocket or lighting up through her clothes in case she does find herself hiding from someone.

Eight minutes have passed since Adams disappeared into the darkness. Madison gets out of her vehicle and crosses the empty road. Within a few seconds, she's on the trail. She glances up at the sky. The stars are out. A chill runs through her at the thought of tomorrow's frost.

After a few minutes, she stops to listen for footsteps or labored breathing. It's creepy enough out here in the daytime, but nighttime is in a league of its own. Hidden creatures rustle in the bushes around her, and her peripheral vision captures movement in all directions. It's like the mountain is alive and watching her. She's suddenly glad Nate's on his way.

Five minutes into her hike, she thinks she hears something to her left. She stops to listen. This isn't anywhere near their four crime scenes.

She hears it again. It's the sound of whimpering.

A chill runs down her spine, and she instinctively moves off the path into the vegetation, using a large tree trunk for cover. She doesn't know what she heard, but she quickly fishes her phone out of her pocket and calls dispatch, turning the incoming volume down low.

When Dina, the night shift dispatcher, picks up, Madison whispers, "It's Madison. I'm on the Juniper Trail. Send backup immediately, but no lights or sirens."

Unfazed, Dina replies, "Doing it now, Detective. Is anyone else present?"

"Detective Adams, but I don't know why he came here. I followed him. And Nate Monroe's on his way with Brody."

She hears another whimper, louder this time, followed by, "Daddy, no!"

"Oh my God." Madison's blood runs cold. "I think Adams's daughters are in danger."

"Understood. Are you armed?"

"Yes. I'm going to hang up to get a better view of what's happening."

"Roger that. Someone will be with you shortly."

Madison ends the call and shoots a quick text to Nate.

Wait in the parking lot. Backup's been dispatched. Do NOT follow me.

She pockets her phone and tries to take a deep breath, but her lungs constrict with fear. Several terrible thoughts run through her head when considering the little girl's words. Has Adams finally lost it? Is he planning to harm his daughters to get back at his wife for cheating on him?

She shakes the thoughts away. No. He received a text. Someone's lured him out here. She remembers the quote he gave to the reporter about serial killers being loathed by their families. Her heart sinks. "Shit." He's angered their killer.

She slowly pushes forward, trying to remain silent, but there are too many twigs and brittle leaves on the ground. Every snap and crunch sounds louder than it would in the daytime.

"What am I supposed to do, honey?" Adams sounds broken. Madison fears her first impression is correct. He's going to harm his daughter.

She's about to run in the direction of his voice when she sees both Summer and Lizzie standing still, facing her direction. They're crying. Lizzie has a red dot aimed at the middle of her forehead. Madison's heart stops.

They're targets.

Adams slowly draws his service weapon.

She gasps. *What the hell is he planning to do?*

She can't tell who's responsible for the red dot. She looks behind her and follows the laser to a higher location on the trail.

Pulling her weapon, she yells, "Adams, no!" She spins around. "Get down, all of you!" She fires blindly in the direction of the armed assailant. The blasts startle the wildlife. Trees and bushes come to life as creatures scarper to safety and her gunshots echo through the mountain.

After three shots, the red laser vanishes, but it's unclear whether she hit the assailant. It's too dark.

She hears movement above her in the distance.

He's on the move.

She turns to look at the girls. Adams clutches one in each hand as he races toward her, dragging them behind him in his panic. Madison leads them all away from the killer's direction, zigzagging through the trees to find a spot capable of protecting them from gunshots. Once they reach a dense area of trees, she stops and kneels down, telling the girls to do the same.

"Try to remain silent," she says, catching her breath. "Back-up's coming."

Both girls look like they've seen a ghost.

"You're going to be okay," she says. "I think I got him." That's not true, but she doesn't want them giving away their location by panicking.

Dazed, Summer nods. Lizzie tears up but tries to cry silently.

Madison looks at Adams in disbelief. "What were you *thinking?*" she hisses. She can't believe he came here alone to face a madman.

He hands her a screwed-up piece of paper. "When I arrived, Summer told me to stay back, then hurled this at my feet." He swallows hard. "I had to choose one of them or..." His voice cracks.

She reads the typed message.

Kill one immediately, or I'll kill them both.

Her eyes widen in horror. She leans in so the girls can't hear her. "You were going to shoot one of them?" she hisses.

He looks grief-stricken. "He had a weapon trained on

Lizzie's head. It would've taken him a second to kill them both. I... I couldn't lose *both* of them."

Madison doesn't believe he would've gone through with it. She can't believe that. Maybe he pulled his weapon to fire at the assailant. Or perhaps he would've shot himself so he didn't have to make a terrible decision that would haunt him for the rest of his life.

Her mouth goes dry as she realizes he had no choice.

She rests a hand on his back and feels his body trembling violently beneath it. He's in shock. "How did you know to come here?" she whispers.

He looks at her. "I got a text from an unknown number. It said my girls were up here and they needed help. If I wanted to find them alive, I had to come alone." He suddenly hugs both of his daughters to him.

Madison spins around at a sound behind them. The snap of a twig to her left startles her. Someone's running toward them. She raises her weapon and prepares to fire.

The footsteps advance. Madison hears panting, and Brody bounds up to her, tail wagging hard. It should make her feel better, but it means Nate's close behind and vulnerable to attack.

She stands and looks down at Adams. "Stay here. I'll be back."

He nods.

Brody runs away from her, and she knows to follow him. Heading closer to the path, she waits behind a tree for the sound of approaching footsteps. She hears voices first. Male and female. Then Nate appears. He's with Officer Shelley Vickers, who has her service weapon drawn. Madison exhales in relief.

She waves them over when they spot her. Keeping her voice low, she gives Shelley the short version of what happened. Shelley's expression changes to alarm. "What direction was he aiming from?"

Madison points. "Up there. I fired three shots, but I don't know if they found the target. Is anyone else here yet?"

"Sanchez was behind me," says Shelley. "We'll block the roads and wait for more officers to arrive." As she walks away, she gets on her radio to notify dispatch that they have an armed suspect on the run.

Madison looks at Nate. "Let's get Adams and his girls out of here. They're hiding back there."

Nate leans in to hug her. "Thank God you're okay." When he pulls back, he looks closer at her nose. "Is that bruising?"

She scoffs as she remembers how bad she looks. "Yeah. Wait until daylight. You might want to rethink our relationship."

He pulls her to him again and strokes the back of her head. She can't stop herself from trembling. "Adams was going to kill one of his daughters."

"*What?*" He pulls away, stunned.

Her eyes well up. "The perp gave him a choice, and Adams told me he was about to pick one to save the other. He pulled his weapon. Can you believe that?"

He shakes his head in disbelief. "No one can ever know. You can say he pulled his weapon to shoot the assailant instead, okay? Because you don't know for sure that he would've gone through with it."

She nods, trying not to think about what would've happened if she hadn't followed Adams here tonight.

CHAPTER THIRTY-EIGHT

After just a few hours' sleep, Madison and Nate stop by the diner together in the morning. Nate, Brody and Bandit stayed at her place last night, which meant the former K9 and Owen's cat met Mrs. Pebbles. It didn't go well. The chihuahua scared Brody so badly that he wouldn't sleep in Madison's bedroom. Instead, he took the couch while Mrs. Pebbles curled up in Nate's armpit. Bandit slept in Owen's room. He tried to get close to the small dog, but she wasn't having any of it.

Madison has no idea what to do with her, so for now, she has the run of the house while Madison's at work. The cat spends most of his day outdoors, so there shouldn't be any drama while she's gone, but she needs to find a new home for Hank's dog.

Adams slept at his own place as he didn't want to leave his daughters' side. Selena turned up at the mountain, frantic about where her girls had gone, and Madison was impressed by the restraint Adams showed his wife. He didn't blame her for letting their daughters out of her sight long enough for them to be abducted.

Madison doesn't yet know how the assailant managed to

abduct Lizzie and Summer. All she knows is that the perp hasn't been caught overnight. He managed to get away before the roadblock was put in place, which isn't surprising since there are so many entry points for the trails. The search of the mountain has intensified as they look for more bodies, as well as clues to the perpetrator's identity. They need to catch him before he strikes again.

She zips up her coat and stuffs her hands in her pockets while she waits for Nate to exit his vehicle. Brody jumps out first and runs over to the woods to relieve himself. It's a bright, frosty morning, but she's consumed with a simmering dread. If the killer is sick enough to go after Adams's young kids, he could go after anyone.

Nate follows her into the diner, where Vince is leaning against the counter looking thoughtful. It isn't busy yet, as it's not even seven, and with it being closed yesterday, the regulars might assume it'll be closed again today.

The welcome aroma of coffee makes Madison realize how tired she is. She walks to the counter. "Morning, Vince. How are you?"

He winces when he sees how bad the bruising has gotten around her nose and under her eyes. "Better than you from the looks of things." He nods at Nate before asking, "Is Hank in custody yet?"

Madison shakes her head. "Today, hopefully." She checks over her shoulder before quietly adding, "Did you hear about what happened overnight?"

"I heard on the news that Detective Adams was ambushed on the mountain. I can't imagine what he was doing up there alone at that time of night." He narrows his eyes. "He's not the Grave Mountain Stalker, is he?"

Madison can't tell whether he's joking, but if he's had that thought, it's likely others have too. She just has to hope the press doesn't go down that road.

"After discussing it overnight, we think it might've been Hank who ambushed Adams," says Nate. "He could've been responsible for some of the victims on the mountain too."

In some ways, Hank fits the profile of a serial killer, and the fact that Carla was killed suggests he was trying to distract them from their investigation. It's not a perfect theory, since he planned to buy this place with Carla, but until they can question him, it seems more likely than Stuart Carpenter being involved in the mountain murders.

Madison looks at the missing person posters on the wall behind Nate's back and spots one for Brandon Dorsey. Nate told her what he'd discovered about Robert Dorsey's wife, and how Brandon might've gotten into a car with someone right before he vanished. The fact that Brandon vanished five years ago, like Tasha Harris and Becky Draper, could mean something. She intends to look into Robert and read the investigation notes from his son's case file.

Vince shakes his head sadly. "Carla didn't stand a chance. Maybe if I hadn't agreed to sell this place to them, she wouldn't have stayed with the asshole."

Madison rests her hand on his. "Don't do that, Vince. If you ask me, she was happier than ever in the days leading up to her death. None of us could've known Hank would kill her if she didn't even suspect it herself."

He straightens. "Coffees to go?"

Madison nods, but Nate says, "Actually, I'm going to stay for breakfast." He gives Madison a look. He probably wants to chat with Vince some more.

Vince pours Madison a coffee to go as she gently kisses Nate goodbye, trying not to hit her sore nose on his. "I'll call you later."

"Sure."

She leaves the diner bracing herself for another day of surprises.

. . .

The station is busy when she arrives, giving her the impression that something's happened. Her heart pounds a little harder as she remembers she missed a call on the drive over here. She checks her phone and finds it was from Steve. She heads straight for his desk.

He's talking to Chief Mendes. It takes a second for them to notice her arrival.

"Morning," she says as they turn. "What's going on?"

Steve takes a deep breath. "We've found Hank Goodman."

Relieved, she glances at the interview room. The door is open. It looks empty inside. "Is he in custody?"

Steve glances at Mendes before responding. "No. He's on his way to the morgue. He's dead, Madison."

"*What?*" She swallows. Whenever a suspect is found dead, the first thought that goes through all their minds is suicide. "Did he kill himself?"

"No," says Mendes. "He called dispatch after suffering a medical emergency. Officer Sanchez was first on the scene, and he believes Goodman either had a cardiac arrest or died from exposure. It looks as though he was hiding in the woods overnight."

Madison's shocked. She tries to feel bad for him, but a vivid flashback to Carla's brutally wounded body makes it impossible. When he fled his apartment yesterday, he wasn't wearing a coat. It was bitterly cold last night. "No justice for Carla's family then."

Steve crosses his arms. "Actually, Hank might not have been her killer."

She scoffs. "Come on! He tried to kill *me*, remember?"

He nods. "I know, but listen to his call." He takes a seat and selects an audio file on his computer. When he hits play, they hear Dina asking the caller how she can help.

"This is Hank Goodman. You record these calls, right?" His voice is strained.

"Sir, what is your location?" says Dina.

"Shut up, would you? You record these calls, right?"

"That's correct. Do you need medical assistance?"

"I didn't kill Carla." He struggles to get the words out in between shallow breaths.

"Sir, you sound unwell. Please confirm your location, then we can talk."

"You have to listen to me!" he barks. "I can't breathe properly. My chest is tight and I don't have much time. I arrived at the diner before Carla and I heard a noise out back." He takes a sharp intake of breath, as if he's in pain. It's unnerving to listen to someone in their final moments.

"Just give her your damn location, Hank," mutters Madison. Even though she knows he didn't make it, she wants to yell at him to give his location. He could've been saved. He could've stood trial.

"It was a guy in a ski mask." His voice gets weaker as his breaths become shallower. "I loved her. Don't let me go down in history as a killer. You got that?"

"Yes, sir. Every word," says Dina, cool as a cucumber. "Now, please give me your location so I can send an ambulance."

"I'm in the White Woods, near the creek." He pauses for the longest time before adding, "I loved her. We were going to grow old together." The call ends.

Unsure what to think, Madison looks at Steve. "But we know he killed her. He was covered in blood on the door cam footage, and he fled the scene. Could he be lying to spare his family?"

Steve sits back and shrugs. "We need to look for the guy he mentioned. But no one dressed in a ski mask has turned up on any surveillance footage we've been through."

"Maybe he came and went through the woods behind the diner," says the chief.

Madison doesn't buy it. "I think Hank knew he was dying and wanted to clear his name. But we can review the footage again, just to be sure."

Alex arrives, shaking his coat off and heading straight for them. "Morning, all," he says. "So, Mr. Goodman is with Dr. Scott for an autopsy later this afternoon, but I attended the scene and there were no indications to suggest he'd harmed himself or that anyone else was involved in his death. I think he was simply in poor health."

Madison wonders how Lena and her team are coping with so many bodies in such a short space of time.

"How's Detective Adams?" asks Alex. "I heard what happened. He must be relieved his daughters are safe."

Madison and Nate are the only ones who know what Adams was almost driven to. She agrees with Nate that it needs to stay that way. She looks at Mendes as she answers. "Adams should see the therapist. Urgently."

Mendes straightens. "You better come into my office."

CHAPTER THIRTY-NINE

Madison's phone rings as she follows the chief. She answers it in case it's urgent. "Hello?"

"Hey, it's Shelley. One of the rookies found a bloodstained knife in Hank Goodman's apartment. It was hidden behind the bathtub."

Madison turns. "Alex?" she shouts. "Officers have found a bloodstained knife at Hank's apartment. If Shelley brings it in, can you check it for prints and then send it to the lab asap?"

He nods. "Of course."

"Thanks." Down the line, she says, "Shelley? Could you bring it to Alex immediately?"

"On my way."

She slips her phone away and enters Chief Mendes's office, closing the door behind her. "So much for Hank being innocent. Shelley just found a bloodstained knife hidden in Hank's bathroom."

Mendes sits behind her tidy desk. "Looks like you were right. The supposed masked assailant he talked about was an attempt to clear his name." She moves some paperwork out of the way and leans forward, elbows on her desk. "So why do you think Detective Adams needs to see Julien?"

Sitting opposite, Madison says, "He's under pressure right now and I think it's getting to him. As you know, his wife cheated on him with his brother. Yesterday, they decided to separate, so he won't get to see his daughters as much. I know that'll be eating away at him. And he chose to venture alone to the mountain last night, knowing someone had abducted and threatened his daughters. He didn't call for backup. Instead, he lied to me." She shakes her head. "Chief, he's making poor decisions, and it pains me to say it, but until he's seen a therapist, I don't think he should be at work." She doesn't mention the brief dalliance with Officer Kent. She doesn't want to get him into trouble.

Mendes leans back in her seat as she considers it.

"I don't want him to think we're punishing him for his poor decisions," says Madison. "I just want him to get help. That's why we hired the therapist, right?"

The chief nods. "Okay. I'll trust your judgment and pay him a visit. Is he at your place?"

"No, he stayed with Selena and the girls. I don't know if he intends to show up for work today."

Mendes looks at her for a second without speaking. Eventually, she says, "And what about you? Do you need to see Julien?"

"No, I'm fine."

The chief shakes her head with a knowing smile. "What if someone was worried about you the way you're worried about Adams? Would you go then? Was there any point in me finding the money for a therapist? I mean, it was *your* idea, Madison."

She can tell the chief is frustrated with her. Maybe she's right to be. "How *did* you find the money?" she asks, deflecting slightly. "It still seems odd to me, given how we never have money for anything around here."

Breaking eye contact, Mendes appears to consider her response carefully. "I'm not supposed to tell you."

Madison frowns. "What does *that* mean?" Before Mendes can reply, Madison suddenly understands. She leans back. "It was Nate, wasn't it? He's funding the therapist?"

Chief Mendes meets her gaze. "Yes. He was worried about you after your father's murder, and he knew you'd been trying to secure a team therapist for a while. He thought that if we got one, you might actually use them."

Madison lowers her eyes. Nate's always looking out for her. It's not something she's used to.

Mendes stands. "I'll pay Adams a visit right away. I think it's a discussion best had in person, so he knows we have his best interests at heart."

Madison gets up and heads to her own desk. Once Mendes has left the building, she picks up her desk phone to call Adams.

He answers on the fourth ring with a long sigh. "I'm not gonna lie, Harper. I'm not in the mood for work today."

She keeps her voice low as she says, "You don't need to come in. Listen, I want to give you a heads-up about something. Are you at your place?" She hears a door click closed and assumes he's walked into an empty room for privacy.

"Yeah, why?"

"I just want you to know that I haven't told anyone about what really happened last night."

He remains silent.

"As far as the team knows, when I turned up and found you, your weapon was holstered. You never touched it."

Slowly, he says, "I wouldn't have done anything."

She hesitates, because that's not what he told her last night, and it's not what it looked like. "I know. I just didn't want to muddy the waters by telling them your weapon was drawn. And I wanted you to know that before Chief Mendes turns up at your house."

"Mendes?" he says, sounding confused. "She's coming here?"

"Right. She just left. We're worried about you, Adams. You're going through a lot, so I told her that I think you need time off to talk to Julien."

He exhales loudly.

"I know, I'm sorry. I wouldn't have told her if I didn't think it was important. You should concentrate on your girls. How are they?"

He scoffs. "Better than me. I guess they don't really understand what happened, or what could've happened."

"What *did* happen?" she asks. "I mean, how did they get there?"

"I tried to question them this morning, but I had to go easy as they're afraid the guy who took them could return. I might be able to get more from them over the coming days. But I know that Selena had gone next door late last night to deliver some packages that came for the neighbors while they were at work, and she went inside for a chat. Summer says the doorbell rang while she was gone, and she thought her mom had forgotten her keys. When she opened the door—something we'd trained her not to do, by the way, or thought we had—a guy dressed all in black with a black ski mask and gloves walked in and grabbed her while smothering her mouth with his hand."

"A ski mask?" Hank said the person who supposedly killed Carla was wearing a ski mask.

"Right. He didn't say a word."

"But they're both certain it was a man?"

"Summer is. Lizzie won't talk about it. I assume he found her after incapacitating Summer and then carried them out to his vehicle." His voice gets thicker as he says, "Selena didn't even notice they were missing right away. When she returned home twenty-five minutes later, she assumed they were still in their rooms as they'd already gone to bed."

She must be kicking herself.

The line goes quiet for a few seconds until Adams asks, "Was it Hank Goodman who did this?"

Madison isn't sure. He could've had time before he died, as the White Woods aren't far from the mountain. But she can't imagine him being strong enough to abduct two children, even if they were incapacitated. They're not infants and easy to carry. They're almost ten years old. "I don't know yet, but I'd be surprised. He's been found dead overnight."

"*Dead?*"

"Yeah. He called dispatch right before he died. Told Dina he didn't kill Carla. That some guy in a ski mask did."

After a few seconds, Adams says what she's thinking. "Could Hank have told the truth and the same guy took my girls?"

She chews her lip as she thinks. "I don't know. Alex is checking a knife found hidden at Hank's place. If his prints and Carla's blood are on it, then Hank's our guy." Steve approaches Madison's desk, so she wraps things up. "I've gotta go. I just wanted to let you know what I discussed with Mendes. I hope you don't think I'm going behind your back. I want you back at work as soon as you're ready."

He clears his throat. "Thanks, Harper. For... you know. I mean it when I say I wouldn't have gone through with it."

She smiles sadly. "I don't doubt it for a second."

CHAPTER FORTY

Steve leads Madison into the briefing room. "Alex is on his way."

Officers Sanchez and Kent follow them in. Kent doesn't make eye contact with Madison. Not wanting the young officer to think she's mad about what happened last night, Madison plans to pull her aside and talk to her when they get a minute. Officer Kent is young and single and can date whoever she wants. It's none of Madison's business. She was just disappointed in *Adams's* behavior. Still, at least he didn't sleep with her.

Through the open door, Madison sees Dr. Stevens appear. Dressed smartly in another beige suit and clutching an umbrella, he asks Stella something. Stella points to the briefing room as Madison heads to the door to greet him.

"Hi, Dr. Stevens."

"Conrad, please. I hope you don't mind me turning up unannounced? I thought you might want an update, and Dr. Scott is busy at the morgue."

"You have perfect timing. Come join us." She closes the door behind him as he enters.

"Will Chief Mendes be joining us?" asks the forensic anthropologist.

"No, she had to head out." When he seems disappointed, Madison adds, "I can ask her to give you a call?"

"No, it's fine." He smiles. "I'm sure I'll bump into her at some point."

Madison wonders if he has the hots for Mendes. The thought makes her smile as she imagines how Mendes will react. None of the team knows anything about the chief's private life, but if she starts dating Conrad, and Alex starts dating Conrad's daughter, Nora, Mendes could end up as Alex's future mother-in-law.

"Ready?" says Steve.

She looks at him. "Yes."

"Okay, things are getting complicated," he tells the team. "So I thought it was a good time to regroup and make sure we're all on the same page." He leans against a table. "First of all, Detective Adams will be off duty for a few days. Madison? Feel free to use me for anything you'd normally need Adams to do."

She smiles. "Thanks."

"I've been steadily working through the cold cases," he continues, "to see if there are any similarities between what our missing people were wearing and what we found with the remains on the mountain. There's nothing so far, but I keep getting interrupted, so I have more to trawl through."

Officer Sanchez asks, "Are we treating Carla's murder separately from the mountain murders?"

"Until we find concrete proof to suggest they're linked, yes," says Madison. "After all, she wasn't killed on the mountain, and we have footage of Hank fleeing the scene covered in blood, plus the knife hidden in his bathroom."

He frowns. "So what about the guy who tried to kill Detective Adams's daughters last night?"

"I think we have to assume that was the person who's been

dumping bodies on the mountain," she says. "Otherwise, why lure Adams to that location?"

"Sure," says Sanchez, thinking aloud. "So that means that Stuart Carpenter wasn't the Grave Mountain Stalker, right?"

Madison chews her lip as she thinks. It's time to decide on a direction for this investigation. If it leads them down the wrong path, they can at least rule it out and move in another direction, which is better than being at a standstill. "It's looking that way." She glances at Steve. "I don't even think Stuart was responsible for Becky's and Tasha's deaths now. I think he confessed because he felt guilty for being the sole survivor. I mean, he told me he attended the meeting at the diner because he needed support. Maybe the perp knew that by killing the two women and leaving Stuart alive, he would make a great suspect. And he did. Which means we've been led astray from the beginning."

Steve looks at her. "Why didn't Stuart tell us someone else killed them?"

"In his statement, he denied harming them," she says. "He explained what happened from his perspective. As far as he knew, they simply disappeared ahead of him into a thick fog. He could've been killed too if he hadn't headed back to his vehicle."

Steve frowns. "How do you explain Tasha's driver's license being found under his floorboards?"

She crosses her arms, frustrated because she *can't* explain it. "Look, I don't have all the answers. I'm just trying to move things forward. Stuart wasn't the one who abducted Adams's kids yesterday, and he didn't kill Carla, so I really think it's time to focus our efforts elsewhere."

He nods. "Anyone who could abduct two little girls and try to make their father choose between them obviously views killing as a blood sport. They're screwed up. They get off on the trauma they're causing. So to capture them, we need to try to think like them."

Officers Sanchez and Kent share a look. Kent seems excited at the prospect, but she wasn't on the team when the Snow Storm Killer was active. Hunting a serial killer is vastly different from watching it play out on a TV documentary while snuggled on the couch with a bag of potato chips for company. Every person involved in the investigation—and their loved ones—is at risk now.

Madison needs to call Owen. He might not be in Colorado anymore, but she wants him to be alert, just in case. When she thinks about Nate, the unnerving dread returns. She should buy him a weapon and train him to shoot, whether he intends to use it or not. The thought brings an image of Stuart Carpenter's last moment to mind. She sees him at the dining table. The shotgun goes off. The air mists with blood. Her ears ring at the memory.

Steve turns to the whiteboard and grabs a marker pen. "If we concentrate on the victims from the mountain, we have the skeletal remains of Tasha Harris, a headless woman who we think is likely to be Becky Draper, a teenage girl, and the woman found between the trees. All are female. Which means the motive for their deaths is probably sexual, but we can't tell whether any of them were sexually assaulted."

He starts a list. *Male killer. Female victims. Motive: sexual?* He turns to look at Madison. "What's Adams said about the person who abducted his kids?"

She shrugs. "All the girls could say is that it was a guy in a ski mask, and he never said a word."

Steve rubs his jaw. "He's careful. I'll have Alex check Adams's house for trace evidence. Does Adams have a door cam or security cameras?"

She shakes her head. "Nothing. Like me, he's been meaning to get something installed, but he's never home to arrange it." She needs to make the time to get her house secured. Unless she moves in with Nate.

"So other than their sex," says Steve, "what do the victims have in common?"

"Well," says Conrad, stepping forward. "Two of the victims were shot, and two appear to have died by strangulation. Attempts were made to hide two of the bodies—between the trees and in a shallow grave—but the other two appear to have been left out in the open."

"Maybe it's down to math," says Officer Sanchez. "Because that's a lot of twos."

"What do you mean?" asks Madison.

"Well, serial killers are weird, right?" he says. "They usually have screwed-up logic attached to their motives or their victims. Maybe ours loves math, and the number two is significant. Just look at Adams's twins. That's another two!"

Madison doesn't think it's significant, but it makes her smile. "Okay, Einstein. You can look into that one."

Sanchez smiles. "Do I get a raise if I'm right?"

Everyone laughs.

Steve looks at Conrad. "Do we know how old the remains are yet, or how long they lay undiscovered?"

The doctor nods. "I've finished my examination of all four sets of remains, and I believe they've all been out there between five and ten years. I'm waiting for several results before I can age them more accurately."

"So now we have a time frame for the kills," says Madison. "Assuming we don't find any more bodies."

"Correct," he says. "Judging by these bodies alone, it seems the killer was active over a five-year span and finished dumping his victims on the mountain five years ago, with Becky and Tasha. Of course, that doesn't mean he didn't just find a new dumping ground somewhere else, or perhaps he served time in prison, which put a hold on his antics. I don't know how wide your search efforts have spanned so far, but you won't know how long he's been killing until you search the entire mountain."

Madison shifts position. That's a lot of ground to cover. "We don't have the resources for that kind of ground search. Even a drone wouldn't be much use unless the bodies were fresh and no attempts had been made to conceal them." She looks at Steve. "Does anyone in the search team have a drone?"

"Not that I know of," he says. "But I can ask. Maybe Chief Mendes will let us buy a couple. Your friend's dog could cut down the search time too. In fact, we could do with ten of Brody."

She smiles. "Wouldn't that be nice? I'll see if Nate can spare some time to take him up there again."

On the whiteboard, Steve writes the years the killer was active.

The door opens. Alex appears excited as he enters. "Sorry to interrupt, but I have an update."

"Go ahead," says Madison.

He winces as he notices the bruising under her eyes. Her nose still feels swollen, but painkillers have taken the edge off the throbbing.

"First of all," he says, dragging his gaze away, "the number used to message Detective Adams last night to lure him to the mountain is a burner phone. It's already been disconnected, and we can't trace its owner as it's prepaid."

Madison nods. She expected nothing less. "Could you swing by Adams's place later to check for evidence? Not this morning, though. Chief Mendes has gone to visit him."

Alex nods. "Of course. Now for some good news. I've discovered a couple of fingerprints on a pair of women's sunglasses found under the body between the trees. They were protected by the elements, so the prints are perfect."

"And?" she says, excited.

"One of them matched with someone who has a criminal record." Alex smiles. "Jordan Payne was arrested years ago for an alleged assault in a bar, but the charges were eventually dropped. His contact details are on the system. He lives in Prospect Springs."

A town north of Lost Creek, Prospect Springs is a two-hour drive away on a good day, although patrol can get there faster. Madison glances at Steve. "I wonder whether he lived in Lost Creek five years ago."

It seems Steve is thinking the same thing. "I'll check."

Alex continues. "We have no way of knowing when he touched the sunglasses, of course, which means he could be the person who sold them to her, or he could be one of her friends."

"And the other print?" says Madison.

"No match on the system, so we can't tell who it belongs to, but it's likely to be the victim's. Of course, we can't compare her prints as she had none left by the time we found her."

Madison's stomach flutters with nerves. "Imagine if this Jordan guy is the serial killer."

Excitement ripples through the room.

"I don't know," says Officer Kent. "I kind of hope it's not some random guy in Prospect Springs." When everyone looks at her, she shrugs. "It sucks when a serial killer turns out to be no one we know. It's not as juicy. Sorry. Just my opinion."

Amused, Madison says, "I don't know. I think I'd prefer that one of my friends, neighbors or co-workers isn't a serial killer."

Kent snorts. "I guess you're right."

"We should bring Jordan Payne in without explaining why," says Steve. "Take him by surprise."

Madison agrees. She looks at Officer Kent. "Ask dispatch to send a patrol unit to his address immediately. Let them know why and that he could be dangerous. He's not to be arrested at this stage. They can tell him we just want to ask him some questions about a cold case. No specifics until he gets here."

Kent nods. "Sure, Detective."

As she leaves the room, Madison spots Shelley arriving. She has something in her hand. She approaches the briefing room, and Madison gestures for her to join them.

"Here you go, Alex." Shelley hands him a bagged knife. "From Hank Goodman's place."

"Thanks. I'll check it right away." Madison's eyes follow him as he practically runs to his office.

Turning to Steve, she says, "Did you do a background check on Stuart Carpenter's father?"

He nods. "Bryan's clean. I haven't managed to find anyone who saw him on his morning run, though."

That's interesting. Her phone rings. She looks around the room. "Anything else?"

The team shake their heads and start to disperse.

Madison answers her phone. It's Nate. "Hey, how are you?"

"Good," he says. "I need a favor."

She smiles. "So do I."

CHAPTER FORTY-ONE

Nate parked by the side of the road to call Madison. He smiles. "See how mutually beneficial our relationship is?"

Madison laughs. He loves her laugh. "You go first," she says.

He takes a deep breath. "It's about Robert Dorsey. Could you run a background check for me? I'm not asking for details, because I know you can't disclose anything—"

"So what do you expect me to tell you if I find something?" She sounds amused.

"I don't know," he says. "Maybe next time we meet, you could blink twice if he has a criminal record or once if not?"

She snorts. "I'll run a check, but I can't flag anything to you. If I find something, I'll look into it. I was going to read his son's case file anyway. Are you any closer to figuring out what happened to Brandon?"

Nate watches traffic as it speeds by. "I've been going door-to-door asking neighbors whether they saw anything, but I've only had one guy willing to talk." Gordon Humphrey was a good witness. "I can't tell you what he said, as you don't work for me. Sorry. Data protection." He smiles.

"To tell you the truth," Madison says, "working for you

again sounds tempting right now. This Grave Mountain Stalker case is killing me." She sighs. "Anyway, I need to hire Brody for the day. Is he available?"

Nate looks at the dog through the rearview mirror. He's lying on his side in the backseat, lazily watching Nate's every move. His tail starts thumping against the seat when Nate says, "Brody? I don't know. I'll need to check his schedule."

"You do that," she says. "He's needed on the mountain. We think there could be more bodies, and we don't have enough manpower to widen the search area by much. I'm hoping Brody can reach places the volunteers can't."

"Makes sense." He glances at the clock on his dash. "Actually, I need to be somewhere, but Vince enjoys helping with searches. I'll see if he'll take Brody up there. It might give him something to focus on other than Carla's murder."

"Good idea. Oh, about that..."

He frowns. "What?"

"We found Hank dead in the woods earlier today," she says. "Could you give Vince and the waitresses a heads-up before they hear about it on the news? I'd do it, but I'm swamped."

His mouth falls open. "Hank's *dead*?" He didn't like the guy, but it's still shocking.

"Afraid so. Possible heart attack. He called dispatch and insisted he didn't kill Carla. Apparently, there was a masked assailant who did it, but we found a bloody knife hidden behind his bathtub." Before he can respond, she says, "Hang on a minute, Nate."

He hears a faint male voice in the background. When Madison comes back on the line, she says, "Alex just confirmed Hank's prints are on the knife. The blood is yet to be tested, but we expect it to be Carla's."

Nate sighs. "I'll let Vince know." Before she can go, he says, "Will I see you tonight?" He doesn't know whether Detective Adams still needs her for moral support.

"I hope so, but I can't promise anything. You know how it is."

"Sure," he says, masking his disappointment. "We'll speak later. Love you."

"Love you too. Bye." She ends the call.

Nate pockets his phone and turns to look at Brody. "Are you up for a hike?"

The dog sits up, alert.

Nate smiles as he starts the engine.

At the diner, Vince jumps at the chance to join the search with Brody. He never turns down the opportunity to help an investigation. The Lost Creek Police Department is lucky to have trusted locals willing to share their workload for free.

"It'll stop me seeing Carla's face everywhere I turn," he says. "I keep expecting her to walk out of the kitchen with her hands full of orders."

Nate feels for him. He glances at Brody, who's waiting patiently by the door. "Brody's ready when you are."

Vince nods. "Leave him with me. I'll just be a few minutes." The diner is packed, the mood somber. As head waitress, Carla did a fantastic job keeping the customers *and* the employees happy. Nate finds himself wondering who will take over from her.

He heads outside after telling Brody to be good for Uncle Vince. With just an hour until his appointment, he slips into his car and opens his laptop on the passenger seat. He finds the flash drive Gordon Humphrey gave him and inserts it into the card reader.

As it loads, he glances at the rearview mirror and sees Vince leading Brody to his vehicle. Vince waves before pulling out of the lot. A pickup truck pulls in soon after and Robert Dorsey gets out. He doesn't spot Nate watching him as he disappears inside the diner.

Robert hasn't called for an update since their first meeting two days ago, which is surprising considering how he came across then. Nate thinks about the guy's deceased wife, Caroline. Richie said she'd had health problems when she sought advice about a divorce, and Robert said she'd died from heart failure. Robert's in his late forties now, and Caroline died six years ago. So unless he married a much older woman, Caroline presumably would've been in her forties too. It seems a little young to be affected by heart issues.

He opens Google on his laptop and types: *Caroline Dorsey death, Lost Creek, Colorado.* An online obituary is the first link. He opens it.

> After a long and brave battle, Caroline Dorsey succumbed to heart failure at age forty. She is survived by her loving husband, Robert, and her son, Brandon, the light of her life. A native of Colorado, Caroline was a devoted friend, a cherished wife and the best mother a boy could have.

Nate stops reading. He must be getting cynical if he thought Robert could've killed his wife. Maybe it's time for a new career. One where he can take people at face value.

Movement in the rearview mirror gets his attention. Robert Dorsey emerges from the diner with a takeout coffee in one hand and something bagged in the other. Grease spots appear through the bag. He gets straight into his truck and quickly drives away. Nate wonders where he's going and whether he's been laid off from his job.

Closing the obituary, he opens the audio file from the flash drive Gordon gave him. It's thirty-eight minutes long. He clicks *play* and immediately hears Detective Douglas's voice as he explains the purpose of the questioning and how it's related to the recent disappearance of Brandon Dorsey. When he's done, an older lady replies.

"You don't need to speak to me like I'm an idiot, Mr. Detective. I taught high school literature. I'm probably more intelligent than you."

Nate smiles. Violet Humphrey sounds like a woman to be reckoned with.

Douglas apologizes and spends a few minutes shooting the shit with Gordon. They sound like they're sipping drinks. Douglas is trying to make Violet comfortable in his presence before getting to the important questions.

Eventually, Violet interrupts them. "He's in the car."

That's the line she repeated over the days that followed Brandon's disappearance.

Detective Douglas clears his throat. "Who's in the car?"

Violet repeats, "He's in the car."

"Can you describe the car for me, Mrs. Humphrey?"

After a few seconds of silence, Violet says, "Gordon? Who is this man? Why's he in our house?" She sounds afraid.

Nate's heart sinks. It's clear Violet's lucid moments didn't last long by this point. Gordon patiently explains everything again.

Violet responds with, "Why are you repeating yourself? Where's my blanket?"

It must've been incredibly frustrating for Detective Douglas to know this woman could hold the key to Brandon's disappearance and was unable to help them.

"Here you go, Vi," says Gordon, presumably handing her the blanket.

The detective asks, "Did you recognize who was driving the car, ma'am?"

"What car?" says Violet, confused.

Nate drops his pen. He can understand why the investigation stalled if this was the best lead the cops had. They didn't even tell Robert about it, not wanting to get his hopes up. They couldn't have done, or Robert would've told Nate what Violet said.

Still, he listens to the entire clip as he watches customers come and go at the diner. Some bring flowers and disappear around the side of the building to leave them near where Carla was killed. Yellow crime-scene tape will stop them from getting too close, and Nate knows an officer is present to keep the scene secure until Alex is done with his forensic investigation.

After twenty minutes of going around in circles with his questioning, the sound of movement on the tape suggests Detective Douglas is ready to leave. He thanks Violet for her time before he and Gordon discuss whether it was useful. Nate's ready to hit *stop* when he hears Violet's voice in the background as the men talk. He doesn't catch what she says, so he takes the recording back a few seconds and turns up the volume to listen again.

He still doesn't make it out, so he tries a third time.

"But who is she?" says Violet.

Nate frowns. He listens to the rest of the recording, but it abruptly ends a few seconds later. Douglas must've stopped it as he left the property.

He makes a note of Violet's question. *But who is she?*

It could be unrelated to Brandon's case, just a memory she's reliving or a question about something in her day-to-day life. Nate knows he can't take her words too seriously, given her condition. But he underlines it anyway.

CHAPTER FORTY-TWO

Madison approaches her desk with a fresh mug of coffee in her hand. Before she gets there, Stella calls over to her from the dispatcher's cubicle.

"Bryan Carpenter's just arrived. He wants to speak to you."

Madison wonders what he wants and how much she can tell him. "Okay, thanks." She places her coffee on her desk and tells Steve where she's going.

"Want me to come?" he asks.

"No, that's okay."

He nods. "By the way, Chief Mendes has issued a press release stating that the three unidentified victims are all female. She thought it might reduce the number of people at the mountain seeking answers. They seem to be congregating there with the press, who are feeding them what little they know."

She wishes she could put their minds at rest, but until they've identified all the victims, she can't. "I'll head over there later in case any of them can help us. It might be quicker than going through every single cold case."

He nods. "Good idea. It's taking me forever because of all the interruptions."

She heads to the front of the station through a secure door and finds several people seated in the waiting area. Bryan stands as she approaches him. He looks like he's aged ten years since she first met him at the lodge just a few days ago. His shirt is badly creased, and his skin looks haggard, as if he's not drinking any fluids. "What can I do for you, Mr. Carpenter?"

He glances over his shoulder at some unsavory-looking characters. "Can we go somewhere more private?"

Madison nods. "Sure. Follow me." She leads him through the office and into an interview room, keeping the door ajar.

Bryan sits opposite her, and although he stares at her swollen nose, he doesn't mention it. "I'm not being recorded, right?"

She frowns. "No. I didn't even know you were coming. What's the problem?"

He takes a deep breath and runs his hands along his thighs as if they're sweaty. "Robert Dorsey needs locking up."

"Why? What's happened?"

"He threatened me! He believes the ridiculous press speculation about my son being responsible for murdering Becky and Tasha, and now he thinks Stuart could've killed his boy too, which is outrageous. There's no way Stuart could've hurt a child."

Concerned, Madison asks, "Did he physically assault you?"

"No, it was verbal intimidation. He said he was going to expose me. That I knew what my son was doing!" Bryan looks exasperated. "Have you even found Brandon Dorsey's body? Is that why he thinks Stuart was involved, because his son was found on the mountain?"

Madison shakes her head. "No, we haven't found Brandon, nor are we actively searching for him. Robert's hired a PI to investigate. The next time he approaches you, tell him to take it up with his investigator." She doesn't know whether Dorsey has any evidence to support his claim or whether he's just hot-headed and the news reports are getting him riled up.

Bryan leans back in his seat. "I've been having palpitations. My doctor says I'm on course for a heart attack. And I'm terrified Jay will follow his brother's example and take his own life. The accusations and the press attention are too much after losing Stuart."

"I know," she says softly. "I'd recommend you avoid the news."

"It's not that easy," he says. "Guests are canceling their bookings at the lodge and swamping our Facebook page with one-star reviews and accusations about Stuart. Every time one of us leaves, some obnoxious reporter takes our photo."

"I'm sorry," she says. "I can imagine how that adds to your pain." She wants to tell him their latest theory: that Stuart might not have killed the women. That he was used as a scapegoat by the real killer. But she can't until she has something solid to back that up.

He leans in. "What's painful, Detective, is knowing that my son has been branded a killer by the media and everyone thinks we were in on it. It makes no sense! Even if he did kill someone —God forbid—how are *we* responsible?" His eyes search her face for answers. "Are *you* responsible for what your sister and her husband did just because you're related? Does your sister's actions make you a bad person too?"

Although she doesn't appreciate Angie being dragged into this, she understands his point.

"I don't believe so," he continues. "Just because someone is related to a criminal doesn't mean they're anything like them. If it were that easy, every serial killer in history would be locked up alongside the rest of their family. It seems to me, from what I've seen on TV at least, that most killers work alone. They're usually estranged from their family and reclusive. That wasn't Stuart." His tone sharp, he adds, "So don't be sloppy, Detective.

While you're wasting your time looking at Stuart for those murders, you're missing clues, and it pisses me off."

"Listen," says Madison, trying not to get angry. "I'm not fixed on any one person right now. I'm considering all the options and going where the evidence leads me."

She needs to ask him something, but she knows he won't appreciate it after everything he's just said. Still, she can't let him leave without checking. "I understand from Mel that you went for a run yesterday morning despite your doctor's advice. Is that correct?"

He answers immediately. "I go for a run most mornings. So what?"

She ignores his question. "And where were you last night?" She's thinking of the time Lizzie and Summer were abducted. "Were you at the lodge overnight?"

He scoffs. "Of course I was. I live there."

"So you never left the premises? Is there anyone who could verify that?"

He licks his lips, and his demeanor changes. He must know that Carla was killed while he was out running yesterday morning and that there was an incident on the mountain last night involving Detective Adams.

He stands. "I find your line of questioning offensive. If you want to speak to me again, I'll want a lawyer present."

Madison stands too. "I'll see you out."

Once he's left the building, she returns to her desk. She doesn't even manage a sip of coffee before Stella calls over to her again.

"I've got Nancy Draper on the line for you."

Madison takes a deep breath. Her to-do list is getting longer by the minute. Selfishly, she wishes Adams were here to help. "Has patrol picked up Jordan Payne yet?"

Stella nods. "He was reluctant, apparently. They're on their way back with him."

Madison's desk phone rings as Stella transfers Nancy. She picks up the handset. "Hi, Mrs. Draper. How are you?"

"Have you found Becky yet?" The older woman sounds exhausted.

Madison's torn over how to answer. Doug told her not to drip-feed his wife information as it's making her more anxious, but she can't just refuse to answer her questions. She sits down. "Not yet, but we still have one set of remains awaiting DNA results. Until we get those, we won't know whether it's your daughter."

"Wait, I'm confused," says Nancy. "You have Becky's dental records. Why can't you use those?"

How does she tell the woman that the body is missing its head without upsetting her? Eventually, she says, "Dental records aren't always viable, which is what's happened in this case. So the forensic anthropologist we have working on the case has extracted a sample of DNA for the crime lab to compare to the one taken from Becky's hairbrush at the time of her disappearance. Unfortunately, it can take some time for those results to come back, but I'll chase them and remind the lab of the urgency."

"Oh, okay." Nancy sounds disappointed. Waiting for your loved one to be identified must make the hours grind to a halt. "Thank you."

"Just... don't get your hopes up. In case it's not her."

"Too late," says Nancy. "I'm making arrangements to be buried in the same plot. Once we have her back with us."

Her words send chills down Madison's arms. "Mrs. Draper. You don't mean you're going to—"

"Harm myself?" She snorts. "I'll wait to hear from you."

Madison clears her throat. "Yes. As soon as I know—"

"Thank you. Goodbye."

Madison puts the phone down. She needs to find Nancy some help. A bereavement therapist or a hoarding support service. She doesn't know if the woman would agree to it, but she has to try.

She runs a hand over her face as she attempts to focus. She can't. Her nose starts to throb again, so she takes two pills with her cold coffee. Grabbing her car keys, she decides to head to the mountain. She needs some fresh air.

CHAPTER FORTY-THREE

When Madison pulls into the parking lot near the Juniper Trail access point, she realizes she's underestimated the public interest in this case. She hasn't been leading the press conferences because Chief Mendes wanted to do that to free up Madison's time, so she hasn't gotten a feel for what the press is asking or how many of them are following the case. The number of media trucks and reporters here today tells her it's big news. And if the media is interested, the public is too, which means more scrutiny of how she and the team investigate.

She gets out of her car, relieved that the sun is shining and the air is warmer than it's been the past few days. A series of loud barks makes her turn to look up at the trail's path. She wonders if it's Brody, but he and Vince are probably much farther away by now.

As she passes a female reporter doing a piece to camera, she hears the woman say, "The unsolved disappearance of two hikers five years ago has triggered this investigation. We understand there are currently no clues, no leads and no eyewitnesses in the case, just a suspect who killed himself as soon as he was cornered. As he wasn't alive when the detective's children were abducted last night, it begs the question: just *who* has been using Grave Mountain as a dumping ground for their prey?"

Madison dodges the press and approaches three men and two women huddled together under a large aspen tree, each holding a takeout coffee or a cigarette.

One of the women sees her coming and her eyes light up. "Detective! Can we speak to you?"

Madison's on the news so often that she's frequently recognized. She smiles. "Sure. How can I help?"

The woman frowns at her. "Oh my God. Are you okay?"

Madison remembers her bruising. "I'm fine. It looks worse than it feels."

One of the men steps forward. "Is it true that no unidentified males have been found up there?"

"That's correct," she confirms. "Just females."

Disappointed, he asks, "Do you think it's likely you'll find more... bodies?"

Cautiously, she says, "I'm sorry. I have no idea at this stage."

"What about babies?" says a voice behind her. "Are there any babies up there?"

Madison turns to the second female. It's the woman who was at the support group meeting on the evening Tasha Harris's body was discovered on the mountain. She was frustrated that Madison was focusing on the Drapers and Robert Dorsey when she was keen to discuss her missing baby.

"I'm Gina Clark." The woman shakes Madison's hand. "My baby boy has been missing for some time. I know you said you haven't found any males, but I guess I'm wondering whether there are any smaller bodies waiting to be examined."

Madison hopes they don't find a baby's body up there. It doesn't bear thinking about. "No infants at all," she says gently. "Out of the three unidentified victims we currently have, two are adults and one is a teenager. I'm sorry."

Gina nods. "I'd like to talk to you about my son one day soon, Detective. I didn't get a chance before."

How can she say no? "Of course. Once this current investigation is over, we should meet." She means it too. She'd like to help this woman find her child. As she can't help her yet, she hands Gina her card.

Satisfied, Gina turns away. The group watches her as she slips into a Honda and pulls onto the road. The two men also walk away, presumably because the person they're looking for is male, so they know they're wasting their time here now.

Madison can't tell whether she's delivering good news or bad to these people.

Only the woman who called her over remains, with what must be her husband or partner, as they're holding hands. They're both tall and slim. The woman is dressed in smart jeans, black boots and a camel-colored woolen coat. The man is dressed more casually. She'd guess they're in their late thirties.

"I'm Sarah Walker, and this is my husband, Tim," says the woman. "We have a missing daughter. Fourteen-year-old Abby Walker." She hands Madison a photo of a pretty teenage girl who looks embarrassed to have her picture taken. Her hair is a beautiful shade of auburn, long and straight, and she looks young for her age. "Could she be who you found?"

"When did she go missing?"

"Almost six and a half years ago."

That fits within the time frame Dr. Stevens estimated.

"Come with me." Madison leads them over to an empty picnic bench. She gestures for them to sit down before sitting opposite them. The wooden bench is damp beneath her, and the sun is in her eyes, but it feels pleasant on her face. Pulling out her pocket notepad and pen, she says, "Tell me what happened."

Sarah looks at her husband. "You tell her. You know what I'm like. I get too emotional."

Tim stubs out his cigarette on the wood and leaves the butt there. The aroma of smoke awakens Madison's yearning, something she regularly has to suppress no matter how long she goes without a cigarette. She tried sucking on candies as a substitution, but her dentist convinced her that was a bad idea.

"Abby and her friend Lauren Moss lied to us," he says. "They told us they had a sleepover planned at a friend's house when actually, they snuck up here to camp alone overnight."

Their daughter disappeared from the mountain. Madison keeps her expression neutral, not wanting to alarm them. Steve can't have reached that cold case yet or he would've immediately suspected that Abby Walker is a good candidate for the teenage remains. She pulls her phone out. "Excuse me for just a second."

She types a quick text.

Abby Walker could be our teenager. I'm currently talking with her parents. Read the case file.

She places her phone on the table face-up and looks at Tim. "Sorry about that. And they both disappeared?"

"No," says Tim. "Only Abby. Lauren returned home on her own later that night. She snuck into her bedroom and never even told anyone she'd left Abby alone up there. At least, we assume she did. We have no real way of knowing."

"How come?" Madison's phone buzzes. She sees a thumbs-up from Steve.

Sarah lowers her eyes as she says, "Because Lauren took her own life that night. Before her parents even woke. They found her in her closet."

Chills run down Madison's arms. She can picture the scene those poor people walked in on. They must've been traumatized. They probably still are. She wonders what was so bad that

Lauren would kill herself over it. She must have either done or witnessed something terrible. "That's awful."

"We were obviously devastated for her parents," says Sarah, pushing her hair behind her ears. "But we've never known what happened to Abby."

Tim continues, "Four days later, some hikers came across Abby's belongings in a tent near the Juniper Trail. They were scattered across a large area as if disturbed by the wind or animals. The police investigated the scene but never found our daughter or her cell phone. The phone was disconnected, which they believed meant it had been destroyed by whoever hurt or abducted Abby."

"It's like living in a nightmare you never wake from," says Sarah. "And there are no coping mechanisms for what we're going through." She tears up. "No one can help us. Not unless they find our daughter."

Madison feels terrible for them. "Were Abby and Lauren really friends?"

Confused, Tim says, "What do you mean?"

She shields her eyes from the sun. "I'm just wondering whether Lauren played a trick on your daughter. Maybe she pretended to be her friend to isolate and then bully her."

"Oh," says Tim, understanding. "That's what the detectives asked at the time. They thought she could've pushed Abby off one of the cliffs or into water, but no, they were close. Abby didn't have many other friends, so they spent a lot of time together."

That's something, at least. "Did Lauren leave any sort of message before she took her life?"

Sarah digs into her purse and pulls out a piece of folded paper. "She wrote this, but her parents didn't show anyone until early last year, and that's only because we begged them to tell us if they knew anything."

Madison takes it from her. It's a photocopied sheet of lined paper with just five words.

I'm sorry. He made me.

"We took it straight to the police," says Tim, running a hand down his face. "But they said it didn't mean anything, and even if it did, it was too late after the fact. Too much time had passed. Maybe if they'd seen it at the time, they could've looked into whether someone else was present when Abby vanished and whether it meant Lauren had harmed her, but we don't believe she would've hurt her. I mean, they were just kids."

Madison wouldn't rule anything out. Teenagers can be worse than adults. She needs to look into the original investigation to see what's already been checked. But first, she needs to confirm that the person they have in the morgue is this couple's missing daughter. "Did the detectives collect Abby's DNA as part of their investigation?"

"Yes, from a comb with strands of her hair in." Sarah's eyes light up. "You can compare her DNA to the teenager you found on the mountain, right?"

Madison nods. "And I think we found some clothes with the remains. Do you remember what Abby was wearing that day?"

"Of course. It's burned into my memory," says Sarah. "Blue jeans, a yellow T-shirt and black sneakers."

Madison makes a note and then stands. "Give me a minute while I make a call."

The couple clutch each other's hands, looking expectant.

She walks away so they can't hear her as she calls Alex.

He answers almost immediately. "Afternoon, Detective."

"Hey, Alex. Can you remember what clothing we found with the teenager's remains? I'm with a couple who think she might be their daughter."

"Ah. Let me find the list I sent to Nora." The sound of shuffling papers can be heard down the line. "Here we go. Teenage victim..." A few seconds pass as he reads. "Partial denim remains that looked like they were once a pair of jeans, and a purple hoody with a zip up the front. No shoes were found."

"Okay. Hold on a second, would you?"

"Of course."

Madison steels herself before returning to the couple. "Do you know whether Abby owned a purple hoody with a zip—" Sarah's hands fly to her face before she can finish.

"Oh my God." The woman gulps for air. "Oh my God. I can't breathe." She pulls her scarf away from her throat.

Tim's eyes go red as he hugs his wife to him. "Does the one you found have a green logo on the front? I forget what brand it was."

Madison takes a deep breath and speaks to Alex. "Did you hear that?"

"Yes," he says. "I'm just looking for the photos I took of it." Almost thirty seconds go by, and Madison can feel the intensity radiating from the couple as they wait. "Here we are," he says eventually. "Ah. Yes. I'm afraid so. It's a tree in a circle. All green. The rest of the item is purple."

Madison nods to the couple.

Sarah sobs into her husband's shoulder. He pulls out a pack of cigarettes with his spare hand.

"Okay, Alex," she says. "Our teenager is likely to be Abby Walker. Her DNA is already on file as part of the original investigation into her disappearance. Would you send the details to Nora and ask her to compare them to the DNA taken from the remains. Or maybe we can get her dental records for comparison. That might be faster. Check with Lena."

"Of course," he says solemnly. "And I'll let the rest of the team know her name."

"Thanks, Alex. Steve's reading the case file as we speak."

Madison ends the call and returns to the bench. The couple

hug again. They're attracting attention from the reporters on the other side of the lot.

"I'm so sorry for your loss," she says. "We'll need to formally identify her to be certain, but for now, I think it's best that you head home." She nods in the direction of the reporters.

Tim briefly glances behind them. "When can we see our daughter?" His voice is thick with emotion.

Madison opens her mouth to speak, but she has to choose her words carefully. "I just need to be clear. What we found on the mountain was only skeletal remains. But I'll let you know as soon as she can be released to a funeral home of your choice. It might be a week or two, I'm sorry. We have to be meticulous about collecting potential evidence. We want to find the person who did this."

"I think it was Lauren," says Sarah through her tears. "That's what her suicide note meant."

Madison wonders whether one of the girls had a boyfriend and their threesome grew complicated. "It's possible. But at this stage, I don't know, so I'd ask you not to say that to any reporters. They can ruin someone's reputation in a heartbeat with speculation. Lauren's parents also lost their daughter, so I don't want to cause them any unnecessary pain. Let me figure out what happened first, okay?"

They glance at each other and then nod. Madison thinks they're sensible people. They won't do anything misguided, no matter how much they're hurting.

She stands as her phone buzzes with a text from Steve.

Jordan Payne's arrived at the station. His lawyer's on his way.

Madison's stomach flips with excitement as she wonders why he felt the need for a lawyer when he doesn't even know what she wants to question him about. Could this actually be the guy they're looking for?

CHAPTER FORTY-FOUR

It's starting to get dark by the time Madison arrives at the station. She pulls her jacket off and heads straight to Steve's desk, where Chief Mendes joins them. "How's Adams doing?" she asks.

The chief chooses her words carefully. "He's shaken up, but he's agreed to attend a couple of therapy sessions before he returns to work. His daughters appear to be fine."

Relieved, Madison nods. "That's something."

"There's some obvious tension between Adams and his wife, though," says Mendes. "He wanted to know whether he can still stay in your spare room. I said I'd ask."

"Absolutely," says Madison. "For as long as he wants." Even though Nate asked her to move in with him, neither of them has mentioned it again. They never really resolved their earlier issue about Nate protecting himself. It got swept under the rug. Once this investigation is over, she'll address everything, but she doesn't have the time right now.

She fills them both in on Sarah and Tim Walker and their missing daughter.

"I read the case file," says Steve. "It sounds like it's her."

"I agree." It's a relief to get some leads at last. Madison looks at Mendes. "By the way, Dr. Stevens was here earlier. He seemed disappointed to have missed you."

For the first time since Madison has known her, Mendes blushes. An awkward silence follows until Madison's phone buzzes with a message. It's from Nate.

Vince called. Brody found a skull on the Lovers' Peak Trail.
It's on its way to the morgue.

Her mouth drops open in surprise. She shows them what it says.

Steve seems as relieved as she is. "So Becky Draper could be formally identified shortly, assuming her dental records match."

She nods. "And assuming the skull doesn't belong to more undiscovered remains." Her stomach flips at the thought. The morgue will be overrun if they keep finding new bodies.

Chief Mendes rubs her temples. "I'm avoiding the district attorney's calls."

"According to the notes about Abby Walker's disappearance," says Steve, "her cell phone was never found, and she didn't have any social media accounts, so we don't know what she and her friend were doing while camping or whether they took a third person with them. Lauren was a prolific user of Instagram, but apart from one sunset photo from that night, there are no clues, presumably because they didn't want their parents finding out where they were."

"Have you seen Lauren's suicide note?" Madison asks.

"Yeah, it was in the case file. I get the impression it didn't lead anywhere, though."

Chief Mendes says, "Do we know why Abby's body wasn't found at the time?"

Steve opens a map of the mountain on his computer. "I checked where we found her body and where the tent was found, and there's some distance between them. I think the killer moved her to make it harder to find her, although she wasn't buried."

Madison finds it odd. How two of their victims were concealed and two weren't. It suggests different killers were involved. If Hank was one of them, who was the other?

Steve stands and collects a bundle of documents together. "Jordan Payne is in interview room one. I checked whether he ever lived in Lost Creek during our five-year window for the murders, and he did."

"Remind me who he is again," says Mendes.

"His prints were on these." He pulls out a bagged pair of broken sunglasses. "They were found between the tree trunks that concealed our second victim."

Mendes nods as she remembers. With the four mountain murders, plus Carla's, it's difficult to keep up.

"So we think he might be able to tell us who the victim is?" she says.

"Right. Or he could be our killer."

With raised eyebrows, she says, "You'll assist Madison?"

Steve looks at Madison, who says, "That would be great."

"Let me know how it goes." The chief heads back to her office as Madison collects a notepad and pen and then follows Steve to the interview room.

Over his shoulder, he says, "The guy's lawyer has turned up. They've had some time together to prepare." He opens the door to interview room one without knocking.

Madison's surprised to find Richie Hope inside. Richie has helped her and Nate out of brushes with the law in the past. She considers him a friend now. "Richie. Nice to see you."

"Always a pleasure, Detective." He nods at Steve. "Sergeant."

Next to him is an attractive man in his early forties. His right arm is covered with a sleeve of tattoos, stopping at the wrist. His eyes dart back and forth between Madison and Richie. Madison knows from his record that he was working in IT at the time of his last arrest. He has a cup of water in front of him.

Steve sits opposite them and hits the record button for the camera that watches them from high up in the corner of the room. "Mr. Payne, this is Detective Madison Harper, and you already know I'm Sergeant Steve Tanner."

Richie and Jordan seem transfixed by the bruising around her nose, so Madison says, "Ignore my injuries. I was head-butted by an assailant, but I'm still standing."

Richie chuckles in awe.

Madison looks at Jordan. "I'm sure you're wondering why we've brought you in."

"I know I am," says Richie amiably. "Isn't it customary to tell someone what they're being questioned for?"

"Sorry about that, Mr. Hope," she says. "But time was of the essence, and we're swamped right now with a fast-moving investigation. The fact that your client came willingly to answer questions is much appreciated, and we'll try not to take up too much of his time."

Jordan remains silent and stony-faced. Beads of sweat line his temples, which is strange as this is the second-coldest room at the station. The first is Alex's office.

"I'll get straight to the point," she continues. "We've discovered the remains of several unidentified females on Grave Mountain, and with one of those bodies was a pair of sunglasses."

Steve pulls out the evidence bag containing the glasses and slides it across the table. Jordan's eyes flicker to them before he glances at Richie.

"A fingerprint was found on the lens, Mr. Payne," says Madison. "And as you have a prior arrest, we were able to match it to your prints."

Jordan shifts in his seat but remains silent.

Madison locks her eyes on him. "Mr. Payne, it would be helpful to our investigation if you could tell us who these sunglasses belonged to. We're trying to identify the remains so we can notify her family of her death."

He swallows and again glances at Richie, who says, "You can answer."

"No, I can't," says Jordan.

Sometimes, suspects who don't want to talk to the cops inadvertently open the floodgates with just one answer, no matter how unhelpful. It gives the interviewer a way in. Madison leans forward. "Is that because you don't know who they belong to?"

He won't make eye contact now. He sits back and crosses his arms.

Madison tries a different approach. "Are you married, Mr. Payne?"

He bristles. "What's that got to do with anything?"

Richie writes something down.

"So you are?" says Steve.

"No. Divorced. Two kids."

Steve picks up a pen. "What's your ex-wife's name?"

Jordan uncrosses his arms. "Leave her out of this."

It's not unusual for serial killers to be married with kids. It's difficult for most people to fathom how someone can kill multiple women while leaving their spouse unharmed. Rather than suggesting his wife was in on it, or at least knew what her husband was doing, it suggests the killer is capable of loving—or sparing—certain people, despite his desire to cause harm. In some ways, that makes it worse.

Madison stands and looks at Steve. "I'll be right back."

CHAPTER FORTY-FIVE

A quick search of Jordan's prior arrest record provides the name of his ex-wife: Deborah Payne. Madison hopes she kept her married name. She searches for a contact number with a Prospect Springs address. Finding only one person with that name, she lifts her desk phone and calls the number. It's 5:30 p.m. She crosses her fingers that Deborah is home from work.

A woman answers. "Hello?"

"Oh, hi. My name's Detective Harper from the Lost Creek Police Department. I'm sorry to bother you, ma'am, but I'm after some information about your ex-husband, Jordan Payne. Do you have a minute?"

"I, er, I don't know." Deborah sounds hesitant. "What is it you want?"

"Did you ever live in Lost Creek when you were together?"

"Sure. We moved away probably six years ago."

Madison's heart beats a little harder. That's just before the killer stopped dumping bodies on the mountain. "Did you and Jordan enjoy hiking in the mountains while you lived here?"

A few seconds of silence pass. "He did. He enjoyed keeping fit."

"Did you ever hike with him?"

"No. I'm not a hiker."

Madison can't tell whether she's giving short answers to avoid incriminating herself or her ex-husband. "So you wouldn't have lost a pair of women's sunglasses while hiking in Grave Mountain?"

"No. Why?"

"Because Jordan's prints are on a pair discovered at a crime scene."

Deborah gasps. After a couple of steadying breaths, she says, "We split because I suspected he was cheating on me. I checked his phone but found no messages or names I didn't recognize. He was too clever to leave an electronic trail, as he's good with computers and tech."

"So what made you think he was cheating on you?" asks Madison.

"My friend told me she saw another woman in his car one day when he drove by her. Apparently, they were laughing, and then the woman leaned over to kiss him."

"Did your friend recognize her?"

"No. Well, not until she saw her face in the paper."

Confused, Madison frowns. "What do you mean?"

With a tremor in her voice, Deborah says, "A woman went missing six or seven years ago, and her face was on the news and in the papers. Lily, my friend, thought she looked like the woman in my husband's car."

Trying to contain her excitement at the possible break-through, Madison asks, "Do you remember the woman's name?"

"Shannon Briggs," Deborah whispers, realizing the implications. "She worked with kids. She was thirty-two years old when she vanished. Jordan was thirty-four. She was in his car just a month before she went missing."

Gently, Madison asks, "Did you ever question Jordan about her? Or about your friend allegedly seeing her in his vehicle?"

"No. I was too afraid. I didn't know if he'd kill *me*." Deborah scoffs. "No one would've believed me if I'd told them what I was thinking, so I decided to leave him, not just for my safety, but that of our children. I never dared to tell him the real reason. I was vague, and just told him I wasn't happy anymore because he'd moved us up to Prospect Springs for no apparent reason. The truth is, he'd changed. He started suffering from depression, which seemed to be getting worse." She sighs shakily. "He didn't exactly fight for our marriage."

"But after the divorce, you never returned to Lost Creek, right?"

"No. I couldn't afford to once the divorce was finalized. I needed my job, and I have friends here. It was just an excuse I used to get away from him. I haven't seen him in over a year, but I think about him often. I wonder whether his mental health declined out of guilt for what he might have done. Other times, I convince myself I'm overreacting. I thought I'd never know the truth."

Madison feels for her. "Well, thanks for answering my questions. I'll be in touch again at some point."

"Wait! You can't tell him I told you any of that," says Deborah, sounding afraid. "He might come after me."

"I'm questioning him at the station right now," says Madison. "And I intend to make sure he can't hurt anyone else."

After a stretch of silence, the woman says, "I need to move, don't I? If he killed Shannon Briggs, it'll be all over the news. People will say I should've gone to the police back then with my suspicions."

"Why didn't you?" Madison asks.

"Because I had no proof! You wouldn't have arrested him just because my friend *thought* she saw someone who looked like Shannon in his car. I know how it works, and that's not enough!"

Madison bites her tongue. The investigating detectives

could've searched for more evidence if they'd had a named suspect. They could've secured warrants for Jordan's home and vehicle and kept looking for Shannon's body. She takes a deep breath. At least now she has a name for the victim, which means she can check to see what was done in the search for her six years ago.

She remembers that the woman hidden in the trees was strangled. "Did Jordan ever get rough during sex?"

Deborah doesn't even have to think about it. "No, never. He wasn't like that. Not with me, anyway."

It's not unusual for men to treat their wives differently to their lovers or their victims. "Thank you, Ms. Payne. I'll be in touch." Madison ends the call.

Out of the four victims from the mountain, they've managed to identify Tasha Harris, Abby Walker and now, hopefully, Shannon Briggs. Just the headless victim remains, and if the skull Brody found belongs to that body, they could identify that victim by the end of the day.

But first, Madison needs to arrest Jordan Payne for murder.

CHAPTER FORTY-SIX

On her way back to question Jordan, Madison finds Officer Fuller and asks him to wait outside the interview room. He's happy to oblige. Once she's inside, she drops her notepad on the desk and takes a seat. "So, you enjoy hiking?"

Jordan remains silent.

"Did Shannon Briggs enjoy hiking with you?" she presses.

His whole body tenses at her name. Richie notices too.

"Do we need a break?" asks the attorney.

Jordan exhales. He raises his eyes to give Madison a cold stare. "If you're going to arrest me, just do it."

She senses he's been waiting a long time for this moment. "I've never met anyone in a hurry to be arrested before."

He looks at Richie. "I'm done here. Am I free to go?"

"I get the feeling the answer to that question is no," says Richie. "Detective? Are you arresting my client based on his print being found at the crime scene?"

Madison stands and opens the door so that Officer Fuller can enter. "That and some information I just obtained from his ex-wife. Please stand, Mr. Payne."

Jordan reluctantly gets out of his seat.

"Jordan Payne, I'm arresting you for the suspected murder of Shannon Briggs." She reads him his rights, but he doesn't react. His face is devoid of expression, suggesting he felt nothing for the woman he killed. Madison's hopeful she just arrested the Grave Mountain Stalker.

Richie stands too. "Once you've been processed, Mr. Payne, I'll be back to see you. In the meantime, I suggest you keep quiet."

Officer Fuller leads Jordan away to the holding cells.

As Madison escorts Richie to the exit, she tells him what Deborah Payne said. "I'll keep you updated."

Richie nods. "Are you considering him for the murder of Carla Hitchins too?"

With a deep breath, Madison says, "I don't think so. But I'll let you know if things change."

"Of course. Meanwhile, I have a date with a takeout pizza." He pulls his car keys from his pocket. "Don't work too hard, Detective, or it won't be a fair fight." He winks.

Madison smiles as she watches him leave. Richie could make it difficult for the prosecution to secure a conviction against Jordan. She needs to stay one step ahead of him.

When she returns to her desk, Alex is waiting for her. "What is it?" she asks.

Steve approaches.

"I've had a call from Conrad," says Alex. "It appears the skull discovered by our lovable friend Brody had enough teeth to compare it to Becky Draper's dental records."

"And it's her?"

"Afraid not."

"It *isn't?*" She's surprised.

Alex leans against her desk. "No. And until we can compare DNA from both the skull and the body, we won't know whether they belong together or whether they're two different people."

Madison's shoulders slump. "I wanted it to be Becky so bad." She drops onto her desk chair. "I need to tell Nancy."

Steve looks at her. "Where did you get Shannon Briggs's name from?"

"Jordan's ex-wife." She tells him what Deborah Payne disclosed over the phone, then adds, "So if you could look into the investigation into Shannon's disappearance, that would be great." She turns back to Alex. "And I need you to confirm that the body found between the trees really is Shannon Briggs. Use the DNA we have on record for her from when she vanished." She pushes her hair behind her ears. "Then I can notify her family that we've finally found her."

Alex nods. "Forgive me for saying this, but with Detective Adams being absent, you look tired."

She nods. "I'm swamped, but we'll get there eventually. I feel like we're finally building momentum with this investigation. We believe we've identified three of our four victims, so now we just need to identify the headless body and find concrete evidence linking Jordan Payne to all four murders." She scoffs. "Easy, right?"

Steve takes a seat next to her. "I don't want to muddy the waters," he says, "but I can't help thinking we're looking for more than one killer."

Madison considers it. "I know what you mean." She sighs. "Maybe the deaths aren't linked at all and we're not looking for a serial killer."

They fall silent as they consider it.

Eventually, Steve says, "So how would things look if there was more than one killer?"

Madison leans back in her seat, "Well, we think Hank killed Carla and possibly abducted Adams's daughters."

"Er, no, actually," says Alex. "Lena recently finished Hank Goodman's autopsy, and she believes he died before Detective Adams's twins were abducted."

"Interesting," she says. "Okay, so let's say Hank killed Carla. Jordan Payne killed Shannon. Our teenager's best friend, Lauren, implied that *she* harmed Abby and then took her own life, possibly from guilt. And Stuart Carpenter implied that *he* killed Tasha and Becky before taking his own life."

"Huh," says Steve. "When you put it like that, it sounds like the murders aren't related at all. The only similarity is that four of the five were discovered on the mountain. But the mountain makes a good hiding place, so I guess it makes sense that multiple killers could've used it as a dumping ground."

Madison thinks about the situation with Adams's girls. She's wondering whether Jordan Payne abducted them, but he doesn't even live here anymore. And what's his motive? He probably killed Shannon to stop his affair from being discovered. But if he didn't kill the others too, why abduct Adams's kids?

"Adams was given a choice," she mutters.

"What's that, Detective?" says Alex.

"Adams was given a choice. Told to pick one of his girls." Something suddenly clicks. "Oh my God."

Steve and Alex exchange a look.

"Oh my God," she repeats, leaning forward. Everything starts making sense. Her arms break out in goosebumps. "What if they were *all* given a choice?"

"What do you mean?" says Steve.

She attempts to explain what she's thinking. "Lauren—Abby Walker's best friend—wrote in her suicide note, 'He made me.' And Hank told dispatch that someone else killed Carla, yet we know he held the knife himself. Did the masked assailant he mentioned *make* him do it? And did someone *make* Stuart kill Becky and Tasha?" She looks at them both.

"Holy crap," says Steve.

"What if we *do* have a serial killer on our hands, but it's not Jordan Payne or Hank Goodman?" she says. "Instead, it's someone who gets off on making other people do his dirty work. It's a control thing. We know killers love being in control, right?"

They nod.

"Well, this is just another way to do it without him getting his own hands dirty."

Steve goes a little pale at the thought, but Alex warms to the idea. "So he stalks people on the mountain, or while they're isolated, and makes one of them kill the other while he watches, taking pleasure from their horrific dilemma."

"Right," she says. "I mean, if he's sick enough to make Adams choose between his daughters, he's sick enough to make other people kill a friend or loved one."

"But if that's the case," says Steve, "why haven't the people who were made to kill their companions come forward to tell us?"

Madison doesn't know. It's a flaw in her theory. "Well, Hank tried to, but he didn't have time to explain it fully before he died." She leans back in her seat. "Maybe the killer has something on them that he uses as blackmail. He could threaten to release it to the cops if they tell anyone what he made them do. Perhaps he keeps the weapon afterward, the gun with their prints on."

"But two of our victims were strangled," says Alex. "What evidence could he keep from that?"

She shakes her head. "I don't know."

"And if he's not even committing the murders himself," says Steve, "what could we charge him with? His defense would argue that his hands are clean and it's his word against the people accusing him. You can bet that if he's smart enough to get others to kill for him, his DNA is nowhere near the bodies."

Alex clears his throat. "Well, even the smartest criminals can slip up, Sergeant. Let's not automatically assume he has us beaten on that score. He may not have left anything on the victims, but his home would be a different story. Once we have a suspect, I can search his property, as well as his phone and computer. We can draw up a timeline to see where he was when the victims were killed."

"If you're right about this, Madison," says Steve, "he's one sick son of a bitch. I mean, I've never heard of a serial killer who doesn't perform the act himself. The fact that he can get pleasure from watching someone else do it is seriously twisted."

Madison says, "I don't think he gets pleasure from the murders. I think his pleasure comes from being able to coerce someone into something so horrendous. It's the power and control he has over *them*. He knows he's ruining their lives forever, and in some cases, causing an extra death when those who can't handle what he made them do resort to taking their own lives."

She's determined to test her theory. She looks up at them both. "We can't ask Lauren why she killed Abby because she's dead. We can't ask Stuart why he killed Becky and Tasha because he's dead. And we can't ask Hank why he killed Carla because he's also dead. But we *can* ask Jordan Payne what really happened between him and Shannon Briggs."

She jumps out of her seat at the same time as Steve, who says, "Think he'll tell us?"

She smiles. "There's only one way to find out. Get Richie back here. I don't think Jordan will talk without his lawyer present."

CHAPTER FORTY-SEVEN

While Madison waits for Richie Hope to return, she starts reading the case files for the newly identified victims, trying to piece together any similarities in their deaths or crime scenes. She can understand why no one has ever linked the disappearances. If her theory is correct, the person responsible for the murders was clever to use other people to perform the homicides.

She stops reading for a second, feeling the start of a dull headache. Her eyes are blurry. It's past 7 p.m., and her energy levels are dipping. Wondering what Nate's doing, she drops him a text.

I have to work late. Sorry.

He replies immediately.

No problem. I'm heading to the diner with Robert Dorsey for a support group meeting.

Madison raises her eyebrows, intrigued. She wonders whether Nancy and Doug Draper will attend. It also reminds her that she was going to look into the report on Brandon Dorsey's disappearance. If Adams were here, she could ask him to read it, but that's a luxury she doesn't have, so it'll have to wait.

She frowns as something occurs to her. She hasn't seriously considered the possibility that Brandon's case might be linked to the others. Mainly because his body was never found, so she can't assume he *is* dead. She looks through her notes to see when exactly he disappeared, and it jumps out at her. It was just a week before Becky and Tasha. But he was last seen downtown, nowhere near the mountain. And he was on his way home from school, not on a hike.

As it's not as urgent as her current cases, she has no choice but to delay reading the investigative report until she has some spare time. Besides, Nate's already looking into it, so she can quiz him on what he knows next time she sees him.

Steve appears with a case file in his hand. He drops it in front of her. "This is a missing person case that's nine years old. The victim was a bartender at a dive bar close to the Lovers' Peak Trail that has since been demolished." He leans over her chair, pointing to a color photograph of the missing woman.

She has a luminous smile that makes her appear warm and approachable. The photo was taken in someone's backyard at a summer barbecue. She's holding a beer and wearing a red flannel shirt and cut-off denim shorts. Two laughing toddlers are frozen in time as they run around her feet in the grass.

Madison's heart aches thinking about how those two little children had to cope with their mother's disappearance. "I remember this one." She glances up at him. "Maria Whitman. She was only thirty-five, I think. She vanished the year before I was arrested for Officer Ryan Levy's murder."

"You weren't a detective then, right?" he asks.

"Right. I was still an officer. Ryan and I taped off the crime scene. Damn. I forgot all about her." It's sad how many victims get forgotten, even by those involved in their investigation. She reads the notes. "Last seen leaving the bar in the company of a truck driver. Name unknown."

Steve says, "Her friend and fellow bartender that night, Janie O'Neill, thought she was going to the guy's truck to make out with him, so she didn't suspect anything was wrong until an hour or so later, when she realized they were taking their time."

"Do we have a description of what Maria was wearing when last seen?"

"Yeah, it's all in there." He nods to the case file.

Madison hands it back to him. "Go check with Alex what was found with the headless victim. I'll call her friend and see if I can get more details."

"Sure." He heads to Alex's office.

Madison calls the cell number they have on record for Maria's friend. As she waits for her to answer, something eats away at her. The fact that Maria Whitman was last seen with a truck driver.

"Hello?"

"Hi," says Madison. "Is that Janie O'Neill?"

"Yeah, but whatever you're selling, I'm not buying."

"No, wait!" She tries to stop the woman from hanging up. "I'm calling from the Lost Creek PD. Detective Harper."

The line falls silent. Eventually, Janie says, "I've been watching the news. It's all about what's going on up there on the mountain. You've found Maria, haven't you?" A sob escapes before Madison can reply.

She gives the woman time to compose herself.

Finally, Janie sniffs back tears as she says, "I'm sorry. It's just... well, I raised her kids because there was no one else to take care of them. I didn't want them going to child services. I guess I feel guilty. I shouldn't have let her leave the bar with that cowboy."

"Listen," says Madison gently. "We don't know whether we've found Maria, but whatever information you can give me could help us figure out what happened to her, okay?"

Quietly, Janie says, "Sure."

"What can you tell me about the trucker she left the bar with?"

After blowing her nose, the woman says, "He was tall, attractive, and I guess he was the silent type as he never said much. I think that's why we liked him, because he was mysterious." She says it with distaste, as if she was tricked. "We didn't even know his name. He was stuck in town because of a storm, but he was due to leave the very next day. Maria knew it was her only chance to, you know, have some fun before he left." She pauses. "Don't judge her for taking her chance, Detective. Her entire life was taken up with being a single mother and working hard to stay off welfare."

"Trust me, I'm not judging her," says Madison. "The only person responsible for her death is her killer. That's if she *is* dead." She takes a deep breath. "Was the trucker ever interviewed about her disappearance?"

"No, they never found him. The cops eventually checked traffic cameras, and his truck was spotted leaving Lost Creek, but he was using fake license plates, and his truck was never found. He probably took the plates off once he was out of town, sold the vehicle and hitchhiked out of Colorado." She sighs. "I got the feeling the cops suspected that Maria saw her opportunity to ditch her kids and start a new life with a hot stranger, but she would never have done that."

If Madison's theory is correct and someone made this trucker kill Maria, he won't want to be found. But she could be wrong. Maybe the person behind all this occasionally does his own dirty work. He might enjoy a mixture of forcing others to kill and killing people himself. Right now, she has to remain open to all possibilities.

"Can you remember his eye and hair color?" she asks.

"Both were brown."

Madison's stomach lurches. "Approximately how old was he?"

Janie sighs. "I'm not good with aging people, Detective. It's dark in the bar, and he kept his cowboy hat on most of the time. Maybe in his early forties? But I couldn't swear to it. Not in court. Not unless you have someone in mind and need me to help you convict the asshole."

Madison smiles. "No, that won't be necessary. Do you know who he worked for? What name was on his truck?"

"It was unmarked. And men like him don't tend to offer much information about themselves. I'm sorry. I feel like I'm not much help."

"It's fine." She's disappointed, but if any of that information had been available at the time of Maria's disappearance nine years ago, it wouldn't be a cold case. "My last question might sound a little odd, but do you know who Maria's dentist was?"

"Her dentist?" The woman sounds puzzled until she says, "Oh no. No. Don't tell me... You need her dental records to identify her, don't you?" She breaks down again. "I mean, I know there's probably not much left of her after all these years, but the thought of *that*..."

"I know," says Madison softly. "I'm sorry to put that image in your head. Just try to focus on the fact that if we have found Maria, you and her children can lay her to rest at last. They'll have somewhere to visit."

Janie's rendered speechless as she sobs, and eventually, she ends the call without speaking again.

Madison puts the phone down and rests her head in her

hands. The woman's grief is still raw, even after all this time. She wonders how old Maria's kids are now.

Steve returns from Alex's office. "Everything okay?"

She looks up. "Janie's devastated." She rubs her temples. "I didn't find out who Maria's dentist was, but I'll try calling her back tomorrow."

He offers her a sympathetic look, then checks his cell phone and sighs heavily.

"What is it?" she asks.

He pockets the phone. "Lena's pissed because I'm still at work. I feel like she should be more understanding, considering she knows what we're doing." He runs a hand over his jaw. "Maybe I'm not cut out to be in a relationship."

Madison feels for him. She's glad Nate doesn't make her feel bad about working long hours.

"Anyway," he says, changing the subject, "Alex confirmed the clothing matches. It looks like our headless victim is Maria Whitman."

Madison nods slowly. "In that case, I think we need to look into Doug Draper's whereabouts on the night she vanished."

"Draper? How come?"

"Because he was working as a truck driver when his daughter vanished. It stands to reason he could've been a truck driver when Maria vanished too." Her theory has some holes, but she thinks it's worth checking out.

Steve raises his eyebrows. "If he killed Maria, could he have killed Becky and Tasha too?" His eyes widen as he adds, "That could be why we haven't found his daughter's body on the mountain. He might've taken it to bury her somewhere he could visit."

Madison feels sick at the thought. She imagines having to explain that to Nancy. Unless Nancy was in on it...

Her skin crawls. "Surely not?" She thinks back to the night the first body was found on Grave Mountain. "Doug was at the support group meeting when Adams told me a body had been found. He wanted to go with us to see it. I thought it was because he was a grieving father who needed to know if it was his daughter, but now I'm wondering whether it's because he wanted to visit one of his victims. Some killers get off on returning to the scene, right?"

Steve nods.

She slowly exhales. "So Doug's worked as a truck driver, his own daughter is missing, and I think he meets the description Janie gave me for the guy Maria was last seen with."

"You don't know for sure?"

"She couldn't confirm his age, but she thought he was in his early forties back then. That means he'd be about the same age Doug is now. And they both have brown hair and eyes."

Steve frowns. "According to the case file, Draper was briefly considered as a suspect for Becky and Tasha's disappearance, but his alibi held up, so he was never formally questioned."

She nods. "Remind me what his alibi was again." She remembers asking Doug directly, but he walked away offended.

Picking up the case file from his desk, Steve rifles through it. "I think I read in the report that he was home all morning with Nancy, which she corroborated. That covers him for the time of his daughter's hike. In the afternoon, before he and Nancy knew Becky and Tasha were missing, he left town to go on a job. I don't know where he drove, but I'm sure he left Lost Creek. I think we have surveillance footage from a traffic camera that confirms it."

Madison's head pounds as she wonders whether Doug moved his daughter's body so Nancy would never know the truth of what he'd done to her. She stands. "Show me the footage." She follows him to his desk.

"Detective Harper?" Officer Fuller appears behind her.

Madison turns. "Yeah?"

"Richie Hope's back."

"Take him to an interview room, would you? And then bring Jordan Payne back up too."

Fuller nods. "On it."

Madison looks at Steve. "We should question Jordan, then return to this."

Steve stands. "Let's go."

CHAPTER FORTY-EIGHT

Madison closes the door to the interview room behind her. With the evening advancing, it's pitch black outside the station, not that you'd know it in this small, windowless room. The bright fluorescent light overhead could trick you into believing it's morning.

Jordan Payne is seated with his lawyer.

Richie looks at her, his expression puzzled. He must be wondering why he's been summoned back so soon.

Joining them at the table, she takes a deep breath and focuses on Jordan. "Mr. Payne, we believe you were having an affair with Shannon Briggs while you were married."

At first, Jordan looks like he isn't going to respond. Eventually, he crosses his arms and says, "I don't know anyone by that name. Never have."

Richie shoots him a look that suggests he should resist making bold statements.

Madison smiles. By lying, he's hurting his defense. "We know of a witness who saw you and Shannon together in your car just a month before she vanished."

A flicker of surprise crosses his face. He resists glancing at his lawyer. "Either you're lying, or your so-called witness is." He tilts his head. "Maybe *they* killed her."

"I'm afraid not," says Madison. She intends to secure a statement from Deborah Payne and her friend as soon as possible, but first, she wants to see if he'll admit what he did. "When I learned that you were seen together, I thought you probably killed Shannon to silence her so that your wife never found out about the affair. However, in light of recent developments, I'm working on a different theory." She rests her elbows on the table and leans in slightly. "I don't believe you killed Shannon to silence her." She pauses, giving him the opportunity to say something. He doesn't take her up on it.

Richie says, "So why on earth *would* he kill her?"

She looks at the lawyer. "Because someone *made* him do it."

Jordan's hands drop to his lap. His mouth opens. He hesitates before saying, "Why would you think that?" He doesn't sound so self-assured now.

"Mr. Payne," she says. "This is your opportunity to tell the truth and defend yourself. The sooner you tell me what really happened on Grave Mountain, the more your attorney can help you."

"Well," says Richie lightly, "I think that depends on what the truth is and what you think you have on my client." He looks at Jordan. "I'd advise against saying anything that could hurt your defense in court."

Jordan lowers his eyes before rubbing them with the palms of his hands. He groans loudly. "I'm so over all this."

"Over what?" says Madison. "Pretending you don't know Shannon or protecting her real killer?"

He keeps his hands over his eyes for a long time as he considers what to do. When he finally removes them, he says, "I want to make a deal."

Madison frowns.

Steve says, "We're not responsible for making deals, sir.

That's the DA's office. But help us to understand why you think you need one."

After a quick glance at his lawyer, Jordan says, "Because I'm being blackmailed, and the asshole doing it will cut a deal before I can. I guarantee it."

Madison sits back and looks at Steve. She was right. Someone blackmailed Jordan to kill Shannon, and their other victims might've been killed the same way. "Tell us everything from the beginning."

Richie leans in to his client and whispers, "Are you sure you want to do this?"

Conflicted, Jordan raises his chin to the ceiling as he thinks. "This has been hanging over me for seven years. One way or another, it has to end."

Madison holds her breath. At last, they're going to get answers. She prompts him to start at the beginning. "What were you and Shannon doing on the mountain in the first place?"

Jordan finally looks at her. "We were in a sexual relationship. We had to find places to go where we wouldn't be seen, so I took her to the Lovers' Peak Trail. Cheesy, I know, but I thought it would be quiet at midmorning on a weekday, and it was. Until someone interrupted us."

"While you were having sex?" asks Steve.

"No," he replies. "But almost. Shannon saw him first. He stepped out from behind a tree wearing a ski mask. I knew right away that something was wrong. I mean, it was midsummer. He must've been sweltering under that thing."

"Can you describe him for me?" asks Madison.

"No. I couldn't see his hair or his face. He was slim, maybe five-ten to six foot. I don't know, it was seven years ago." He shakes his head.

"Did he get close enough for you to see his eye color?" asks Steve.

"No. I was more focused on the gun in his hand."

"Do you know what kind of firearm it was?" he presses.

Jordan shakes his head. "I don't know the first thing about guns."

"Okay, so what happened next?"

"He told me I had to kill her, or he'd kill me. I mean, he pointed the gun at my head, so what was I gonna do? He said I had sixty seconds to decide." The look on his face suggests he's reliving his dilemma. His brow is furrowed as sweat beads at his hairline. "Shannon tried to get away, but I held on to her, afraid she was going to get *me* killed."

Madison swallows. Shannon must've been terrified.

Jordan takes a sip of water. He's fidgety now. "I can't believe I'm telling you this." He wipes his brow with the back of his hand before continuing. "I told the guy I couldn't kill her because I didn't have a weapon, and he said my hands were my weapon. I realized I'd have to strangle her. I knew I couldn't beat her to death. It was too brutal."

Steve says, "So you went ahead and strangled her with your bare hands?"

Jordan nods. "I had no choice. I didn't want to die." He clears his throat, while Richie furiously scribbles everything down on a legal pad. "She fell to the floor as we struggled. I got on top of her and pinned her down. It took three attempts for her to stop breathing. The guy had his gun trained on me the entire time."

The room falls silent for a few seconds as they picture what Shannon went through.

"Who stuffed her body between the tree trunks?" asks Madison. The trees would've been less mature back then. Alex believes they grew around her over the years she lay undiscovered.

"I did. I had to hide her so I wouldn't be arrested."

Surprised, she says, "The assailant didn't make you do that?"

"No, he disappeared as fast as he'd arrived, leaving me to clean up the mess. I couldn't fit her all the way in because she kept slumping to the ground, so I left her sitting up and covered her bottom half with branches and shrubs. Her top half slouched into the gap. I was convinced she'd be found within days."

Madison's shocked at his choice of words. He called Shannon *the mess*. He viewed her lifeless body as something to be hidden. She was good enough to use for sex but not good enough to try to save. It sounds like he never considered how her family would feel when she didn't arrive home. Just because he was forced to kill her to save his own life doesn't mean he's completely innocent in all this. He was cheating on his wife. Maybe he's always had a low opinion of women.

"At some point, it occurred to me that he might kill me afterward anyway," he continues. "That it was some kind of sick trick. And ever since, I wished he had. It probably would've been better than the alternative."

"Why?" says Madison.

"Because I didn't know when he'd go to the police or the press. It's been hanging over me ever since."

So, not because he'd killed a woman, but because he was worried about being caught for doing it. Madison has some sympathy for the position he was in, but he could've at least tried to run or fight the guy instead.

"What I don't understand," says Steve, "is how he could blackmail you if you killed her with your hands? What evidence did he have?"

Jordan looks at him. "He filmed the whole thing and threatened to release it online for the cops to find. And he kept Shannon's bra. I'd touched it. My DNA was all over it."

Madison swallows. *He filmed it.* Does that mean he filmed the other murders too? Are they eventually going to find a computer filled with snuff movies? She realizes Alex was right when he said there could be a way to catch the person behind all this. Even though the perpetrator left no evidence of himself at the crime scenes, he *is* holding on to something that can place him there. All they need to do is find the camera and the footage. His voice might be on the recordings.

"What kind of camera did he use?" she asks.

"It was one of those GoPro things on a small tripod. He placed it on the ground while he threatened me." He didn't even have to hold the camera as he watched his victims play out his sick fantasy.

"What was he wearing?"

"I don't know," says Jordan. "Shorts and a T-shirt, I guess." He's not much help, but he was under an incredible amount of stress, so it's not surprising that his memory is sketchy.

"Forgive me for asking," says Madison, "but did you notice whether the perpetrator became aroused at any point?"

He balls his fists as he nods. "The son of a bitch was turned on by the power he had over us."

"What did he sound like?" she asks. "Did he speak with an accent?"

Jordan leans back. He looks exhausted. "I don't know. He sounded like any other guy. I don't remember an accent."

Madison looks at Steve. They both stand. "Thank you," she says. "We need a moment."

As they leave the room, she hears Jordan ask Richie, "What's going to happen to me now? I was forced to kill her. Her death wasn't my fault."

She doesn't hear Richie's response.

"What does happen now?" asks Steve as they return to the office.

She takes a deep breath. "We find out whether he's telling the truth. But first, I want to check Doug Draper's alibi for the day his daughter disappeared."

CHAPTER FORTY-NINE

At the diner, Nate glances out the window behind him as heavy rain lashes against the glass. Condensation builds as the coffee machine loudly whirs into life. It's too dark to see outside, but Vince's security lights occasionally flicker into life as a car passes or someone enters the parking lot.

Vince hands him a black coffee.

"Are you okay?" asks Nate. He's worried about Vince blaming himself for failing to see what Hank Goodman was capable of.

"No," says the older man. "But I'm sure I will be in time. If I can learn to live with my wife's murder, I'll come to terms with what happened to Carla eventually." He sighs. "I learned the hard way that I've got to keep busy. Distraction is the only way through grief."

Nate wishes there was something he could do to help, but grief is a deeply personal experience.

Vince changes the subject. "Where's Brody? I hope he was rewarded for finding that skull."

Nate smiles. "You needn't worry about that. He's

exhausted, so he's staying home. When I left, he was stretched out on the couch watching *Law & Order*."

Vince snorts. "Once a cop..."

Nate takes his coffee and turns to find eight chairs in a circle behind him. He chooses a seat next to Robert Dorsey, who's dressed in a blue flannel shirt over a T-shirt and dirty jeans. He's checking his watch. They're the first to arrive.

"Why did you want me here, Robert?" asks Nate.

The older man looks him in the eye. "I thought that if you could hear the impact a missing family member has on people's lives, you'd work a little harder to find my son."

Nate looks away. He doesn't need any more motivation. "If I didn't intend to find him, I wouldn't have taken the case."

The door opens and Bryan Carpenter enters. Robert sees him and mutters, "Asshole."

Nate wonders what his problem is, since there's been no suggestion that Stuart Carpenter had anything to do with Brandon's disappearance. Before he can ask, Vince asks Bryan to leave.

"It's nothing personal," he says. "It's just that I've closed early for a prior engagement, sorry."

Bryan looks around the room, his eyes settling on Nate and Robert and the empty chairs in the circle. "How come they're here?"

Vince moves toward him, ready to usher him out. "With all due respect, Mr. Carpenter, that's none of your business."

"Get out of here, jackass," says Robert.

Bryan glares at him before leaving.

When he's gone, Nate says, "What was that about?"

"Guys with money like him think they can do whatever they want. That they own the roads all because they can afford nice cars." Robert angrily shakes his head. "We butted heads years ago, when he was in my neighborhood visiting his son. He had a bad case of road rage, even though it was *him* who cut *me* off. I almost called the cops on him, but his son talked me out of it. He's been an asshole ever since. We got into it again recently too. I don't trust the guy."

Nate thinks about it for a second. "When you found out Stuart had killed himself after admitting to killing Becky Draper and Tasha Harris, did you ever think he could've been the person who took Brandon?"

Robert's face turns to stone, making Nate regret saying anything. "I had considered it, yeah, thanks to the news reports about him." He eyeballs Nate. "Are you telling me that Stuart Carpenter *did* hurt my boy? Is that why he came to the last meeting? To get off on my grief?"

"No," says Nate. "That's not what I'm saying. I just wondered whether it was ever considered by you or the cops, since Brandon went missing just a week before the women disappeared."

Robert's brain is ticking over. "What if it was *Bryan?*" he says slowly. "I mean, the guy clearly hates me."

The door opens again, and Nancy and Doug Draper appear. A younger woman follows them inside. Nate doesn't recognize her. They spend a couple of minutes talking to Vince while they order drinks.

"Let's not jump to any conclusions," says Nate. "I'll ask Madison if she can disclose what's in the police report." He thinks about what Violet Humphrey said in her recording about someone getting into a car. It's been bothering him. "Did Brandon's friend Erin drive?"

Robert shrugs. "She does now, but she was only thirteen when Brandon vanished."

Nate nods. Just because she wasn't legally old enough to drive doesn't mean she didn't know how to. She could've taken her parents' car without permission. Maybe she offered

Brandon a ride home. They could've gotten into an accident and her dangerous driving killed him. Given that most options have been exhausted in the attempt to find him, it's worth considering whether Erin has been lying all this time. Her parents could've helped with the cover-up so she didn't get jail time.

"What is it?" asks Robert, studying his face.

Nate sips his coffee. "Probably nothing, but one of Erin's neighbors might've seen Brandon getting into a car after leaving Erin's house."

Robert's eyes widen. "What car?"

"She wasn't able to say, unfortunately. She had dementia, and she just kept repeating, 'He's in the car' and 'Who is she?'"

Robert falls silent, lost in his thoughts. Eventually, he mutters, "Why didn't Detective Douglas tell me that?"

"Because it didn't lead anywhere," says Nate. "And there's no telling whether she was talking about Brandon. She could've meant anyone."

Nancy and Doug take a seat opposite Nate and Robert. Nancy says hi before introducing the young woman. "This is Susie Harris, Tasha's sister."

Nate smiles. "Nate Monroe."

Robert doesn't speak.

"I hope no one minds me being here," says Susie nervously. "It's just that Tasha's remains were found on the mountain, and, well, Nancy invited me. My sister and her daughter were inseparable."

"I'm glad they found your sister," says Robert, leaning forward and resting his elbows on his knees. "I'm looking for my son. I've hired this guy." He nods to Nate. "He's a PI. Did you know my son? Brandon Dorsey."

Susie shakes her head. "I don't think so, but I remember the news reports. I'm sorry for what you're going through. I wouldn't wish it on my worst enemy." She lowers her eyes.

Robert looks at Doug. "Did they find Becky up there yet?"

Nancy answers. "No, not yet. But they will. I have faith in Detective Harper."

Nate suddenly feels all eyes on him.

An awkward silence settles over the room as they sip their drinks and think of their missing loved ones. It's only broken when the door to the diner opens again and Madison walks in, followed by Sergeant Tanner.

Nate frowns as Madison's eyes search the room. Her coat drips rainwater all over the floor. He wasn't expecting to see her here.

"Madison?" says Vince from behind the counter. "I didn't realize you were coming. What can I get you both?"

"Nothing for us," says Steve, who runs a hand over his wet hair to remove the rain.

Madison offers Nate a tight smile before approaching the Drapers. "Doug, can we have a word outside?"

The blood appears to drain from Doug's face. Nate watches him closely. He looks like he's been caught red-handed at something.

Nancy stands, clasping her hands together in front of her. "You've found her body, haven't you? I knew you would. It's okay, you can tell me. Finally learning the truth will bring me peace, no matter how painful it is."

Madison seems hesitant to talk in front of the group. "No, Nancy. I'm so sorry. I've just had confirmation that Becky wasn't one of the people we found on the mountain."

Nancy looks crestfallen.

"So why do you want to speak to me?" says Doug, tipping his damp baseball cap backward slightly. He remains seated.

"Let's go outside," says Steve. "You don't want to discuss this in here."

Nate thinks about getting the others to leave to give the

Drapers some privacy, but Doug inexplicably erupts before he can do so. He bolts upward and gets in Madison's face.

"You two need to stop talking down to me and just say what you've come to say!"

Nate jumps out of his seat.

CHAPTER FIFTY

"Everyone needs to just take a second and calm down," shouts Steve, getting between Doug and Nate.

Madison's worried someone's going to get hurt. She looks at Doug. "Fine. We'll do this here if you'd prefer."

Susie Harris walks to the corner of the room, trying to avoid the fallout.

The force of the wind outside pushes the door open a little, letting rain cover a small section of the floor. Madison can see everyone reflected in the large window, including herself. It's like watching a play on stage, except *they're* the actors.

"Sit down, Doug," she says forcefully. "You too, please, Nancy."

He slowly sits. A quiet intensity radiates off him, and she suspects he could lash out again at any minute. She sits next to him. Steve remains standing in case someone does something stupid.

Nate doesn't move, so Madison gives him a look. "Maybe you should wait outside."

He doesn't do as she says, which surprises her. He's not the type to get into a fight. If he won't carry a weapon for protection, how does he think he'll do in a physical altercation?

Nancy clutches the gold cross she wears around her neck. Her eyes search Madison's face for answers. Madison has to look away. She's filled with guilt over what she's about to do.

Pulling out her cell phone, she says, "Doug, I need you to explain this." She hits play. It's the surveillance footage they found in the case file from the investigation into Becky and Tasha's disappearance five years ago. She watches Doug and Nancy closely as they stare at the screen.

Robert Dorsey creeps over to get a look. "That's you in that truck," he says, looking at Doug.

Nate touches his arm and gives him a look that suggests he shouldn't get involved.

"So what?" says Doug. "I was working."

He and Nancy watch as a truck drives out of Lost Creek at midmorning on the day of the hike. The day Becky and Tasha vanished. Doug can be seen clearly at the wheel.

Madison says, "We have footage of you returning to Lost Creek later that day. Before Stuart Carpenter alerted the police to your daughter's disappearance."

Robert quietly walks away, his hands on the back of his head. Maybe he's guessed where she's going with this.

She and Steve believe this footage could suggest that Doug transported his daughter's body out of town before returning home in time for dinner. But she wants to give him the opportunity to offer an alternative explanation.

Susie Harris approaches the couple and stands in front of them. "Was it you, Doug? Did you kill my sister?"

Nancy looks puzzled. "I don't understand," she says. "What's this got to do with anything? He had to work that afternoon. So what?"

Madison looks at Doug. "I think you should tell your wife

what you did, because I don't want to be the one to break her heart." The words catch in her throat.

Doug fixes his eyes on hers and doesn't speak for the longest time. "I was trying to *protect* my wife," he says eventually. "You've ruined everything." He lowers his head into his hands.

Nancy stands on shaky legs. "Doug? What did you do? What's going on?"

When he doesn't answer, Madison turns to her. "Nancy, we believe this is footage of your husband transporting your daughter's b—"

She doesn't get to finish her sentence because the door to the diner opens behind her. She turns as a woman enters.

"Sorry, we're closed," says Vince, stepping out from behind the counter. "This is a private meeting."

"Oh my God!" exclaims Susie, her hands flying to her mouth. "Oh my God! I don't believe it!"

The stranger's eyes fill with tears. She's staring at Nancy.

Madison frowns. It takes her a second to recognize the woman, because she's five years older than in the photograph taken on the morning of the hike. Her hair is platinum blonde instead of brown, and she's wearing heavy makeup. Madison's mouth falls open when she realizes who she's looking at. She turns to Nancy, who's still staring at her husband, waiting for answers.

Doug's eyes are fixed on the ground.

Madison doesn't know what he was about to admit to, but it's not what she thought it was. She goes to Nancy's side. "Nancy, look." She points to the newcomer.

When the older woman's eyes meet Becky's, she stops breathing, and her whole body tenses.

Doug looks up, but instead of being exhilarated, he shakes his head before standing to face his daughter. "You shouldn't have come."

Madison wonders why he'd say that. She was wrong about

him killing Becky, but he could still be responsible for Tasha's murder. And the others.

She suddenly feels Nancy leaning into her. She clutches the woman's arm and holds her up. "Nancy? Are you okay?"

Nancy passes out, with Madison taking her weight.

Nate and Steve rush forward to help ease her onto her back on the floor. Madison crouches down and listens to her chest to check she's still breathing. She isn't. Pressing her fingers to the woman's neck, she shouts, "Call an ambulance!"

"On it," says Nate.

Steve begins CPR as Vince clears chairs out of the way. Nancy looks dead already. It doesn't take long for her lips to turn gray.

The room falls silent, with the only sounds coming from Steve as he tries to keep Nancy alive.

Madison's heart is in her throat as she watches. "She can't die like this," she says, panicked. "She can't. She needs to at least speak to Becky first."

No one answers, but she feels Nate's hand on her shoulder. She listens as he speaks to dispatch.

When he ends the call, he says, "The ambulance is seven minutes away."

"Keep going," says Madison to Steve.

"They've gone," says Robert Dorsey behind them. "Why would they run?"

Madison's confused until she turns and realizes that Becky and Doug have disappeared. "*Shit.*" She retrieves her cell phone and calls dispatch.

Dina answers immediately. "They're not far away now," she says, obviously assuming it's about the ambulance.

"Dina, listen," says Madison. "I need patrol to bring Doug Draper in for questioning. He's just fled Ruby's Diner with a twenty-four-year-old blonde woman named Becky Draper."

"Becky *Draper*? His missing daughter?"

"Yes."

Dina only hesitates for a second before confirming she understands. "I'll notify all units immediately."

As Madison drops her phone, Robert runs for the door. "I'll try to follow them."

"Mr. Dorsey, stay here! Do not..." It's too late. He's gone.

Nate turns. "I'll go after him."

"Nate, no!" She doesn't want him getting caught up in whatever's about to happen.

"I'll be careful!" he shouts over his shoulder as he runs.

Madison turns back to the woman on the floor. She can't leave her. She has to keep her alive long enough to speak to her daughter.

The pallor of Nancy's skin suggests it might be too late.

CHAPTER FIFTY-ONE

Seated next to Nancy's hospital bed, in the soft glow of the bedside light, Madison's waiting for news from Nate about what happened after he and Robert Dorsey raced after Doug and Becky Draper. Officer Sanchez is stationed outside the hospital room. Madison doesn't *think* Doug would hurt his wife, but it's not a risk she's willing to take. In his desperation at recent developments, he might decide Nancy's better off not knowing what he did.

Madison's still getting her head around the idea that Becky Draper is alive. It leaves so many unanswered questions that she feels exhausted just thinking about unraveling it all. The clock above the bed tells her it's almost 10 p.m. She stifles a yawn.

A nurse enters the room, smiling. She leans over the bed and checks Nancy's pulse by lifting her hand and holding her wrist. "The doctor has given her a sedative, so you can leave if you want to. She'll be asleep until the morning."

Madison hesitates to leave her all alone. "Was it a stroke? Or her heart?"

"We won't know that until a doctor has examined her test results."

Madison nods and sits back in her chair. When the nurse leaves, she's alone for a while, listening to the steady beeping of machines and Nancy's soft breathing. It would be peaceful if her mind wasn't buzzing with everything she still has to do.

Approaching footsteps make her look at the door in anticipation.

Nate appears. His hair is soaking wet and his jacket drips rainwater all over the floor. He pulls it off. She stands as he comes over to hug her.

He holds on for longer than usual before pulling away. "Are you okay?" he says.

"I am." She feels the cold air clinging to his skin when he kisses her.

"I talked Robert into going home," he says. "I said I'd call him in the morning with an update."

"Why does he need an update about Doug Draper?" she asks.

Nate brings a second chair over as Madison sits back down. He glances at Nancy and keeps his voice low as he explains what he's discovered during his investigation into Brandon Dorsey's disappearance.

She gasps when he tells her what the neighbor's wife said about Brandon possibly getting into a car with a female driver. "So, what, he thinks Becky was involved?"

He shrugs before taking her hand and absently resting it on his knee.

"Did Becky and Brandon know each other?" she presses.

"Not according to Robert. And remember, Violet Humphrey had dementia. I can see why Detective Douglas didn't want to base his whole investigation around her statement, although I don't think he heard her final words, as he was saying goodbye to her husband when she said them."

"So he might not have known that Violet thought the driver was female," she says.

"Right. I plan to question Brandon's girlfriend, Erin, again tomorrow since it could've been her in the car." He pauses. "Erin suggested Robert might not have been happy about her and his son dating because of her skin color."

Madison raises her eyebrows. "Racism could be a motive?" She studies Nate's face. "You think Robert was involved in his son's disappearance, don't you?"

He rubs the back of his neck before answering. "God, I hope not. But there's something about the guy that bothers me. What with his wife trying to leave him before she died, and the fact that he seems to hate everyone."

"Everyone?"

Nate nods. "Before you arrived at the diner, he had a run-in with Bryan Carpenter. There's some bad blood between them because of a road rage incident years ago. Apparently, Bryan blew up at him, and let me tell you, Robert Dorsey is a man who holds grudges."

"Huh." She thinks about it. "I wouldn't have thought Bryan was the type to fly into a rage. Remind me again why Robert's wife stayed with him even though she consulted a lawyer."

"She suffered with ill health and died a few years later."

"Did she die, or was she killed?"

Nate smiles. "That's what I wondered, but I looked into her death. She was definitely in poor health."

Madison thinks about it. "Bryan Carpenter's wife is no longer with us either."

Nate squeezes her hand. "Are those cogs turning?"

She laughs. "You know me. It's not a proper investigation until I've suspected everyone of killing someone. Hold on a second." She retrieves her phone from a pocket and heads outside the room, not wanting to disturb Nancy.

Dina answers immediately, and Madison asks whether Steve is still at the station.

"Afraid not," says the dispatcher. "He said he had to get home."

Disappointed, Madison says, "What about Chief Mendes?"

"No, she left an hour ago. It's quiet here. The rookies are shadowing me to learn what I do. Can they help?"

Madison considers it. She needs to sleep, so she has no choice but to delegate. "Sure, put one of them on."

Officer Kent comes on the line. "Hello?"

"Hi, Lisa. I need a favor. How are you with research?"

"Well, I can find an ex-boyfriend's new girlfriend on social media in less than two minutes. Does that count?"

Madison snorts. "Sure, why not? I need you and Corey to look into the cause of death for Bryan Carpenter's wife, Lucy Carpenter." She only knows Lucy's name because Mel told her that she and Jay intend to name their baby after the woman.

"Sure thing. Should we call you if we find anything?"

"No. I'm heading home soon, but I'll be in early tomorrow."

"Okay," says Kent. "Have a good evening."

"Thanks." Madison ends the call and re-enters Nancy's room. The older woman is still sleeping soundly.

Nate stands. "Can you leave her for a few hours and get some rest?"

Madison nods.

"Then let's go home." He picks up their jackets and takes her by the hand, leading her out of the room.

She smiles as they walk. Nate's a hand-holder and a hugger. In fact, he's so open with his feelings for her that she suddenly decides to accept his offer. She wants to live with him. The thought doesn't scare her anymore. She stops. "Nate?"

He turns to look at her. "Yeah?"

"Do you still want me, Bandit and Mrs. Pebbles to move in with you?"

A smile breaks out, making him appear younger. "I don't remember Mrs. Pebbles being part of the deal."

She shrugs. "Sorry, I come with baggage. It's an age thing."

He laughs as he cups her face with his hands. "Lucky for you, I have plenty of room for baggage." He kisses her before leading her to the elevator.

CHAPTER FIFTY-TWO

The following morning starts bright and sunny, with a crisp chill to the air and a mist rising off the mountains from the overnight rain. Madison calls in at the hospital on her way to the station. She's hoping Nancy is awake and can answer some questions about her missing husband and daughter. Patrol didn't locate them overnight, and there are no signs of them returning home, so she's worried they've left town.

When she enters Nancy's room, it's clear the older woman didn't wake up during the night as she's in the same position as when they left yesterday. Madison takes the opportunity to check her messages. She has one from Alex to say he didn't find anything at Detective Adams's house that could help identify who abducted Lizzie and Summer. And Steve ran a background check on Robert Dorsey for her, but there's nothing of interest there, so Nate could be wrong about him.

A noise behind her makes her turn. She's shocked to find Doug Draper standing in the doorway. She reaches for her service weapon, but Officer Sanchez is waiting behind him.

Doug holds his empty hands out in front of him. "I'm not

here to cause trouble. I want to see my wife. Then you and I need to talk."

"Where's Becky?" asks Madison.

Doug folds his arms over his chest. "I'll answer your questions once I've seen my wife."

She nods to Sanchez, who leaves the room.

Doug approaches Nancy's bed and stands opposite Madison. Her heart beats a little faster in anticipation of what he might do.

He takes his wife's limp hand in his. "Is she going to pull through?"

"No one knows yet. We should learn more later this morning." Feeling pressed for time, Madison says, "What's going on, Doug? What did you do?"

He looks across at her with weary eyes. "I tried to protect my wife."

"From what?"

He doesn't answer. Frustrated, Madison says, "You knew Becky was still alive, right?" That's what it sounded like in the diner last night.

"Yes. I knew."

"And you didn't tell Nancy?" She's incredulous. "How could you keep that from her all this time? I mean, the state of your house... And the state of her mental health. *You* did that to her. You and Becky." She pauses as something dawns on her. "Oh my God. Becky killed Tasha, didn't she?"

"Don't be so stupid," he hisses.

Madison doesn't understand why he won't open up now she knows Becky's alive.

Doug turns away from her and Nancy. "I want a lawyer."

Madison shakes her head. He's left her with no choice. "Officer?" Sanchez reappears, and she gestures for his handcuffs. She takes them from him and cuffs Doug Draper.

"You've caused this, Doug. By remaining silent about what you know, you've made yourself a suspect."

He doesn't reply as Sanchez leads him out of the room.

When Madison gets to the station, she notices the parking lot is filled with empty news trucks. Sanchez arrives with Doug Draper. Inside, she processes Doug's arrest and has Sanchez take him to the holding cells while they wait for a lawyer. After fixing herself a cup of coffee, she passes the conference room and sees it's full of reporters.

A message on her desk tells her the Prospect Springs PD is currently searching Jordan Payne's house. Madison doesn't expect they'll find the footage of Shannon's murder there because she doesn't think he's the mastermind behind all this, but she could yet be proven wrong.

She finds Steve in Chief Mendes's office. He stands as he says, "Patrol hasn't found Doug or Becky Draper, but someone's informed the press that Becky's alive. They've been calling the station all morning, so the chief's about to hold a press conference."

"Delay the press conference," says Madison. "I just brought Doug Draper in for questioning, so we might finally get some answers."

Chief Mendes raises her eyebrows. "Where was he?"

"He turned up at the hospital to see Nancy. He wants a lawyer." Madison sips her coffee. "He wouldn't tell me where his daughter is. I suspect he told her to flee, so she could be anywhere by now. Dispatch has issued a BOLO for her."

Officers Kent and Fuller appear at the door. "Can we come in?" asks Fuller. His shirt is undone at the collar, and Kent is holding her purse. They must be heading home after a long night shift.

Madison nods. "Find anything on Bryan Carpenter's wife?"

Officer Kent says, "We sure did. Lucy Carpenter drowned in the family's pool back when they lived in Nebraska. We spoke to one of the investigating detectives, who told us that she and her partner disagreed about what happened to her." She swings her purse strap over her body as she adds, "Her partner thought it was an accidental drowning, so it was never investigated as a homicide, even though *she* suspected foul play. As she couldn't find any evidence of that, and because Lucy was dressed in a swimsuit at the time of her death, she was overruled."

"Bryan Carpenter's alibi was that he was at work at the time," says Fuller. "He managed a chain of motels, and enough employees backed him up, but there were also chunks of time where no one could vouch for him."

Madison's heart beats a little faster. She looks at Steve. "Bryan could've killed his wife."

"Do we have a motive?" asks Mendes.

Madison tries to think. "No, but he's a businessman with a lot of money to lose in a divorce, so it might be worth checking whether his wife was planning to leave him."

Mendes doesn't seem convinced. "Even if he killed his wife, that doesn't mean he killed our victims."

Madison desperately tries to think of a link between Bryan and any of their victims. "His younger son, Stuart, was friends with Tasha Harris and Becky Draper. It's likely Bryan met Tasha at some point. And let's not forget he was out running alone when Carla was killed."

Chief Mendes considers it. "It could be why Stuart took his own life. Maybe he knew his father was a killer."

Steve checks his notepad. "Bryan fits the height description Jordan Payne gave us for the perp who made him kill Shannon Briggs."

"What about Doug and Becky Draper?" says Chief Mendes. "Where do they fit in?"

Madison takes a deep breath. "I don't know."

"What if Bryan was sleeping with Becky?" says Officer Kent, her eyes lighting up.

Madison hadn't considered that. "Nancy suspected Becky was seeing someone in the months before her disappearance, but she didn't know who. Bryan could've wanted to keep it a secret because of their age difference and how it would look."

Mendes nods. "Okay, fine. It's worth questioning Bryan. See how he reacts to the suggestion that his wife was murdered. And find out how well he knew Becky and Tasha. His reaction should tell you everything you need to know."

Madison smiles at the rookies. "Good work, guys."

Officer Kent fondly nudges Fuller in the ribs as she smiles up at him. Fuller's serious demeanor finally cracks.

CHAPTER FIFTY-THREE

The parking lot at the Pine Shadows Lodge is less than half full when Madison and Steve arrive, and a sign states the venue is closed for the foreseeable future. Madison wonders whether the recent negative publicity has irreparably damaged the business or whether Bryan intends to cut his losses, sell up and leave town.

He won't be going anywhere if she gets her way.

Steve gets out of his car and approaches her. "Ready?"

She nods.

They walk toward the glass-fronted entrance, which is closed. The faint sound of violin music reaches them. Madison stops. "Oh no."

"What?" Steve stops behind her.

She turns to him. "They're getting married today."

"Who?"

"Jay and Mel. The family talked them into going ahead with the wedding."

Steve raises his eyebrows. "Seriously?"

"Think we should wait until they're married?" she asks.

He rests his hands on his hips. "Bryan's probably less likely to cause a scene at his son's wedding. He might come quietly if we approach him now."

The decision is made for them when the automatic glass doors slide open and an elderly man appears.

"You better hurry if you want to catch the vows," he says. With thick lenses and fine white hair, he's dressed in a navy-blue suit with a single white rose pinned to the lapel. "I'm slipping out for a cigarette." He winks at them. "Don't tell anyone."

Madison steps into the lobby. The warmth from the open fireplace greets them, and bunches of white and pink flowers adorn the entrance, giving off a pleasantly sweet scent. The violin music lowers, suggesting the bride has made it up the aisle. Madison follows the sound to an oak-paneled library. The impressive room is decorated beautifully, with flowers everywhere and pink ribbons tied to each seat with large bows. Red rose petals line the aisle, and the room contains an intimate gathering of approximately thirty guests: men in smart suits, a few well-behaved children, and women wearing pastel dresses and heels, some with fancy hats.

Madison feels a sharp pang of envy. Not because she wants to be a bride with a lavish wedding, but because of the smiling guests, who appear to be happy for the young couple. Her own family is decimated, with just her son and a criminal sister left. She can't imagine who would attend if she were ever to get married. It would probably need to be a small affair at the courthouse to avoid embarrassment. She shakes the thought away. It's unlikely she'll ever marry anyway.

She and Steve hover in the doorway, trying to stay out of view so they don't interrupt the wedding. Madison wants eyes on Bryan Carpenter. He's standing behind his son, dressed smartly in a navy suit. The bride's dress is carefully crafted to minimize her protruding belly, and the bouquet of pink and white roses also helps disguise it. Madison can only see Mel's side profile as she gazes into Jay's eyes. She's beaming with happiness. With her spare hand between his, Jay gazes lovingly back at her. He looks like his younger brother, but Stuart will never reach this age, thirty-six.

Jay and Mel have been through so much this week that Madison can't help but feel happy for them until she realizes Stuart's funeral will look eerily similar, with rows of family members seated like today, except with far less color involved and, instead of being held at the lodge, it will take place in a church.

It's a grim thought.

She notices a wedding photographer off to the side. He's switching between taking photographs and checking a video camera that's fixed to a tripod at the end of the aisle as it captures the occasion. She frowns. Something bothers her about it, but she can't quite grasp what.

Steve leans into her as he whispers, "Step back. Jay's spotted us."

She locks eyes with Jay. He looks concerned at their presence. He must wonder whether they're bringing more bad news about his brother's involvement in the Grave Mountain Stalker case. She hopes he can forget about them and concentrate on exchanging vows with his beautiful bride.

Bryan follows his son's gaze and scowls when he spots them. His face quickly reddens, and Madison wonders whether he's angry they showed up at his son's wedding or because he knows why they're here.

Part of her feels guilty. They should've held back until the wedding was over. Now that they know Bryan's definitely here, she thinks they should wait until the ceremony is finished before trying to speak to him. This family has had enough upset already.

She turns to Steve. "Let's wait in the lobby."

They quietly retreat. A few minutes pass as the couple exchange vows. Steve warms his hands in front of the fire.

Madison gets a whiff of some tantalizing food; roast chicken, perhaps. The caterers must be busy preparing for a sit-down meal. As they wait, everything seems so peaceful it's almost relaxing.

Until a woman's scream tears through the air.

Madison straightens and looks at Steve. "What the hell was that?"

More screams follow.

A cold knot of fear builds in her stomach. Something terrible has happened. She races to the library and finds the guests are no longer seated. A flurry of people rushes past her, getting in her way. She's confused. She can't see Bryan anywhere.

"Police!" she yells. "Let us through!"

"Over there!" Steve points to the front of the room as guests clear out of the way.

The wedding officiant is crouched over someone, a pool of blood spreading at his feet. Madison holds her breath, fearing that Bryan has caused a devastating distraction to give himself time to escape.

She looks at Steve. "What if it's Mel? She's five months pregnant!"

Steve rushes ahead of her, moving people out of their way. Madison follows. When she sees who's lying on the ground, she gasps.

It's Bryan.

Confused, she crouches down, wondering whether he's taken his own life. When she can see no obvious injuries, she looks up at the officiant. "What happened?"

Clearly shaken, the man points to a knife on the floor. He then opens Bryan's tuxedo jacket, and Madison sees blood spreading across his crisp white shirt. He's been stabbed in the chest, possibly more than once.

She hears Steve on his cell phone behind her, calling for

backup and an ambulance. She stands. "Who did this?" she asks the crowd.

A male guest steps forward. "Jay. He suddenly flipped out! One minute he's saying his vows, the next he's pulling a knife from his jacket." He looks down at Bryan. "Holy crap. Will he be okay?"

Madison spins around, pulling her weapon. She can't see Jay and Mel anywhere. She suddenly realizes why watching the wedding photographer gave her a bad feeling. The day she came here to notify Stuart's family of his suicide, Jay was recording his and Mel's arrival at the lodge. Jordan Payne told her that the perpetrator who made him kill Shannon Briggs recorded the murder. And Jay no longer lives in town. Did he leave after the day of the hike?

She swallows. "What happened after he stabbed his father?"

The guy has a hand to his mouth. He looks like he could vomit.

"Sir," she says urgently, "I need you to answer me."

A woman rushes over to them. She's the spitting image of Mel, except older. Tears have wrecked her makeup, leaving mascara smeared under her eyes. "Where's he taking my daughter?"

Madison steps closer to her. "Which way did they go?"

The woman points to the French doors. "He dragged her out there. She was screaming." She grips Madison's arm as desperation fills her eyes. "My daughter's pregnant. You can't let him harm her and the baby. She's my only child!"

Madison races out of the French doors and into the cool daylight. She finds Mel's ivory high heels discarded on their sides on the lawn. She must've lost them as Jay dragged her away, but there's no sign of the newly married couple. Her heart races a mile a minute as she fears the worst.

The property beyond the lawn consists of densely wooded

areas and a narrow creek. As it's his father's property, Jay will know this place like the back of his hand. She has no hope of finding him. It would be too dangerous to enter those woods alone as she doesn't know if he's armed with a gun.

Steve approaches her. "EMS are on their way. I found a nurse among the guests. She's applying pressure to Bryan's wounds." He takes a deep breath. "I don't understand why things went south so fast."

Madison spins around to look at him. His shirt is covered in blood. "Because it wasn't Bryan behind the murders on the mountain. It was Jay. *He's* the Grave Mountain Stalker."

CHAPTER FIFTY-FOUR

THIRTEEN YEARS AGO

Watching the flashing lights of an approaching emergency vehicle hits differently when they're arriving for *your* loved one. It's easy to ignore them when you're passing some drunk driver by the side of the road or when they're speeding to someone else's house for someone else's emergency. But when they're responding to something that affects you or your family, that *should* hit differently. So Jay can't understand why it doesn't.

He watches the scene unfold from his parents' bedroom window. First responders appear like actors on a stage. They're dressed for the part in their blue uniforms, with heavy bags of medical equipment. They're soon followed by lazy cops, hands on their hips, surveying the scene with boredom. It's just another day at work for those guys.

While the EMTs fish Jay's mother from the pool, the cops try to figure out whether this is a homicide or an accidental death. Jay knows which they'd prefer. Accidental drowning is less paperwork, which means they could still be home in time for dinner and leave the real work to the medical examiner. They can entertain their spouses over meatloaf and mashed potato by describing what they were called to.

We found an overweight white woman floating face-down in the pool at her home, her blonde hair fanned out around her. She was bobbing around like a seal in her black swimsuit. We learned she was forty-five years old with two kids. Boys. Poor bastards. One of them watched as the EMTs took her away. No doubt he'll be scarred for life.

Jay hates cops, mainly because Stuart always wanted to be one. As a kid, his younger brother had an annoying obsession with all things emergency and an unhealthy admiration for police officers. He played with toy cruisers, ambulances, guns and fire trucks, all with real siren sounds and flashing lights.

Now, though, Stuart is nowhere to be seen. He's probably disgusted with himself and fearful of being caught and going to jail. Not only did Stuart obsess over cops, but he's always been obsessed with their mother too. And their mother loved the attention. She favored little Stuey because he was the youngest. He could do no wrong in her eyes.

In contrast, Jay was always thought of as a bad influence. Or the reason why Stuey was upset. He got the blame for every single argument. Every single light switch left on, or broken dish in the kitchen.

Yet it was Stuart who ended her life.

Jay captured the moment on camera as Stuart, almost fifteen now, and strong, held their mother's head under the chlorinated water. He zoomed in on the air bubbles as she gasped her final water-filled breaths. Then he focused the lens on Stuart's face as she went limp in his hands.

Stuart must've felt eyes on him because he glanced up at Jay, his expression oozing self-hatred.

Jay might have coerced him into killing their mother, but Stuart could've refused if he weren't so easily manipulated. It was easy to ruin their relationship. Jay's been feeding his brother lies for a long time now. He'd told him their mom laughed about him behind his back. That she thought he was pathetic and a huge disappointment to her. He explained how she took him everywhere she went because she knew he couldn't stand up for himself against other kids. And over the past few months, Jay has made him see how twisted his relationship with their mother really is.

"How do you hope to get a girlfriend one day when everyone knows you're infatuated with Mom?"

Stuart soon started distancing himself from her. Jay saw the pain in their mother's eyes when she noticed. He enjoyed it. The more she hurt, the more he fantasized about her death. Ever since he was small, Jay's always known he was on a slippery slope of hatred. But he's never wanted to carry out the act of murder himself. He wanted to watch Stuart kill her. So he planted the seed in his brother's weak mind.

Stuart thinks Jay looks out for him like a big brother should, and as his hatred for their mother grew, Jay gave him a way to release his confusion and hurt. He suggested making a move when their mom was swimming because it would be easy to make it look like an accidental drowning.

He wasn't at all surprised when Stuart went right ahead and did it.

It occurs to him now that if he can get Stuart to kill someone, imagine what he could make strangers do.

The thought arouses him as he stares at his mother's lifeless body, hastily flopped onto the concrete next to the pool. Her breasts are in danger of slipping out of her swimsuit. Her lips are gray. Her eyes are glassy. She's staring in his direction. One of the EMTs follows her gaze and spots Jay peeking out of the upstairs window. He moves in front of the woman at his feet so her son won't remember her like this.

But Jay *wants* to remember her like this. This moment will fuel him in low times. Who needs pills for poor mental health when you can watch your mother die over and over again?

CHAPTER FIFTY-FIVE

PRESENT DAY

Madison's forced to leave Steve at the lodge to coordinate the search party for Jay and Mel as she's been recalled to the station by Chief Mendes. All she's been told is that it's urgent. She can't imagine what's more urgent than apprehending the Grave Mountain Stalker, but she has no choice.

It's midafternoon when she arrives, and Mendes is waiting for her. Before Madison can update her on the stabbing at the lodge, the chief says, "Becky Draper is here."

Madison stops in her tracks. "Are you serious?"

"Yes." Mendes walks fast, heading for the interview room. Madison tries to catch up. "She heard her father was brought in for questioning, so she wants to talk. For what it's worth, I think the only thing Doug Draper's guilty of is covering for her."

"And lying to his wife about her daughter being missing," says Madison.

Chief Mendes glances at her. "You never know, he could have a good reason for that."

"Just stop for a second," says Madison. "We need to talk about Jay Carpenter."

Mendes stops, and Madison tells her why she believes Jay is

their serial killer. The chief listens, her expression grave. "So he's on the run with his new wife as a hostage, and his father's on his way to the hospital?"

Madison nods.

Stella approaches them with her unplugged headset resting around her neck. "Sorry to interrupt, but I've had an update from EMS."

"Go ahead," says Mendes.

"Bryan Carpenter's dead," says Stella. "The EMTs were unable to revive him. He passed away in the ambulance."

Madison closes her eyes briefly as she runs a hand through her hair. "This just keeps getting worse."

Stella returns to her desk, as the phones are ringing nonstop. News must be spreading fast.

"I'm going to look into Lucy Carpenter's drowning," says Mendes. "To see if it could've been a homicide after all."

Madison looks at her. "You think Jay killed his mother?"

Chief Mendes shrugs. "We need to know what kind of man we're dealing with."

Madison agrees. "Hopefully, not the kind who's also capable of killing his wife and unborn baby." An adrenaline rush causes her to break out in a sweat. She can't let them die.

Mendes pulls out her cell phone. "I'll alert the media that a manhunt is underway and arrange a roadblock near the One-Way Bridge. Patrol will find him. He can't stay hidden for long, not with his hostage dressed as a bride and the whole town on the lookout." She nods to the interview room. "We also need to see what Becky Draper's excuse is for vanishing and whether she knows who killed Tasha Harris before she changes her mind and walks out of here."

Madison stops her from entering the room by stepping in front of her. "I can do that. I need you to get a search warrant for Jay Carpenter's house. I don't know where he lives, but Mel told me they'd traveled here for the wedding, so it could be out of state."

Mendes bristles slightly at the order.

"Sorry," says Madison. "But with Adams taking time off and Steve managing the scene at the lodge, I need help. Once you have the warrant, tell whoever performs the search that we're looking for footage of the murders. We need to seize all his tech equipment: cameras, computers, phones, flash drives, hard drives... *everything*."

"Understood. But on the subject of being short-staffed, we need to discuss Adams."

Madison frowns. "Now?"

"I'll be quick. When he returns to work, it won't be as a detective."

Madison's stunned. "*What?*"

Checking over her shoulder before continuing, Mendes says, "As you know, he was a sergeant at his last PD, and he agreed he's more suited to that role. To tell you the truth, he seemed relieved when I suggested it."

Confused, Madison says, "But we need more detectives, not sergeants."

Mendes smiles briefly. "I know, Madison. That's why I plan to offer Steve the detective role. I should've listened to you when it was first vacant and chosen him then. I think the pair of you will make a good team."

Madison couldn't agree more. She just has to hope he'll accept. For all she knows, he might think she's a nightmare to work with like Adams does. Although, she thinks she won Adams over eventually.

Before heading to her office, Mendes adds, "Don't mention it to Steve yet. I want to be the one to explain it." She walks away.

Madison's phone rings. It's Adams. "Hey," she says. "I'm about to talk to Becky Draper, so I don't have much time."

"Sure," he says. "Things sound crazy there. Mendes filled me in. I just wanted to tell you something before word spreads, since you're my partner and all." He sounds exhausted.

"Mendes just told me," she says gently. "You're swapping roles with Steve. Are you sure you're okay with that?"

He sighs. "You know what? I am. I never enjoyed investigating. And the criminals in Lost Creek are something else." He takes a deep breath before putting a positive spin on things. "Besides, I've been told I look great in uniform."

Madison unexpectedly laughs. "Well, I'm glad you're staying with us. I spent too long breaking you in for it all to go to waste."

He snorts. "I'll let you get back to it. I promised the girls I'd make popcorn and watch a movie with them. But I'll be back at work as soon as they're settled."

"Good," she says. "I wouldn't want you getting used to time off. I'll try to keep you updated on the case, okay?"

"You do that," he says. "See you, Harper."

Madison ends the call and realizes she misses having him around. But she doesn't have time to think about the change in partner. With everything moving at breakneck speed, she takes a deep breath before entering the interview room. She has absolutely no idea what Becky Draper wants to tell her.

CHAPTER FIFTY-SIX

Officer Shelley Vickers is seated opposite Becky at the table in the center of the room. She stands to leave when Madison enters.

"That's okay," says Madison. "Stay seated." She'd rather have an officer present than do this alone. There's a reason why Becky vanished, and it won't be good.

Becky's nursing an almost empty coffee cup and watching Madison with interest. Wearing a designer dress under a thick woolen coat and with a full face of makeup, she doesn't look like she's been living in fear of being found, but Madison knows looks can be deceiving.

She takes a seat opposite the young woman. "I'm Detective Harper. I'm afraid I don't have much time, so we have to be quick."

"How's my mom?"

Madison meets her gaze. "Isn't it five years too late to ask that question?" She feels Shelley's eyes on her. Maybe she's being too harsh, but she's been in Nancy's house. She's seen firsthand what Becky's disappearance did to the woman.

"I guess I deserve that." Becky straightens in her seat. "Okay, I'll get to the point. You need to arrest Jay Carpenter." She pauses, expecting Madison to be surprised.

Without missing a beat, Madison says, "I know. We're looking for him right now."

Becky frowns. "You already know? How long have you known?"

Madison looks at the clock above the door. She's busy, and she doesn't owe this woman any answers. "He made you kill Tasha, didn't he? It wasn't Stuart. It was you who killed your friend."

"What? No. I could *never*." Becky's face crumples in disbelief at the accusation. "We were like sisters."

Madison thinks she's lying. "So what happened on your hike? Where did you go, and what happened to Tasha?"

"Why are you being so cold?" says Becky. "I came here voluntarily to give you answers. I could easily have skipped town again."

"So why didn't you?" Madison asks. "What's in it for you?"

Tears spring from the young woman's eyes and run down her face.

Madison reminds herself that Becky was only nineteen when she vanished from the mountain. And who makes good decisions at that age? But she could've come to them years ago about Jay. She could've stopped him from orchestrating countless more deaths since then.

In a gentler tone, she says, "Were you dating Jay? Is that how you got mixed up in all this?"

Becky wipes her eyes with her hands as she nods. "He was twelve years older than me. He wanted me to keep our relationship a secret even though we were both single. At first, I liked the attention, but he soon became controlling. I wanted out but didn't know how to end it. I felt like I shouldn't upset him."

Pushed for time, Madison needs to move her along. She can learn the details later. "Did Stuart know you were dating his brother? Because you were friends with Stuart, right?"

"Right. He's more easygoing than Jay. Stuart's nice but easily led, and he looks up to his older brother. He always does whatever Jay wants. I think he has self-esteem issues."

Madison realizes she's talking about Stuart as if he's still alive. Her heart sinks. "You haven't heard what happened to him, have you?"

Becky tilts her head. "What do you mean?"

After a quick glance at Shelley, who looks like she'd rather be anywhere other than here, Madison says, "Stuart took his own life last week. I'm sorry."

Becky's mouth drops open. "Are you serious? Why? Because of Jay?"

"Because we found Tasha's body on the mountain and he thought we were going to arrest him for it. He told us he was responsible for your deaths. He was covering for you."

Becky lowers her head into her hands. "No. He wasn't covering for me. He was covering for Jay."

Madison's getting confused. "Why did you suggest a hike that day, Becky? Were you luring your friend to her death for Jay? Did your boyfriend make you kill Tasha?"

Becky looks up. Her mascara is smeared around her eyes. "No. He didn't make me kill *Tasha*."

Madison's heart rate spikes. She thinks she knows what happened, and it's even worse than she imagined. "He made you kill someone else, though, didn't he?"

Becky slowly nods, her tears dripping onto the table. "He tricked me."

Shelley finds a box of tissues in a cabinet behind them and slides it across to the young woman. "Here."

Madison's phone buzzes in her pocket. She pulls it out and

sees Nate's name on the screen. She can't answer now, so she switches it to silent.

She gives the woman in front of her time to dry her eyes, but the tears keep coming. Gently, Madison says, "Tell me what you did, Becky."

CHAPTER FIFTY-SEVEN

FIVE YEARS AGO

As Becky drives downtown, she thinks about how she regrets getting involved with Stuart's brother. Seeing an older man was initially exciting, but Jay quickly changed from charming and flirtatious to domineering. She feels claustrophobic around him because he constantly tests her feelings for him and accuses her of flirting with other men. He likes to embarrass her too, like when he told a hot woman in the grocery store that Becky wanted her to join them for a threesome.

He also has a cruel side, where he's overly critical about how she dresses. She has this one dress that's tight around her hips, which she thinks accentuates her curves, but when he saw her in it, he laughed and said she was too young for saddlebags. Usually, she wouldn't let unkind words affect her, but when they come from an older guy, it hurts.

Because of all that, she hopes to break up with him today, depending on what mood he's in. She's worried about how he'll react, and knows she has to time it right. Hopefully, Stuart's with him. He's the only person who knows they're dating, which means Jay's probably ashamed of her. In which case, why the hell is he even with her?

She sighs heavily. Trying to understand Jay Carpenter is exhausting.

Her cell phone rings beside her on the passenger seat. She checks the rearview mirror before grabbing it. It's Jay. She hits accept. "I'm almost there."

"Good," he says. "But I need you to collect Brandon Dorsey from Ash Street first. He should be on his way home from school by now, and I have something for him."

She rolls her eyes. "Can't you get him?"

"No. I don't have time. Tell him his package is at my place, and he needs to come here to collect it." He hangs up.

She drops the phone into her lap. She's met Brandon twice before at the house Jay and Stuart share. Jay obtains steroids for him to help him bulk up. Becky doesn't agree with it, but the poor kid is so grateful that she can't begrudge him wanting to do something to stop being a target at school. He's really skinny and tall for his age, which means he stands out like a sore thumb.

She pulls onto Ash Street. It doesn't take long to spot Brandon. He's heading away from a large property. He walks fast, probably to avoid the kids from school. He's another four houses away before she pulls alongside him. "Hey, Brandon!" she says through the open window.

He stops and comes over when he recognizes her. He leans close to the passenger window, making his heavy backpack slide off his shoulder and hit the car door. "Hey."

"Jay told me to pick you up. He's got your stuff."

A wide smile breaks out on the boy's face. "Cool." He gets into the car, and she pulls away.

"How was school?" she asks.

"Good."

She glances at him. "Good? Since when was school ever good?"

He laughs. "Okay, it sucked."

She feels for him. At his age, nothing can make you feel worse than being targeted by other kids. "Do you have many friends?"

He reddens. "I mostly hang out with my girlfriend."

Becky smiles widely. "Cool." She's glad he has someone to look out for him.

Traffic is light. They make it to Jay's place in two minutes. The door is unlocked. Brandon follows her into the house.

Within seconds, Jay appears from the kitchen. Tall, with dark hair, and always well-dressed thanks to his dad's money, he's probably the best-looking boyfriend she'll ever attract. It's a shame he's an asshole.

"Hey, kid." Jay goes to the door and locks it behind Brandon. He has his cell phone in his hand.

Brandon sits on the couch, looking a little awkward.

Becky is about to sit beside him when Jay says, "I have some new stuff. You drink it instead of injecting it."

Brandon's face lights up. "No more shots?"

Jay smiles. "Right. I know you hate them, so I thought we'd try it this way." He looks at Becky. "It's in the brown mug on the counter. Go fetch it, would you?"

She goes to the kitchen and sees a single mug with what looks like cola in it. When she brings it into the living room, she notices that Jay's recording her on his phone. She frowns. "Why are you recording?"

He grins. "Because I've heard it tastes like crap, so I want to capture his reaction."

Jay may be older than her, but he's still immature, like most men. She hands Brandon the drink. "Here you go. The best way to drink something that tastes rancid is to knock it back fast. Don't sip it."

Brandon stares at it briefly and looks a little dubious, but he surprises her by downing the whole cup. When he's done, the bubbles from the cola cause him to burp loudly, which makes them laugh.

"Good?" says Becky.

He nods, but within sixty seconds, his hand goes to his chest. "My heart's racing." He tries to laugh it off, but it turns into a gulp as he starts gasping for air. "Something's. Wrong. I. I. Can't breathe."

Becky's smile fades. "What's the matter?"

Brandon can't speak. He clutches his shirt and leans his head back to open his airway.

"Jay, help!" she shouts, kneeling in front of the boy. As she pulls his shirt open, the buttons go flying. Her hand on his chest tells her his heart is thudding too hard.

Jay's still recording. "Becky, what have you done to him?"

She panics. "I only gave him a drink! We need to call 911! I think he's having a heart attack."

Brandon collapses forward with one word. "Dizzy." He falls onto the floor head-first and starts convulsing. He vomits, but it sounds like it gets stuck in his throat.

"We have to help him!" Becky yells. But Jay doesn't move. She tries to move the boy into the recovery position, but he's thrashing around, choking on his own vomit. His face has turned purple. Within seconds, he falls still.

Becky stares in disbelief.

Jay gets closer, filming Brandon's contorted face.

"What are you doing?" she yells, jumping up to hit him across the arm. "Turn that thing off! We need to help him!"

Jay finally slides his phone into his pocket. "Can't you see it's too late? He's dead. You killed him."

Stunned, she falls to the floor and sobs as she watches the life fade from Brandon's eyes. "This can't be happening." Several minutes pass. The only sound is the tick of the clock on the kitchen wall. Becky has to focus on that, because if she concentrates on what just happened, she'll lose it.

Eventually, Jay says, "We need to hide his body."

"*What?* Are you out of your mind? We need to call the police!"

"Becky, think about it," he says. "If the cops come here, they'll watch the footage on my phone. They'll see it was *you* who made him drink it. You even told him to down it in one. It won't look good for you. They'll say it was premeditated murder."

Lost for words, she doesn't understand how her life has changed in just a few minutes. Eventually, she says, "You told me to give it to him. You knew it was poisonous, didn't you?"

He smiles.

Her body trembles uncontrollably. He's sadistic. He made her do this. "I'll tell them you got the poison."

He smirks at her. "They'll never find a link between me and the substance in his body."

Bile burns the back of her throat. "Delete the footage."

He scoffs. "It's not that simple. Nothing's ever deleted from your cell phone or your computer. The cops can retrieve *everything*. You'd be locked away for life. Think about your parents. What would that do to them? To your mom especially?"

She lowers her eyes. Her mom wouldn't be able to cope. *She* wouldn't be able to cope. Not in prison.

"There's nothing we can do for Brandon," says Jay. "We need to hide what you did. And if you don't help me, I'll bury you alongside him. Maybe your mom too."

Her head snaps up to look at him. She sees it in his eyes. The certainty that he wouldn't hesitate to kill her and her mother. All this time, she's been dating a killer. She should've trusted her instincts and escaped before now.

But it's too late for that. She has to appease him if she wants to get out of here alive.

CHAPTER FIFTY-EIGHT

PRESENT DAY

Madison leans back in her seat, horrified at Becky's description of Brandon's murder. Now she understands why Becky never went to the police. Jay was blackmailing her. Threatening to kill her mother. The videos he took from the various crime scenes were sick mementos he could watch back whenever he wanted to, but they were also weapons to use against those who could alert the police to what he was doing.

She turns to Shelley. "Would you bring Doug in?"

"Sure." Shelley stands before quietly leaving the room.

Becky's eyes widen. "Before my dad gets here, I need to tell you something he doesn't know." She tries to compose herself, but struggles to find the words. Her lip quivers as she says quietly, "Jay raped me afterward."

Aghast, Madison says, "After you buried the body?"

"No. On the floor of the living room, next to Brandon." Becky shivers. "It excited him, knowing we'd just killed someone. He got off on the power he had over me and Brandon. I kept my eyes shut the entire time."

Madison can't believe what she's hearing. There's something seriously wrong with Jay Carpenter if he's aroused by having sex in the presence of a corpse. She feels terrible for judging Becky too harshly before she had all the facts. "I'm so sorry. I can find you someone to talk to."

Becky dismisses it with a wave of the hand. "I've tried therapy. It didn't work for me because I couldn't tell anyone the truth. I could only skirt around the real issues." She leans back, her hands trembling in her lap. "In the days that followed, I almost drank myself to death. I couldn't see a way out from the guilt and the shame. And the fear that he'd kill my mom. When drinking didn't help, I asked Tasha if she'd go for a hike. I wanted to get her alone and see if she'd leave town with me. I was going to confide in her about everything. But she invited Stuart along, and it was obvious he had no idea what Jay had done to Brandon."

"How can you be so sure?" asks Madison.

"Because Jay ambushed us on the Juniper Trail and told them that I'd killed Brandon. Stuart had inadvertently told him the night before that we were going there. Jay showed them a clip of Brandon writhing on the floor at my feet. Tasha believed him."

Madison shakes her head in disgust. "He was jealous of your friendship with Stuart." She can see how someone as evil as Jay Carpenter would hate for his girlfriend to enjoy his brother's company. It's about control again. Stuart probably never reached his full potential because of Jay. And that's exactly how Jay wanted him: downtrodden and easy to manipulate.

A thought comes to her. "Did you know that their mother drowned when they were younger?"

Becky lowers her eyes and nods.

"I initially thought Bryan killed her," says Madison. "Was it Jay?"

"I don't know for sure, but I'd guess it's more likely that Jay made Stuart do it."

Madison pictures Stuart's final moments in his dining room

before he pulled the trigger on his shotgun. He was tormented, and she had no idea it was because of everything Jay had put him through. Yet, still, he protected his brother from the police. He took Jay's secrets to the grave. She closes her eyes against the memory of what the blast did to his face. "We found photographs in Stuart's nightstand of him and his mother together."

"That doesn't surprise me," says Becky. "He told me more than once that he missed her." Wiping away a tear, she adds, "I never understood why Jay was jealous of our friendship. He had everything: the looks, the charisma and the money. Stuart was the complete opposite."

"But *that's* why," says Madison. "Stuart was likable. People liked him even though he wasn't as attractive or successful as his brother. Jay would've hated that because he's shallow and mean. He's a narcissist."

Becky nods. "That's a good word to describe him. On the mountain, he handed Stuart a gun and made him choose between me and Tasha. If he didn't kill one of us, Jay said he'd kill all three of us." She clears her throat as she wipes away a tear. "Tasha was frozen to the spot. Our cell phones were in my backpack, but I couldn't call for help without being seen, and cell service is patchy on the mountain anyway. I didn't know what to do. I was sure Stuart would pick me because of what I'd done to Brandon, but now, I think that made him sympathetic. Maybe because he'd been forced to kill his mother. He knew the torment I was going through." She pauses. "So he shot Tasha instead."

Madison realizes that's why he admitted to it the night he died. He *did* kill Tasha, but not because he wanted to.

The door suddenly opens, and Doug appears, followed by Shelley. He takes a seat next to his daughter, leaning in for a long hug. Pulling away, he says, "Have you told them everything?"

Becky nods, using a tissue to wipe her face.

Madison realizes Doug knows everything. He must've helped his daughter flee town afterward. "Was Jay holding a gun to Stuart's head so that he couldn't back out?" asks Madison.

"No," says Becky. "He had a gun, but he didn't need it for his brother to comply. He knew Stuart had no way out. Stuart could never get away from him."

If only he'd confided in their father. But Bryan viewed Stuart as a disappointment compared to Jay, so he must've known his dad wouldn't believe him.

"As soon as he shot Tasha, I fled," says Becky. "I ran without stopping and without looking back. I knew that hesitating would mean the end of my life. And I knew that if I told anyone what had really happened, Jay would release the footage of me killing Brandon, and he'd probably kill my mother too, out of spite."

Madison looks at Doug. "She called you to ask for help?"

"From a payphone," he says. "She wouldn't tell me much, just that she needed to leave town immediately or she'd be locked up for murder, *and* Nancy would be killed. I never knew the specifics back then, but I assumed something went wrong on the hike and Becky was responsible. I had to make a split-second decision. It was either get my daughter out of town with no questions asked or visit her in prison after burying my wife." He swallows. "I'll admit, I didn't consider the repercussions of helping her. I had no idea how badly her absence would affect Nancy. But on the other hand, I think Nancy would've made the same decision as I did and chosen our daughter over me." His voice catches as he adds, "I just hope she'll forgive me one day. If she gets the chance."

"Why not just confide in her about what had happened?" asks Madison.

"Because Nancy's maternal instincts would've kicked in

eventually," he says. "She'd have wanted to see Becky if she knew she was alive. She'd have wanted to follow her wherever she went, and I never knew who was blackmailing my daughter, so I didn't know whether we were being watched. I couldn't risk it."

Madison looks at Becky. "You didn't tell him it was Jay?"

"No. Not until earlier today. I thought the less he knew, the safer he was. And I had to be sure he wouldn't go after Jay for what he'd done to me. I couldn't risk him getting arrested for murder. I had to deal with it alone."

Madison takes a deep breath. "Did you two stay in touch?"

Doug takes his daughter's hand in his. "We messaged each other once a month to check in. When you found that first body on the mountain, I assumed it was Tasha. Turns out I was right. I'd put some of the story together over the years. I obviously knew Tasha went missing that day and assumed that's whose murder Becky would be framed for. So when it looked like you'd found Tasha's body, I messaged her and told her she needed to run."

"You never suspected Stuart of being the person black-mailing your daughter?"

He nods. "Sure I did. So I asked her in a message. She assured me it wasn't him."

Madison can't imagine how torn Doug was after helping Becky flee. Seeing his wife's mental health seriously declining while also knowing their daughter was alive must've affected him deeply.

She looks at Becky. "Where did you go?"

"A women's refuge up north. I told them I was fleeing a murderous boyfriend. They were amazing. I stayed there for two months until one of the women secured a fake ID and social security number for me. That allowed me to get a job. I moved to New York City, knowing it would be easier to hide there than in Colorado. I don't know if Jay ever looked for me, but I felt him behind me every step of the way. I expected a hand on my shoulder every waking minute. I got a job at a check-in desk at LaGuardia Airport, and eventually, thanks to the kindest boss I've ever had, I was offered a place in the training program for flight attendants. I realized it would be safer to have no fixed address and spend most of my time in the air than to be a sitting target for Jay or any private investigator he might've hired to find me. But now, I believe he let me go. I think he knew that I'd be living in fear, and that was more satisfying to him than any physical damage he could do to me."

The stress of the past few years is evident in every word she speaks. She's been living a half-life since the day she handed Brandon that mug of poison.

"After I left, I stalked Jay's social media," she goes on. "I learned he moved away from Lost Creek the year after the hike. So I thought my parents would be safe then, but I knew I wasn't. Not while he had that footage of me. So I stayed away. I've been hoping he'd die from cancer or get into a car wreck or something so I could return home and see Mom. But evil people never die young."

Overwhelmed by everything she's heard, Madison looks at the clock. It's almost 4 p.m. It'll soon be dark, making it harder to find Jay. "Why did Jay choose Brandon?"

"Because Jay's dad had a problem with Brandon's dad. Jay was in the car when Bryan and Robert had an altercation over a stupid near-miss. He saw how pissed his dad was about it, and Robert humiliated Bryan in front of passersby, so Jay decided to get back at him."

Disappointed that that's all it took to make Brandon a target, Madison thinks Robert will blame himself if he finds out, and she has no idea how to help him. "I need to tell Brandon's father what happened. He's never stopped looking for his son."

Becky lowers her eyes. "You have to tell him I didn't mean for it to happen."

"I will. But you have to tell me where you and Jay buried Brandon's body."

The young woman nods.

Madison might be unable to bring Brandon home alive, but she *can* bring him home.

CHAPTER FIFTY-NINE

Madison's phone rings as she races through the streets, running multiple red lights. A quick glance tells her it's Nate. She answers it hands-free. "Hey, I'm driving," she says.

"I'll be quick. I've just learned that Stuart and Jay Carpenter lived near Brandon Dorsey in the same house where Stuart killed himself. According to Brandon's girlfriend, Jay was selling him steroids. Erin never told the police because Brandon didn't want his dad to know he was using them. She didn't tell me when we first spoke either, but I contacted her again to see if she was the person who picked Brandon up the day he vanished. She wasn't."

Madison keeps her eyes on the road. "Nate, I know everything. Jay Carpenter is the Grave Mountain Stalker. He's abducted his bride and gone on the run."

"Are you serious?" he says. "Is that why there's a roadblock near the One-Way Bridge?"

"Right. We're looking for him. Mel's pregnant, so we have to be quick."

"Sure. I'll let you go."

"Wait," she says. "Don't hang up. I need you to meet me at Stuart's house. Bring Brody."

"Got it. We're not far away. See you there."

Madison almost hits a white sedan that tries to pull out in front of her without warning. She slams her foot on the brakes and hits the horn. The sedan reverses, giving her room to get by. When she reaches Stuart Carpenter's house, it's dark, and two cruisers are already there. She rushes out of her vehicle and into the house.

Officer Kent greets her. "Detective? That guy we're looking for, Jay Carpenter?"

Madison stops. "What about him?"

"Well, I'm really sorry, but I let him into the house after his brother's death."

Madison frowns. She fails to see why that matters. "And?"

"It was before Tasha Harris's driver's license was found upstairs. When I heard Jay was our prime suspect, I realized he could've planted it that day."

Madison's shoulders sag as she exhales.

Seeing the disappointment on her face, Officer Kent says, "I know. I'm sorry. He was telling me how devastated he was and how he just wanted to get some of his brother's clothes so they could dress him for the funeral." Her face is full of worry. She knows she screwed up. "It'll never happen again, I promise. I feel like an idiot. Corey wouldn't have fallen for it."

Madison agrees that Officer Fuller wouldn't have, but Jay wouldn't have tried it with a male officer. She rests a hand on Kent's shoulder. "It's fine. We all make mistakes. However, in *this* job, you can't repeat the same mistake twice."

Kent nods. "Trust me, I won't."

Movement behind them makes her turn. Brody has arrived, ready for action. The big dog runs into the house, stopping in front of Madison, where he sits awaiting instructions.

Nate quickly follows. "Hey, so what's going on?" he asks.

"Follow me." She leads Brody and Nate through the house and out to the backyard. It's long and rectangular, surrounded by overgrown bushes and trees. At the far end is a patch of concrete where an outbuilding used to stand. Madison knows that because Becky told her. Nearby is a small fir tree, planted five years ago. It looks lonely in the middle of the lawn.

Officer Sanchez approaches them with a shovel. "Is this the one?" he asks.

Madison nods.

While he digs, she tells Nate what Becky and Jay did to Brandon.

Upset, Nate lowers his eyes. The news comes as a blow. "This will kill Robert." He runs a hand over his face and watches Sanchez. Suddenly understanding, he says, "Wait. Is Sanchez digging because Brandon's down there?"

"Right. I don't know if Jay ever told Stuart he'd buried the dead boy in his backyard. I hope not."

Brody helps Sanchez to dig, which means there's no doubt Becky was telling the truth about the location of Brandon's remains. The tree comes up easily. Sanchez dumps it on the ground and keeps going.

Madison takes Nate's hand. He probably thought he could find Brandon alive. But it's been five years since the boy vanished. The chances were beyond slim. She squeezes his hand. "I can tell Robert."

"No," he says. "I should do it."

Madison will go with him.

"Detective Harper?" Officer Kent runs over to them. "Chief Mendes just called. She said you need to check your phone. She's sent you an urgent email."

Madison's stomach flips with dread. She pulls out her phone, opens the email and reads: *He's just uploaded footage of every single murder.*

She looks at Nate. "Oh my God. Jay must be trying to

discredit our case against him. If the public watch the murders, they'll assume these people wanted to kill their victims. They won't understand that they were blackmailed."

She clicks on the first link in Mendes's email. It takes her to YouTube. She and Nate watch in silence as they recognize the scenic mountain terrain. At odds with the summer sunshine, Jordan Payne brutally strangles Shannon Briggs with his bare hands near the Lovers' Peak Trail. Shannon begs for her life between gasps, but her pleas go unanswered.

Madison's body feels numb. She lowers the phone, unable to watch.

Nate takes it from her and clicks on the next link. She finds herself watching this one too. It's her job. She has to.

Maria Whitman from the dive bar is lying on her back in the cab of a truck. It's dark, but the scene is lit in places by the camera's light. A man's large hands squeeze her neck. His thumbs apply pressure to her hyoid bone. Maria's eyes bulge as she desperately tries to remove them. Tears roll down either side of her terrified face. Despite her fear, part of her will be wondering who will raise her children if she dies.

The footage is shot over the shoulder of the cowboy Maria left the bar with. It gives the illusion that he secured the camera to the front seat in order to film his actions, but in reality, Jay is sitting there, sexually aroused as he watches these strangers carry out his sickest fantasy.

The cowboy glances back at the camera, and when she sees his face, Madison realizes she was wrong to think he could've been Doug Draper. She doesn't recognize him. But she'll need to find him to tell him they know he was forced to kill Maria. Fear is etched on his face. He looks like he wants to fight the assailant, but the shadow of a gun's barrel appears in the bottom left corner of the screen, just for a second, confirming that he's being forced to do this. The public might not spot that. They'll jump to conclusions. They'll think this guy is intentionally murdering Maria. Anyone who recognizes him will make his life hell and probably report him to the police.

Madison's mouth goes dry. Maria wasn't killed on the mountain. The cowboy likely carried her lifeless body up the nearby trail to hide it before taking off.

She doesn't need to watch the whole video. She takes her phone back from Nate and moves on to the next. She doesn't want to watch any of them in detail.

Fourteen-year-old Abby Walker appears. Madison groans. "Oh God."

Abby's best friend, Lauren, is standing some distance away, pointing a gun at her. Jay has positioned himself and the camera behind Lauren, making it seem like no third person is present. A beautiful sunset surrounds the girls and their small tent.

"Please don't hurt me," says Abby, clearly terrified. Her eyes are wide and her face is bloodless.

"I'm so sorry!" sobs Lauren. "But it's you or me. And if I choose me, my mom will die."

It becomes apparent that Jay threatened young Lauren with the same thing he threatened Becky with. He told them both that he'd kill their mothers if they didn't carry out his twisted demands.

Abby suddenly yells, "Lauren, no!"

A gunshot goes off. Madison quickly stops the clip and takes a breath while fighting back tears.

Eventually, she forces herself to click on the next link.

This video is shot in black and white, with no audio. Somehow, it adds to the creepiness, making the viewer feel like a voyeur. Nineteen-year-old Tasha Harris stands a few feet away from Becky Draper near the Juniper Trail. A dense fog has encased them, just like Stuart said it did. Stuart's profile is visible as he holds the weapon out in front of him with shaky hands. Tasha suddenly drops to the ground. Becky turns and flees.

Each clip is edited to be short and impactful, leaving plenty of questions for the viewer. They don't show Jay, the build-up to the murders or the devastating choices Jay gave these people. His voice isn't in these brief clips.

What can't be denied from watching them is who's physically responsible for each murder, and it's clearly not Jay Carpenter.

Madison moves on to the next video, which shows Brandon Dorsey seated on the couch at Jay and Stuart's house. Becky Draper unwittingly hands him a mug of poison.

She passes the phone back to Nate. "Turn it off." She won't watch another child die. She wants to throw up. Bile burns the back of her throat.

"There's one more," says Nate.

Madison frowns. "What? Who?"

He hits play.

Her throat seizes as Carla Hitchins appears on the screen. The waitress looks puzzled as she comes into full view, thanks to Vince's security light illuminating the area near the dumpsters. "Hank?" she says. "What are you doing back here, honey?"

Hank appears. "He's making me do this, Carla. I'm so sorry."

Carla laughs nervously. "Who's making you do what?" She spots the knife in Hank's hand as he raises it.

Madison quickly turns before dry-heaving. She spits saliva into the grass. "Turn it off," she says.

Nate rubs her back as she tries to regain her composure. "I'm sorry."

She won't watch Carla's murder. Chief Mendes can do that.

It's gut-wrenching to know the victims' final moments are online for everyone to watch. She wishes she could protect them and their families. She wipes her mouth with the back of her hand. "I haven't even had time to notify Shannon's and Maria's families that they've been found, never mind warn them about what happened to them."

"No names are listed in the descriptions," says Nate. "And YouTube will act fast to remove the videos. They violate content rules. You might still have time to contact the women's families and warn them not to watch any of this before their names are revealed."

Madison straightens just as Brody barks forcefully behind them. She turns.

Officer Sanchez steps out of the hole he's dug and wipes his brow. He looks at Madison. "Bones."

Madison's eyes lower to Brandon Dorsey's grave. He was just thirteen years old. "Officer Kent?"

Kent steps forward. "Yes?"

"Get Alex Parker here. And Dr. Scott. And tell Chief Mendes that she and Steve need to get on the phone and notify every victim's family about what's happened. Everyone except Brandon Dorsey's father. We'll do that."

"Sure, Detective." Officer Kent runs back toward the house, her phone to her ear.

Madison takes a deep breath before turning to Nate. "Ready?"

Nate nods, but he looks like he could vomit too.

CHAPTER SIXTY

Madison approaches Robert Dorsey's front door. It's pitch black out, but his porch light is on. Nate follows her, leaving Brody behind in his vehicle. Madison turns to look at him. "You sure you want to do this?"

He nods before knocking on the door. "He hired me to find answers, no matter how bad those answers might be."

After a few minutes, Robert appears. He's holding an empty box, and when he sees Nate has brought Madison with him, his face freezes.

"Sorry to arrive unannounced," says Nate. "Can we come in?"

Robert reluctantly steps aside. Nate enters the house first. As Madison follows, she takes in the sparse room, with boxes piled high along one wall. He's moving. There's no couch for them to sit on while they break the news, just one camping chair in the middle of the room. He doesn't even own a TV.

Nate moves to the chair. "You might want to take a seat."

"Just tell me." Robert's voice is barely a whisper. He clears his throat. "Give it to me straight."

Nate takes a deep breath. "I'm sorry, Robert, but it's not

good news." He pauses. "We've just learned that Brandon was killed on the day he vanished."

A few seconds of disbelief pass while the devastating news sinks in. Robert silently drops to his knees on the hardwood floor.

Nate crouches next to him, his hand on the man's back.

Finally, Robert says, "I don't understand. Who would want to hurt my boy?"

Nate looks up at Madison. He appears to be struggling, so Madison crouches in front of them both. "Brandon was using steroids to try to bulk up—"

"No, he wasn't." Robert shakes his head.

"He was. I'm sorry. He was being bullied at school, and he thought steroids would help him. His friend Erin confirmed it for us."

Robert is struggling to come to terms with the fact that his son kept secrets. All teenagers do, but that doesn't make it any easier. No parent wants to learn their child does harmful things when they're not around. Because how can they protect them if they don't know about it? No one can watch their children twenty-four seven. That's what makes parenthood so terrifying.

"Even if he was, how did that get him killed?"

Madison considers how to explain the boy's death without going into too much detail. "Jay Carpenter was supplying the steroids. And on that day, he tricked Brandon into drinking poison."

Robert jumps up. "He *what*? Bryan Carpenter's son killed Brandon?" He marches to the door. "I'll kill Bryan for this. And then I'll kill his son."

"Mr. Dorsey," says Madison, going after him. "Jay killed his father earlier today."

He stops and turns.

"Bryan's dead," she says. "And now Jay's on the run with his wife as a hostage. We're doing everything in our power to catch him. We've set up a roadblock so he can't get out of town, and the press is aware there's a manhunt underway." She pauses. "You'll be able to face him in court after he's charged with your son's murder."

She doesn't explain Becky Draper's involvement. He has enough to take in right now, and she doesn't want him driving to the Drapers' property to seek revenge on them.

The thought of facing his son's killer in court seems to settle him for now. He goes to his solitary chair and sits with his head in his hands.

Madison and Nate share a look. The silence is deafening.

Suddenly, Robert looks up at them. "Where's my boy? Do you know?"

Nate nods. "He was buried on the property Jay shared with his brother."

Robert's eyes fill with tears. "You're telling me he was only two streets away from me this entire time?"

Madison rests a hand on his shoulder. "You'll be able to bury him soon."

"Is there someone we can call for you?" asks Nate.

Robert doesn't answer right away. He shakes his head before wiping his eyes. "I'll go next door. My neighbor knows what I've been through. She'll want to know what happened to Brandon."

Nate glances at Madison. They need to tell him about the video. "Mr. Dorsey," he says. "There's something else you should know."

Robert stares up at him with wet eyes. "What?"

"Jay just released a series of videos online," he says. "He was responsible for the deaths of several people, and it appears he liked to record them."

Robert freezes.

"I'm sorry, but Brandon's murder is one of the videos he's

released. We want you to know so that you can avoid watching it."

The man goes deathly pale as he stares into space. Eventually, he shakes his head. "I thought my son disappearing was the worst thing that could ever happen to me."

Madison steps closer. "We'll get the videos removed as fast as possible. YouTube may have already acted, as I'm sure viewers will flag them as inappropriate."

He looks her in the eye. "Have you seen it?"

She nods.

"Did he suffer?"

Madison's eyes well up. She didn't watch the whole video, but she'll never forget the detailed description Becky gave her of Brandon's final moments. She swallows before speaking. "We'll get it removed. Please don't focus on that. Focus on organizing his funeral and telling people what an amazing son he was."

Robert looks away.

Madison worries that if he ever learns why Jay targeted Brandon, he might take his own life. She hopes not. She hopes he surprises her and turns his devastation into something positive, as so many bereaved parents somehow manage to do.

Her phone buzzes with a message.

There's been a sighting of a woman in a wedding dress on the Lovers' Peak Trail. We're on our way to check it out. Officer Kent.

Madison tenses. She quickly replies.

On my way.

She looks at Robert. "I'm sorry, we have to go. I'll call you with an update as soon as I can. If you need anything, call the station and ask for Chief Mendes. She's fully up to date with the case and can find someone to help you with your grief. We can refer you to—"

Robert nods to cut her off. He looks like he's aged twenty years since he answered the door.

Madison doesn't want to leave him alone, but knows she has no choice. She heads to the front door. Nate follows her. Once outside, she turns to him. "Jay Carpenter's wife has been spotted on the mountain. Jay must be hiding up there."

He nods. "Then let's go get the son of a bitch."

CHAPTER SIXTY-ONE

Madison reaches the parking lot near the Lovers' Peak Trail before Nate. The ride over here has given her anxiety time to build. She can't shake off the ball of dread that first settled in her chest after watching Stuart Carpenter take his own life.

Something terrible is going to happen here this evening. She can feel it.

Headlights flash in her rearview mirror as Nate arrives. He pulls into the space next to her. They're the only ones out here. Any hikers have long since descended the trails, not wanting to get caught on the mountain after dark. Madison briefly wonders how long the uniforms will take to arrive. Most of them are still searching the grounds of the lodge. That's on the other side of town. If she waits for them, Mel could be dead by the time they get here.

Nate opens her door. "Ready?"

She gets out. Before he can let the dog out, she says, "Leave Brody behind."

"Why? He can help us."

"I know. But he could also give away our position."

"He won't do that," says Nate. "He knows when to keep quiet."

Exasperated, she looks at him. "Nate, Jay Carpenter is evil. He might kill Brody to distract us. He'll target areas where we're weak, and I'm sorry, but Brody is one of your weaknesses."

Nate glances at the dog, who barks at him from behind the glass, eager to be let out of the car and put to work. "Brody would attack anyone trying to hurt us."

Madison takes his hand in hers. "Brody can't outrun a bullet, Nate, no matter how hard he'd try. Leave him behind." After a few seconds of hesitation, she adds, "In fact, you should stay behind too."

He scoffs. "Madison, I'm not letting you go up there alone."

Her chest tightens with anxiety. He never listens to her. But she can't risk losing him. Because he's *her* weakness.

She goes to her trunk and pulls out her only bulletproof vest. "If you're coming, you're wearing this."

He glances at it. "No. That's for you."

Frustrated, she rolls her eyes. Before she can talk him into it, a woman's scream pierces the silence.

Madison pulls her weapon and spins around, running for the path that leads to the trail. She hears Nate close behind her. She can't waste time arguing. It's better to at least locate the perpetrator and have eyes on him until backup arrives.

A few minutes in, Nate stops her and slips the vest over her head, securing it in place. She doesn't fight it, but if something happens to him tonight, she'll never forgive him.

Quickly getting off the main path so that Jay doesn't have a clear view of them, they stick to the shadows. The deeper they go, the more the woods seem to come alive around them. They keep heading north, but it's impossible to know which direction the scream came from. Even stopping to listen doesn't help. By the time they get close to where Shannon Briggs was strangled, Madison's out of breath.

"How did you know they're on the mountain?" whispers Nate behind her. He sounds suspicious of the situation.

Madison stops. "Officer Kent texted me. She said someone spotted a woman on the trail wearing a bridal gown." She frowns. "But there's no one out here to spot anyone."

Realization hits her. Her body goes numb. "Shit! It's a trap."

"What do you mean?"

She turns to look at him. "I don't know Kent's phone number, so I took the message at face value, but it could've been Jay who messaged me, pretending to be her. I gave his dad my card, so he has my cell number. He wanted us up here, Nate." Her throat tightens as she realizes backup's not coming. She grabs his arm. "You need to leave. *Now*."

Another shrill scream to their left makes them duck before changing direction. They try to maneuver quietly through the woods in the dark. Madison winces every time one of them steps on a fallen branch. She's aware she should stop and call for backup. Get Nate out of here.

"Help!" yells a woman's voice. It sounds close. "I can't hold on much longer!"

Madison changes direction sharply and comes to the edge of a cliff. She uses her cell phone to light the darkness beneath her. "Oh my God."

Mel Carpenter is standing on a small ledge, desperately clinging to the rocky wall. "He pushed me!" she yells, seeing Madison's light. "Please, you've got to help me. I don't know how long I can stay here. The rock is crumbling!" Panic is etched on her face.

Madison swallows. "Try to stay calm. We'll get you, but you need to stay still."

She and Nate should be strong enough to pull the woman up. She turns around to look at him, and stops dead. Jay is standing behind Nate, holding a gun to his head.

Her heart drops into her stomach as she realizes her worst nightmare has come true.

"Throw your weapon over the side, or I'll shoot him right now," says Jay.

Madison's legs go numb. She struggles to inhale. This is what she was dreading all along. The second it looked like they were dealing with a serial killer, she knew what would happen. She was foolish to ignore her fears. She should have left Nate with Robert Dorsey. She should never have told him where she was going.

The hand gripping her weapon is slick with sweat.

"You have three seconds," says Jay.

Madison has no choice. She throws her weapon over the edge, ensuring it's wide enough to miss Mel, who's gone deadly silent beneath her.

She must know there's no hope for any of them now.

CHAPTER SIXTY-TWO

Nate sensed Jay creeping up on him just a second too late. It wouldn't have happened if he'd brought Brody with them. A terrible thought occurs to him as he stands dead still. Did leaving Brody behind make the dog a sitting duck? Has this asshole already killed him before following them up here and making sure they fell for his trap?

It doesn't bear thinking about. But his fists ball in anger all the same.

Madison looks frozen in fear. Nate can tell by her bloodless expression that she's already blaming herself for this situation, which means he needs to remain focused. He won't let anything happen to her.

Now unarmed, she takes a step forward.

"Stop!" says Jay.

"Why?" says Madison. "Are you really afraid of the damage an unarmed woman could do to you?"

Jay steps back, so Nate risks a glance at him. The asshole is still pointing the weapon at his head, which is better than aiming it at Madison, but he isn't filming this. It makes Nate wonder whether that means he's come to the end of his killing spree, and he intends to either escape for good or take his own life when he's done here. Perhaps he couldn't prepare properly, given that Madison took him by surprise at his wedding.

"You know," says Jay. "The only time anyone ever respects me is when I have a weapon in my hand."

"They respect the weapon, not you," spits Madison. "Why don't you make it a fair fight for once in your sick life and use your hands?"

Jay appears amused as he replies, "No. It's far more exciting this way. The stakes are higher."

Nate realizes that this is Jay's twisted way of exerting power over people. He gets off on their fear. He feels like a bigger man because he's able to control them. He must have no control in his real life. Maybe his father's success overshadowed his child-hood. Or perhaps he's just deranged. Whatever the reason, seeing the effect his coercion has on people must offer a bigger thrill than he'd get from committing the crimes himself. He knows that the people he blackmails have to live not only with what they've done but also with the fear that he could expose them one day. Their lives are effectively ruined the minute he steps out of the shadows.

"What do you want?" says Madison.

She looks as though she's desperately trying to devise a plan to get them out of here alive. Her eyes dart back and forth, searching for a means to overpower him.

"Eleven people have already died thanks to your narcis-sism," she says, probably trying to buy time.

Nate's surprised by the number, but it includes both of Jay's parents, his brother, the four victims found on the mountain, Brandon Dorsey, young Lauren Moss, plus Hank and Carla.

"Isn't that enough?" she goes on. "You're already going to be famous if that's what you're after."

"*Eleven?*" Jay laughs, but it lasts too long, making him sound unhinged. "There are far more victims than that," he says. "Not that you'll ever find them all. Lost Creek may have been where I learned my trade, but it's not where I excelled."

Nate's blood runs cold as he imagines other victims in other towns. Other families like the Drapers and Robert Dorsey, all trying to live alongside the unanswered questions. He knows then that their chances of escaping are slim. He needs to act.

He lets instinct take over as he turns and lunges for Jay Carpenter. Jay drops his gun in the altercation. The element of surprise gives Nate time to land two hard blows to the guy's jaw before Jay pulls something from his pocket and fights back.

"Nate, no!" yells Madison.

Jay's elbow meets Nate's kidney, sending a flash of pain through his back. As he collapses to his knees, winded, he sees Madison stepping forward. He shakily gets to his feet in an attempt to stop her. Their eyes meet, and he shakes his head to warn her off doing anything rash.

Behind him, Jay retrieves his gun and aims it at Nate's head.

"Try that again," he dares them with a sick smirk. He touches his jaw. "You cracked a tooth."

Pain radiates through Nate's side, making him feel like he's been stabbed. He touches the area and feels something warm and wet. He glances at Jay. He's pocketing a knife with his spare hand.

Nate swallows. It wasn't Jay's elbow that hit him. If his kidney's punctured, he could bleed out. He discreetly wipes his hand on his jeans so Madison doesn't notice the blood.

Jay's standing too far away for Nate to lunge again.

"Becky Draper's back in town," says Madison.

Jay's smirk fades. He obviously wasn't expecting her to return. Maybe he always feared she would approach law enforcement to tell them what he was capable of. He's probably wishing he had hunted her down and finished what he started.

Shifting his position, Jay stares at Nate with pure hatred. "You're going to push your partner off the cliff now, Monroe."

Nate spins around to look at him properly. His mouth goes dry. "What?"

"You have a choice," says Jay calmly. "You can either jump off yourself and die what would probably be a slow and painful death, or you can push your girlfriend off and watch *her* die."

Madison groans behind him. "You sick bastard."

Nate turns around to lock eyes with her. He can tell she's trying to hide her fear, but he sees it anyway. He's surprised she's afraid, because she should know he'd never hurt her. Maybe it's because the last time they talked about this being a possibility—that he would be a target for the serial killer—he refused to arm himself.

He can tell, though, that she's not afraid for her life. She's afraid for him. She's afraid he's going to get himself killed in a bid to save her.

But what can he do? His choices are limited.

He turns back to Jay. "If you knew anything about me, you'd know I'd die for Madison."

"Nate, no. Don't say that!" Her voice breaks, and Nate knows then that they either both need to live or they both need to die, because neither of them wants to survive the other's death.

"Backup will be here any minute, Jay," she says, trying to keep her voice steady. "You'll be shot if you try to escape. But if you drop the weapon and come with us, you'll get to meet your baby one day."

A sob behind them reminds Nate of Mel's precarious situation. He can't imagine what's going through the poor woman's head. Even if she survives this, she'll have to live with the fact that her baby was fathered by a serial killer. How will she ever break that news to the poor child?

Jay laughs. "I think we both know that no one's coming to save you. And do you really think I'm bothered about my child? I pushed my wife off the cliff, didn't I?"

Madison falls silent, seemingly lost for words.

"Can I at least hug her before I jump?" asks Nate.

"What?" He hears Madison step closer. "Nate! Don't be stupid. You're not jumping!"

He turns to her. "It'll be okay, Madison. You have Owen to think of. He needs you."

She angrily wipes tears from her eyes. "If you go anywhere near that cliff, I'll jump too."

Jay laughs. "This is great. I wish I'd brought my phone." He takes a deep breath. "No hugging, Monroe. Just get it over with before I shoot both of you."

With a surge of adrenaline coursing through his veins, Nate slowly approaches the edge, with Madison on his left and Jay behind him. The blackness below doesn't show him how high the cliffs are, but he's been here before, so he already knows. The way down is littered with sharp edges, boulders and thick tree trunks.

He knows that Jay will pull the trigger if he doesn't jump, and is probably aiming the weapon at Madison now instead of him.

He slowly brings his hand to his inside coat pocket.

"What are you doing?" says Jay sharply. "Drop your hand."

Nate stops. Over his shoulder, he says, "I have a ring in my pocket. I was planning to propose tomorrow."

Madison covers her mouth with her hands and silently turns away.

Nate's throat seizes. He hates seeing her upset.

"My God, it's like a Shakespearean tragedy," says Jay, amused. "Fine. Just throw it to her. You can look at that ring every day after your boyfriend's death and remember that you caused this, Detective Harper." He spits her name like he's insulted by it. "You caused this by coming after me and ruining *my* life."

Nate finds what he's looking for. He slowly draws it out,

keeping it in front of him. Madison won't look at him. "Madison," he says. "Take it."

"No!" She keeps her back to him. "I won't watch you die, Nate." Her voice breaks.

He has no choice. He knows he has to act.

Tightening his grip, he spins around as fast as he can and fires his brand-new Glock pistol at Jay Carpenter's chest. The one firearms lesson he attended before tonight taught him to aim for the largest body part when under attack.

The gunshot rings out through the woods, sending birds flying. Madison exclaims in surprise.

Jay Carpenter is forced backward by the blow to his body. Nate doesn't think he hit his heart, but he's disabled him long enough to shout, "Madison, get down!"

He's too late. Jay hits the ground and fires two shots in quick succession with his outstretched hand. Madison screams in pain before dropping to the ground.

Behind them, Mel sobs loudly. "Help!" she yells, desperate now. "Someone help us!"

Devastated that he didn't stop Madison from getting shot, Nate walks up to Jay Carpenter and steps on the hand that's holding the gun. As he looms over the killer, he feels blood oozing down his back from his own wound. He sees stars, and his head feels heavy, as though he could pass out any minute. It hurts to stand upright now.

Jay looks up at him, panting from the effort of breathing with a gunshot wound. "Looks like you and I aren't husband material, Monroe."

Madison is silent behind him. Nate can't look. Not until he's dealt with this asshole.

His hands slick with sweat, he aims his weapon at Jay's head. An internal conflict rages through him. Technically, Jay is no threat to him right now. If Nate shoots him, it would be out of anger. Revenge for what he's done to Madison. So he shouldn't pull the trigger.

He already knows he couldn't live with himself if he kills someone. It goes against everything he believes.

His hesitation gives Jay time to free his arm and lift his weapon.

A shot rings out. Nate hears Madison scream again. Relief washes through him as he realizes she's still alive. But it's quickly followed by the overwhelming urge to vomit.

His ears ring from the blast. He gasps for air. Everything goes hazy.

He looks down.

He was a faster shot than the dead man at his feet. Jay Carpenter has a bullet through his forehead.

The dense vegetation rustles behind him, and someone yells, "Drop the weapon *now*!"

Somehow, backup has arrived. Nate turns slowly, wincing in pain. A young male officer he doesn't know is advancing toward him, aiming his weapon at his chest. The officer must've witnessed him killing Jay Carpenter.

"Get on the ground, now!" yells the officer. He pulls cuffs from his belt with his spare hand and speaks into his radio. "Shots fired! Shots fired on Grave Mountain. Officer down!"

Nate's been through this before. His last arrest landed him on death row for seventeen years. Ever since his release, he's feared he would be sent back to prison.

His body suddenly trembles uncontrollably as he realizes he's about to be arrested for murder. The only difference this time is that he's guilty.

CHAPTER SIXTY-THREE

Madison's shoulder burns. The first bullet hit her just above her heart. It would've killed her if Nate hadn't insisted that she wear the vest. The second skimmed the fleshy part at the top of her left arm. Her wound is a mess, but not life-threatening. She still has to see a doctor before she can leave the hospital. She just wants to bandage it and take a ton of painkillers, but she doesn't want to fall asleep yet. She can't. There's too much going on.

As she was helped to the waiting ambulance, Nate was taken in for questioning. She wasn't allowed to speak to him first. Brody's being cared for by Vince. Apparently, he'd torn Nate's car apart in a bid to get out and reach them on the trail, sensing something was off, but he wasn't able to break out.

Steve told her that a reporter followed her and Nate to the mountain from Robert's house, his instinct telling him something was going down from the way they raced out of there. He heard Mel's screams for help from his position in the parking lot and called 911. Unfortunately, he also captured footage of Nate being taken away in the back of a cruiser. It's already being shown on TV, which means Nate will once again find himself the subject of public scrutiny.

The scene must've looked bad to Officer Fuller, arriving alone to shots fired, Madison wounded, and an armed man he didn't know looming over a dead guy. Fuller had no idea what had preceded events, so Madison's not going to complain, but she's told Chief Mendes that if Nate isn't released immediately, she'll quit the department.

Mendes is considering what to do with him. She's pissed that Jay's dead because she thinks it means they'll never know who his other victims were. Madison disagrees. Jay would never have willingly given up the information if he'd survived. Besides, he probably has videos of all his kills somewhere.

She slips off the hospital bed and glances at her cell phone. Nate hasn't replied to any of her messages yet. She knows Jay wounded him somehow, but she doesn't know how badly, and it's driving her crazy.

Outside her room, she finds a nurse and asks for an update on Mel Carpenter.

The nurse seems in a rush to be somewhere and is clutching a handful of files to his chest, but he stops to answer her. "The doctor assessed her. She has no serious injuries, just raised blood pressure."

"And the baby?" she asks.

He glances over his shoulder as though he shouldn't be telling her this. "The baby's going to be fine too."

Madison breathes a sigh of relief. She'll visit Mel shortly, but she wants to check on Nancy Draper first.

Nancy's awake and already has three visitors: her husband, her daughter, and Officer Shelley Vickers, assigned to keep an eye on Becky Draper until the DA decides what charges to bring. Whatever happens, it'll be controversial, not just for Becky but for Jordan Payne and the cowboy truck driver, if they ever find him. If Stuart Carpenter, Hank Goodman and young

Lauren were still alive, they'd likely be charged too. It doesn't seem fair somehow, and yet they *did* all take someone else's life.

Madison's glad she's not in charge of those decisions.

Becky Draper is seated on the bed, holding her mother's hands. Nancy's face gives away her joy at having her daughter back, but it's clear the ordeal has weakened her. The last five years have taken a terrible toll, and although the outcome is better than she ever could've expected, she might now lose her to a prison sentence.

"Have you found him?" asks Becky.

Madison nods. "Jay's dead. He can't hurt anyone else."

Becky swallows. "Jay's entire family is dead because of him. I can't help wondering how many other victims there are that we don't know of."

Madison remains silent. Chief Mendes notified the Feds about Jay's claim that the mountain murders only scratched the surface of his crime spree. They'll get to the bottom of it. There will be an extensive investigation. She's relieved it's not up to her, although she's certain they'll want to interview her at some point.

"I should've gone straight to the police after Brandon died," says Becky. "I should've risked a prison sentence, since I've been living a sentence of my own making anyway. At least if I'm incarcerated, I can see you guys. You can visit me."

Nancy squeezes her hand. "I'm sure that won't happen." She turns to look at Madison. "Thank you for helping me through a stressful time, Detective."

Madison smiles sadly. "I feel like all I ever did was deliver bad news. I'm glad you've been reunited at last." She looks at Doug, who smiles at her for the first time since they met. She wonders if the couple will make it through this. She suspects they will. They have their daughter back. That should hold them together.

Not wanting to intrude for long, she leaves quietly and

walks back to her own room, hoping she can be discharged soon and with some good pain meds. When she steps through the door, she gasps.

Nate's standing by the window, looking out at the darkness. He turns when he sees her reflection in the glass. His face is lined with worry. Or maybe more than that. Guilt.

She goes to him, and he gently embraces her. She feels his throat constricting, holding back emotion. As she strokes his hair, she silently thanks God that he's safe.

He pulls away, wincing.

"What's the matter?" she asks.

He turns and lifts his jacket and T-shirt. A large bandage covers his lower back. The waistband of his jeans is blood-stained. "He knifed me."

"He *what*?"

"It's okay. He missed my kidney. I'll be fine, but I've got to stay until I've seen a doctor."

Madison kisses him. When she pulls away, she says, "So, you actually purchased a weapon?"

"You told me to."

She laughs. "What, you suddenly do everything I tell you now?"

"I thought you'd leave me otherwise," he says. "You were pretty pissed. I only managed one lesson before…"

Despite her attempt to lighten the mood, he seems broken, and she knows why. "You're going to be okay, Nate," she says, squeezing his hands. "No one is going to lock you up for what you did. What you *had* to do. They're just going through the formalities."

He lowers his eyes. "Maybe I *should* be locked up."

She swallows the lump in her throat. "No. Please don't say that."

He fixes his blue eyes on hers. "Madison, I killed someone."

She strokes his face, unable to find the words to ease his

conscience. Nate wanted to be a priest when he was younger. His faith is strong, or at least it was until someone took it from him. Gently, she says, "You have to look at it another way if you don't want it to eat away at you. You saved *my* life, Nate. And what's worse, killing a murderer or watching the woman you love die because you didn't act?"

He nods, but she knows he'll never forgive himself. And maybe he's right not to. Taking another person's life *should* make him feel this way. But not forever. Because had he gotten away, Jay Carpenter would undoubtedly have gone on to kill others in the future.

"You saved more lives than just mine tonight." She makes him look at her. "For starters, you saved Jay's wife and unborn daughter." She watches him battle with his conscience.

He nods again. "Don't worry, I'll see someone about it. I'll have to, or it'll eat away at me. I know because I'm already craving things I shouldn't."

She feels tears creeping up on her. She hates seeing him in pain.

He must see it in her eyes, her memories from when they first met and how he coped with his pain back then. He gently embraces her. "I'll figure it out. I don't want it to come between us."

Into his warm neck, she says, "It won't come between us, I promise." She has faith that he'll find a way to cope with this. He's been through so much already and has come out the other side. She can help him through it.

She pulls away and rests her hands on her hips, ignoring the pain in her arm. "Now, about that supposed engagement ring," she jokes.

Nate smiles properly this time. He moves his hand into his jacket pocket and pulls out a small box. "You mean this one?"

Madison gasps. She had no idea. She thought it was all a

ruse on the mountain so he could pull out his weapon. She looks up at him. "You were *serious?*"

He opens the box to reveal a beautiful platinum band set with several diamonds. It's perfect. Her hand flies to her mouth.

Nate takes her other hand and slips the ring onto her finger. "I'm always serious about you, Madison. You should know that by now."

She's only just agreed to move in with him, and part of her feels it's too soon to get married, but that's okay; they can have a long engagement. She leans in and kisses him.

Someone enters the room behind them, but they don't pull apart.

"Wait, you're proposing to her in her *hospital* room? Dude, that's lame."

Madison spins around to find her son standing there.

Owen's hair is shorter, and styled differently from when he left home months ago, and he looks older somehow. She's not ready for him to be all grown up. She suddenly yearns for the years she missed with him as a little boy when he was stuck living with Angie. Thoughts of her sister's impending release from prison threaten to ruin the moment. She hasn't told Owen about Angie's plea deal yet because she knows he'll worry about it after everything Angie and her husband put him through. She shakes the thought away. She can worry about that another time.

Owen sighs heavily as he drops his backpack by the door. "I was told you were in a life-or-death situation, so I raced here, which means you can't blame me for any speeding tickets I got along the way."

"You drove dangerously?" she says sternly.

"Mom!" he says exasperated. "I thought you were *dying!* How was I supposed to know you were well enough to make out with your boyfriend?"

She laughs as he comes in for a hug. He aggravates her wound by squeezing her too tight, making her wince.

Nate rests a hand on both their backs, making Madison finally feel safe. Despite knowing they'll have their challenges over the coming months as Nate comes to terms with what he did, the menacing feeling of dread that's been hanging over her for days has finally lifted.

A LETTER FROM WENDY

Thank you for reading *Grave Mountain*, book seven in the Detective Madison Harper series.

You can keep in touch with me and get updates about the series by signing up to my newsletter.

www.bookouture.com/wendy-dranfield

I hope you enjoyed this latest book in the series. I never thought we'd reach book seven, but there's still plenty more to come, thanks to Madison and Nate regularly finding themselves in trouble! I feel for Nate and wonder how he'll cope with what he's done. I think we know by now that he's his own worst enemy when under pressure.

But never mind that! More importantly, how will Brody, Bandit and Mrs. Pebbles live together in harmony when Mrs. Pebbles is such a diva?! I probably say this every time, but nothing bad will ever happen to the pets. I just wish I could promise the same for Madison and Nate! I try to keep them safe, but they tend to do the complete opposite of what I want them to do. At least it makes it more interesting for us.

I hope you'll join me for book eight next, and if book seven is your introduction to the series, I recommend going back and reading them from the start, beginning with *Shadow Falls*. You'll learn how Madison and Nate first met, how they acquired former police dog Brody, and how Nate helped Madison to overturn her conviction and find her long-lost son.

If you enjoyed this book, please leave a rating or review (no matter how brief) on Amazon, as this helps it stand out among the thousands of books published each week, allowing it to reach more readers and ensuring the series continues. And do follow me on social media or my website for updates on future books and photos of my cats!

Thanks for reading.

Wendy

www.wendydranfield.co.uk

 facebook.com/WendyDranfield1

ACKNOWLEDGMENTS

Thank you to the readers who have followed me from the beginning of my career and cheer me on with each new book. Also to the advance readers and book bloggers who review my books with so much enthusiasm. I love reading your reviews.

As always, thank you to everyone at Bookouture who worked on my latest book.

And special thanks to my wonderful husband, the reader of all my first drafts.

PUBLISHING TEAM

Turning a manuscript into a book requires the efforts of many people. The publishing team at Bookouture would like to acknowledge everyone who contributed to this publication.

Audio
Alba Proko
Sinead O'Connor
Melissa Tran

Commercial
Lauren Morrissette
Jil Thielen
Imogen Allport

Cover design
The Brewster Project

Data and analysis
Mark Alder
Mohamed Bussuri

Editorial
Claire Simmonds
Jen Shannon

Copyeditor
Jane Selley

Proofreader
Ian Hodder

Marketing
Alex Crow
Melanie Price
Occy Carr
Ciara Rosney

Operations and distribution
Marina Valles
Stephanie Straub

Production
Hannah Snetsinger
Mandy Kullar

Publicity
Kim Nash
Noelle Holten
Myrto Kalavrezou
Jess Readett
Sarah Hardy

Rights and contracts
Peta Nightingale
Richard King
Saidah Graham

Milton Keynes UK
Ingram Content Group UK Ltd.
UKHW012246290324
440241UK00004B/156

9 781835 253847